Acclaim for *Unknown No More*

"In the 1930s Sanora Babb created an American literary masterpiece with her Dust Bowl novel, *Whose Names Are Unknown*. But by a cruel twist of fate, it was not published for more than sixty years. We believe it to be a much fuller account of the terrible conditions and the resilient people living through those toughest of times. This collection of essays explores Babb's eloquent writing in this novel and in all her other work and helps set the record straight on an important American author."

—**Ken Burns and Dayton Duncan**
producers of *The Dust Bowl*

"These thirteen new essays on Sanora Babb are a great development in the rescue from obscurity of her marvelous literary work. With an engaging style, scholars, researchers, academics, and a friend of thirty years offer new perspectives on her fiction, poetry, nonfiction, and her unusual early life in the Dust Bowl area, then in Los Angeles among the literati, filmmakers, and progressives of the 1930s and '40s. *Unknown No More* is a valuable contribution to the ongoing campaign to rediscover the beautiful Sanora, a forgotten writer and a vital, brilliant woman, and include her in the American literary canon, where she belongs."

—**William Kennedy**
Pulitzer Prize winner and author of *Ironweed,*
Quinn's Book, and *Roscoe*

"These timely and engaging essays about the immensely talented author Sanora Babb finally restore the writer to her due place in American literary history. Offering insights about a politically engaged figure who was of her era yet also ahead of her time, the contributors make a convincing case for positioning Babb at the center of our conversations about ecology, labor, race, gender, and regional belonging."

—**Susan Kollin**
editor of *A History of*
Western American Literature

"*Unknown No More* represents a heartfelt and compelling tribute to a writer and activist whose work deserves to be read and studied today. Building on but working to avoid the blunders of previous scholarship that often paid insufficient attention to gender, class, and region, the essays in this volume explore the emotions and experience of overlooked and often misunderstood individuals and communities. The book revives a crucial yet nearly lost component of literary history in a way that seems destined for a readership inside and outside the academy."

—**Julia L. Mickenberg**
Professor of American Studies,
University of Texas at Austin

"*Unknown No More* is the book that devoted readers of Sanora Babb have been waiting for and new readers will greet as an invitation to join her fan club—a wide-ranging set of essays that examine her life and work in their fullest dimensions. Whether addressing Babb the poet and storyteller of the West, the labor activist, the environmentalist, or the champion of feminism and equality, the essays together record the full dimension of Babb's pivotal contributions to twentieth-century American life and letters."

—**Lawrence Rodgers**
coeditor of *America's Folklorist:
B. A. Botkin and American Culture*

"*Unknown No More* is the first collected volume focused entirely on this important author and covering all of her work—her wide-ranging poetry, short fiction, novels, memoir, journalism, field notes, reviews, and letters. The authors whose essays are gathered here advance Babb scholarship and revive her literary and political reputation while also promoting a broader understanding of the history of left-wing protest, the roots of ecofeminism, and the sweep of Great Plains environmental history. These powerfully written, pathbreaking contributions argue convincingly that Sanora Babb was an immensely gifted, deeply committed writer and activist whose time has come and whose courageous life and vivid art can inspire a wide range of present-day general readers, scholars, and activists."

—**Michael C. Steiner**
editor of *Regionalists on the Left:
Radical Voices from the American West*

UNKNOWN NO MORE

Sanora Babb in her Hollywood Hills home, circa 1970. Courtesy of Joanne Dearcopp.

UNKNOWN NO MORE
Recovering Sanora Babb

Edited by
JOANNE DEARCOPP and CHRISTINE HILL SMITH

Foreword by DAVID M. WROBEL

UNIVERSITY OF OKLAHOMA PRESS : NORMAN

Library of Congress Cataloging-in-Publication Data

Names: Dearcopp, Joanne, 1944– editor. | Smith, Christie, editor. | Wrobel, David M., writer of foreword.

Title: Unknown no more : recovering Sanora Babb / edited by Joanne Dearcopp and Christine Hill Smith ; foreword by David M. Wrobel.

Description: Norman : University of Oklahoma Press, [2021] | Includes bibliographical references and index. | Summary: "Thanks in part to the Ken Burns documentary *The Dust Bowl*, Sanora Babb is perhaps best known today for her novel *Whose Names Are Unknown* (2004), which might have been published in 1939 had her publisher not thought the market too small for two Dust Bowl novels, hers and Steinbeck's *The Grapes of Wrath*. Into the twenty-first century, Babb wrote and published lyrical prose and poetry that revealed her prescient ideas about gender, race, and the environment. The essays collected in *Unknown No More* recover and analyze her previously unrecognized contributions to American letters. Editors Joanne Dearcopp and Christine Hill Smith have assembled a group of distinguished scholars who, for the first time in book-length form, explore the life and work of Sanora Babb. This collection of pathbreaking essays addresses Babb's position within the literature of the Great Plains and American West, her leftist political odyssey as a card-carrying Communist who ultimately broke with the Party, and her ecofeminist leanings as reflected in the environmental themes she explored in her fiction and nonfiction. With literary sensibilities reminiscent of Willa Cather, Ralph Ellison, and Meridel LeSueur, Babb's work revealed gender-based, environmental, and working-class injustices from the Depression era to the late twentieth century. No longer unknown, Sanora Babb's life and work form a prism through which the peril and promise of twentieth-century America may be seen."— Provided by publisher.

Identifiers: LCCN 2021001181 | ISBN 978-0-8061-6936-1 (paperback)

Subjects: LCSH: Babb, Sanora—Criticism and interpretation. | BISAC: LITERARY CRITICISM / Modern / 20th Century | LITERARY COLLECTIONS / Women Authors

Classification: LCC PS3552.A17 Z89 2021 | DDC 813/.54 [B]—dc23

LC record available at https://lccn.loc.gov/2021001181

The paper in this book meets the guidelines for permanence and durability of the Committee on Production Guidelines for Book Longevity of the Council on Library Resources, Inc. ∞

Copyright © 2021 by the University of Oklahoma Press, Norman, Publishing Division of the University. Manufactured in the U.S.A.

All rights reserved. No part of this publication may be reproduced, stored in a retrieval system, or transmitted, in any form or by any means, electronic, mechanical, photocopying, recording, or otherwise—except as permitted under Section 107 or 108 of the United States Copyright Act—without the prior written permission of the University of Oklahoma Press. To request permission to reproduce selections from this book, write to Permissions, University of Oklahoma Press, 2800 Venture Drive, Norman OK 73069, or email rights.oupress@ou.edu.

To my sister Janet, Luke, and Zachary
—JD

To my mother, father, Steve, and John
—CHS

CONTENTS

Foreword ▪ ix
David M. Wrobel

Preface ▪ xiii
Joanne Dearcopp

Introduction ▪ 1
Joanne Dearcopp and Christine Hill Smith

1. Sanora Babb in Her Time and Ours ▪ 14
   Alan M. Wald

2. Thinking like the Plains: The Creation of Sanora Babb's Land Ethic ▪ 27
   Jessica Hellmann

3. Discovering Ecofeminism in Sanora Babb's Narratives ▪ 40
   Erin Royston Battat

4. The Real West in Sanora Babb's Short Stories ▪ 54
   Iris Jamahl Dunkle

5. Maternal Thinking in Sanora Babb's *An Owl on Every Post* ▪ 63
   Katherine Witt

6. Resilience in Sanora Babb's Life and Characters ▪ 72
   Amy Strickland Smith

7. Sanora Babb's *An Owl on Every Post* in the Canon of American Literature ▪ 83
   Daryl W. Palmer

8. "Today Is a Terror": *Whose Names Are Unknown* and the "New" Dust Bowl Novel ▪ 95
   Christopher Bowman

9. Farm Fiction: Cather, Wilder, and Babb ▪ 110
   Tracy Sanford Tucker

10. The Radical Voice of Sanora Babb ▪ 123
    Christine Hill Smith

11. Erratic Orbit: Sanora Babb, Poet ▪ 140
    Carol S. Loranger

12. Transcending Regional Literature: Teaching Sanora Babb ▪ 155
    Jeanetta Calhoun Mish and Cullen Whisenhunt

13. No Longer Unknown: Exploring the Archive of Sanora Babb ▪ 172
    Caroline Johnson and Mariah Wahl

Acknowledgments ▪ 187

List of Contributors ▪ 189

Index ▪ 195

DAVID M. WROBEL

■
FOREWORD

Unknown No More is the first comprehensive collection of essays charting the life experiences that undergirded the remarkable work of Sanora Babb, her empathy, advocacy, and creativity, and the impressive range of genres she employed as a writer. Babb's vital contributions to western American regional literature, to the national literary canon, and to the cause of social uplift and understanding are thoroughly and insightfully explored in the pages that follow. The essayists collectively make a powerful case for the depth and breadth of her footprint on the American past and the pertinence of her legacy to the present.

Sanora Babb's time has come, and *Unknown No More* will help bring it fully into being. In his landmark study *Exile's Return: A Literary Odyssey of the 1920s* (1934), renowned literary critic Malcolm Cowley charted the rediscovery of America by expatriate writers—including T. S. Eliot, John Dos Passos, F. Scott Fitzgerald, and Hart Crane. Cowley described how these formerly disillusioned writers "found a home" and "ceased to be exiles" by embracing the struggles of ordinary Americans during the Great Depression. Babb embraced those struggles as fully and forcefully as any of Cowley's subjects. In the *Portable Faulkner* (1946), Cowley revived interest in a great American writer whose works were not being widely read and were often viewed as obtuse and inaccessible. Faulkner's place at the tables of public and critical recognition needed reviving, and in that anthology, Cowley brought the full weight of Faulkner's contribution to American letters into focus. For Babb, it has been a long-term and sustained recovery project, and *Unknown No More* is a milestone in the growing appreciation of one of America's great literary voices.

Babb understood the culture and the hardships of the people she helped and then wrote about; her empathy grew from her experience. She was herself born in Oklahoma Territory, in April 1907, seven months prior to statehood. Babb experienced extreme poverty as a child, both in Oklahoma and eastern Colorado, where her family moved when she was seven to take up homesteading and reside in a primitive dugout dwelling. Her memoir recounting the family's homesteading struggles, *An Owl on Every Post* (1970), is one of the most beautifully detailed, compelling, and moving works in the entire genre of western settlement fiction. Her appreciation for her Otoe Indian neighbors back in Oklahoma is on full display as she reflects on what has been lost in the family's gamble on homesteading in Colorado. The theme of loss is seared into the reader's consciousness and heart when Babb chronicles being caught with her pregnant mother and younger sister in a wild storm they tried to outrun, the consequent premature birth and instant death of her brother in the dugout, and the pain of her father as he immediately dug the grave while Sanora held the lifeless body. This is one of the most powerful scenes in western American literature.

Although written earlier, Babb's first published novel, the heavily autobiographical *The Lost Traveler* (1958), recounts the family's nomadic existence after leaving Colorado because her father was a professional gambler. She began to write during these years and worked at local newspapers. Having earned her Associated Press credentials, at twenty-two Sanora traveled to Los Angeles to find a job in journalism, but the Depression was just beginning; opportunities had dried up before she arrived. On her visits to her mother in Garden City, Kansas, in the mid-1930s, Babb witnessed firsthand the terrible poverty in the area. A few years later she would volunteer to help poverty-stricken migrant families in the Farm Security Administration's government camps in California.

Drawing on her personal experiences, her deep feelings for the suffering of others, and her remarkable ability to capture the seasonal rhythms and the beauty and danger of the natural environment, Babb crafted her first novel in the late 1930s, though it would be the last of her work's published in her lifetime. *Whose Names Are Unknown* (2004) is the subject of excellent discussion in several essays in this volume. Suffice to say here that Babb's novel provides a harrowing and captivating account of the Dunne family's Dust Bowl struggles in western Oklahoma and their experiences in the presumed promised land of California. *Whose Names Are Unknown* would have entered the public consciousness and the literary canon upon publication at the beginning of the 1940s if the stars had aligned differently for Babb. And surely the book market at that time could have handled a second inspired and advocacy-driven novel on the contemporary California migrant crisis in addition to John Steinbeck's *The Grapes of Wrath* (1939).

Whose Names Are Unknown should become required reading for anyone interested in the American West, the human struggles of the Depression years, the connection of people to place, the plight of migrant families, the exploitation of the working poor, and the power of women to effect change. The novel should be read alongside *On the Dirty Plate Trail: Remembering the Dust Bowl Refugee Camps* (2007), a collection of Babb's unpublished field notes, letters, published articles, and short stories about the migrants' experiences, accompanied by photographs taken by her sister, Dorothy. In addition to the works already mentioned, two collections of Babb's short stories, *The Dark Earth and Other Stories* (1987) and *The Cry of the Tinamou* (1996), and her collection of poems, *Told in the Seed* (1998), deserve the attention of readers today. Babb's short stories were twice included in Martha Foley's important anthology *The Best American Short Stories* (1950 and 1960).

Babb's legacy as a poet, short story writer, novelist, memoirist, nature writer, feminist, labor activist, champion of the marginalized, and celebrator of racial and ethnic equality is realized in this important work of recovery. *Unknown No More* is a clarion call for Babb's enduring importance in the American literary canon and to the role of her activist writing in the struggles for social justice both during her lifetime and in our present moment. It is long since time for the nation to catch up with Sanora Babb.

JOANNE DEARCOPP

■
PREFACE

When Hy Cohen, an editor at McCall Books, came into my office late one afternoon in 1969 with a manuscript to read, little did I suspect it would be the start of a long and rich relationship with Sanora Babb. His description of the story—a family living in a dugout on the Colorado plains and struggling to survive—didn't sound very appealing to me as a young New York City gal. To my surprise, it captivated me. *An Owl on Every Post* shines with an exaltation of life despite its hardship story. It gave me my first sense of the author's undaunted exuberance for living.

The following year, when Sanora's memoir was soon to be published, I was in Los Angeles for a convention and was asked to take our author to lunch. She chose to meet at the Farmers Market (not my first choice on an expense account), and I was early. Killing time, I wandered the booths and bought a dramatic Navajo turquoise and coral pin. Then I joined Sanora, a striking, white-haired woman who flashed a warm smile that never left her face. She was smothered in turquoise jewelry—bracelets on both wrists, multiple rings, and a Zuni squash blossom necklace. Undeterred by her extravagant display, I enthusiastically showed her my new piece, and she admired it with generous praise. During our lively conversation, imbued with her joyous spirit, I began to suspect that here was a woman who wanted to squeeze all the juice out of life. My strong feeling of rapport was echoed years later when she wrote "there's some affinity here." After our lunch, she invited me to join her and her husband Jimmie (renowned cinematographer James Wong Howe) for dinner that evening in Chinatown. Thus began the evolution of our relationship—from professional to deeply personal—a friendship that lasted until her death.

Sanora's life changed markedly after Jimmie died in 1976. There were periods of grieving and lassitude. Attending to his legacy was demanding, yet she took time to write expressive poems about him. When I visited, I stayed at her Mediterranean-style white stucco home, perched high in the Hollywood Hills. We developed a ritual that was repeated at every visit: Sanora would remove tall stacks of books from atop a cabinet, open the top, and bring out her Indian jewelry piece by piece for us to admire and handle as one would fine art. It wasn't just jewelry; it was imbued with connective tissue to her memories of the Otoe Indians. Another ritual was our long talks—the main attraction of our time together. We would sit by the ceiling-to-floor arched window that filled half a wall with the view of Los Angeles spread below. In late afternoon, we'd have our tea, shifting to cocktails as the gloaming moved in.

First, we caught up on the activities of our lives and publishing news; we discussed our work, shared travel stories, speculated on life and death, reflected on men and romances in our lives. Yes, Sanora loved men and they loved her— our affinity on this led to lively shared stories. Being a creative storyteller and a romantic, her stories were sometimes embellished in the various tellings, but they always had a positive tone—even those of her hardship years. The way she told the story of her volatile family life in *The Lost Traveler*, for example, was deemed by her mother as "quite tame." Her most recurring stories grew out of her childhood memories of Chief Old Eagle, who wanted to buy her when she was a child, and the pinto pony and name he gave her: Little Cheyenne Riding Like the Wind. She didn't speak much about her times on movie locations with Jimmie, but I recall her saying that the best camaraderie of crew and cast she remembered was on *The Molly Maguires*. Neither did she talk much about her years in the Communist Party, and I didn't ask. How I wish I had. What came across in the stories and reminiscences was her fierce drive and determination to be free and independent. Our rich exchanges kept us talking as the lights of Los Angeles came on, first here and there, until finally, the entire city spread sparkling below us.

Dinner always seemed an intrusion. Sanora was never keen on cooking, but sometimes she would cook a boiled chicken and rice. She proudly told me, "Jimmie said I make the best rice." This was significant because she never wanted to be a housewife, which caused some rough periods early in her marriage as she strove to maintain her independence as a writer. "Jimmie was fully responsible to his gifts. I have been scattered; to me almost everything is interesting. I have not been fully responsible to my gift of writing, but I have always been very serious and respectful of it. Life is so full of possibilities, so rich that I could never resist living it in many ways. I don't regret that. I used to regret that I had not been more ruthless about writing and time for it. But I don't regret that anymore. I just accept it as a fact of my being." (February 23, 1977)

In her seventies and early eighties, Sanora was back to writing: a screenplay for *The Lost Traveler*, a treatment for a film on Jimmie, short stories and poems she wrote and sent out. Years after Jimmie's death, she startled me with this news in an April 7, 1986, letter: "I am indulging myself in a love affair with a Mexican Indian—age 29! and am delighted and super *alive* again in that special way. It got me writing again—poems mostly—but a pressing desire to write more than I have been."

In the early 1990s, we embarked together on a publishing campaign. I acted as her agent, and we succeeded in getting two out-of-print books republished, as well as her first collections of short stories and poetry. We both enjoyed this meaningful and productive period of constant contact: sharing ideas, selecting stories and poems for the collections, and engaging with publishers. Initially, I suggested we approach the Feminist Press, to which she sternly objected. "I'm not a feminist writer, I want to be known as a literary writer." The flurry of books coming out reactivated her identity as just such a writer, a confirmation of her life-long passion.

Unfortunately, it was during this same time Sanora began to experience serious medical issues. Major surgery in 1996 drained her energy but not her will. Writing to me on September 2, 1996, she said: "At present, no writing news from here.... when I leave dear old planet Earth. Until then I hope I can write a story or two and poems. Work is such a vital part of being alive, truly alive. But I love all kinds of being alive. Every minute!" Sanora's strong will, determination, and unfailing optimism were still at work. She was even optimistic about death. One time after returning from her cardiologist, she admitted she was disengaging from life. I asked her, "Do you fear death?" She quickly replied, "No. Who knows, it could be interesting." At my visits during these years, there was still much publishing activity to discuss, and we continued our rituals of enjoying her Indian jewelry (and new pieces I had bought) and our evening cocktails.

Six years later, the gloaming settled over Sanora's life. In her letters to me, her beautiful handwriting had deteriorated, revealing her physical decline. Yet the sun hadn't totally set—she saw her first written novel, *Whose Names Are Unknown*, finally published in 2004. She was bedridden by then, sleeping most of the time and hardly speaking. When I handed her the book, her smile was nonetheless luminous. I asked her to autograph my copy and with great effort she tried. Her illegible scrawl was shocking. I had all I could do to not cry in front of her, to maintain my smile and upbeat mood of the moment. That was the last time I saw her. A year later, identifying as she did with the planet Miranda in her poem, she left for a new adventure.

Miranda

I am in love with Miranda.
She is a free spirit.
How she escapes the celestial rules
Is a mystery not even science understands.
She whirls the opposite of Nature's whirls,
Lurching, tumbling: it's called erratic orbit.
She even wobbles in fun sometimes,
That is, for millions of years,
And wanders on impulse.
Miranda is a little planet, a little moon
Of Uranus, just three hundred miles across,
A good day's drive, but rough
Over "cliffs, craters, and oddly stacked terraces."
She lives among the stars, too small
To shine in Earth's far sight,

But her non-conformist ways
Puzzle the searcher's mind
And nudge his heart.

NOTE

All letters quoted herein are in the personal collection of Joanne Dearcopp.

JOANNE DEARCOPP AND CHRISTINE HILL SMITH

■ INTRODUCTION

> I always wanted a lot of experiences and I've certainly had them. But best of all I love being alive every minute; I love the earth, I love animals, wild and tame and wild birds, and weeds and trees and all growing things, and our magnificent and still unknown universe.
> —Sanora Babb

Since the democratic upheavals of the 1960s and 1970s, scholars in a range of disciplines have endeavored to recover the voices and experiences of women, people of color, and other groups excluded from historical narratives and the literary canon. Sanora Babb remained relatively unknown then, but now in a new era of social and political struggle, her time has come. Babb's long career began as a prolific and award-winning poet and short-story writer in the 1920s and 1930s. Her work appeared in the *Prairie Schooner, Midland, The Magazine, Southwest Review, Southern Review*, and other journals along with young writers such as William Saroyan, John Sanford, Meridel LeSueur, Tillie Olsen, Nelson Algren, Carlos Bulosan, and W. C. Williams and established writers Genevieve Taggard, Dorothy Parker, Nathanael West, and Katherine Anne Porter. She also published essays and short stories in the leftist journals *New Masses*, *The Anvil*, *California Quarterly*, and *The Clipper* alongside Thomas McGrath, Ernest Hemingway, Ralph Ellison, and Ray Bradbury.

Her first novel, *Whose Names Are Unknown*, written in the late 1930s, chronicled the Dust Bowl migration to California. It was praised by editors but rejected because of its unfortunate timing—she had just finished the manuscript when John Steinbeck's *The Grapes of Wrath* made a national sensation in 1939. Babb's subsequent books—her novel *The Lost Traveler* (1958) and memoir, *An Owl on Every Post* (1970)—earned critical acclaim but soon faded from view. Yet Babb's life and writings now speak to a new generation of readers. Her defiance of social conventions and her zest for life offer hope in a time, like hers, marked by inequality and division. Babb's stories, books, and poems offer a lens into a countercultural way of being marked by self-determination, open-mindedness, compassion, and love. They do so not through explicit political commentary, but with a complex exploration of the emotional experience of her protagonists as they make their way in the difficult world. Babb also captures the multisensory experience of the natural world, rendering remote and desolate landscapes beautiful and intimate.

Essays in this volume investigate how Babb's lived experience gave rise to a unique voice that has been overlooked by earlier recovery projects. Many current scholars now see her work within the context of her experience in the western lands of her childhood, her marginalized status growing up poor in small towns, her fierce loves across boundaries of race, and her work with the displaced farmworkers in the California migrant camps. Momentum is building for Babb's recovery as evidenced in the growing scholarship and proliferating conference papers and the eagerness of contributors to this volume. Taken together, the essays in this first collection of critical analyses make an argument for the recovery of an "unknown" writer—or, more accurately, one who was once known and then lost. In doing so, they add to the decades-long recovery projects that have breathed new life into the study of American literature and cultures.

A WRITER KNOWN AND UNKNOWN

Sanora Babb's childhood on the plains—from the Oklahoma Territory to a dugout in Eastern Colorado—followed by her family's frequent moves to small

Oklahoma and Kansas towns fueled a great deal of her writings. As a young woman eager to pursue a literary career, the choice was either Los Angeles or New York City; being a gambler's daughter, the decision was made with a coin toss by her father. In 1929, she moved to LA, experienced poverty and often homelessness, published her short stories and poems, and enjoyed the camaraderie of fellow writers and leftists.

In 1938, she volunteered to help in the California migrant camps, working with Tom Collins, the federal migrant-camp manager whose work and documentation would influence both Babb and John Steinbeck. She began to write her first novel and sent four chapters to Bennett Cerf, editor and cofounder of Random House, who was impressed enough to pay for her to come to New York City to finish the manuscript. On July 27, 1939, Cerf wrote her that "our first reader's report on your book is exceptionally fine." Yet on August 16, 1939, Cerf wrote that they would not publish her book and included the readers' reports. One, KB, wrote, "The book stands up to Steinbeck quite well. . . . Its people have more background. . . . I think this is a very fine book, solid and rewarding. The GRAPES was first, and many will follow. This will be one of the best. I hope we take it."[1]

Other publishers concurred on the book's merits, yet the consensus that the market could not support two Dust Bowl novels prevailed. Deeply disappointed, Sanora put her manuscript in a drawer, and there it stayed. She went on to publish two other books, but by the 1990s, these were out of print. One balmy evening on Sunset Boulevard, Sanora Babb and Joanne Dearcopp, Babb's long-time friend and soon-to-be agent, were finishing their al fresco dinner when out of the blue Sanora lamented, "I wish my books were back in print." Whether from the mellow mood or the lovely wine, Joanne instantly replied, "No problem. We can do that."

Babb and Dearcopp had met twenty years earlier when Dearcopp was with McCall Books, publisher of Babb's memoir, *An Owl on Every Post*, and her assuredness arose from the belief that Babb's work had literary merit. And so it happened—*Owl* and *The Lost Traveler* were republished (in 1994 and 1995, respectively). The goal then became to get more of her work out in book form. A collection of short stories, *Cry of the Tinamou* (1997), and a poetry collection, *Told in the Seed* (1998), followed. Finally, Joanne, along with the encouragement of Doug Wixson, convinced Sanora to get out the manuscript of *Whose Names Are Unknown*, and it was published in 2004, the year before she died. Sanora always considered it her "most important book," and it was quite an emotional moment for them when she first held the book; neither she nor Joanne had to speak.

It is impossible to know how Babb's career might have changed had Random House published *Whose Names* sixty-five years earlier, but we know that she was not unknown at that time. Her poetry was recognized in national magazines and newspapers, with her first poem published at age ten in the Forgan *Eagle*. This life-long pursuit, from the 1920s to the 1990s, gained her recognition, with poems included in the 1928 *Grub Street Book of Verse*, best poem in the 1928 March–April issue of *The Prism*, and a 1932 gold medal award in the *Mitre Press Anthology* (London). In his long-running Kansas Grass Roots column of the *Topeka Capital*, E. E. Kelley quoted praise from the *Wichita Eagle* and the Elkhart *Tri-State News*, concluding, "Sanora Babb is not only a talented young woman but she has the genius of industry: which is a right good thing for a writer of any sort to have."[2]

A major portion of Sanora's oeuvre written from the 1930s–1980s are her short stories, which appeared in diverse publications, from the *California Quarterly*, *New Masses*, and *The Clipper* to the *Saturday Evening Post*, *Antioch Review*, *Redbook*, and *Southern Review*. In a review of "The Dark Earth" and "The Refugee" in *Small Press Magazine* in 1987, Hugh Crane noted that "Babb can sing, and thereby convince us, at least for a while, that to touch bottom is to find hope."[3] And a *Publishers Weekly* review of the collection *Cry of the Tinamou* called her stories "evocative," noting with approval that "most of the tales feature strong female protagonists . . . [and] surprise a reader with their poignancy and sensitivity to character."[4]

Contemporaneous reviews of Babb's other book-length works were received with critical acclaim as well. *The Lost Traveler* (1958) was deemed "a brilliant first novel" by the *Los Angeles Times*. The *New York Times* noted, "There is a good deal of laughter in *The Lost Traveler*. There is a good deal of tragedy in it, too, for Miss Babb has given us a living and unflinchingly honest picture of a wandering gambler and his family. . . . a searching storyteller." When the book was published the same year in the United Kingdom, the London *Sunday Times* lauded, "Strongly recommended. A fascinating story . . . occasionally embarrassing, frequently funny, and as an account of the development of family relationships good by any standards."[5]

Babb's memoir, *An Owl on Every Post*, was mined from a portion of her earliest draft of *Whose Names*. It stands out as perhaps her most beautifully written book, showcasing her talent and passion as a vivid environmental writer. When originally published in 1970, Ralph Ellison considered it a "thought-provoking description of the mystery, wonder and poetry of growing up in a pioneering environment," and William Saroyan called it "an enchanting true story of a childhood on the plains. Absolutely Great." In a 1997 letter to Babb, long-time friend Ray Bradbury praised its "quiet humor, and . . . great all encompassing love for a land and her people."[6]

Similar to *The Lost Traveler*, *Owl* had wide appeal outside the United States in other English-speaking countries. With the headline "Magic Touch and Beauty in this Writing," the *Pretoria News* said that "the author has achieved a small miracle with this book for she has turned hunger, poverty, loneliness and depression into incomparable beauty by the magic of her writing." The London *Times* called it "Masterly. Hers is a small song, and not grand opera. But hearing it is a significant and salutary experience." And the London *Sunday Telegraph* called *Owl* "a quietly beautiful tale, haunted by the harsh splendor of the plains." Babb's ability to depict the beauty of a stark landscape and the spirit of the people who live there appeals to readers across geographic and cultural boundaries.[7]

When Babb's Dust Bowl novel *Whose Names Are Unknown* was published in 2004, it was, not surprisingly, almost universally compared to *The Grapes of Wrath*. The *Tulsa World* said that it "is one of the best I have ever read about Oklahoma Panhandle farmers during the 1930s . . . Is it better than Steinbeck's *The Grapes of Wrath*? I think so, but you be the judge." *Booklist* praised it as an "authentically compelling narrative. A slightly less political, more female-oriented, companion piece to *The Grapes of Wrath*." Mike Conklin interviewed Babb for a feature article in the *Chicago Tribune*, in which he notes that "those who have read both books say Babb's novel is a better read for today's market than *The Grapes of Wrath*—leaner, faster paced and full of details that give a more insightful look at a tragic time in American history."[8]

The backstory of the book's delayed publication and often sensationalized if inaccurate telling of Steinbeck's access to Babb's field notes gained as much attention as the book. A reviewer in the *Dallas Morning News* began with, "It is rare for the story behind a novel to be as compelling as the novel itself, especially when the book in question is as authentic and powerful as Sanora Babb's *Whose Names Are Unknown*" (Watt). The *Women's Review of Books* celebrated "At last we hear the whole powerful story from the point of view of a woman . . . a welcome addition to my canon of American working-class literature" (Annas).[9]

Complementing *Whose Names* is the nonfiction *On the Dirty Plate Trail: Remembering the Dust Bowl Refugee Camps* (2007) which publishes for the first time Babb's detailed field notes, as well as published articles and short stories, about the migrant worker. It is a vivid, firsthand account of the Dust Bowl refugees, migrant labor camps, and growth of labor activism among the farmworkers in California. It is a newer companion to the famous photojournalistic documentation of the Dust Bowl by the iconic couple Dorothea Lange and Paul Taylor in their 1939 *American Exodus*. *On the Dirty Plate Trail* features dozens of unmediated, even naïve photographs by Babb's sister Dorothy, which, while not as epic as those of Lange, nonetheless give one a candid sense of the migrant camps. The camp dwellers knew and trusted Sanora and her sister, and it shows; they didn't get to know Lange. Douglas Wixson, volume editor, provides extensive commentary in *Dirty Plate* and places the sisters' work in relevant historical and sociopolitical contexts; the book was a runner-up for the 2008 National Council on Public History Book Award.

While *Whose Names Are Unknown* had itself been a finalist for several awards, it took the Ken Burns Dust Bowl PBS documentary in 2012, in which he featured Babb and the novel, to immediately catapult it to best seller on Amazon and to reach a wide audience. Scholars, however, have been exploring her work for well over two decades. They recognize Babb as an important unexplored voice of mid-century America. An early advocate, Douglas Wixson, discovered Babb while researching proletarian authors for his 1994 book *Worker-Writer in America: Jack Conroy and the Tradition of Midwestern Literary Radicalism*. His in-person interviews and exhaustive research led to papers and presentations at academic conferences where he was often a lone advocate. Owing to Wixson's indefatigable efforts, Sanora Babb's work—primarily *Whose Names Are Unknown* and to some degree *An Owl on Every Post*—has featured in dissertations, essays, and books on the Dust Bowl migration, Depression-era culture, proletarian literature, farm fiction, regionalism, and western women's writing.

Recently, Babb has been discussed in relation to regionalism and "the Other" by Ken Hada; Great Plains women's work and identity by Jamie Rhoads-Coley; Oklahoma women's Dust Bowl history by Carly Fox; and as farm fiction by Nicholas Coles. She might be explored even more by analyses of her work in relation to that of Mari Sandoz, who in *Old Jules* shows us a domineering father governing an isolated prairie family, and the work of Oklahoma historian and pioneer Angie Debo. Like Babb, Debo had great respect for Native American history and culture and, more than Babb, suffered for her radical, revisionist work, being denounced in the 1930s and 1940s for writing accurate and damning histories exposing the US government's duplicitous policies toward the tribes.

Babb's memoir can be usefully compared to the famous 1927 novel *Giants in the Earth* by Ole Rolvaag, since its stark, perilous prairie setting and depressed frontier wife reflect the family situation in Babb's *Owl*. Family isolation on the plains as a new and unique challenge had been documented in the *Atlantic Monthly* in 1893 by E. V. Smalley in his excellent and wise "The Isolation of Life on Prairie Farms." Babb's mother suffered from the isolation in Colorado, though as a child, Babb herself loved it.

Robert V. Hine's classic *Community on the American Frontier: Separate but Not Alone* is a relevant study, with its progressive awareness of many of the environmental, feminist, and social issues that captured Babb's imagination and voice of protest. Recent scholarship on Babb reflects on her leftist politics, antiracism, and environmental consciousness and gives voice to women, the rural poor, and other marginalized communities. Books by Hughes Manzella, Gioia Woods, and Erin Royston Battat (and a promising dissertation by Natasha O'Neill) link Babb's work to the issues of American migration, race, and citizenship in a period of economic collapse and social upheaval. Douglas Wixson explores Babb's involvement with the Communist Party and California's leftist circles in Michael C. Steiner's collection *Regionalists on the Left*, while Kate Weigand examines the intersection of radical politics and gender in *Red Feminism: American Communism and the Making of Women's Liberation*. Similarly, Jennifer Marie Harrison and Francisco Eduardo Robles situate Babb alongside activist and antiracist writers Muriel Rukeyser, Zora Neale Hurston, Tomás Rivera, Lydia Mendoza, and Alice Walker and the singers Woody Guthrie and Odetta. Babb's Depression-era writing has also drawn scholars interested in the intersection of social class and the environment in this period. Sarah D. Wald fleshes out details of Sanora's time in California's fields in her study of race, citizenship, and farming since the Dust Bowl. Nicholas Coles and Janet Zandy's anthology of American working-class literature includes Babb's description of dust storms in *Whose Names Are Unknown* based on her mother's letters from Kansas. This scholarship recovers a rare voice—female, western, environmentally conscious—in the tradition of anticapitalist, antiracist dissent.

Scholars have begun to probe Babb's significance to the life and work of important writers of her era—John Steinbeck, William Saroyan, Ralph Ellison, B. Traven, Carlos Bulosan, and others. She is included in James Edward Ponzo II's discussion of jazz in Ralph Ellison's *Invisible Man* and in E. San Juan Jr.'s analysis of the anti-imperialist life and themes of Bulosan, a good friend of Babb and her sister Dorothy. Taking a new approach to Babb's work, Sharon Kristen Tang-Quan discusses her short stories about Chinese immigrant women in California, which focus on their successful efforts to counteract their often circumscribed lives. While Babb was first known as a voice of the rural West, scholars are beginning to recognize the broader universality of her writing.

The essays in this volume contribute to the growing body of Babb scholarship with fresh and critical perspectives that explore the complete range of her oeuvre, along with biographical and social circumstances of her life. As Alan M. Wald notes in his essay, "Sanora Babb in Her Time and Ours," it is important to view "her art as well as her life as interactive elements of the same analytical framework." With his encyclopedic knowledge of progressive writers, having known Babb and been an early supporter, Wald places Babb's leftist writing in the broader context of her life and work. Others, likewise, look at her life circumstances for clues to explain her prescience—be it environmentalism or feminism. In "Thinking like the Plains: The Creation of Sanora Babb's Land Ethic," Jessica Hellmann shows that in *An Owl on Every Post* and her two other longer works, Sanora depicts a world where humans are a respectful part of a living community, not just taking advantage of the land but instead "living in conversation and relationships." Just as Babb advocated for women's autonomy decades before feminism's second wave, she was ahead of her time in depicting a holistic connection of humans to the land and its ecology. She wrote of a "land ethic" well before Aldo Leopold defended rights for the environment in the late 1940s. As Wald notes in this volume, she "became a promising subject for eco-criticism before eco-criticism had a name."

In "Discovering Ecofeminism in Sanora Babb's Narratives," Erin Royston Battat presents Babb's environmental consciousness and nascent feminism as rooted in her rural western childhood. The essay explores Babb's feminist alternative to the frontier myth by looking at pioneer patriarchy, western masculinity, and a feminist revision of the western hero. Further analyzing this theme in another of Babb's genres, Iris Jamahl Dunkle's "The Real West in Sanora Babb's Short Stories" shows Babb's strong female protagonists living full lives in the American West. They unseat the classic cowboy stereotype and give us a more authentic and accurate depiction of the storied region. Focusing also on the upending of gender roles, Katherine Witt examines Babb's family dynamics to shed light on the fluid gender parenting in "Maternal Thinking in Sanora Babb's *An Owl on Every Post.*" In *Owl*, Sanora's grandfather, who had lost some decades of his life to alcohol, gets the chance to redeem himself by nurturing Sanora and her sister and taking charge of their education. Amy Smith's essay on "Resilience in Sanora Babb's Life and Characters" digs into Babb's personal history for the biographical underpinnings of her strong female characters. She explores how Babb's lifelong optimism, courage, and flexibility allowed her to overcome the deprivation and poverty she encountered in early life. This personal resilience explains Babb's focus on strong, autonomous female characters in her writing, although she knew women like her mother and sister who were constrained by life's vicissitudes and domineering men.

While momentum is building for the rediscovery of Sanora Babb, it is helpful at this stage for some comparative analysis with more established authors. Daryl W. Palmer, in "Sanora Babb's *An Owl on Every Post* in the Canon of American Literature," argues that Babb should be taught alongside Willa Cather and other more mainstream authors. He examines her transformation of the pioneer memoir and argues that its late arrival is a genuine strength, opening the door for innovations that her predecessors could not have imagined. Christopher Bowman compares Babb's authentic depiction of the Dust Bowl to John Steinbeck's more universally known version. In "Today Is a Terror: Whose Names Are Unknown and the 'New' Dust Bowl Novel," he explains how Babb's deep knowledge of the High Plains, dryland farming, and the California migrant labor conditions makes her novel more compelling if less epic than Steinbeck's. Tracy Tucker also places Babb in the canon, showing how her voice as farm-fiction writer compares to Willa Cather and Laura Ingalls Wilder in "Farm Fiction: Cather, Wilder, and Babb."

Although lesser known, Sanora Babb's earliest published work is her poetry, radical journalism, and proletarian short stories. Like her contemporaries on the Left, Babb was hampered by the anticommunist purges of the Cold War that silenced leftist writers and continue to tarnish critical evaluation of their work. Christine Hill Smith uncovers the literary and historical value of Babb's Depression-era, proletarian, and communist attitudes and writings. Using the Harry Ransom Center's deep Babb archive, Smith reviews Babb's leftwing journalism and fiction written during her communist years in "The Radical Voice of Sanora Babb." A critical evaluation of Babb's work would not be complete without an exploration of her lifelong engagement with poetry. Carol S. Loranger's aptly titled "Erratic Orbit: Sanora Babb, Poet" explicates her common themes and unique ones from her teen years into her eighties. In tracing the development of Babb's craft she maps out the stages, identifying characteristic themes and concerns—many reflecting events in her life.

Two essays offer valuable guidance to teaching and researching Babb's body of work and in so doing may help facilitate broadening awareness of her writing. In "Transcending Regional Literature: Teaching Sanora Babb," Jeanetta Calhoun Mish and Cullen Whisenhunt lay out the variety of classes in which one might teach Babb, for even though she has a coherent vision of humanity and larger societal forces in her writings, it's also true that Babb resists simple categorization. They provide a rationale and readings for courses that might include Babb in the literature of the West, migrants and immigrants, the Great Depression, and ecology/sustainability, as well as the proletarian novel, memoir, and biography. The Babb archive and librarians at the Harry Ransom Center serve as great partners for Babb scholars and interested readers alike. Caroline Johnson and Mariah Wahl relate an instance of this in "No Longer Unknown: Exploring the Archive of Sanora Babb." Taking a book group of local citizens through a reading of *Whose Names Are Unknown* and sharing HRC materials on the genesis of the book, they reveal the importance of archival access even for nonscholars.

The stars aligned beautifully for a number of years to culminate in this volume, *Unknown No More*. Douglas Wixson's passionate commitment to Babb and the many papers he presented and published have been a starting point and foundation for subsequent scholars. Sadly, ill health slowed and ultimately precluded his writing his intended Babb biography/social history of the High Plains. For years, he and Joanne Dearcopp worked to gain awareness of Sanora's work. Joanne organized panels at American Studies and Western Literature Association conferences, at which she blatantly would state, "I'm here to recruit champions." Christine Hill Smith was at the 2016 WLA Big Sky, Montana, conference, grabbed a copy of *An Owl on Every Post*, and started teaching it. The next year, she presented on Babb and the seeds of this volume were sown.

Unknown No More captures some of the current blossoming of interest in Sanora Babb's oeuvre. Her stories and ideas speak to the concerns of her historical time, place, and culture and to ours today. The lyricism of her writing and her ability to sense the extraordinary in the ordinary elevate even the bleakest of her stories. Babb's timelessness and current relevance reflect her embrace of life and love and her commitment to crossing boundaries and defending human dignity. Most of her characters are marginalized people—farmers, migrants, immigrants, and the displaced—who are depicted with understanding and compassion. She celebrates the multiplicities of ethnicities and backgrounds in America and hopes for intercultural connections and solidarity. Perhaps because of her youth on the late frontier, Babb has a capacity for envisioning a better future for her characters despite their real disadvantages. Her inclusive and progressive attitudes about race, gender, and the environment speak to contemporary readers as we become more aware of social inequities and looming environmental problems. Sanora Babb internalizes what Wallace Stegner called "the geography of hope," and she has much to say to us and to later generations.

NOTES

1. Bennett Cerf to Sanora Babb, 27 July and 16 August 1939, Joanne Dearcopp personal collection (copy; originals of all letters in the Dearcopp collection are in the Harry Ransom Center, University of Texas at Austin, Austin, TX).
2. E. E. Kelley, "A Shortgass Poetess," *Topeka Capital*, n.d.
3. Hugh Crane, *Small Press*, October 1987.
4. Review of *Cry of the Tinamou*. *Publishers Weekly*, 22 September 1997.
5. "From the Daily Book Report." *Los Angeles Times*, 5 April 1958, p. 89; Charles Poore, "Books of the Times," *New York Times*, 20 March 1958, p. 27; Review of *Lost Traveler*, *London Sunday Times*, Aug. 1958.
6. Ralph Ellison, William Saroyan, and Ray Bradbury on cover copy for *An Owl on Every Post*, by Sanora Babb (Muse Ink Press, 2012).
7. "Magic Touch and Beauty in this Writing," Review of *Owl*, *Pretoria News*, 29 March 1972; Review of *Owl*, *London Times*, 1 November 1971; Review of *Owl*, *London Sunday Telegraph*, 16 January 1972.
8. Mike Nobles, "Book Puts Human Face on Depression-Era 'Okies,'" *Tulsa World*, May 2, 2004; Margaret Flanagan, "Babb, Sanora: Whose Names Are Unknown, May 2004," *Booklist*, 15 April 2004; Mike Conklin, "'Whose Names Are Unknown' Finally Becomes Known," *Chicago Tribune*, 13 October 2004, https://www.chicagotribune.com/news/ct-xpm-2004-10-13-0410160157-story.html.
9. Donaley Watt, *Dallas Morning News*, 2 June 2005; Annas, *Women's Review of Books*.

WORKS CITED

Annas, Pamela J. *Women's Review of Books*, vol. 21, nos. 10–11, July 2004, 10–11.
Battat, Erin Royston. *Ain't Got No Home: America's Great Migrations and the Making of an Interracial Left*. University of North Carolina Press, 2014.
Coles, Nicholas. "Working the Fields: Love and Labor in Farm Fiction from 1890 to the Dust Bowl." *A History of American Working-Class Literature*, edited by Nicholas Coles and Paul Lauter, 215–31. Cambridge University Press, 2017.

Coles, Nicholas, and Janet Zandy, editors. *American Working-Class Literature: An Anthology*. Oxford University Press, 2006.

Debo, Angie. *And Still the Waters Run: The Betrayal of the Five Civilized Tribes*. Princeton University Press, 1940; University of Oklahoma Press, 1984.

Fox, Carly. *Radical Genealogies: Okie Women and Dust Bowl Memories*. 2015. Sarah Lawrence College, master's thesis.

Hada, Ken. "Voices in the Earth: How Regional Writing Validates the Other." *Journal of the American Studies Association of Texas*, vol. 37, November 2006, pp. 69–78.

Harrison, Jennifer Marie. "Oppositional Narratives: Embedded Tales, Social Justice, and the Reader." 2014. University of Maryland, PhD dissertation.

Hasslestrom, Linda. Introduction. *Old Jules*, by Sandoz, Mari. 1935. 2nd ed., Bison Books, 2005.

Hine, Robert V. *Community on the American Frontier: Separate but Not Alone*. University of Oklahoma Press, 1981.

Kelley, E. E. "A Shortgrass Poetess." *Topeka Capital*, n.d.

Lange, Dorothea, and Paul Taylor. *An American Exodus: A Record of Human Erosion*. Reynal & Hitchcock, 1939.

Manzella, Abigail. "Permanent Transients: The Temporary Spaces of Internal Migration in Four 20th-Century Novels by U.S. Women Writers." 2010. Tufts University, PhD dissertation.

Manzella, Abigail, and Genée Hughes. *Migrating Fictions: Gender, Race, and Citizenship in U.S. Internal Displacements*. Ohio State University Press, 2018.

O'Neill, Natasha. *Race and Hunger in Depression-Era Literature*. 2017. University of California, Santa Barbara, PhD dissertation. *ProQuest*, http://search.proquest.com/docview/1937923307/abstract/46122A84E89C4004PQ/7. Accessed 1 June 2020.

Ponzo, James Edward, II. *Order, Jazz, and Chaos in Ralph Ellison's "Invisible Man."* 2016. State University of New York at Buffalo, master's thesis. *ProQuest*, http://search.proquest.com/docview/1810153845/abstract/46122A84E89C4004PQ/3. Accessed 1 June 2020.Rhoads-Coley, Jamie. "Gendered Power on the Great Plains: Women's Work and Community Identity in the 1930s." 2016. Texas A&M University Commerce, master's thesis. *ProQuest*, http://search.proquest.com/docview/1861177644/abstract/46122A84E89C4004PQ/5. Accessed 1 June 2020.

Robles, Francisco Eduardo. *Migrant Modalities: Radical Democracy and Intersectional Praxis in American Literatures, 1923–1976*. 2016. Princeton University, PhD dissertation. *ProQuest*, http://search.proquest.com/docview/1796054415/abstract/46122A84E89C4004PQ/2. Accessed 1 June 2020.

Rolvaag, Ole. *Giants in the Earth*. Harper, 1927.

San Juan, E., Jr. "Excavating the Bulosan Ruins: What Is at Stake in Re-discovering the Anti-Imperialist Writer in the Age of US Global Terrorism?" *Kritika Kultura*, vol. 23, 2014, pp. 154–67, doi: http://dx.doi.org/10.13185/1885. Accessed 28 May 2020.

Smalley, E. V. "The Isolation of Life on Prairie Farms." *Atlantic Monthly*. September 1893. pp. 378–381. https://www.theatlantic.com/magazine/archive/1893/09/the-isolation-of-life-on-prairie-farms/523959/. Accessed 26 August 2020.

Steiner, Michael C. *Regionalists on the Left: Radical Voices from the American West.* University of Oklahoma Press, 2013.

Tang-Quan, Sharon Kristen. *Transpacific Utopias: The Making of New Chinese American Immigrant Literature, 1945–2010.* 2013. University of California, Santa Barbara, PhD dissertation. *ProQuest,* http://search.proquest.com/docview/1505373102/abstract/46122A84E89C4004PQ/6. Accessed 1 June 2020.

Wald, Alan M. Introduction. *Cry of the Tinamou: Stories,* by Sanora Babb. University of Nebraska Press, 1997.

Wald, Sarah D. *The Nature of California: Race, Citizenship, and Farming since the Dust Bowl.* University of Washington Press, 2016.

Weigand, Kate. *Red Feminism: American Communism and the Making of Women's Liberation.* Johns Hopkins University Press, 2001.

Wixson, Douglas. "Radical by Nature: Sanora Babb and Ecological Disaster on the High Plains, 1900–1940." *Regionalists on the Left: Radical Voices from the American West,* edited by Michael C. Steiner. University of Oklahoma Press, 2013, pp. 111–33.

———. *Worker-Writer in America: Jack Conroy and the Tradition of Midwestern Literary Radicalism.* University of Illinois Press, 1994.

Woods, Gioia, editor. *Left in the West: Literature, Culture, and Progressive Politics in the American West.* Nevada University Press, 2018.

ALAN M. WALD

1
SANORA BABB IN HER TIME AND OURS

In her illuminating foreword to *The Dark Earth & Other Stories from the Great Depression* (1987), Sanora Babb (1907–2005) is blunt about the sources and sensibilities of her fiction, poetry, and journalism: "No matter what form writing takes, writers are writing out of their experience and their times. Even when they are indifferent, they are holding up their personal mirrors."[1] For the scholar and critic of today, Babb's dictum, which she reiterates on several occasions, is an admonition against inquiries into an author's literary creativity while one is ill-informed about, or even just unconcerned with, biographical and social circumstances. We are not talking here of a search for mechanical causality between literal and fictionalized events or of correlations between actual people and literary characters; rather, we are speaking about her art and her life as interactive elements of the same analytical framework.

Babb's note of guidance is imperative for those of us who encounter Babb's work amid the alarm bells of the present. After all, in 2020, United States government policies menace the hopes and security of immigrants, the inequality of wealth endangers the health and well-being of the poor, rapacious exploitation by corporations proceeds unabated against the environment, misogynous legal decisions endanger the fundamental right of women to control their own bodies, and the COVID-19 pandemic has created the deadliest medical crisis for the poor in half a century. Such a time could hardly be more conducive to appraising the social intelligence and artistic ingenuity of a writer such as Sanora Babb, who so often presents us with a view through the eyes of the "other" to reveal how unrecognized facets of humanity are all around us. So how does one approach Babb on her own terms?

THE PERSONAL MIRROR

The years of a woman who lived nearly a century can be divided in myriad ways and then have their peaks and dips reassembled to meet an assortment of agendas. Yet biographical studies confirm that a writer is never completely independent of the context and purposes that attended the dawning of her art; the writing that comes afterward stays affected by that inaugurating emotional architecture. That is why the preponderance of scholarship about Babb accurately acknowledges that her upbringing in western High Plains poverty gave a singularity to her life not only as an artist but as a woman as well. As all her book-length works attest, she was an offspring of the windswept plains of both Oklahoma and Colorado. And this became a life tasted twice over, once in the living and again in the telling in the pages of two novels (*The Lost Traveler* [1958] and *Whose Names Are Unknown* [2004]), a book-length memoir (*An Owl on Every Post* [1970]), several short stories (especially "A Good Straight Game" [1951]), and at least one poem ("Old Snapshots" [1965]).[2]

It was first and foremost the personal encounters with hunger and insecurity in her childhood that gave birth to a marked sensitivity to the intricate feelings and conflicts that drive her impoverished and outcast characters—those homeless, facing discrimination, and politically repressed. She knew first-hand about women accustomed to being unseen and never being fully known, and of the diverse ethnic constituents in a community of oppressed but determined people. Whether or not she inserted an avatar of herself as the engine of a particular story, she carefully deployed moments related to her own experiences (sometimes through personally conducted research) to open new emotional territory. As if rewriting the same story throughout her entire life, interweaving the personal with social history, Babb employed members of her immediate family as a prime source for complex characters depicted in layered and nuanced ways.

And then there were the violent dust storms on the plains, of which she and her mother were keen observers. Such memories probably aroused in her a passion for nature so that she became a promising subject for eco-criticism before eco-criticism had a name. Her poetry in particular specializes in relocating emotions to flora and fauna, as in "Again":

> And we were happy again
> As close as the veins of leaves
> As lyric as larks
> As destined as seeds[3]

This is typical of the manner in which her verse uses images gleaned from the landscape to comment on human behavior.

Other poems, however, seem like celebrations of repeated amazement at nature:

> The stars have fallen down.
> The western sky is big over the wide valley.
> It meets the sea like the lid of a box closing
> Over jewels. Small diamonds gleam on the sea
> And wink in the air. A ruby bracelet circles a tower.[4]

In addressing other topics (such as "At Mama's Grave"), Babb's poetry reveals itself as both intimate and cosmic.[5] And the many verses treating love (such as "Love Song" and "The Verge") exhibit a sparsely elegant and at times judicious use of environmental material in inventive ways to articulate subjective material.[6] As with passages in her fiction, these suggest that some of the smallest and most fleeting events in our lives are also the most significant.

However, when we move beyond the elements that formed her initial, and enduring, deepest emotions, we encounter more elusive and problematic aspects of Babb's life. First came a bohemianism that drew her toward the "New Woman" ethos of writers such as Edna St. Vincent Millay, an intense (and still not fully revealed) relationship with William Saroyan, and immersion in the milieu of diversely radical and untamed writers and artists who were pulled to the Communist-led John Reed Club in the early 1930s. Then came two decades as an activist allied with the Communist Party (CP-USA), most of that time as an organized member. Under new literary inspirers, such as the radical poets

Ralph Cheney and Lucia Trent and novelist Sherwood Anderson, her literary skills were intensively honed by participating in the editorial groups of three journals led by CP-USA supporters and the submission of her own draft manuscripts to the Hollywood Writers Clinic supervised by CP-USA cultural leader John Howard Lawson.[7]

LOVE AND REVOLUTION

Investigations into these two areas of Babb's past—the personal and the political—have until recently been stymied by an understandable secrecy about her intimate life and the persistence of misleading Cold War perceptions about Communist politico-cultural identity. By 2020, however, cracks have opened providing at least a beginning insight into both aspects. The centrality of her romantic and Communist experiences to her psyche starting in the mid-1930s was suggested, albeit somewhat cryptically, by her statement of intention in 1987 to write directly about them: "Through new acquaintances, old friends or old loves or destiny, I met my future husband, James Wong Howe [1899–1976], the Chinese cinematographer, a fine artist, a fine man. In those years such a union was taboo, and a whole new set of experiences began, both terrible and wonderful, about which I hope to write someday."[8]

Why she never wrote that story of these "terrible and wonderful" things during the next twenty years is not known. In regard to Babb's intimate life, Howe had died a decade earlier, after six years of illness, so amorous revelations would not personally wound him. But perhaps her own age and health slowed her down, or maybe the subject matter turned out to be more painful and recalcitrant than she had anticipated. Fortunately, Arnold Rampersad, Erin Royston Battat, John F. Callahan, Marc C. Conner, Panthea Reid, and Larry Ceplair have provided preliminary information on the complicated marriage of Howe and Babb, although Howe's inner life still remains obscure.

What these scholars reveal about Babb is that her insistence on independently maintaining male friendships, several of them sexual, caused repeated crises in her marriage followed by healing reconciliations.[9] Erotic liberation, eighty or ninety years ago, could be complex, especially for a woman.[10] Research into the life of Ralph Ellison, confirmed by correspondence, shows that Babb might have been candid about taking the initiative in regard to her own sexual passion, somewhat beyond the conventional norms of her society.[11] On the other hand, she was no uninhibited Janis Joplin, and she was quite censorious of her friend Tillie Olsen's behavior; to an Olsen biographer, she complained that Olsen's amorous conduct could be too casual, without emotional involvement or commitment.[12] A letter to Jewish American Communist producer and screenwriter Paul Jarrico (1915–97) offers some insight into Babb's own heterosexual preferences:

> it seems to me that you are generous and warm, rather than cautious and shy; that you are gentle and tender, that you have a quietness that has nothing to do with an uncertainty, that you are capable of simple gaiety, which is rare. . . . I like the way you behave with women—a kind of promiscuous and sincere attention which seems to contain no real promiscuity or emotion, but a fairly large liking for them.[13]

Jarrico, like Ellison and, earlier, Saroyan, was younger and from an ethnic minority. Also, the first two were married at the time, like Babb, and shared her political devotion.

Lovers are one thing, and siblings are another. An additional dimension of her intimate life that must receive far more attention involves her fraught relation to her younger sister, Dorothy. In many ways, Dorothy was a less successful Sanora, due in part to psychological problems that tormented her mature years. Like her older sister, Dorothy aspired to write fiction, and she even hoped to be known as one of "The Writing Babb Sisters."[14] Also like Sanora, she was involved with men of color around the Communist movement—Carlos Bulosan, Lal Singh—although she never realized a long-term committed relationship.[15] Endlessly aspiring and endlessly frustrated, Dorothy's illness kept her mainly housebound and often dwelling with Sanora, an additional source of conflict with Howe.[16]

The literary implications of these experiences have barely been addressed. Babb reportedly read *Madam Bovary* six or seven times, studying it carefully, although the novel has yet to be cited as an influence.[17] In her book-length works, Babb's mature women are mired in economic circumstances such as to constrain sexual freedom of any type, and the autobiographically based females are of a young age. However, the story "Reconciliation" appears to address a troubled marriage, likely derived from her own relationship to Howe, and "The Vine by Root Embraced" is a commentary on the challenges awaiting a professional woman who seeks a fulfilling partnership.[18] The plot of the latter, one of several stories set in China, concerns a nurse who realizes her dream of marrying the doctor for whom she works, only to find him insistent that she abandon her career and also refusing sexual consummation. When she discovers his incestuous relation with his overbearing mother, a woman who demands others conform to old-fashioned gender roles, the protagonist turns for support to a wise uncle, who encourages her to obtain a divorce.

NO REGRETS

Babb's loyalty to the Communist Party was a deep one in the sense that she never publicly expressed political disagreements with any of the numerous political twists and turns of the movement. Here we have documentation of a general trajectory, but many specifics remain uncertain or simply unknown, leaving many blanks to be filled in by subsequent scholarship. For example, Douglas Wixson, probably the dean of Babb scholars and an admired expert on the literary Left, stated in *Worker-Writer in America* that Babb "broke" with the CP-USA at the end of the 1930s as a result of "CP censors who insisted on scrutinizing her work before publication."[19] Yet fifteen years later, Wixson wrote that she "left it [the CP-USA] in the 1950s, convinced that it had lost the progressive aims that first attracted her," and he made this point, about her severing connections, a second time after citing the Khrushchev revelations of Soviet terror, which he misdates as 1958.[20]

In contrast, Babb insisted to me that she had no problems with the CP-USA in the 1930s that resulted in rupture, including some negative opinions she received about her manuscripts, and the accurate date of the Khrushchev revelations is early 1956.[21] Nevertheless, it remains possible, pending further investigation, that Babb dropped out for various periods (especially during World War II when she was engaged in civil defense work), or shifted from a CP-USA branch to a writers unit or some other status, or that she was disquieted by the 1956 revelations but, like others, held off on a total break until 1958 to see if there were any real changes. Although it may defy conventional beliefs about writers who left Communism, Babb's stated objection that led to her ultimately disowning the CP-USA was not that it was authoritarian or too tied to the USSR, but that it was no longer progressive.

What is certain is that her attraction to the CP-USA emerged during the ultra-revolutionary early 1930s (when Franklin Delano Roosevelt was characterized as a fascist) and blossomed into a formal commitment during the Popular Front (when Roosevelt transformed into a hero and ally). Thus, her allegiance was not a response to conjunctural politics and was not shaken during the era of the Hitler-Stalin Pact (when anti-fascist organizations were disbanded), the Browderite dissolution of the CP-USA into the Communist Political Association, the subsequent left turn after Browder's expulsion, or during the early 1950s when she and others believed that the US was on the verge of fascism. Indeed, her fears about this last episode are well-documented in correspondence with Communist editor Charles Humboldt (a pseudonym for Clarence Weinstock).[22] Her effort to evade a subpoena to testify before a congressional body explains why she temporarily relocated to Mexico, where she was especially close to the Communist dancer Waldeen.[23] The only evidence of any uneasiness with the CP-USA leadership came through her participation in a literary debate, "The Maltz Affair," which I will discuss below.

Even after separating herself from CP-USA institutions, Babb never voiced bitterness or criticisms of the movement in any way that I have seen. Although she would later call herself a "liberal," there is no known record of her coming to terms with the seriousness of Soviet despotism, and she affirmed that she had "no regrets" about her CP-USA past.[24] On the contrary, one can find a surprising number of continuing literary associations. For example, in 1958, her short story "Young Boy, the World" appeared in a pro-Communist collection, *The American Century*, edited by Maxim Lieber. Lieber, who had been among Babb's literary agents, was a member of the CP-USA implicated in Whitaker Chambers's espionage activities and fled the United States for Mexico in 1951 and then to Communist Poland in 1954. Seven Seas Books, an East German publishing house, published his anthology, and the vast majority of contributors can be readily identified with the CP-USA. One wonders what she thought of the crude, propagandistic postscript by Lieber, which would have met the approval of Andrei Zhdanov, the notorious Stalinist cultural ideologue.

Then, in 1987, Babb jointly published a story collection in a volume with Lew Amster, a former party member who never abandoned his political beliefs, and she was also maintaining a friendship with novelist John Sanford, whose views about Communism were the same as those of his good friend Amster.[25] After that, in 1998, Babb published her sole collection of poetry with the radical West End Press, edited by the former Communist journalist John Crawford, who devoted extraordinary efforts to keeping alive the memory and writing of many cultural workers with Communist backgrounds—Don West, Meridel Le Sueur, Thomas McGrath among them.

Still, one shouldn't overplay the role of the CP-USA in Babb's life and deny her the force of her own decisions and creativity. By my own estimation, her close emotional connection with the movement lasted about twenty years, and a formal organizational affiliation may have spanned close to fifteen. But it always seems to have been more of a moral than an ideological commitment. Babb was not a polemicist but an activist, hyper in her own assessment; she claimed that this was a cause of her lack of productivity, which led to a belief that she would be remembered as a good minor talent.[26] Starting in the late 1930s, evidence is strongest for her prioritizing literary and editorial involvement in three publications steered by pro-Communists, not only *The Clipper* and *Black and White*, where Babb played a leading role, but especially in *California Quarterly*.

To retrieve memories of the Communist cultural movement is simultaneously to realize how much has been forgotten. Among the many surprises of research is to discover that there are almost no references to Babb in the substantial scholarship and memoir writing about the Hollywood Left, including the period of exile in Mexico, where she resided for a four-month and then a six-month period. She was, after all, hardly invisible, serving on the executive committee of the Communist-led League of American Writers (LAW) in 1937; as executive secretary of the LAW in 1938; and as the secretary-treasurer of the Hollywood chapter in 1939, 1940, 1941, and 1942 (the LAW's final year). One explanation for this absence was the desire to protect the reputation of Howe from any hint of Communist association; as the cinematographer on many films by radicals and also as the owner (through Babb) of a Chinese restaurant that, among other things, was a sometime hang-out for the Progressive crowd, Howe was a well-known figure among Leftists in the film industry.[27] Not only was there a danger of Howe's being blacklisted, but Howe lacked US citizenship (he could own no property, such as a house) and could face deportation. In addition, Babb herself tended to work quietly behind the scenes, never seeking the limelight, and this was at a time when women were not taken seriously as leaders.

Nevertheless, her CP-USA commitment was palpable. She was no fellow traveler, but she signed up and participated in party affairs, not as a pontificator of the party view but as an activist-organizer. She traveled to the USSR, then worked for a while on the pro-Communist publication the *Week*, edited by Claude Cockburn, in England, and on her return was reported (by an informer) to have bragged about meeting Stalin himself.[28] She took a party assignment of volunteering to work among agricultural workers, collaborating with Tom Collins, manager of the Arvin Sanitary Camp, whom she considered a potential CP-USA recruit.[29] Back in Hollywood, she raised funds for defense of the Spanish Republic and was a volunteer in the office of the Hollywood Anti-Nazi League.[30] It was in Babb's apartment that editorial meetings were held for the pro-Communist publications *Black & White* and *The Clipper*, and she later used her home to host fundraising events for the *California Quarterly*.[31]

Babb's participation in the well-known Albert Maltz Affair is also not as simple as it might seem from the straightforward fact of her defense of the well-known Communist screenwriter and novelist. In February 1946, Albert Maltz published an article in the CP-USA's *New Masses* titled "What Shall We Ask of Writers?" in which he criticized fellow Communist writers for placing political concerns above artistic ones in judging literary quality. The result was primarily venomous attacks on Maltz from fellow CP-USA members, both in print and in person at party meetings. He was accused of "Browderism" (diluting Communist principles) and in order to retain his good standing, he was obligated to repudiate his own article.[32]

Although the dispute might be boiled down to the question of whether the slogan "Art as a Weapon" should remain the watchword of the literary Left, Babb herself was not opposed to proletarian literature. Her story "Young Boy, the World" and book *Whose Names are Unknown* would qualify as much as other writings in the genre.[33] Nevertheless, it was difficult for Babb to sustain a quantity of writing in that style, especially in the 1930s, when Lawson and others put pressure on her to be more socially conscious in her fiction. Not only was her primary focus on fresh language, but she relied mainly on her own experiences and preferred to depend in her writing not "on the merit of shock, but on the pull of emotion."[34] Nevertheless, her objection to the attacks on Maltz was not a defense of aestheticism or complete artistic freedom, but mainly that he was being misrepresented as a heretic or renegade through "quick judgments." She insisted that Maltz's essay fell within the norms of the Communist cultural movement as articulated by *New Masses* critic Isidor Schneider in his opening of the debate.[35]

THE BOUNDARIES OF EMPATHY

As a Communist writer, Babb was hardly unique in speaking to the broadening roles of women in United States literature. Like Agnes Smedley, Josephine Herbst, Tillie Olsen, and others, she was in the vanguard of cultural shift that revealed the invisible burdens that can weigh down the lives of those oppressed by gender and class. Through her regional emphasis in her book-length works, she staked out her own territory, but in the twenty-first century, she mostly remains a minor figure. The one exception is that the late publication of her rediscovered novel of the 1930s, *Whose Names Are Unknown*, has given her a somewhat popular niche in literary studies as the feminist anti-Steinbeck.

In my view, however, the reconstruction of Babb's entire career is still very much in progress as we await more scholarship about the shape of a life that largely remains to be seen. After Communism, a core identity as a political radical may still have existed in Babb but in increasingly scrambled form. To be sure, even when removed from her original geographic settings, her postwar fiction and poetry take her female characters on an emotional journey that touch on the mid-century's racial and social attitudes as she skillfully weaves bright threads of nuance and exacting observation of the social mores. Babb may have commenced as our plebeian Jane Austen of the plains, with the motive of committing acts of earnest witnessing. Over time, though, her art increasingly suggests a socialist Vermeer, patiently observing and chronicling daily life from angles odd and slanted. But what she thought of the new styles of radicalism of the 1960s and issues such as Vietnam and Black Power was not made explicit. Here one will have to dig very deep to find the person beneath the superficial images that appear on book covers, in blurbs, and in Wikipedia.

Craft conscious as well as class conscious, Babb's writing can be bittersweet, elegant, and faintly wistful, sometimes with a grim documentary frisson. She can pour herself into nooks and crannies of her characters' contradictions even as her vision is undergirded by a Marxian awareness of the structures of oppression. The result is that she pushes the boundaries of empathy to value humanity as undivided and seemingly catches the zeitgeist of at least two ages—the Great Depression and the New Millennium. No wonder the faces staring out from much of her fiction at times have a startling immediacy. Do we really want to treat her recreations of the 1930s and after as antique artifacts to be scrutinized through glass cases? Are they not, in so many respects, living and breathing with much to reveal about our own times?

It is one thing to note connections between cultural works from another era and today in order to commend how the artist makes history feel contemporary. It is another to treat Babb too facilely as "one of us," as if her notion of social change is of a piece with the anti-Trump "resistance," or to conclude that her acute attentiveness to women's oppression is effectively a version of third or fourth wave (or even second wave) feminism. The impulse to consider Babb as our contemporary is understandable and not without merit, but it can also threaten to take away a crucial specificity from her art, the generation that came of age in the 1930s, and episodes in literary history during the post-Depression decades. Babb must be seen from a multiplicity of angles through the prism of her life and times, her predecessors and contemporaries, as well as preoccupations of a new cohort of readers. This is foundational—and it is what Babb herself desired—if future scholars are to enhance their understanding of what is distinctive in her personal-political narratives of the mid-twentieth century that gave her license to speak for suppressed and marginalized voices of her time.

NOTES

1. Babb, *The Dark Earth*, 9.
2. Sanora Babb, "A Good Straight Game," in *The Dark Earth*, 65–78; "Old Snapshots."
3. Babb, "Again," in *Told in the Seed*, 56.
4. Ibid., 29.
5. Babb, *Told in the Seed*, 41.
6. Ibid., 50, 52.
7. In the Wald interview with Babb in Los Angeles, July 1989, Babb cited the sequence of literary influences. Babb also reported to me that while many pro-Communist writers never submitted their drafts to the Writers Clinic, she did it when it was suggested, although she was not always happy with the results.
8. Babb, *The Dark Earth*, 10.
9. Battat, *Ain't Got No Home*, 45.
10. I attempted to address some of these gender issues in Wald, "Introduction: Soft Focus."
11. See Rampersad, *Ralph Ellison*, 48. More documentation can be found in Callahan and Conner, *The Selected Letters of Ralph Ellison*, 148–54.
12. Reid, *Tillie Olsen*, 106.
13. Ceplair, *The Marxist and the Movies*, 77–78.
14. See correspondence from Dorothy and Sanora Babb, 1951–54, in the McCoy papers.
15. Wald interview with Roxanna Ma Newman, 21 February 2008, Ann Arbor, MI.
16. McCoy papers.
17. Wald interview with Babb, Los Angeles, July 1989.
18. These are reprinted in Babb, *Cry of the Tinamou*, 31–40 and 89–104.
19. Wixson, *Worker-Writer in America*, 396.
20. See Wixson, "Radical by Nature," 123.
21. Wald interview with Babb. In regard to the Writers Clinic, Sbardellati reports in his article about Albert Maltz: "Communists in Hollywood were not obliged to submit their work to Lawson or to follow his advice. Indeed, Maltz himself 'never submitted an idea with Lawson.'" See Sbardellati, "The Maltz Affair Revisited," 5. Nevertheless, Babb may well have been hurt by criticism, as her later correspondence with Charles Humboldt suggests a defensiveness in regard to her approach to social issues.
22. See Babb to Charles Humboldt, 5 February 1952, Charles Humboldt papers.
23. See Babb to Charles Humboldt, 11 October 1951, Charles Humboldt papers.
24. Babb interview with Wald.

25. See correspondence between Sanford and Amster in the John Sanford Collection. In discussing her collaboration on the joint volume, Babb's only criticism of Amster was that he lived off women. Babb sent an inscribed copy of *The Cry of the Tinamou* to Sanford in 1997. See Box 20 of the Sanford Collection.

26. Babb to Charles Humboldt, 11 October 1951, Charles Humbolt papers.

27. Howe's restaurant was called Ching How and was located in Studio City. Since Howe could not own property, it is likely that Sanora was listed as owner and worked as manager, while Dorothy kept the books. When Babb left for Mexico in the early 1950s, the restaurant shut down. Email from Joanne Dearcopp, 23 January 2020.

28. Horne, *Class Struggles in Hollywood*, 89.

29. See Wixson, *On the Dirty Plate Trail*, 102.

30. Babb interview with Wald.

31. See Endore, Introduction, 4; and Babb to Charles Humboldt, 11 October 1951, Charles Humboldt papers.

32. The episode has received considerable scholarly attention, although there is no discussion of Babb's contribution. See Burnett, "The Albert Maltz Affair; and Sbardellati, "The Maltz Affair Revisited."

33. "Young Boy, the World," was reprinted in Lieber, *The American Century*, 112–21.

34. Babb to Charles Humboldt, 11 October 1951, Charles Humboldt papers.

35. Babb, "Another Viewpoint." As far as I can tell, her contribution was ignored.

WORKS CITED

Primary Sources

Charles Humbolt papers, Yale University
Esther McCoy papers, American Archives of Art
John Sanford Collection, Boston University, Gottleib Manuscript Library

Secondary Sources

Babb, Sanora. "Another Viewpoint." *New Masses*, no. 58, 12 March 1946, p. 10.
———. *Cry of the Tinamou: Stories*. University of Nebraska Press, 1997.
———. "Old Snapshots." *Prairie Schooner*, Winter 1965–66, pp. 302–3.
———. *The Dark Earth and Other Stories from the Great Depression*. Capra Press, 1987.
———. *Told in the Seed*. West End Press, 1998.
Battat, Erin. *Ain't Got No Home*. University of North Carolina Press, 2104.
Burnett, Colin. "The 'Albert Maltz Affair' and the Debate over Para-Marxist Formalism in the *New Masses*, 1945–46." *Journal of American Studies*, vol. 48, no. 1, February 2014, pp. 223–50.
Callahan, John F., and Marc C. Conner. *The Selected Letters of Ralph Ellison*. Random House, 2019, pp. 148–54.
Ceplair, Larry. *The Marxist and the Movies: A Biography of Paul Jarrico*. University of Kentucky Press, 2007.

Endore, Guy. Introduction. *Black & White*, Greenwood, 1968.

Horne, Gerald. *Class Struggles in Hollywood, 1930–1950*. University of Texas Press, 2001.

Lieber, Maxim, editor. *The American Century: A Collection of American Short Stories Reflecting the Nature of Society in the United States*. Seven Seas, 1958.

Rampersad, Arnold. *Ralph Ellison: A Biography*. Knopf, 2007.

Reid, Panthea. *Tillie Olsen: One Woman, Many Riddles*. Rutgers University Press, 2010.

Sbardellati, John. "The Maltz Affair Revisited: How the Communist Party Relinquished Its Cultural Influence at the Dawn of the Cold War." *Cold War History*, vol. 9, no. 4, November 2009, pp. 489–500.

Wald, Alan. "Introduction: Soft Focus." *Cry of the Tinamou: Stories*, by Sanora Babb, University of Nebraska Press, 1997, ix–xvi.

Wixson, Douglas. *On the Dirty Plate Trail: Remembering the Dust Bowl Refugee Camps*. University of Texas Press, 2007.

———. "Radical by Nature." *Regionalists on the Left: Radical Voices from the American Left*, edited by Michael C. Stein. University of Oklahoma Press, 2013, 111–33.

———. *Worker-Writer in America: Jack Conroy and the Tradition of Midwestern Literary Radicalism, 1898–1990*. University of Illinois Press, 1994.

JESSICA HELLMANN

2

THINKING LIKE THE PLAINS
The Creation of Sanora Babb's Land Ethic

We Americans exist in a constant state of manifest destiny. We don't care that Frederick Jackson Turner closed the West in 1893 or that the climate is rapidly changing. The sovereign, seemingly endless landmass of North America protected by oceans that we call home has influenced how we view and treat this land. Some visionaries in our history have tried to change this careless, expansionist, rapacious approach. Environmentally concerned readers know the name Aldo Leopold from his seminal, posthumously published *A Sand County Almanac* (1949). But it's obvious that his essays haven't found a true home in our cultural understanding. Reading Leopold's writing now leaves one only frustrated and angry that we seem to be taking steps backward from 1949 in how we view our relationship with our continent and patria, despite the world's undergoing catastrophic, anthropogenic climate change. Leopold asked us to view the land as something we are in a relationship with, that we be citizens of this world, not rulers of it. He held that we need to be fellow members of the biotic and abiotic communities that surround us. It is disappointing that we as a nation—as a world—have still not adopted this ecologically minded ethic, one where the land has equal rights to our own.

Aldo Leopold is credited with creating the term "land ethic" in his *A Sand County Almanac*, in the essay "The Land Ethic." In this short piece, Leopold posits that "a land ethic changes the role of *Homo sapiens* from conqueror of the land-community to plain member and citizen of it. It implies respect for his fellow-members, and also respect for the community as such" (Leopold 204). Leopold proposes that we recognize that we are merely members of an ecological community and citizens of the natural world. Once we remove those Abrahamic barriers, a land that we expect "to drip milk and honey" (205) into our mouths, we can see what our actual role should be: citizens of the land in respectful relationships with the biotic and abiotic communities that surround and support us. He writes that "we see repeated the same basic paradoxes: man as conqueror *versus* man the biotic citizen; science as the sharpener of his sword *versus* science the searchlight on his universe; land the slave and servant *versus* land the collective organism" (223). *An Owl on Every Post* and *Whose Names Are Unknown* are Sanora Babb's contributions to the land ethic conversation. Through these books, Babb creates a land ethic that is similar to Leopold's, one where humans need to be respectful members of a biotic and abiotic community, not simply living *on* the land but instead living in conversation and relationships *with* the land.

The first time I read Babb's novel *Whose Names*, I was frustrated that it took until 2004 for her Dust Bowl novel to be published and that the author had put this manuscript in a drawer for over sixty years. It was odd that in my years of reading and researching the Dust Bowl and the novel that defined it, *The Grapes of Wrath*, I had never come across Babb's name. I picked up her novel just as I started teaching a college literature course on environmental disasters and the American West. Though I had scheduled a couple of weeks for the class to read *The Grapes of Wrath*, thirty pages into *Whose Names* I changed my mind. Babb's candor and care for the people of the High Plains, and the High Plains itself, forced me to include her novel and not Steinbeck's in my class. The students were happy, particularly as her book is about half the length of Steinbeck's, and I was happy because I had found something and someone I didn't know I had been looking for.

When I finally read Babb's memoir of her childhood in southeastern Colorado, *An Owl on Every Post*, I knew I had found my literary home. I grew up in western Colorado near the banks of the Colorado River and in the shadow of the Grand Mesa. My world is one of the High Plains desert, a harsh, treeless place filled with rabbit brush and gray-brown dirt that blows in the summers. It's not the eastern plains of Babb's Baca County, but it's similar. In this memoir, I read the story of my great-grandparents' childhoods growing up on homesteads near and around Routt County, in remote, northwestern Colorado. This feeling intensified when I reread *Whose Names*. I could see my recently widowed great-grandma Effie DuBeau Clark trying to feed her three surviving children in the middle of the Depression on her salary from delivering mail by horseback. I could see my great-grandmother Myrtle Blake Frentress delivering her second child on the floor of her farmhouse alone, her husband and doctor stuck somewhere in the spring mud. Something inside me resonated. Babb was writing about my land and my people.

But she was not. She was writing about her land and her people. She wrote about them in a way that made them feel like they were my own. And her land ethic, though it isn't explicitly laid out like Leopold's, is my own as well. It permeates her compassionate and attentive writing about a misunderstood, hostile, and misused place and how the people living there related to their homes. The lonely, widely spaced farms on the High Plains were not as independent as they looked. The people who homesteaded this land quickly realized that community was the only way to survive—and that community included the land, the animals, and the plants of their homes. For me, Sanora Babb's ethic is informed by my readings of John Wesley Powell and Aldo Leopold. But Powell's relationship with the land is one of a detached scientist-bureaucrat, and Leopold writes in vague terms about a place that has easy access to water. Babb's land ethic, and the care and love with which she presents it, is wholly her own.

Babb's ethic is echoed in the writings of modern-day environmental scientists reckoning with the rapidly changing American landscape through the use of scientific understanding and personal essay. This includes writers such as Ellen Wohl in her 2009 collection *Of Rocks and Rivers: Seeking a Sense of Place in the American West*, which deals with how the geology and myth of the West sit in opposition to one another and how we as a nation need to learn to "live within" the land and not "impose on it" (234). Botanist and essayist Robin Wall Kimmerer engages with this land ethic in her books *Gathering Moss: A Natural and Cultural History of Mosses* (2003) and *Braiding Sweetgrass: Indigenous Wisdom, Scientific Knowledge, and the Teachings of Plants* (2015). She combines her ancestral Potawatomi stories with scientific knowledge to explore how we relate and how we should sustainably relate to the natural world around us. She discusses how the relational, symbiotic existence with the land practiced by her ancestors has been damaged by our white, American, transactional view of the environment. If we begin to view ourselves as partners with the land and not owners of it, Wall Kimmerer asserts, a balance may be restored. In her own way, using the novel and memoir form, Babb's creation of a communal land ethic may seem to take a backseat to her storytelling. But it is through our engagement with her narratives that we, her readers, begin to perceive how central her land ethic is to her writings and understanding of the world. In her books *An Owl on Every Post* and *Whose Names are Unknown*, Babb challenges two American myths about the West—that of the Jeffersonian yeoman farmer and of western rugged individualism. Through these two works, her readers begin to understand what it is to think like the plains, where the vast harshness of the lands informs the communal relationships that we form with the ecologically connected world around us.

HOSTILE, MISUNDERSTOOD LAND

The High Plains of Sanora Babb's memoir *An Owl* and the first half of her Dust Bowl novel *Whose Names* is a difficult place to love. It makes up the space once labeled the Great American Desert and was at times thought to be uninhabitable (Worster 81). It has few redeeming features. No purple mountains' majesty to mine for precious metals, no desert valleys transformed by irrigation into flowering Edens. On the face of it, these High Plains appear to be useless, open wasteland, though manifest destiny and the Homestead Acts pushed people into settling this marginal landscape. In his 1878 report to Congress on "the lands of the arid region of the United States," John Wesley Powell writes:

> The redemption of all these lands will require extensive and comprehensive plans, for the execution of which aggregated capital or cooperative labor will be necessary. Here, individual farmers, being poor men, cannot undertake the task. For its accomplishment a wise previson, embodied in carefully considered legislation, is necessary. It was my purpose not only to consider the character of the lands themselves, but also the engineering problems involved in their redemption, and further to make suggestions for the legislative action necessary to inaugurate the enterprises by which these lands may eventually be rescued from their present worthless state. (8)

In his report, Powell pushes for legislative foresight and acceptance of the particularities of these High Plains. Unfortunately, Congress was deaf to his suggestions and warnings. These places were settled with the same expectations that drove homesteaders to the rain-filled parts of the middle of the country, states like Indiana, Illinois, Iowa, and Ohio, where a homestead of 160 unirrigated acres was enough to provide for a family.[1] But while this arid grassland was home to fertile soil, its rainfall was insufficient to support this single-farmer style of agriculture. The land detailed in Babb's books push back against this eastern, well-watered system of land management: the Jeffersonian yeoman farmer system of the East and old West.

In her memoir *An Owl*, Babb writes about her family's being belated early-twentieth-century homesteaders in World War I era Baca County.[2] On the train with her family traveling to her grandfather's broomcorn farm in Colorado, Babb details her first reaction to seeing this open, unpeopled space. She is "utterly unprepared for the desolation viewed from the train windows," and "the lackluster autumn landscape was like an old gray carpet spread to the far, far circling horizon. There was nothing more to see. This was an empty land. A primordial loneliness was on it" (*An Owl* 7). Babb's first impression of this space is one that is out of step with her newly technological era. She and her family leave a thriving bakery and town with cars, trees, and telephones and travel backward in time to the days of dugout, pioneer living. The Babbs join her grandfather, Alonzo, who has been homesteading, poorly, for the last fifteen years. He proved up a government claim of 160 acres, which he lost "to taxes ten years later, unable to raise crops without water" (8). He convinces his son, Babb's father, Walter, to buy 320 acres of grazing land, and they attempt to make a living with broomcorn—the only crop that somewhat reliably grows on these waterless, wind-swept plains.

Sanora Babb, showing more foresight and understanding about these arid lands than the Congress of Powell's time, writes that "the government had opened these margin lands for settlement, and so powerfully inviting is the ownership of land that people came; many left, a few remained" (*An Owl* 8). It is here, on the second page of her memoir, that Babb lays out that Jeffersonian yeoman myth propagated by manifest destiny, the Homestead Acts, the tenet that "rain follows the plow" (Worster 81–82), and how and why all these fail on the High Plains. For those moving "swiftly ahead" in other, wetter parts of the country, these ideals still manifest with success (*An Owl* 8). But on the dry plains, it is a different story, and it is only through desperation for land ownership and the freedom which accompanies this, that people move into these marginal spaces.

The first Homestead Act was passed by Congress in 1862. According to revisionist historians, it was designed as a response to slavery in the South and presented as a way to combat the morally corrupt plantation system (Reisner 41). The act allowed any American citizen (naturalized, a woman, an African American, etc.) twenty-one years of age or older who had never taken up arms against the United States and was a head of household to file for a quarter section of public domain land.[3] All they had to do was put in the patent at the local land office, pay a modest fee, occupy the land for five years, and make improvements on it (United States 392–93). In *Cadillac Desert*, Marc Reisner describes the original 160 acres as a "mythical allotment of land" and "the ideal acreage for a Jeffersonian utopia of small farmers" (41). He goes on to discuss how this system worked in the East and old West by climatic happenstance. Most of the land settled east of the hundredth meridian receives enough rain on a yearly basis to support quarter-section yeoman farmers. But that's not the case on the arid High Plains. One hundred and sixty acres and an individual farmer is not enough to produce a thriving farm and family. As the Babbs would find out, it is just enough to starve on.

Even though the Babb family began homesteading in Colorado in 1913 (*An Owl* 7), the indications of the environmental collapse to come in about twenty years are present. The Babbs plow up huge swaths of ecologically balanced short and tall grass prairie, leaving the fertile top soil exposed to the high winds and little precipitation that defines the High Plains. They have entered into an alien space and are flailing about trying to figure out how to make the land fit into their farming paradigms, instead of allowing the land to shape how it should or should not be used. Babb remembers her father saying: "'Maybe we aren't supposed to open this grass' . . . 'Maybe the land's fighting back, pushing us off.' We had plowed the grass under, opened the rich unmolested soil" (209). He, and the other dryland farmers, sense that what they are doing is wrong. The land is telling them. The broomcorn and wheat markets are telling them. The banks are telling them. And yet, the pull of land and the power associated with land ownership is too strong for them to listen to the warnings. They plowed up a fragile, balanced ecosystem in search of a version of the American Dream which the land could not support. And the consequences of this were one of the worst, human caused environmental disasters in the history of the United States.

Many of the homesteaders of Babb's Dust Bowl novel *Whose Names* came from places with more water than these arid plains offer. Babb writes that "Milt had grown up in the corn country" and had dreamed of the wheat country that lay west for years (*Whose Names* 3). When he gets there, he finds a land that can barely support a wheat crop "two out of every four or five years" (3). The dryland farmers of the novel constantly lament that "this is a good country if common folks could just afford water" (72). Unfortunately, the common folks could not afford water. They could not drill deep enough to tap into the Ogallala Aquifer, and they could not buy water from distant reservoirs. And without water their temperate climate farming practices and habits simply could not succeed. Even the introduction of Turkey Red winter wheat in the 1870s (Worster 87 and 175) did not yield a level of success beyond something Milt later calls "a kind of left-handed starvation in more ways than one" (*Whose Names* 82).

This starvation extends beyond their stomachs. Their entire way of life is being starved out, either by the dust or the banks or some combination of both. Farmers, like the Brennermann family in *Whose Names*, who can afford water can also afford to buy foreclosed land from the banks and then rent it back to the farmers already living there. Babb uses the Brennermanns as an example of what success looks like out on the High Plains. But it is not a flattering picture that she draws. The Brennermanns have water, alfalfa fields, hogs, and a milk house, and they seem successful. But that success comes with a price. They cannot be good neighbors or generous to those around them who are struggling (*Whose Names* 30–33). This myth of small, independent, yeoman farmers succeeding off the fruits of their own labor cannot survive in the face of the dust that starts to blow and the pressure of taxes being due. Once again, this illustrates the indifference of the land toward those not listening and adapting to what the land had to say.

SILENT, MISUNDERSTOOD PEOPLE

The people in Babb's novel *Whose Names* and memoir *An Owl* are like those she encountered growing up on the High Plains and later helped in the California migrant camps and agricultural fields. She writes in the afterword of *An Owl* that "like many people, our parents and grandfather had only grade school education, and only a few grades at that. But they were not ignorant. Somehow, they must have learned by reading newspapers and a few books; and grown in themselves from experience. They were casually informed. Perhaps we forget about the various degrees of native intelligence and the variety in quality of mind" (252). They were not the ignorant Okies of Steinbeck's Dust Bowl novel. They were also not the vaunted American yeoman farmers of yore. The farmers of the High Plains were, and still are, a part of a complicated ecosystem where isolation is a function of the land, but rugged individualism has no place.

The people who farmed these far reaches of the plains came to understand that their land was sparsely populated for a reason. Isolation was thus not an indication of a rugged individualism but of a "collective respect" for each other that Abigail G. H. Manzella coins and details in her book chapter, "The Environmental Displacement of the Dust Bowl: From the Yeoman Myth to Collective Respect and Babb's *Whose Names Are Unknown*." Manzella writes that "this form of communal bonding stands in stark contrast to the individualistic and atomistic mentality of the yeoman myth, pointing to the incongruity between these ideas of movement for individual ownership and movement for community togetherness and showing how, even as the characters believe in the myth at this point, they are still trying to engage with each other using what I am calling 'collective respect'" (80).

This "collective respect" can be found in Babb's memoir *An Owl on Every Post* even more than in *Whose Names*. The child narrator, Cheyenne, details nonhuman communities on the plains from their first moments there. Babb and her sister were fascinated one day watching "a large anthill, the great red ants hurrying, carrying prey, sticks, enormous loads they put down and picked up again, moving in an ordered, inexorable way toward their destination" (*An Owl* 25). The ants are busy individually working toward a common goal, much like the far-flung farm families coming together at harvest and seeding time. Babb describes that late summer ritual as "a general exchange of labor among the distant farms. Men and women enjoyed a release from isolation and loneliness in the hard shared work" (145). The families are happy to complete the labor needed for their neighbors in a communal fashion. They bring together not only food, but the tables and benches necessary to enjoy the community meal. The work needed to get a crop from planting, to harvest, to sold is not the work of solitary individuals or single families but of a community forming despite their isolated living situations.

Interestingly, John Wesley Powell factored in the land's need for isolated farms and the human need for connection in his suggestions to Congress. In 1878, he wrote:

The homes must necessarily be widely scattered from the fact that the farm unit must be large. That the inhabitants of these districts may have the benefit of the local social organizations of civilization—as schools, churches, etc., and the benefits of cooperation in the construction of roads, bridges, and other local improvements, it is essential that the residences should be grouped to the greatest possible extent. This may be practically accomplished by making the pasturage farms conform to topographical features in such manner as to give the greatest possible number of water fronts. (Powell 33–34)

He also suggested that pasturage, or grazing lands, should not be fenced and that herds roam in common. Such environmentally sensitive practices would have helped prevent the Great Die Up of the winter of 1886–87. We now know that this communal method of settlement is an ancient solution to the problem of the aridity of the High Plains. The people who settled there had to live and work together cooperatively with their fellow humans and the land. By conforming settlement to the topography, instead of attempting to manage the land according to an imposed grid system, both people and ecosystem would have a better chance of flourishing. But this took forethought and respect for the land, something that most people who only knew how to enact the yeoman myth could not imagine.

The need for human connection on the vast High Plains was as real to Babb and her family as their almost constant hunger. Her mother, Ginny, struggles with the isolation on the plains, and it is through Babb's characters that the readers can come to understand female friendship on the plains serving as the backbone holding the communities together. On their first foray into the town of Two Buttes, folks tell the Babbs, "Woman will *sure* be glad to see you" (*An Owl* 21). This "woman" may be one man's wife or all isolated women living on the plains. Either way, the women of the Two Buttes area crave each other's companionship. Ginny cries when she first sees Carrie Mayo Whitehead, and it is no surprise that these two lonely women become fast friends. Carrie is the first person to help the Babbs after the family experiences a stillbirth. She takes charge and rides into town to fetch the doctor to care for Ginny. Later, Babb tells her readers that "Carrie Mayo Whitehead had stopped by and left, as she put it, 'just some neighborly food.' Even at my age, I realized that she was being careful of Papa's pride; but we all knew, too, that when the woman of the house is down, neighborly help is right and proper. He could not object" (125). While Carrie respects the cultural norms and Walter's pride, she will not let that stop her from taking care of her friend's family while the woman of the dugout is recovering.

In her books and other writings, Babb centers not only on female friendship but also on women's stories. The women of these two books feel real in a way many canonical western women do not. They are not some young man's fantasy of strong western womanhood like Willa Cather's Ántonia in *My Ántonia* or the allegorical matriarch of Ma Joad in *The Grapes of Wrath*. Ginny is Babb's mother, dreaming of her tree-filled streets and comfortable home back East. And Julia in *Whose Names* is the only character in this novel who gives the reader a true first-person perspective when she decides "to keep a record of the strange phenomenon of dust" (90). For the rest of chapter 17, Babb gives us access to Julia's deepest thoughts along with a record of the awful dust storms during the month of April (90–95). Babb allows Julia to breathe on these pages and doesn't distance her readers from the calamity the Dunnes are experiencing. Through Babb's record, the reader is able to tell that Julia is not a middle-aged man's nostalgic remembering of a childhood love or an uneducated Okie like Ma Joad. Instead, Julia is her own person, working tirelessly to keep her family fed and clean during the never-ending dust storms plaguing her home. Through her books, Babb gives voice to the people of the High Plains, accurately depicting their strength of character and sense of community that enabled them to survive.

A WAY FORWARD: SANORA BABB'S LAND ETHIC

Through these two books, Sanora Babb introduces her readers to a world and a people rarely featured in American, and specifically western, writing. She centers the relationship between the settlers and one of our country's last wildernesses. Babb's books push back against the common narrative of the American farmer, the isolated individual concerned primarily with his bottom line and production for whom the land is nothing more than a medium to be used to achieve his American Dream. Babb counters this myth with the reality of homesteading on the prairie in the World War I years and then in the epicenter of the Dust Bowl in the 1930s. It is through Babb's relationship with this land that her readers can see her land ethic forming, one in which people build community relationships with the land they settle on and the others (both human and nonhuman) living there.

Babb's grandfather plays a central role in how she comes to view the land of her childhood. Alonzo views his High Plains home with the scientific eye of a modern-day ecologist. He embodies the second half of Leopold's paradox, one who uses science as a searchlight and not a weapon against the land (Leopold 223). Alonzo champions his friends the coyotes and defends them against Walter's pro-culling, rancher-backed, "modern" argument (*An Owl* 62–63). When Alonzo teaches young Cheyenne about the connection between yucca and a specific species of moth that pollinates the plant, he ends his lesson by saying, "I read about it and never forgot it because it just goes to show there's a pattern. Pull a few threads and you undo nature's pattern" (130). Alonzo sees this web laid out before him and attempts to live within it. He spends his life on the High Plains literally living in the earth in a dugout and eschewing the comforts of progress and middle-class life that his daughter-in-law Ginny so longs for. He teaches his granddaughters to be citizens of the natural world and to respect and love the wild place that they live in.

In the afterword to *An Owl*, added to the second edition of the book in 1994, Babb sums up the land ethic that she presented through the whole of her memoir:

> I always felt grounded in the plains. The impact of those years is still potent. I treasure the deep influence of those years: a sense of living on a grand earth under a big sky, not just within walls. The darkness on the plains was as black as space and the stars so thick and brilliant they seemed touchable while they seemed eons away, all of this mysterious and awesome. Long before I read that everything in the universe is connected, that all life is One, I knew it intuitively when I was seven years old. This was an awareness, not a discovery. It gave me a mystical sense of being in the universe, related, belonging, as transient as a flower but just as welcome. It gave me freedom from the need for specific beliefs and dogmas. It gave me tolerance. Perhaps it was the bigness of the plains and the sky that stretched my thoughts. Quien sabe? It is important to have mysteries. They urge us to seek and change and grow. (251)

Babb sees the natural world of her childhood as an interdependent cosmos of individuals, each just trying to survive, whether a grasshopper or a farming family. To both her seven-year-old and eighty-seven-year-old minds, each creature has just as much right to survival as the other. This complicated understanding wasn't a hard-fought prize achieved after years of ecological study. It was an awareness that came from living in a place that makes survival very difficult for all its inhabitants. The land is a collective organism, one that is bigger and more complicated than we could hope to understand and not something to be enslaved for our own purposes. According to Babb's land ethic, we need to care for and love the land and its nonhuman inhabitants as if they were members of our own families.

Sanora Babb's entry into the land ethic conversation is as unique and complicated as the land and people she detailed. Made famous by an environmental disaster that reshaped them and the people who remained, this land is relegated to the history books and typically discussed only in its relation to the Dust Bowl and the Great Depression. Babb's books rescue this place from the historical dustbin. She breathes real life into the people from the myth-making images captured by Dorothea Lange and the other Farm Security Administration photographers. The Babbs of *An Owl* and the Dunnes of *Whose Names* become real people to her readers. And it is through these characters and the stories she tells that she creates her land ethic. The land and the people she loved are more than what our cultural memories tell us they are. They aren't the yeoman farmers of Jefferson's dream or the epic Okies of Steinbeck's allegory. They are a community of people who love and accept the harsh reality of the land that they call home, who attempt to extend their ideas of community to cover and welcome their biotic and abiotic neighbors. They are the people I myself come from and the sort of people that I hope to become. My son is a seventh-generation Coloradoan, and I hope, if we adopt a land ethic like Babb's, there will be a wild, hostile West for him to call home.

NOTES

1. I refer to these states as the old West in an attempt to recognize the ever-shifting nature of the frontier and the concept of the West in American history. This is in opposition to the idea of the new West, which refers to the lands west of the hundredth meridian, or the line of aridity, detailed in chapter 1 of Powell's *The Arid Lands*.

2. Baca County is located in southeastern Colorado and would later become part of the epicenter of the Dust Bowl. Timothy Egan's book *The Worst Hard Time* details this area and the people who lived through the disaster.

3. The history of public domain lands and how they were acquired by the federal government is a deeply troubling and racist one. The government purchased or outright stole the land from the indigenous people, then forced these peoples onto smaller and smaller and poorer and poorer reservations, kidnapped their children, destroyed their distinct cultures and languages, and then sold that land to white settlers. *High Country News* in its April 2020 issue did an in-depth analysis of land-grant universities and how they are still profiting off this stolen land today (Lee and Ahtone). Rebecca Nagel, a

member of the Cherokee (Tsalagi) Nation, created the podcast *This Land* to cover the land right and sovereignty issues of the recently decided Supreme Court case *Sharp v. Murphy* (*This Land* and Sharp v. Murphy). These are just two recent examples of the exploration of the long and disconcerting history of public lands in the United States.

WORKS CITED

Babb, Sanora. Afterword. *An Owl on Every Post*, Muse Ink Press, 2012, 251–56.
———. *An Owl on Every Post*. Muse Ink Press, 2012.
———. *Whose Names Are Unknown*. University of Oklahoma Press, 2004.
Egan, Timothy. *The Worst Hard Time*. Mariner Books, 2006.
Lee, Robert, and Tristan Ahtone. "Land-Grab Universities: Expropriated Indigenous Land is the Foundation of the Land-Grant University System." *High Country News*, vol. 52, no. 4, April 2020, pp. 33–45.
Manzella, Abigail G. H. *Migrating Fictions: Gender, Race, and Citizenship in U.S. Internal Displacements*. Ohio State University Press, 2018.
Nagle, Rebecca. *This Land*, Crooked Media, https://crooked.com/podcast-series/this-land/.
Leopold, Aldo. *A Sand County Almanac: And Sketches Here and There*. Oxford University Press, 1968.
Powell, John Wesley. *The Arid Lands*, edited by Wallace Stegner. Nebraska University Press, 2004.
Reisner, Marc. *Cadillac Desert: The American West and its Disappearing Water*. Penguin, 1993.
Sharp v. Murphy. 591 US __. Supreme Court of the US. 2020. https://www.supremecourt.gov/opinions/19pdf/17-1107_0759.pdf.
United States Congress, "Chapter LXXV—An Act to secure Homesteads to actual Settlers on the Public Domain." *Public Acts of the Thirty-Seventh Congress of the United States*. 37th Congress, 2nd sess., chapter 75, 20 May 1862. Pp. 392–393. www.loc.gov/law/help/statutes-at-large/37th-congress/c37.pdf.
Wohl, Ellen. *Of Rocks and Rivers: Seeking a Sense of Place in the American West*. University of California Press, 2009.
Worster, Donald. *Dust Bowl: The Southern Plains in the 1930s*. Oxford University Press, 2004.

ERIN ROYSTON BATTAT

3

DISCOVERING ECOFEMINISM IN SANORA BABB'S NARRATIVES

I first came across Sanora Babb's writings in 2006, when researching American migration narratives of the 1930s. Reading her novel of the Dust Bowl migration, *Whose Names Are Unknown*, was like finding a hidden treasure, a lost voice of the era that spoke intimately of the High Plains people and included women and people of color in the story of California's migrant labor crisis. The recent outpouring of feminist protest in the United States urged me to return to Babb's writings through a different lens. In rereading her three life narratives, what stands out to me is the connection between her environmental consciousness, rooted in her western upbringing, and her feminist thought.

Since the publication of Annette Kolodny's groundbreaking study *The Land before Her* in 1984, scholars have recovered western women's narratives to understand how they reconfigure the frontier myth—a story of white male conquest of western lands and indigenous peoples—to carve a space for women and imagine alternative relationships to the land and to one another.[1] Much of this scholarship has focused on women's representation of domestic spaces. While Kolodny argues that pioneer women recreated a familiar "garden in the wilderness," more recent scholars show how women transformed domestic spaces into sites of adventure where gender roles blurred (Halverson; Stout). In her influential review of western women's writing, Melody Graulich acknowledges that many women also embraced western freedom and wilderness, but few were able to fit women's experiences into masculine plotlines ("'Oh Beautiful'" 191–92). Babb's narratives offer an unexplored avenue for scholars of western women's literature, as they eschew the domestic and offer a feminist alternative to the western hero. Babb expresses an ecofeminist vision through her deep connection with nature, which promotes female freedom and self-discovery, as well as an ethic of care for all living things.

Babb has begun to attract the attention of scholars of western American literature, as indicated by an increasing number of papers presented on her work at regional conferences. Yet her writings also offer insights to readers interested in the literature of feminism more broadly. Babb has been overlooked by critics of western literature in part because she wrote of the High Plains region that was settled in the 1910s, decades after the period that brackets most anthologies.[2] Writing in the middle decades of the twentieth century, she has also been overlooked by scholars of feminist thought. Babb was in her sixties by the time second-wave feminism emerged, and she did not formally associate with the organized movement. Yet Babb's writings—created during a supposed lull between the waves—help us see the continuities in the timeline of feminism. Historians have recently challenged the wave metaphor, recovering a range of feminist resistance during the postwar period, often spearheaded by women of color, labor organizers, lesbians, and others who fell outside the white middle-class norm (Hewitt; Meyerowitz). However, very little attention has been given to western and rural women, perhaps because their often traditional values and conservative politics are at odds with mainstream feminist principles. Yet Babb stands apart. Her feminism was rooted in her love of the natural environment and her family's struggle to survive on the remote plains, and it was often inextricably tied to her antiracist and anticapitalist commitments. While her writings focus on the experience of white women and do not confront this racial privilege, they reflect the antiracist ideology and environmental consciousness that speaks to intersectional feminists of the late twentieth century.[3]

This essay explores Babb's feminist alternative to the frontier myth in her three autobiographically informed narratives. In her memoir of a pioneer childhood,

An Owl on Every Post (1970), Babb views all living things as interconnected and charts the development of an autonomous self through her interactions with the natural world. Babb places this ecofeminist vision in tension with the experiences of her mother and other poor women, notably the migrants she encountered in California and depicted in her novel *Whose Names Are Unknown* (2004), who suffer from poverty and the lack of reproductive freedom under patriarchal capitalism. Finally, Babb's ecofeminist thought culminates in her last novel, *The Lost Traveler* (1958). The autobiographically based heroine, Robin, defines freedom not through rugged individualism or the power to dominate, but through economic autonomy and the expression of love and friendship unfettered by social conventions. Throughout these western life narratives, written "between the waves" of modern feminism, Babb imagines human freedom that is compatible with ecological interdependence and caregiving.[4]

AN ECOFEMINIST VISION IN *AN OWL ON EVERY POST*

The Babb family—Walter, Jennie, Sanora (aged seven), and Dorothy (aged four)—moved to the arid high plains of eastern Colorado in 1913, more than twenty years after Frederick Jackson Turner had famously declared the frontier "closed." When the Babbs were breaking land and living in an earthen dugout, the frontier myth was fully embedded in the popular imagination, shaping their consciousness of their experience. Nostalgic for the pioneer past, grandfather Alonzo Babb attempts to put a positive spin on his family's poverty, reminding them that "we're living about the same as those early times again. . . . How many other Americans are living like old pioneers?" (46). Synthesized by Frederick Jackson Turner's famous essay of 1893, "The Significance of the Frontier in American History," the frontier mythology celebrates the rugged individualist who leaves the genteel social hierarchies of the "civilized" East to conquer the "savage" wilderness, giving new life to American democracy. This mythology is coded in both gender and racial terms. It imagines the rugged individualist as male, and women are both the constraints on male freedom and, as the metaphor of "virgin land" suggests, the object of male power and desire. This tale of conquest often entails violent conflict with native peoples as a test of white manhood and the crucible of democracy, as violence purges the frontier hero of the elite decadence of bourgeois civilization. As Richard Slotkin famously put it, "The myth of regeneration through violence became the structuring metaphor of American experience" (*Regeneration through Violence* 5). In highlighting her grandfather's nostalgia, Babb's memoir suggests the power of myths to motivate masculine ambitions.

While grandfather Alonzo instills the pioneer myth in his granddaughter, he also teaches her an ecological ethic that counters the archetypal narrative of conquest. When her father, Walter, condones killing animals "as a man living in the wilds has to protect himself from them," Alonzo posits that it is "mostly the other way around," that the wilderness needs protection from man (62). Alonzo's ecological ethic also looks to indigenous peoples as models for environmental stewardship: "The Indians killed buffalo for food and hide and still the plains were black with them, millions of them. The white man slaughtered them all in just a few years. What's wrong with man that he can't think in a pattern? Everything has a purpose" (63). In rejecting the assumption that human beings have a natural right to dominate nature, Alonzo expresses a worldview of ecological interdependence that anticipates modern environmentalism.

Sanora was profoundly influenced by her grandfather, echoing his ethic of interdependence as she walked on the prairie one night: "We were not separate from all of nature; we were not looking on, we were a part" (101). Babb articulates a sense of self that according to ecofeminist scholar Greta Gaard is "most commonly expressed by women and various other non-dominant groups—a self that is interconnected with all life" (2). This interconnected self, Gaard argues, counters a Euro-American worldview that separates the self from the "other" and from the natural world. Whereas the separate self gives rise to ethics based on individual rights, the interconnected self fosters an ethic of care and responsibility for others (Gaard 2). Gaard's notion of the interconnected self risks gender essentialism, naturalizing the caregiving roles conferred to women within patriarchal societies. However, Babb's writings resist the feminization of connection and care by highlighting her grandfather's role as a caregiver and by embracing female autonomy and adventure outside the home.

Babb's ecofeminist vision not only rejects the masculine trope of conquest, but also resists prescribed roles for women. In *The Land before Her*, Annette Kolodny argues that women pioneers attempted to recreate a "garden in the wilderness," transplanting the familiar features of the eastern woodlands that allowed them to resume their domestic roles. In contrast, Babb participates in what Janis Stout calls a "countertradition" of western women's writing, forged by writers such as Willa Cather and Mary Austin, who embraced harsh, arid landscapes and viewed them as a site for female autonomy and freedom (24). Cather, for example, was "able to appreciate the prairie on its own terms," exhilarated by its dramatic storms, sudden changes in weather, and unobstructed sky (Stout 26). Similarly, Babb urges readers conditioned by eastern standards of beauty to appreciate the High Plains landscape. She often turns to aural imagery—the sounds of birds, insects, coyotes, wind, and thunder—to capture ecological diversity and sensory richness and of an environment devoid of vegetation, color, and depth. Like Cather, Babb was enthralled by the "perfect meeting of earth and sky" on a vast, treeless plain (Babb, *Owl* 4), and her narrative is punctuated by awe-inspiring storms. Babb's lyrical descriptions of the sky express a yearning for new knowledge and experience. Walking across the prairie, the narrator imagines "a time when I should reach that far land's end and lift up the sky to enter the lives and worlds I had no need to know until then" (18). She repeats this motif later in the narrative (188) and in the afterword, written decades later (256).

In addition to narrating self-discovery through her interactions with the natural world, Babb shows how pioneer conditions break down prescribed gender roles in the home. Babb's depiction of her family dugout and the broomcorn farm reflects what Stout calls the "dual gendering" of the West (41). The family's one-room earthen dugout never becomes the "potential sanctuary for an idealized domesticity" found in the women's pioneer narratives studied by Kolodny (xiii). Instead, both men and women in the family find it to be a confining space, "like a grave" (14), as well as a protective one, "a safe burrow as welcome as that belonging to any animal pursued by the elements" (96). Just as the harsh weather breaks down gendered notions of space, the demands of the harvest break down gendered divisions of labor, as men, women, and children work together in the fields (142). Finally, the remoteness of their farm places men in a caregiving role when Ginny suffers a miscarriage. Far from a doctor, the father and grandfather tend to the mother, and Babb emphasizes the men's emotional reactions to the loss of the child, which fall outside the norms of white western masculinity.

In her book *Radical Ecology*, ecofeminist philosopher Carolyn Merchant proposes a "partnership ethic" that "treats humans (including male and female partners) as equals in personal, household, and political relations and humans as equal partners with (rather than controlled-by or dominant-over) nonhuman nature" (187). Babb offers an early glimpse of this ecofeminist ethic of partnership and care by imagining herself as a part of nature and by embracing the gender fluidity of the broomcorn farm. Conversely, she also reveals the cost of patriarchal expectations for women, particularly the poor and marginalized.

EXPOSING PIONEER PATRIARCHY

In an *Owl on Every Post*, the young narrator awakens to systems of patriarchal power and the suffering of poor women under capitalism, which she observes through her mother's experiences with marriage and childbearing. While Walter Babb celebrates Ginny's pregnancy, dreaming of the son he had always wanted, Ginny retorts, "Has it occurred to you, Walt, what it means to have a new baby in this hole in the ground? . . . This poor baby doesn't know what he's getting into" (104). Tragically, Ginny suffers a miscarriage after she is caught in a thunderstorm and forced to run for home. This emotionally intense scene—replicated in the fictional *Whose Names Are Unknown*—reminds readers of the gendered impact of poverty and the dire consequences of women's lack of control over their reproductive choices.

Impacted by her mother's experience, Babb explored the effects of poverty on childbearing women in her reportage on the Dust Bowl migrants in the 1930s. Her article, "Farmers without Farms," published in the Marxist *New Masses* magazine in 1938, reported on the high rates of infant mortality in the San Joaquin valley and describes women's experiences giving birth "without proper medical care, lying on a dirty mattress or a spring on the ground floor, with newspapers for sheets and possibly the help of the camp neighbors" (Babb and Babb 115; Battat 57–58). Babb uses the artistic license available in fiction to give voice to the class-conscious migrant mother, who shouts, "I have to suffer like this because we're poor, that's why, only poor!" (*Whose Names* 141). Another migrant woman expresses a feminist demand for reproductive rights: "What we need is one of them nurses to come out and tell us about birth control" (*Whose Names* 142). Scenes of miscarriage, stillbirth, and infant death in *Owl*, *Whose Names*, and Babb's reportage point to poor women's lack of reproductive autonomy, which is denied within patriarchal marriages (even loving ones) in a capitalist society.

At the end of *Owl*, the narrator, on the cusp of adolescence, becomes dimly aware of the patriarchal power structures that govern her parents' marriage. After bantering with her husband, Ginny says to her daughter, "Your dad always tells me what I think" (225). The narrator reflects, "I had heard these affectionate, half humorous exchanges many times, but some new awareness in me heard what was submerged, unsaid, not just between Mama and Papa" but between other couples as well. She grapples with his newfound gender consciousness through engagement with landscape: "This knowledge so engaged me that

I wandered out again into the yard and beyond the fence, where I could look over the unbroken distance to the sun going down" (226). Observing "the stillness of the land with its life, secret and hidden," she experiences an awakening: "An eye—not the eyes with which I looked toward the horizon—an eye within opened for an instant and flashed me a message, a coded message. . . . I felt on the verge of a discovery" (226). Echoing her moments of self-reflection on the open prairie, the narrator discovers a sense of self and feminist consciousness through her engagement with the natural surroundings.

WESTERN MASCULINITY IN *THE LOST TRAVELER*

Babb extends this ecofeminist vision of female autonomy and critique of capitalist patriarchy in her novel *The Lost Traveler*. This fictional story is based on the Babb family's experience after they left their broomcorn farm and eventually settled in Garden City, Kansas, where the novel is set.[5] The novel follows the downward spiral of the father figure, Des Tannehill, a charismatic, fiercely independent gambler who fits the mold of the quintessential western male hero. Babb reveals the underside to the masculine myth of rugged individualism through the experience of the mother, Belle, who endures unrelenting domestic labor, verbal abuse, physical violence, sexual assault, and the erasure of self.

The structure of the novel, which centers on the male protagonist and offers little insight to Belle's perspective, may explain why feminist critics have not included Babb in the recovery project that has led to the reprinting of works by contemporaries such as Tillie Olsen and Meridel Leseur. Babb identifies more with her father than her mother in *Owl*, as do the fictional daughters in *The Lost Traveler*. Robin emulates Des's free spirit, and both daughters scoff at Belle's submissive desire to please him. The novel offers little to counterbalance their scorn; an omniscient narrator probes Des's interior, but we mostly see Belle from other characters' perspectives rather than her own.[6]

Yet Babb explores the social forces behind the stereotype of the long-suffering pioneer woman, revealing how Belle's early marriage stunted her sense of self, leaving her economically powerless and vulnerable to domestic violence. Belle explains how her marriage at fifteen prevented her from growing into a fully actualized human being: "I just got blotted out" (129). Marriage also instituted, in a socially acceptable way, the exploitation of her labor and economic dependency. Des refuses to let Belle work outside the home yet relies on her thrift, resourcefulness, and unpaid domestic labor to support the family. Toward the end of the novel, Belle reflects on this painful irony: even though she kept the household running through lean times and never asked Des for money, he "considered her a burden, an extra expense ... indissolubly mingled with the groceries, rent, electricity, and coal" (174). Though Belle remains frustratingly acquiescent to Des throughout most of the narrative, she sheds light on women's invisible labor and exposes the hypocrisy of a frontier myth that views women as constraints on male freedom.

Like Agnes Smedley, a fellow western woman writer on the Left, Babb suggests that economic inequality in marriage enables domestic violence, which is further valorized by a frontier myth that celebrates violence as a national virtue (Graulich "Violence against Women" 14, and "'O Beautiful'" 199). In *The Lost Traveler*, Des's "thought of the pleasure of fighting" is connected to his physical assaults of his wife. Troubled by his failing career, Des went out on the town and "fought a man on in the street" with little provocation (112). When he arrived home, Des still felt like "he could have stood another fight," and he struck Belle "harder than he knew" (112). Des also assaults his wife sexually, asserting his dominance when they quarrel about money (178).[7] Ultimately, an intense scene of domestic violence serves as the turning point in the novel, motivating Robin, and eventually Belle, to leave Des. Babb suggests multiple causes for domestic violence and sexual assault: Des's feelings of weakness and financial stress, patriarchal imperatives to control women's sexuality, and western myths that glorify violence and characterize women as fetters to male freedom.

Eventually Belle liberates herself from her abusive husband. Empowered by her female friend, Belle gets a job at a local store and imagines "herself as a clerk in the Emporium, as a soloist in the choir, as a member of the community, known and respected" (202). Although Belle's decision is momentous—a feminist act of self-determination that would not find a political support for decades—Babb glosses over this experience in a few pages, giving us spare details and little access to Belle's interiority. She does, however, devote the last line of the novel to Belle's particularly domestic declaration of independence: "They heard Belle come in the back and lock the door that had always been open for Des" (273). Rather than "lighting out for the territory" like Huck Finn, Belle asserts her freedom by staking a claim to her own home.

In writing *The Lost Traveler*, Babb applied her keen insights on the effects of poverty and patriarchy on women, developed through her life in the rural West, to craft a fictional account based on her mother's experience. She did so without the language, theories, and political goals of the 1970s women's liberation movement, which may have urged her to explore her mother's perspective more deeply. Instead, the protagonist of *The Lost Traveler* is the father, whose descent drives the plot, while its true hero is Robin, "her father's daughter."[8]

A FEMINIST REVISION OF THE WESTERN HERO

Like her father, Robin fits the mold of the western hero, the rugged individualist who seeks freedom, rejects domesticity, and revitalizes herself in connection with nature. Yet freedom has a different meaning for Robin. She does not seek freedom from her own responsibility as a provider within a white patriarchal society, but from male power that constrains her economic, sexual, and spiritual autonomy. In her quest for freedom, Robin must redefine what it means to be a woman, must carve a middle way between two socially available roles to her: the mother and the whore. *The Lost Traveler* expresses this gender hybridity, blending freedom with and an ethic of caregiving.[9]

In telling Robin's story, Babb invented a romance plot that deviated from her own life experience. But she illustrates fictionally the sexual freedom that she herself bravely asserted as a young woman. Babb began a life-long relationship with Chinese American cinematographer James Wong Howe in the early 1930s and married him in 1948 after the repeal of California's anti-miscegenation laws. Babb also had intense but platonic friendships with Carlos Bulosan and William Saroyan, as well as a passionate love affair with Ralph Ellison, which affected them both deeply. In a letter to Howe written from Russia in 1936, Babb expressed the ethic of sexual freedom that she replicates in *The Lost Traveler*: "When I just knew you, I told you I believe in *complete* freedom of women. Why is *freedom* in men called promiscuity in women? I have always lived, I suppose, like a man—I've *never* been tempted into anything = I've made my own choices."[10] Babb advocated for women's sexual freedom, rejecting the trope of the "fallen woman" and affirming her agency as an empowered woman embracing sex as a choice.

In *The Lost Traveler*, Robin rejects patriarchal social norms by asserting economic and sexual freedom despite the social costs. She repeatedly rejects her boyfriend Blackie's marriage proposals: "What do I want with a nest?" she asks, "I want wings!" (144). She draws the link between marriage and economic dependence by vowing not to get married "until I know how to support myself. And a long time after that" (131). Rather than viewing the purpose of sex as male pleasure or procreation, Robin seeks sexual experience as a form of human bonding and self-expression. Like Edna in Kate Chopin's feminist novel *The Awakening*, Robin follows her own sensual desires rather than the desires deemed appropriate by her male-dominated society. This desire, as critic Claire Watkins puts it, "is the mechanism of [Edna's] deprogramming" and is a political act within a society that denies women the right to seek sexual pleasure for their own sake. Robin experiences sexual desire as a "trembling urge towards this new knowledge," a physical experience that fosters her growth as a person (151).

Just as Babb asserted her right to both sexual and nonsexual relationships with men in her letters, Robin develops a nonsexual relationship with a black male neighbor that offers a model of racial and gender equality. Robin's relationship with Chris is based on intellectual parity and deep emotional connection. They bond over a shared love of literature; as Robin explains to her father, Chris "seemed to respect my mind" (90). When Robin retreats to the wilderness after being severely beaten by her father, Chris comes to find her—at great risk to himself in the Jim Crow era—and "there was such an agreement of affection and empathy between them that she let it be felt in silence" (239). Like Garrison, the black union organizer in *Whose Names Are Unknown*, Chris is not a fully developed character. But Babb offers a literary representation of an interracial, male-female friendship that questions gender and racial barriers to human connection.

While Robin rejects racial codes of respectability in her friendship with Chris, Des is enraged when he discovers that a black family lives next door. In response to his racist invective, Robin reminds him that he was friends with black men and Indians. "But I live out in the world," he responds. "Things are different out there. Besides, I'm a man" (55). Des reconciles his contradictory racial attitudes using the logic of the frontier myth; as exemplified by Huck and Jim, male interracial friendship flourishes in the wilderness, but reverts to social hierarchies in feminized civilization. Robin, the new frontier hero, revises this trope, connecting with Chris across gender lines in both town and wilderness.[11]

Babb's most significant revision of the frontier myth, in my view, is the integration of freedom and caregiving. At the end of the novel, Robin receives money from her lover, Blackie, who wants her to run away with him. Determined to remain unencumbered, she does not plan to join him but fantasizes about taking the money and hopping a train for anywhere else, liberating herself from both her abusive father and from her dependent sister, Stevie, who is debilitated by grief and depression. As the train approaches, "she saw herself leaving—free, free!" (266). However, Robin does not get on the train but rather returns home to take Stevie with her. Her closing thoughts turn with hope and confidence toward an uncertain future: "Beyond the thicket of tonight's emotions there was an irresistible little clearing of happiness at the thought of the prospective journey. Stevie would get out of bed in order to leave. Further than that, except for the knowledge of her own resilience, Robin could only guess" (272–73). Like Huck Finn and a host of frontier heroes before her, Robin thus "lights out for the wilderness." Yet her version of rugged individualism incorporates an ethic of care that makes her a new kind of western hero.

In an age that is increasingly urban, digital, and global, why should we care about a young girl's experience on the remote High Plains and the western heroes she later imagined? While America's fascination with the pioneer story may be waning, "regeneration through violence," as Slotkin puts it, continues to shape America's sense of itself and its role in the word. The myth of rugged individualism informs policy on guns, the environment, and healthcare, while heroic battles against dark-skinned enemies animate the rhetoric behind our border security and military interventions abroad. The glorification of virile masculinity influences our elections and the sexual politics of our workplaces. The voices of western women have been obscured by this dominant mythology of rugged individualism and conquest, and they offer a range of alternative ways of imagining the self in relation to western lands and peoples. Babb's writings challenge human dominance over nature and reveal how this ideology of patriarchal control denies women economic autonomy, physical safety, and sexual freedom.

If "regeneration through violence" is the masculine metaphor of American historical consciousness, Babb offers "interconnection through care" as its counterpoint. She does so while maintaining a love of freedom, wilderness, and discovery, calling into question the gendering of both these categories of human desire. In a time marked by stark political and cultural divisions, Babb reminds us of our connectedness to each other and to the earth we all inhabit.

NOTES

1. For an excellent review essay that traces several decades of scholarship of western women's writings, see Lamont, "Big Books Wanted." Krista Comer, Lamont notes, challenges the notion of a cohesive tradition of women's writing. Comer's book *Landscapes of a New West* focuses on western woman of color who opt for postmodern aesthetics to tell western stories far different from white American pioneer narratives (317).

2. My work adds to the recent studies by Comer, Halverson, and Rosowski that explore a handful of mid- to late twentieth-century writers.

3. Intersectional feminism is an inclusive approach to human liberation that understands systems of power (such as gender, race, class, and sexuality) as overlapping and mutually reinforcing. It thus recognizes women's experiences as multidimensional, shaped by privilege as well as oppression. The concept of intersectionality was first theorized by black feminists and other women of color during the 1970s and 1980s, most notably by the Combahee River Collective in "A Black Feminist Statement" and by other contributors to the anthology *This Bridge Called My Back: Writings By Radical Women of Color* edited by Cherríe Moraga and Gloría Anzaldúa. The term was first coined by Kimberlé Crenshaw in 1989. These feminists of color are often considered a "third wave" that resisted marginalization within a feminist movement dominated by white women.

4. Coined by French feminist Francoise d'Eaubonne in 1974, "ecofeminism" posits that the domination of women in a patriarchal society is linked to the destruction of the environment under industrial capitalism. In other words, the same worldview that authorizes human domination of the natural world also authorizes male domination within the family and society (Buchanan; Kheel 246). Recently, ecofeminist writers have extended this concept to include indigenous peoples, people of color, and other marginalized groups (Cook 5)—a project that, I argue, Babb advanced many decades ahead of her time.

5. In the novel, the town is called Apache.

6. Passive and self-effacing, Belle resembles other western mothers depicted by Babb's contemporaries, such as Mari Sandoz, Tillie Olsen, Agnes Smedley, and Meridel LeSueur. Melody Graulich's assessment of the daughters in these stories applies to Robin: they "find themselves torn between their attraction to their fathers, who they see as creative and colorful figures, and their recognition of themselves as women, as destined to occupy their mother's role" ("Violence against Women" 17). Yet, as Graulich argues, layered beneath these stories of western manhood are the painful realities of western women's lives: patriarchal marriage, domestic violence, and "the exploitation of pioneer women, supported by tradition, by law, and by simple brute force" ("'O Beautiful'" 193).

7. Notably, marital rape is present in three of the four narratives studied by Graulich—Mari Sandoz's *Old Jules*, Tillie Olsen's *Yonnondio*, and Meridel LeSueur's *The Girl*. Like Des, the husbands in these families believe "that he has sexual rights to his wife, upon demand, and he uses violence to assert his rights" ("Violence against Women" 15).

8. Melody Graulich's reflection about her own family experience lends insight to Babb's sometimes frustrating choice to center the novel on the male protagonist: "My mother told me secrets [about domestic violence] she and my grandmother had kept for thirty-five years, yet I used these secrets not to understand their lives, but to explore my grandfather and my identification with him. I did not conceal the story, but like Sandoz, I thought it was about the man, and I did not see that perhaps the story was really about the teller, 'her father's daughter,' my mother. Although I am a feminist, I rendered her invisible and thoughtlessly covered up the real costs of woman abuse" ("Violence against Women" 19).

9. While the rugged individualist is coded male, it is not difficult for women to insert themselves into this myth, as the desire for freedom is a universal human quality (Baym

132–33). Yet Graulich cautions against celebrating the simple replacement of a male hero with a female one in Western women's writing, but rather looks for "the overlap" in the male tradition of freedom and "female concerns with human interdependence," which tend to be undervalued ("'Oh Beautiful'" 196). More recently, feminist critic Rita Felksi argues that women writers have successfully revised male plotlines, "adapting and tinkering with the old structure so that it fits the new protagonist" and creating a "hybrid of masculine and feminine, the old and the new" (101).

10. Babb, Letter to Howe.

11. Although this kind of relationship would be dangerous and unlikely in rural America in the 1920s, Babb recognizes the risk, and Chris pays a price for this interracial friendship, as he is fired from his job when false rumors are spread about a romance between them. The narrator mentions that, as a skilled mechanic, he eventually finds a new job with a competitor. This implication that capitalist market forces can counteract racism reflects Babb's turn toward more liberal politics.

WORKS CITED

Babb, Sanora. *An Owl on Every Post*. Muse Ink Press, 2012.

———. Letter to James Wong Howe. 29 August 1936. Box 46, Folder 6, Sanora Babb papers, Harry Ransom Center, University of Texas at Austin.

———. *The Lost Traveler*. Muse Ink Press, 2013.

———. *Whose Names Are Unknown*. University of Oklahoma Press, 2006.

Babb, Sanora, and Dorothy Babb. *On the Dirty Plate Trail: Remembering the Dust Bowl Refugee Camps*. Edited by Douglas Wixson. University of Texas Press, 2007.

Battat, Erin Royston. *Ain't Got No Home: America's Great Migrations and the Making of an Interracial Left*. University of North Carolina Press, 2014.

Baym, Nina. "Melodramas of Beset Manhood: How Theories of American Fiction Exclude Women Authors." *American Quarterly*, vol. 33, no. 2, 1981, 123–39, https://doi.org/10.2307/2712312.

Buchanan, Ian. "Ecofeminism." *A Dictionary of Critical Theory*. Oxford University Press, 2010. www.oxfordreference.com/view/10.1093/acref/9780199532919.001.0001/acref-9780199532919-e-208.

Comer, Krista. *Landscapes of the New West: Gender and Geography in Contemporary Women's Writing*. University of North Carolina Press, 1999.

Cook, Barbara J., editor. *Women Writing Nature: A Feminist View*. Lexington Books, 2008.

Felski, Rita. *Literature after Feminism*. University of Chicago Press, 2003.

Gaard, Greta. "Living Interconnections with Animals and Nature." *Ecofeminism*, edited by Greta Gaard. Temple University Press, 1993, pp. 1–12, www.jstor.org/stable/j.ctt14bt5pf.4.

Graulich, Melody. "'Oh Beautiful for Spacious Guys': An Essay on the 'Legitimate Inclinations of the Sexes.'" *The Frontier Experience and the American Dream:*

Essays on American Literature, edited by David Mogen, Mark Busby, and Paul Bryant. 1st ed., Texas A&M University Press, 1989, 186–201.

———. "Violence against Women in Literature of the Western Family." *Frontiers: A Journal of Women Studies*, vol. 7, no. 3, 1984, 14–20, https://doi.org/10.2307/3346235.

Halverson, Cathryn. *Playing House in the American West: Western Women's Life Narratives, 1839–1987*. University of Alabama Press, 2013.

Hewitt, Nancy, editor. *No Permanent Waves: Recasting Histories of U.S. Feminism*. Rutgers University Press, 2010.

Kheel, Marti. "From Heroic to Holistic Ethics: The Ecofeminist Challenge." *Ecofeminism*, edited by Greta Gaard, Temple University Press, 1993, pp. 243–71.

Kolodny, Annette. *The Land before Her: Fantasy and Experience of the American Frontiers, 1630–1860*. University of North Carolina Press, 1984.

Lamont, Victoria. "Big Books Wanted: Women and Western American Literature in the Twenty-First Century." *Legacy*, vol. 31, no. 2 (2014): 311–26.

Merchant, Carolyn. *Radical Ecology: The Search for a Livable World*. Routledge, 1992.

Meyerowitz, Joanne J., editor. *Not June Cleaver: Women and Gender in Postwar America, 1945–1960*. Temple University Press, 1994.

Moraga, Cherríe, and Gloría Anzaldúa, editors. *This Bridge Called My Back: Writings by Radical Women of Color*. 4th ed., State University of New York Press, 2015.

Rosowski, Susan J. *Birthing a Nation: Gender, Creativity, and the West in American Literature*. University of Nebraska Press, 1999.

Rampersad, Arnold. *Ralph Ellison: A Biography*. 1st ed., Knopf, 2007.

Slotkin, Richard. *Regeneration through Violence: The Mythology of the American Frontier, 1600–1860*. University of Oklahoma Press, 2000.

Stout, Janis P. *Picturing a Different West: Vision, Illustration, and the Tradition of Cather and Austin*. 1st ed. Texas Tech University Press, 2007.

Watkins, Claire Vaye. "The Classic Novel That Saw Pleasure as a Path to Freedom." *New York Times*, 5 February 2020, www.nytimes.com/2020/02/05/books/review/kate-chopin-the-awakening.html.

Wixson, Douglas. Introduction. *The Lost Traveler*, by Sanora Babb, xi–xxiii. Muse Ink Press, 1995.

IRIS JAMAHL DUNKLE

4

THE REAL WEST IN SANORA BABB'S SHORT STORIES

When one examines Sanora Babb's short stories, it is no wonder that she thought her best genre was short story and that she practiced that craft for many decades. Her use of character, imagery, and symbol, her ability to let the form of the story be chosen by the story, and the deep-seated sense of place that runs deep into the ravines of her stories are just a few of the reasons why her stories about life in the true West should be remembered and studied.

Babb's short stories are in varied tones and in varied settings. She wrote many proletarian stories of men and women down on their luck in the Dust Bowl Midwest and in Depression-era California. She ventured into the gothic genre, with unsettling tales from rural farms and odd neighborhoods in Los Angeles alike. One of her most original legacies, however, is her lifelong commitment to portraying strong women who take control of their fate and who are connected with the environment they inhabit.

Babb knew the West because she lived her life in it. She knew the independence it could afford women. Born in Oklahoma the year it became a state, she grew up in the Oklahoma panhandle and nearby Kansas, on the prairie of eastern Colorado, and in California. She began writing at a young age, working in newspapers from the age of twelve, and later moved to Los Angeles just months before the stock market crashed in 1929. Early on, she published poetry and soon stories, novels, and memoirs, but she primarily identified herself as a short story writer, a craft she took seriously. When challenged by a young writer who claimed, "The only real writing is what comes out naturally," Babb responded dryly, "I have great respect for what comes out naturally, but I call it my first draft." Babb thought "the summit of art is form," which she defines as "the total result of intuition and craft" ("A World of Forms" 11). We know that Babb wrote many drafts of each of her stories. Babb also workshopped them with her esteemed LA writing group, which had been started by Ray Bradbury. She kept careful records of her drafts and often sent these drafts to friends, who provided feedback that she would later incorporate. She taught courses on writing short fiction in the UCLA extension program, where her lectures revealed a deep commitment to putting in the work. Babb believed that the development of strong and memorable characters controlled form in a piece of writing.

In the late nineteenth century, Frederick Jackson Turner equated Americanization with cultural traits of what it meant to be a western American: "coarseness and strength combined with acuteness and acquisitiveness; that practical inventive turn of mind, quick to find expedients; that masterful grasp of material things . . . that restless, nervous energy;" perhaps most importantly, he added the phrase "dominant individualism," which he believed had been shaped by forging new lives in the western frontier (37). This ideas of individualism, entrepreneurship, and strength were embodied in the characters popularized in the western literature that followed, even though the West was populated by women as well as men and by Native Americans and immigrants of many nationalities. For the most part, dime novels and more serious western literature depicted white men, and not these others, with "dominant individualism." An androcentric literary West was created, which then was taken up by Hollywood and immortalized. Writers such as Owen Wister, Andy Adams, Jack Schaefer, Zane Grey, Jack London, early John Steinbeck, Wallace Stenger, and Walter Van Tilburg Clark had few female or minority protagonists who might exhibit masterful cowboy and pioneer traits.

Another glaring reason the literary West is phallocentric is because fewer early western women writers are celebrated. Those who are now recognized, such as Willa Cather and Mary Austin, are often relegated to the regionalist bin. Contrary to this representation on the page, however, the West was a place of ethnic diversity and strong women. As Joan M. Jensen and Gloria Ricci Lothrop explain in *California Women: A History*, "From the days before Europeans ventured into the area, California women have possessed several characteristics, most of them not reflected in their public image" (1). These women dwelt in "a multicultural, multilingual, densely populated culture . . . [with] variety of beliefs, customs, and conditions" (1). This essay explores how the work of Sanora Babb shows us women who were dominant individualists in the West. By looking closely at the West through Babb's short stories, we see a version closer to the true West, one where women were more than weak helpmates and where diversity was not only showcased but depicted as the integral and indeed ancient fabric of the region.

Babb published her stories widely and to much success during the 1940s–1980s. Surprisingly, she didn't publish a collection of stories until 1987, when *The Dark Earth and Other Stories from the Great Depression* was published by Capra Back-to-Back. Most of the stories from this collection were originally published in magazines from 1935 to 1949. Her second short story collection, *Cry of the Tinamou*, was published ten years later in 1997; its tales had been published individually from 1951 to 1986, except for the title story, which first appeared in this book. Of the fifteen stories collected in that volume, ten are written from the perspective of a female protagonist who is usually acting under her own agency.

One of Babb's most interesting female protagonists is found in *Cry of the Tinamou* in "A Scandalous Humility," originally published in *Northwest Review* in 1968. This is Mrs. Tsiang, a determined Chinese immigrant mother who has never accepted American customs and who has been shunned in the United States for a past that was beyond her control. Although she is othered, both in America as an immigrant and within her own Chinese American community as someone who has lost face, she is a strong protagonist as Babb depicts her: "small, sleek as a blackbird" with "dark alert eyes" and a mind "folded tight like a green bud" (13, 16). Mrs. Tsiang believes that in order for her soul to be at rest in her homeland, her bones must be shipped and buried in China. She's driven by a need to "become the dust on [her] own hills" (19). Nothing can stop her. She exhibits many of Turner's famed traits, including an "inventive turn of mind," and ironically, it is this western state of mind that enables her to return, after death, to China.

In addition to giving this female protagonist western traits usually assigned to men, Babb also allows Mrs. Tsiang to cross gender lines. She eats with the men in the restaurant because they are offered a wider variety of foods, and when she prays, she leaves her fate in the hands of a goddess instead of a god. Babb takes her time to reveal the past that has left Mrs. Tsiang shunned. As a young girl, she left her village an orphan and traveled to Canton to become a picture bride. But, as Babb describes it, "something went wrong, and the group of young girls on the long cruel trip by sea were not delivered to husbands but to an old woman with straw hair and blue eyes, a foreign ghost, who paid for them and owned them and set them to their tasks" (20). After years of sexual enslavement, she finally escapes and marries her husband, but soon her past comes back to haunt her. When the people of Chinatown find out about her life as a prostitute, they spurn her and "nothing [she] did won her face" (21). However, by the end of the story, through sheer determination, Mrs. Tsiang has overcome these obstacles by devising a way to save face and at the same time arrange to have her bones returned to her homeland. Babb celebrates this triumph in the end with an image of Mrs. Tsiang looking out her window and seeing moonlight on the dirty stones of the street. The moon illuminates her path forward, a new path created by her own agency. Babb's character of Mrs. Tsiang is striking. Even in literature of the 1960s, it is rare to find autonomous female protagonists, let alone outcast older Chinese women given their own agency to change the path fate has set them on. Babb's choice gives formally marginalized types power over their own lives and is an example of what Alan M. Wald called in his introduction to *Cry of the Tinamou* her "incipient" and organic feminism (xv). Babb depicts a multicultural West where strong female characters survived despite their circumstances and where not only men enacted Turner's traits.

Another example of Babb's use of a strong and unlikely female character can be found in her short story "Davy," originally titled "Snow as Promise." She began writing the story in 1946 and first published it in *New Story* in July 1951. The protagonist is another unlikely hero, whose gender is at first ambiguous. She is named Davy after her father, whose gambling finally drove her mother to kick him out. Though her father is gone, his shame still haunts their household. The story is set in a desolate winter landscape. Like Mrs. Tsiang,

Davy is associated with natural imagery, in this case a nature subdued by winter. In the first paragraph, Davy is struck by the beauty of a dried morning glory vine that she sees "still clinging to her window by its rotting summer strings. How lovely to again see its delicate purple trumpet! Would they live here then?" (145). Winter is the time of the year when poverty often is felt most keenly. But Davy copes with privation well, reading books for company, keeping the stove lit with the little coal the family has, and tending to her emotionally exhausted mother.

Davy's mother has been flattened by trying to support their family on her own. Babb emphasizes this failure by making her a two-dimensional character whose life choices act as a terrifying cautionary tale for young Davy. What frightens Davy is how her mother equates her own fate of suffering with the fate of all women. One sees this when Davy and her mother discuss her father's leaving and the choices men and women have in life:

> "I thought he wanted to be alone," Davy said.
> "Well, he does and he doesn't. That's the way men are."
> "What about women?" Davy asked innocently.
> "Does it matter what a woman wants?" Mama grumbled.
> "Of course, it does! Stop sounding like a worm, Mama."
> "I only wish I were. I'd certainly go underground after today." (148)

Davy resolves to not repeat her mother's defeat, vowing, "I won't be like that.... I'll run away from it" (149).

At one point, Davy leaves the safety and seclusion of their rented house to visit her father in the county jail; this visit will be the catalyst through which she finds her identity. During the short walk to the jail, she is self-conscious, thinking that everyone is staring at her. Even the "tall trees that almost hid the jail in summer" had become "black skeletons . . . baring the paths and the grey stone buildings to every eye" (149). Although Babb claimed in a letter to a friend about the revision of another story that she felt she had little command over her use of symbolism, her use of nature as symbol in this story is expert. When Davy encounters her father in his cell, it is as if she is encountering her own shadow in the Jungian sense: the parts of herself that have been revealed by the black skeletons of her own bare trees, a vision of the failure she could be if she followed the logic of her upbringing. Her father tries to manipulate her into play-boxing with him as they used to when she was little. When she demurs, he complains that she's "got to be such a damn girl lately" (154). Instead of giving in, Davy stands up to his pleas, replying, "I am a girl," realizing in that moment that the love she once felt for her father is now gone. She has seen through his bravado to his limited, damaged essence. He was a man she never could rely on, and she sees that she will never be able to in the future. Instead of being upset by this realization, the moment becomes a catalyst from which Davy's independence surges forth and blossoms. Neither her father's intransigence nor her mother's weakness is for her; self-reliance will be her only successful mode forward.

As she leaves the jail, Davy feels a sense of agency. Babb shows us this with the final image of the story: "The jail door closed after her just as people were walking along the paths going home from work. If anyone stared, and of course they did, it seemed to her now a reasonable curiosity. She was coming out of the jail. I'm myself, she thought rather grandly and then she felt how absurd she must be and added, whatever that is. It's I" (154). Davy finds her path, one of autonomy and liberation, which again are the very tenets that Turner claimed defined the West. In the end, Davy is the most western of all of the characters of the story. We are left with the idea that she, like the purple flowers of the morning glory, will climb to new heights come spring.

With male and female protagonists, the West and its landscape are at the heart of all of Babb's stories, where she uses setting to convey the emotions her characters sometimes cannot express themselves. She also uses setting as an antagonist, a force that puts the protagonist into a drastic situation she otherwise might not have found herself in. In "The Journey Begun" (published in the anthology *Cross Section of New American Writing* [1948] and later collected in *The Dark Earth*), Babb gives another strong female character a male name: Damon Shane. Like Davy, Damon sees her mother destroyed by her father's gambling and drunken beatings. When she was younger, Damon hadn't been able to protect her mother from becoming the victim of her father's rage. But once she gets older, she realizes "that she was his equal. Once she had thrown a knife, not wanting to, and after that she could frighten him with her eyes and her words. . . . That part of her was in everything she was, as natural as laughter, not, as he thought, a segment he could shatter and pluck out" (*Dark Earth* 35). When Damon realizes that she is not a victim like her mother, but despite her gender a fighter like her father, she gains confidence. In this story, Babb uses natural imagery to convey her character's agency and connection to her environment. Damon is connected with the wind, as when "she put her arms around the wind. It was strong enough to hold but leapt away. She felt like the wind, like this clean western wind with its strength and disturbing urgency" (*Dark Earth* 32).

In the end, Damon plucks herself from her father's life in the remote and conventional small town. When the police break up his gambling game, and he makes a run for it, telling her to join him in a few days, she decides not to follow him. The sound of the train and the wind over the prairie awaken something in her that had been dormant before. She thinks "no music, no song would ever speak for her spirit as truly as the wind and the beckoning and farewelling call of a train going through lonely places" (*Dark Earth* 47). It was as if the wind has finally awakened in her the wildness and freedom that was always at her core. When she boards the train and the conductor asks her name, she immediately replies "Delores O'Shea," and with those small words separates herself from her father (*Dark Earth* 48). Damon/Delores survives because she bends the boundaries of gender, in the way many women had to leave behind conventional gender norms to survive the demands of living in the West.

In a sense, "The Journey Begun" works against many of the naturalist themes present in western writers' depiction of the West, especially the idea that humans are fated from the beginning to a life controlled by the environment in which they live. For unlike Jack London's young protagonist Johnny in "The Apostate," whose teenage body was transformed into a machine through his grueling life working in Oakland sweatshops and whose fate was nearly set from the beginning of the story, Damon is able to escape the boundaries imposed on her by her environment by not acting like a woman. "The Apostate" was originally published in *Women's Home Companion* in September 1906 as a political piece against child labor. Johnny has been working his entire life in different sweatshops, but he eventually becomes too ill to continue and decides he's had enough of being a work slave, much to his mother's chagrin, for he is the main breadwinner in the family. When London's protagonist finally escapes by hopping a freight train, he is so sick that the reader is left uncertain if he will survive to enjoy his freedom. In sharp contrast, Damon/Delores is able to step on the train, her pockets lined with her father's money, and start a new life, one where she is no longer controlled by her father's folly. She gains freedom through daring and the invention of a new identity. Under her new name, her father will not be able to locate her.

One finds another sharp contrast to these three strong female characters in one of John Steinbeck's most anthologized stories, "The Chrysanthemums," which was first published in 1937 in *Harper's* magazine. In this tale, Elisa Allen, the protagonist, is trapped in her California valley by fog that "sat like a lid on the mountains and made of the great valley a closed pot" (227). Elisa's fate seems sealed by the gender limitations placed on her. She has a green thumb and wishes she could use her skills to help her husband with their orchard. She thinks, "Maybe I could do it, too. I've a gift with things, all right. My mother had it. She could stick anything in the ground and make it grow" (228). Elisa, however, is not allowed into the spaces of real agriculture and commerce. The only place she has agency is her fenced garden where she grows incredible chrysanthemums. When a peddler stops by and asks her if she might send a few of her flower-starts with him so he can give them to another woman on a farm nearby, Elisa eagerly agrees. The idea of her work passing over the threshold of the garden fence and reaching another woman who might respect the hard work she has done intoxicates her. Equally intoxicating is the peddler's freedom that she thinks about as she readies a pot full of her sprouts. In fact, Elisa is so empowered by the act of passing along her work and for once feeling like it has value that she becomes obsessed by the idea of escape. She tells the peddler just before he leaves, "You might be surprised to have a rival some time. I can sharpen scissors, too. And I can beat the dents out of little pots. I could show you what a woman might do" (232).

But Elisa's strength is short-lived. Later, as she and her husband drive to town, she spots something she knows immediately to be her precious chrysanthemums starts. The peddler had thrown out her plants and kept the pot she had sent them in. To him, her work had no value. He had just tricked her into giving him her pot. The irony in Steinbeck's story is the fact that the very things that make Elisa strong work against her. Had she kept her dreams small enough to fit into her garden, she would not have been disappointed. Out of the confined space of her garden, where she is able to dress like a man and have control over her work, she cannot be strong.

By contrast, in Babb's stories, Mrs. Tsiang, Davy, and Damon develop and retain their strength beyond the confined spaces of their lives. Mrs. Tsiang is forced to live apart from her community because she was sold into prostitution, but she slowly but surely is able to find a path to freedom from this ostracism, albeit posthumously. Davy is forced to live in the isolation of poverty and shame caused by her manipulative, gambling father, but she is able to finally confront her father in jail and become her own person. Damon escapes the vagabond life her father has forced on her and catches a train that will take her identity to a new life. These female protagonists overcome their difficult environments and each, through this adversity, is able to transform into a stronger, freer, more independent version of themselves.

The West that Babb recreates is full of strong female protagonists, bolstered by imagery and symbolism that she expertly employs to underscore female agency, even when the odds seem against it. It is a story we are rarely told in tales of the West. Not for her the cowboy riding in and rescuing the woman from her hapless fate. Babb wasn't one to adhere to gender stereotypes in her writing. As a strong, independent woman herself, she wrote from what she knew and what she saw around her. She wrote about a frontier where some women crossed gender lines to survive, thus transcending gender stereotypes. When we revisit Turner's traits—"coarseness and strength combined with acuteness and acquisitiveness; that practical inventive turn of mind, quick to find expedients; that masterful grasp of material things . . . that restless, nervous energy;" and "dominant individualism"—we clearly see the traits of many of Babb's female characters.

WORKS CITED

Babb, Sanora. "A World of Forms." *The Writer*, vol. 86, no. 7 (July 1973): 11–13.
———. *Cry of the Tinamou*. University of Nebraska Press, 1997.
———. *The Dark Earth and Other Stories from the Great Depression*. Capra Press, 1987.
Jensen, Joan M., and Gloria Ricci Lothrop. *California Women: A History*. Boyd & Fraser, 1987.
London, Jack. "The Apostate." *Women's Home Companion*, September 1906.
Steinbeck, John. "The Chrysanthemums." *The Long Valley*, Penguin, 1995, 1–13.
Turner, Frederick Jackson. *The Frontier in American History*. Henry Holt, 1921.
Wald, Alan. "Soft Focus: The Short Fiction of Sanora Babb." *Cry of the Tinamou*, by Sanora Babb, University of Nebraska Press, 1997, ix–xvi.

KATHERINE WITT

5
MATERNAL THINKING IN SANORA BABB'S *AN OWL ON EVERY POST*

Conceptually, historically, and politically, the woman and the mother are often linked, but as prominent feminist philosopher and author Sara Ruddick points out, that does not necessarily mean that the woman, or birth giver, is always the best at mothering. In Sanora Babb's memoir, *An Owl on Every Post*, the grandfather successfully mothers the children, while the mother is fully occupied, stressed, and burdened with the daily chores of homesteading on the High Plains. Using Sara Ruddick's *Maternal Thinking toward a Politics of Peace* and other theorists, this essay analyzes Babb and offers a new way of thinking through questions of gender roles.

In 1913, Sanora Babb, seven years old, moved from Oklahoma to the desolate plains of eastern Colorado with her father, thirty-two, mother, twenty-four, and four-year-old sister to join Grandfather Alonzo on his homestead land. *An Owl on Every Post* closely reflects Babb's time living in a one-room dugout with her family prior to the Dust Bowl and the Great Depression of the 1930s. Upon meeting her grandfather for the first time, Sanora likes him immediately: "[He] greeted us with no words at all. He did not seem unfriendly but he only nodded. I looked at his long dark face and black eyes and black hair. A full black mustache drooped over his upper lip and mouth. I liked him at once, his darkness and his silence. He was like an Indian" (Babb 12).

Sanora gravitated toward her grandfather and had to share a cot with him while her father, mother, and sister shared the only other bed. Sanora's mother, Ginny, performed the work of cleaning, cooking, crocheting, warming the dugout, and other chores around the property. Her loneliness and the harsh conditions of their environment prevented her from being an attentive nurturer to Sanora (Cheyenne in the story) and her sister, Dorothy (the character Marcy). Cheyenne solemnly relates the realities of her family dynamic: "Mama favored us all with her care and concern, swallowed her frustrations in favor of an atmosphere of kindness, and when she failed, she kept stubbornly quiet until she could find a free moment and a private place to cry" (Babb 18). Ginny relieves Grandfather of some of the household chores, but her frustration and fits of what she herself calls "the blues" sometimes overwhelm her and prevent her from fully giving her time and attention to her children. Ginny's distractions create an opportunity for Grandfather to engage with the children, and he falls into the mothering role quickly and naturally.

The memoir reveals the complexity of mothering in the family. Babb survived and grew to be a successful writer, perhaps made possible because there was an "other" who assisted in the act of mothering. According to Ruddick, a mother is the one who takes the most interest in meeting the children's demands of preservation, growth, and social acceptability. In Babb's story, that figure is often Grandfather Alonzo. He is not considered a mother, however, because he is a man and mothering is not tied to the ideology of masculinity, especially in the American West. Nonetheless, I will here bring attention to this "other mother" and show how Babb depicted and internalized this as a child. She portrays proto-feminist—and indeed, feminist—views in her writing before they might have been labeled as such. She is probing gender roles and motherhood in the 1910s, though academic feminist studies didn't appear until decades later. An important aspect of an analysis of Babb's unconventionally gendered parenthood can be revealed by probing the relationships among both labeling and enacting familial responsibilities in Babb's writing. At several moments in *Owl*, Walter, the father, speaks clearly about what men and women should be responsible for, but in reality, the roles in his story are much more blurred, and indeed the sharing of responsibilities is the reason the family is able to survive such brutal conditions.

Shortly after the Babb family moves to Colorado, Cheyenne notices that her mother is not happy on the plains. She misses having friends to visit and feels lonely in the dugout. Ginny's two luxuries are coffee and stationery to write letters, though later the family is not always able to afford both. If forced to decide between the two, Ginny chooses coffee. Babb comments, "Coffee meant something more to her than a hot drink. Now and then in the afternoon she sat for a while in a fresh apron, slowly drinking warmed-over coffee, her face passive, her gaze rapt in faraway memories or in dreams of escape. She did not mind the hard work, only the terrible loneliness. In that solitary rite she reached backward or forward to friends, perhaps, or simply retired within herself to renew her forces" (Babb 153). Ginny does not hide her loneliness from anyone. Upon meeting a new family in Two Buttes, she quickly admits to the woman, "This is the lonesomest place" (Babb 72). Although young Cheyenne does not fully understand the feelings of her mother or the other members of her family who sometimes deal with discouraging feelings, she gives a name to those feelings: the blues. "In our small, crowded room, each managed to achieve an occasional moment of desperately needed privacy called the blues" (Babb 154). While Cheyenne cannot exactly comprehend these extreme feelings of solitude or desperation, she and her younger sister understand that the adults with "the blues" need to be alone and are not available to give the children attention. Somehow, Cheyenne knows that her mother sometimes can't function the way Cheyenne would like. Although Ginny failed at mothering on multiple occasions, Babb later expressed only gratitude, not blame, toward both her parents equally for those early years.

Adrienne Rich, a contemporary of Sara Ruddick, who also wrote about motherhood as experience and institution decades after the eras in which Babb's stories are set, comments, "What, anyway, is this primal idea which seems to take women—not only in childbirth—in its grasp and press the self out of us, or, even worse, to *become* our selfhood?" (158). Rich challenges the idea that a woman's identity can only revolve around motherhood after having a child. Ginny removes herself from her family when she feels overwhelmed with loneliness. Rich's ideas support the idea that Ginny should be able to preserve her selfhood and take care of her feelings in private without suffering from censure. Rich continues, "The depths of this conflict, between self-preservation and maternal feelings, can be experienced ... as a primal agony" (161). Rich understands and defends a mother's choice to remove herself from the family, when necessary, and rely on the other adults to care for the family.

Preservation is an important way a mother meets a child's needs, though one can make a distinction between intent and action. Mothers' emotional connections to their children may have their ups and downs, but ultimately, mothers have "a *commitment*" to them that informs their lives and deeds (Ruddick 70). Ginny's despairing moods and dislike of the plains often occupy her thoughts and sometimes makes her unavailable to Cheyenne and Marcy, but those feelings do not affect the choices she makes to preserve the lives of her children. Ginny's wedding ring, for example, is the one material item that she never wanted to give up or barter. No matter how poor the family became, her wedding ring was her most important possession; she had no intention to sell it for money or food. However, Colorado homesteading was difficult, and as the family becomes weak with hunger, Ginny sells her cherished ring on a trip to town with the girls' father. When they return, Cheyenne helps her mother unload the wagon and suddenly notices something: "When I reached to take a bag from her hands, I saw it. A wide white band circled her finger where her wedding ring had been. I stared. Her blue eyes glistened with tears. She did not permit the tears to roll down her cheeks but shook her head once so that the drops flew away. 'Let's go in now and fix something to eat'" (Babb 206). Although Ginny is devastated, her commitment to her children's health and lives is more important. Ginny is sometimes absent emotionally from the family when loneliness overwhelms her, but in this instance she acts selflessly for her children because she knows that they must eat to live.

Grandfather Alonzo and Walter also play significant roles in preserving the lives of the Babb children. Alonzo has been living on the property and doing minor improvements for five years before the family's arrival. He's built the dugout and barn, and he lovingly maintains the horses for plowing and transport to town. As we will see, no single adult in the family could have taken care of the children and survived without the others. Ginny, Grandfather Alonzo, and Walter all have their roles. When one falters, another steps up to ensure survival and support. Ruddick points out that "as a child grows, so does the work of protection" (80). Ginny acts to preserve her children physically, but her feelings are often in the way of developing her children in mind and spirit. Since he advances the progress of the children's minds and curiosity, Grandfather Alonzo becomes a larger part of the mothering effort for Cheyenne and Marcy. Cultural, political, and feminist philosopher Virginia Held, who writes on the ethics of care, notes in *Feminism and Community* that "human mothering is no more 'natural' than any other human activity. . . . On a variety of grounds there are good reasons to have mothering become an activity performed by men as well as by women." From reading the memoir, the reader does not know how poorly Grandfather raised his own children, Walter and a daughter. As we now know, he mostly failed, since after the death of his wife he had a breakdown, took to drink, abandoned the children to his parents, and lit out to the territory to homestead in eastern Colorado. For the next generation, however, he compensates for his earlier botched job and redeems himself. After years on the High Plains by himself, Grandfather adjusts to living with a family again, rising to the occasion to mother Cheyenne and Marcy.

A second part of mothering is "to foster growth [and] nurture a child's developing spirit—whatever in a child is lively, purposive, and responsive" (Ruddick 82). While living in the dugout, Grandfather is the adult mainly responsible for the children's education. This is the area where he performs his greatest act of mothering: "Mama and Papa were concerned that there was no school within a hundred miles, but it was Grandfather who set about teaching me what he could" (Babb 77). Ginny and Walter express concern about the lack of formal education in the area of Colorado that they settled, but Grandfather never did. Through his actions, Grandfather demonstrates that there were ways to teach children outside of the classroom and with few resources. The narrator Cheyenne relates: "[He] taught me how to handle a knife, or bridle a horse, or distinguish grains, or he read to me from his only book, *Kit Carson*" (Babb 78). Grandfather introduces Cheyenne and Marcy to practical skills on the farm and to take care of themselves, and he also teaches the girls to read and write. Cheyenne seems to love it all: "The book gave me also my first formal source of education. I studied it to learn words; I copied from it to learn to spell; I read it to myself and aloud; I copied numbers from its pages; I wrote lessons on what I had read" (Babb 78). Ginny had pasted *Denver Post* newspapers in the dugout to hold up the mud walls and act as insulation. Grandfather teaches the girls to read the articles and discusses with them what was written. He forbids some articles because he thinks the content is inappropriate, but Cheyenne reads them anyway: "I was fascinated by all the pieces in the newspaper; each showed me a facet of the world beyond the far circle of horizon" (Babb 79). Cheyenne and her sister did not have friends their same age and barely interacted with people outside of the family. Their only shelter was the dugout, so in good weather and bad, they spend the majority of their days on the vast open land. However,

Grandfather provides for them a way to explore beyond their isolated prairie by bringing to their attention articles on big city life and discussing the contents.

Grandfather informs the girls that "all my people were educated from the Bible by their mothers. They were well-spoken people because of it. By the time they went to school, they had some learning. It was the same with your father and me. His grandmothers looked after that" (Babb 78). Since the family does not own a Bible, Grandfather uses *Kit Carson* instead. The detail in this speech that stands out most for our purposes is that when Grandfather talks about the mothers and grandmothers being responsible for teaching the children about reading and writing, in his own situation, he, not Ginny, takes on that responsibility for Cheyenne and Marcy. The dugout household is a beautiful blending of gender roles and societal expectations that no one questions. At certain points in the story, Walter makes clear his traditional views on gender distinctions, but no one, not even he, comments on Grandfather's being the educator. Both Ginny and Walter worry about the girls not being in school, but neither of them acts to address it. Grandfather steps in and provides one of the fundamental aspects of mothers, which helps the children thrive.

Ruddick also brings light to the importance of stories for nurturing children: "Through good stories, mothers and children connect their understanding of a shared experience. They come to know and, to a degree, accept each other through stories of the fear, love, anxiety, pride, and shame they shared or provoked . . . It is also true that storytelling at its best enables children to adapt, edit, and invent life stories of their own" (Ruddick 98). Grandfather is the storyteller of the family. Cheyenne remembers that almost every question she asked prompted a story. Grandfather even worked stories into his arithmetic lessons: "The problems Grandfather gave me were about acres, horses, cows, chickens, prairie dogs, coyotes, skunks, cane, feterita, and broomcorn, which he raised" (Babb 82). Ginny and Walter contribute to the stories, but Grandfather usually kicks them off. These stories allow Cheyenne's imagination to blossom and explore the world surrounding her: "My imagination was also afire. I visualized the rancher, his family and cowhands, the great roaring windy fires such as I was to see later; I was concerned with the safety of the cattle, with larks nesting in the grass and there was certain to be a prairie dog town burned over or in danger" (Babb 83). Grandfather's ability to develop curious thought and exploration in Cheyenne is inspiring. Their short time together jump started Cheyenne's lifelong curiosity and thirst for learning. His way of teaching caused Babb to create stories in her head even before she began writing them down.

Ginny becomes pregnant, and Walter is convinced that the unborn baby is a boy. While sharing the news with the family, Walter tells his daughters, "'I don't want you mothering him, understand? You can play with dolls. I don't want any sissy'" (Babb 103). This line feels out of place so soon after the description of the education that Grandfather is providing for the girls. Walter has fantasies of the boy playing baseball and thinks he will be very different from the female children he already has. He does not elaborate on his insulting, tone-deaf pronouncements, and Cheyenne, the narrator, leaves the ideas unexplained. This small example demonstrates that the family, or at least Walter, still believes in traditional gender roles; no one challenges Walter's comments. But in such a harsh environment, gender roles are necessarily fluid. While Walter may speak as if there were clearly defined attributes and responsibilities for men and women, the family would not survive if they put those beliefs into practice.

A major part of mothering, according to Ruddick, is addressing social acceptability for the children. She notes that "to be responsible for children's moral well-being means helping them to become people who will be reliably moral when they are along or among peers. This means turning over moral initiative to the children themselves" (Ruddick 108). Children typically spend time with peers in their own neighborhoods, communities, or schools. Cheyenne and Marcy do not spend much time with other children their age until they return to the classroom. Toward the end of the memoir, when the family moves to the Kansas community of Elkhart after four years of living on the eastern plains of Colorado, Cheyenne's education from her grandfather allows her, amazingly, to transition seamlessly into a class appropriate for her age. The principal of the school wants Cheyenne to begin again in second grade, since her last formal schooling had been first grade. However, he agrees to have her tested for placement, and she relates that her teacher, Miss Temple, was "astounded that I could have learned so much from reading only *The Adventures of Kit Carson* and a collection of tales and poems. I tried to explain about Grandfather, but she sped on to questions and problems and discovered gaps in my education that made her frown" (Babb 239). Cheyenne did not answer all the questions correctly, but Miss Temple gave her the opportunity to study for a week and jump her up to the seventh grade. Cheyenne made her own study schedule and was self-motivated to learn all that she could to prepare for school. Grandfather's dugout education and his ability to cultivate Cheyenne's curiosity enabled a smooth return to organized learning in this pioneer community. Acting as a nurturing parent, he taught Cheyenne and Marcy in a way that makes Cheyenne want to set high educational and social goals for herself. Part of teaching social acceptability is fostering inquisitiveness and teaching a child to thrive in an environment filled with peers. Once enrolled in school, Sanora Babb did thrive and went on to graduate high school at the top of her class.

Ruddick writes that "mothers are meant to train children in the conventional behavior acceptable to their social and cultural group. If a child doesn't know how to dress, act politely, play happily, and pass to the next grade in school, her mother will probably be blamed. But when morality turns 'serious,' it is the Father's will that must be placated, the Public Law of the Fathers that holds sway" (110). This is another example of blurred gendered parenting in Babb's story. Babb reflects in her afterword about her father's change from farmer to professional gambler soon after they left the high plains. She likens the uncertainty of dry-land farming to her father's gambling. While Babb earned the honor of valedictorian of her high school class and wrote the class poem, her father's reputation disqualified her, and the school superintendent and local church ministries would not allow her to be recognized. Thus in the Babb family, Walter is not the figure who enforces morality. In the example of Babb's being denied the position of valedictorian, Walter is the cause of that public shame because his morals are suspect due to his career choice.

Cheyenne is taught morality by a host of characters who act as collective mother, rather than by one singular figure, male or female. Commenting on the teaching of social acceptability, which is largely based on the judgement of whether someone has conventional morals, Ruddick explains, "Mothers could not give, nor do children need, constant attentive love. What children and mothers require of each other is proper trust.... She learns to trust a child she loves and to love a real, and therefore trustworthy, child" (123). Cheyenne and her parental figures, Walter, Ginny, and Grandfather Alonzo, share a mutual trust. She trusts her family to provide for and protect her, and the family instructs and trusts Cheyenne to behave conventionally and grow into a wholesome adult. Babb writes in her afterword to *An Owl on Every Post* in 1994 (twenty-four years after the book was originally published and eighty-one years after the start of her family's Colorado homesteading experience) that "it was our concerned parents who suffered the most. They worried about food, clothing, winter shoes, health, warmth, schools. I remember clearly how often I saw our mother put most of her scant food on our plates. I remember our parents' anxiety about no school in that hardly inhabited vast plain; of their talk of the importance of education" (Babb 252). Babb's tone demonstrates nothing but appreciation and love for her family, not frustration or distrust.

As a woman who wrote from her personal perception of her family dynamics, Sanora Babb became a journalist, poet, and author who demonstrated progressive feminist views before such labels existed. Clearly, Ginny took her role as a mother seriously and sacrificed her own comforts and well-being for her children. She loved the girls fiercely. But motherhood alone did not define Ginny. She was also a musician and wanted close, personal friendships with other women. In a similar manner, Grandfather did not simply take care of the land and horses. In a community such as a family, it is inconducive to strictly take on one role and stay within those confines. Her family's experience on the plains made a significant impact on her, so much so that she focused this memoir on that short time and experience. Babb never became a mother, so it is impossible to say how she would have performed that role with her own children.

Sanora Babb witnessed her family members challenge traditional gender roles, and one can assume that this influenced her future writing. I believe her experiences on the plains led her to have unconventional and progressive views very early in her life. Babb broke down the cultural distinction of gendered parenthood well before scholars began studying and challenging these beliefs.

WORKS CITED

Babb, Sanora. *An Owl on Every Post*. 3rd ed. Muse Ink Press, 2012.
Held, Virginia. "Non-contractual Society: A Feminist View." *Feminism and Community*. Temple University Press, 1995.
Rich, Adrienne. *Of Woman Born*. W. W. Norton, 1986.
Ruddick, Sara. *Maternal Thinking toward a Politics of Peace*. Beacon Press, 1995.

AMY STRICKLAND SMITH

6
RESILIENCE IN SANORA BABB'S LIFE AND CHARACTERS

Sanora Babb's complex family ties and her transient early life in which she experienced poverty, hunger, and social alienation not only shaped her outlook but revealed an innate resilience and strength despite her fully inhabiting a marginalized status. Her place on the periphery provided a rich foundation from which to create her written art. Using her early economic and personal deprivations as a springboard, she became an important member of a generation of proletarian writers of the mid-twentieth century. In her memoir of her early life, *An Owl on Every Post*, Babb revealed traits of resilience that gave her the courage to unflinchingly explore her stark physical environment and the interpersonal relationships of her family. Despite her hardscrabble childhood, Sanora thrived and became a skilled writer, ultimately forging a perspective of optimism and joy. Her intense curiosity allowed her to flourish in adversity while other family members struggled to cope. Babb's resilience is integrated into the characters of *An Owl on Every Post*, as well as in her novels *Whose Names Are*

Unknown and *The Lost Traveler*. In *Owl* and *The Lost Traveler*, the characters based on herself reveal an abundance of adaptability and deep-rooted openness to exploration and novel experience.

A review of resilience research is necessary to understand the nexus of Sanora's outlook of hopefulness with her life experiences. Resilient individuals can possess "the capacity of a dynamic system to withstand or recover from significant challenges that threaten its stability, viability, or development" (Shiner and Masten 508). This chapter will show how well Sanora endured deprivation and was able to overcome a harsh physical and familial environment. Resilient people "have been exposed to significant risk that increases the likelihood of negative development [but . . .] display positive adaptation in spite of that risk" (508). Certain experiences and conditions may deprive children or adolescents of crucial developmental relationships, opportunities, and experiences, as was the case for Sanora and her younger sister, Dorothy. The presence of these factors can increase a child's vulnerability to ill health and social isolation, which indeed affected both girls. Interparental conflict and psychopathology can create a harmful environment that has a detrimental developmental effect on children's own interpersonal relationships (Kirby and Fraser 11, 22–23). Sanora's semi-functional family caused uncertainty and stress for the children, but nonetheless, Sanora went on to live a life filled with creative work, solid friendships, and a long marriage.

In studying resilience, researchers have found that protective factors, including individual coping abilities, family protective factors, and community or support outside the family unit, mitigate risk in children (Kirby and Fraser 16; Werner 82–83). Sanora was able to draw on her innately buoyant spirit to capitalize on several of these factors in her early life. She had a fluid "capacity for adaptation" (Shiner and Masten 508). Her own protective factors included a supportive Native American community early in her life, and later, her wise and stoic grandfather. Researchers have identified five personality traits that, by their presence or absence, indicate levels of resilience in individuals: extraversion, conscientiousness, agreeableness, openness to experience, and neuroticism (Campbell-Sills et al. 594). Sanora exhibited these traits, except for neuroticism. However, neuroticism was evident in Dorothy, even as a child. The protective factors in Sanora's life were not enough to overcome damaging experiences for Dorothy. Children with neuroticism may experience the world through agitation, distress, and anxiety, which can result in a decline in life satisfaction (Shiner and Masten 509; Liu et al. 833).

For Sanora and Dorothy, the challenges, significant adversities, and trauma in their young lives are attributable to the two most influential men in their lives: their father and, indirectly, their paternal grandfather. Sanora was devoted to her grandfather Alonzo Babb and enjoyed a close relationship with him, but his early alcoholism and neglect of his son when a boy profoundly affected the entire family, even decades later. While Walter Babb did not turn to alcohol, his life was marked by a series of poor decisions and an incapacity to manage anger. Alonzo's and Walter's lack of ability to navigate hardship resulted in extreme poverty and further social marginalization for the family, especially when Walter later took up gambling as a career. The generational repercussions of these circumstances were ultimately represented in the divergent outcomes of Sanora and Dorothy. Sanora was able to adapt and overcome early traumatic events. She was able to negotiate childhood adversity through writing, while Dorothy suffered lifelong damage from the same events.

Babb's grandfather Alonzo was a baker and later claimed a homestead in southeastern Colorado. He had been devastated by the death of his wife in childbirth and spent several years drinking heavily to cope with the loss (Babb, Wixson interview 4). His alcoholism and delinquent parenting exposed his son Walter to insecure environments. In the years between the approval of the Organic Act in 1890, which separated Oklahoma Territory from Indian Territory, and statehood in 1907, Oklahoma Territory saw an explosion in the establishment of saloons. "Whiskey towns" sprang up all over the new Oklahoma Territory, but especially along the borders of Indian Territory, where sale and consumption of liquor was prohibited (Gumprecht 146–48). In this rough and often violent setting "where saloons lined the streets, bootleggers came to stock up, gambling was widespread, and brothels did a brisk trade in upstairs rooms" (Gumprecht 146–47), young Walter Babb learned the gambling trade (Wixson, "Radical by Nature," 116–17).

Walter Babb married Jennie Parks, and in November of the year Oklahoma became a state, Sanora Babb was born. Her parents made their home in Red Rock, Oklahoma Territory, which was occupied by the Otoe-Missouria Tribe (Wixson, *On the Dirty Plate Trail* 3). Babb relates that her maternal grandmother sent money to her mother for travel to Kansas so Sanora could be born in a proper hospital (Ivy interview). Her grandmother, Anna Parks, had other motives for sending the money. Sanora's birth occurred in Leavenworth, Kansas, because her "aristocratic Southern maternal grandmother could not tolerate" having a grandchild born inside "Indian Territory" (Babb, Wixson interview 1). Anna Parks hailed from an established Kentucky family, and this was an unacceptable birthplace for close kin. Simply by living there, the Babb family occupied a marginalized geographical and social space. In childhood, however, Sanora knew nothing else.

However her extended family may have viewed Otoe-Missouria land, the young Babbs had been an accepted and integral part of the community, where Walter Babb owned and operated a bakery. He spoke several native languages, and both Walter and Jennie counted Native Americans as friends (Babb, Wixson interview 4–5). Sanora's adventures and connections with the Otoes are recounted in *Owl*, and as a young child, Sanora spent much of her time with the tribe (Babb, Wixson interview 5). Sanora later reflected on those days: "It was just a normal way of life for me. Most of my childhood friends there were Indians and I was in camp a lot, mainly lived there. I don't recall thinking of it as different—it was just my life" (Babb, Wixson interview 7). Sanora felt a special kinship toward Red Rock and the Otoe tribe that inhabited the area. Her exposure to the Otoe culture was in direct contradiction to white stereotypes of native populations, and her experience was one of support and acceptance. During this time, she and her family encountered rare years of social stability. The relative security the family found in Red Rock had laid a resilient foundation in Sanora and was one factor that later allowed her to recover emotionally from extreme hardship and thrive. After Red Rock, Babb lived the humiliating reality of poverty and did not look away from suffering when confronted with desperation and hunger in the Great Depression and Dust Bowl. In later life Babb wrote, "Years have passed since my life on the plains, but living in a true wilderness had a profound effect on me. Regardless of what unusual or unexpected professional or personal path I was on, throughout my life I always felt grounded on the plains. The impact of those years is still potent" (Babb, *Owl* afterword, 251).

Alonzo Babb moved to Colorado in 1910 to sober up, stake a 160-acre "proving-up" claim, and begin farming broomcorn. The area was sparsely populated; the closest town was seven miles away. The distance between the homestead and temptation achieved the desired effect: Alonzo stopped drinking. The landscape, which Sanora describes in *An Owl on Every Post*, though unadorned and lonely, was attractive for men like her grandfather: "In such distant and desolate places, and in new towns where no one knows another, a few come to hide, to forget, to start over again" (Babb, *Owl* 40).

Suffering from loneliness, Alonzo wrote letters to his son romanticizing the idea of pioneering spirit in the unsettled West, eventually convincing Walter to join him and farm broomcorn (Babb, Wixson interview 1). Walter was attracted to the pioneering ideal, but he was unsuited to the realities of farming on the dry plains. Nonetheless, in 1914, he uprooted his family and moved to Baca County, Colorado, and into Alonzo's one-room dugout, which Sanora recounted as "a square hole in the ground, dirt floor, with a 2 or 3 ft. wooden wall & roof. No amenities of any kind, save 2 windows which look onto the ground" (Babb, Wixson interview 2).

Walter Babb's lack of business sense and inexperience in farming had disastrous economic results. The attempts to cultivate broomcorn as a cash crop were unsuccessful, and the broomcorn boom market that had first brought Alonzo to southeast Colorado ended after World War I (Wixson, *On the Dirty Plate Trail* 3). As a result, the Babb family suffered economic devastation, physical hunger, and social isolation. During a particularly lean stretch of weeks, the family subsisted on Russian thistle boiled with black pepper (3). Kept inside during harsh winters, the one-room dugout became an intense and unhappy environment. Later, in a 1935 letter to her cousin, Sanora described both the physical and emotional trauma the family endured because of the inept decisions made by her father: "My sister and I began as very healthy youngsters and were quite sturdy looking until my father took a notion to do a little pioneering in an unsettled part of Colorado, and the several hopelessly failing years there, when we were all starved into shadows and broken by his furious vents of temper at misfortune, took such toll of our young bodies that we have never really known health since" (Babb to Pollard 2).

After Colorado, Babb's father's turn at professional gambling forced the family into a nomadic lifestyle, moving from one small High Plains town to another in the region that later became the center of the Dust Bowl (Wixson *On the Dirty Plate Trail* 3). It was here that Sanora experienced the social constraints of small-town Oklahoma and Kansas that could have curtailed her later accomplishments. Her father's unwillingness to seek more legitimate employment relegated her and her family to a space outside the bounds of "decent" society. Sanora suffered social punishment for her father's sins; as senior class valedictorian, she was denied the opportunity to give the customary speech by members of various churches in Forgan since "it would be a disgrace to the town to have a gambler's daughter so honored" (Babb, *Owl* afterword, 254).

Her father's oppressive patriarchal control at home required that Sanora, her mother, and her sister situate their lives around a domineering male, which escalated psychological stress. The women in the family were subjected to various forms of mistreatment by Walter Babb while they lived with him. Sanora's mother Jennie was, for most of the marriage, unable to confront her husband's increasingly mercurial behavior. She lacked agency in her life and marriage. As a girl, Dorothy idolized her father but was wounded by his behavior and never grew into an autonomous adult. Sanora, on the other hand, challenged her father and successfully interrupted gendered helplessness in her own life while still living in the home. Even as a teenager writing poems, she began to use her observations of the unequal balance of power in the family to illuminate unjust power structures. They often appear in her fiction.

The material deprivations and psychological stress of her youth took a physical toll on Sanora. She was hospitalized in early adulthood for an unnamed illness that made her unable to walk for several months, and she suffered a heart attack at the age of forty-five (Babb, letter to Pollard 10; Letter to Dorothy Babb). Though Sanora kept in contact with her father until his death, and despite his helping her with the details of a gambler's life depicted in *The Lost Traveler*, Sanora recounts his failure as a farmer and provider in the novel and lays blame on him for causing the family distress and dysfunction. As strong-willed as her father, Sanora was the only family member brave enough to confront him openly.

Even her child character in *Owl* displays this innate courage: The frustrations his mistakes had created drove him to angry outbursts and formidable declarations of his will over us. It was I who challenged him, even as a child, causing his furies to soar. Behind my back he boasted of my spirit, but in the fray he was my enemy and I was his" (Babb, *Owl* 77–78). In *The Lost Traveler*, this dynamic continues. Robin, the teenage character based on Sanora, is even more defiant and self-reliant. Her defiance is not merely a competitive device for matching wits with her controlling father, but reveals a deep desire for freedom. Robin longs for a life of her own making—free from the constant turbulence at home and the accepted social conventions of a small, rural town. She rejects the idea of marriage and children as a woman's only route to a fulfilling life. Unlike her mother and sister, Robin does not seek a life of relative comfort and safety, but one of new intellectual, creative, professional and relationship experiences. As she states, "I want my own door, my own key" (Babb, *The Lost Traveler* 181).

Unwittingly, her father pushes Robin toward self-reliance through the volatile atmosphere he creates in the home, and his inability to bring in steady income. As Robin earns her own money working for a newspaper, she begins to envision a future without economic dependence on men. The character of Robin's mother, Belle, weary of financial insecurity, also takes a job outside the home. Subsequently, a change in the family's balance of power occurs, as Des, the father, finds himself less necessary to the women in his life.

Though Sanora's relationship with her father in *The Lost Traveler* is continually combative, the one with her grandfather, as revealed in her memoir *Owl*, consists of trust and understanding. She portrays a strong, quiet bond between the two. Grandfather Konkie is a steadying force that usually attempts to smooth over raised tempers in the dugout. He finds an eager student in Cheyenne (Sanora), who is curious about and observant of her surroundings. Sanora reveals her own resilience and curiosity and a keen sense of wonder of the natural world. Her grandfather and father encourage her to appreciate their locale on the High Plains—the seasons, weather, animal behavior, and the night sky. Curiosity is also seen in Cheyenne's insatiable desire for education, which ceased formally during the family's time in Colorado. The nearest schoolhouse was miles away from the homestead. She and her sister were homeschooled by their grandfather, who taught them from the only book he possessed—*The Adventures of Kit Carson*. Cheyenne also read the walls of their crude dugout, wallpapered with the *Denver Post*. These articles were significant as they showed her "a facet of the world beyond that far circle of horizon" (Babb, *Owl* 79).

Sanora remained devoted to her grandfather and was influenced by his spirituality. She described him as "innerly," "mystical," "intelligent," and "interested in nature" (Babb, Wixson interview 3), though in *Owl*, she characterized both her grandfather and her father as "non-believers" (Babb 78). In the narrative, Konkie places some value on Christianity and his early family education based on the Bible, but does not personally subscribe to the tenets of organized religion (Babb 78–79). His spiritual leanings had a lasting effect on Sanora: he was "more mystical in a non-religious sense, as am I" (Babb, Wixson interview 4). She would later state that this mysticism and a rejection of organized religion gave her a "freedom from the need for specific beliefs and dogmas. It gave me tolerance" (Babb, *Owl* afterword, 251).

Sanora's curiosity and open-mindedness were noticed by other adults in her life. Teachers provided Sanora stability and injections of self-confidence and this is also seen in her characters. When the family moves from the homestead to a small town, the girls enter school. In *Owl*, the teacher, Miss Temple, quickly identifies Cheyenne's sharp intellect and knowledge base, despite her lack of much formal education, and is willing to help her succeed in a new school. Kind and sensitive to Cheyenne's obvious poverty, Miss Temple provides the necessary books and materials for her new student to catch up to an appropriate grade level. She gives Cheyenne the opportunity to prove herself academically, a challenge Cheyenne welcomes (Babb, *Owl* 239–40). In Sanora's life, high school teachers and college professors also recognized her exceptional intellect and writing abilities, providing emotional support and encouragement (Babb, *Owl* afterword, 254–55).

Sanora also embraced opportunities for social interaction in her teenage years in Forgan, Oklahoma, and later in Garden City, Kansas. There, despite the family's marginalization because of her father's gambling career, she was still socially active. When she began high school at age twelve, she also signed on for a job at a newspaper as a printer's devil (printer's apprentice). This was one of two newspaper jobs she had where the publisher was female. In her time between work and school, she created extracurricular activities by writing, producing, and performing plays with her sister and classmates: "Every week we produced a new play for a Saturday matinee. Farmers' and ranchers' families came to town on Saturdays and their children and town children filled our 'theater'" (Babb, *Owl* afterword, 253). Sanora had the capability to center herself in new towns and situations and construct new social opportunities and outlets for her own creativity. In *The Lost Traveler*, Robin is acutely aware of her status as an outsider in the town of Apache, but she is not bitter toward her classmates who politely ostracize her, nor does she covet their social position town. She looked forward to a decidedly different future "beyond this time and place, beyond this self she was now" (Babb, *The Lost Traveler* 148–49).

This ability to look hopefully toward the future was one of Sanora Babb's many resilient characteristics and was in stark contrast to the outlook of her sister. Dorothy was intelligent, creative, and a fine amateur photographer, but she did not possess the confidence and motivation of her older sister. Although Dorothy finished a four-year degree at UCLA, she was unable to work consistently as an adult and struggled with insecurities, ill health, and depression. She is portrayed as a young child in *Owl* as shy, compliant, and a favorite of her father. In the character of Stevie in *The Lost Traveler*, glimpses of Dorothy's emotional issues are evident. Notably, Sanora did not describe someone like the adult Dorothy in her stories, depicting strong women instead, but letters between members of the family reveal Dorothy's significant psychological problems (Kempler letter to Sanora Babb, Babb letter to Dorothy Babb). This correspondence also reveals their parents' inability or unwillingness to accept practical responsibility for Dorothy's illness, and much of Dorothy's care and support fell on Sanora. The gravity of this burden is depicted in *The Lost Traveler* as Des is forced to leave town and Robin struggles to come to terms with the lifelong liability of her "invalid" sister's care (Babb, *The Lost Traveler* 257–58). In life, however, this was an obligation that Sanora accepted. The two had a mutual love of literature and art, and they were close throughout Dorothy's life. Sanora observed that happiness often eluded Dorothy: "I hope, if there's an afterlife, she's happier. She never felt at home in this world" (Babb, letter to Dearcopp).

Though Sanora portrayed the beginnings of her sister's troubled emotional life in *The Lost Traveler* in the character of Stevie, she also focused on resilient characters, who serve as symbols of hope in hard circumstances. In *Owl*, the two sisters formed a friendship with a local boy, the physically disabled and terminally ill Fred Shibley. Fred fires their imaginations with stories and games of faraway South Asian locales, though he is physically confined to his home in Baca County. The girls are at first fearful of him and his unnamed condition. Soon they see how access to a few geography books and a fertile imagination engenders his love of the larger world outside the plains. Fred hasn't visited any of the places he reads about, yet he revels in the idea of new and unknown experiences. His open mind represents freedom, strength, and a world worthy of exploration. He tells them, "You see, you must keep the door open. Your mind is better than a thousand legs, but it is no good with the door closed" (Babb, *Owl* 71). His optimism and energy, despite his severe health problems, are a role model to Cheyenne, and his early death a lesson in carpe diem.

Although Sanora Babb's early years were often framed in disappointment and deprivation, her resilience allowed her to embrace and write of human complexities through a lens of hope; circumstantial resentment is not projected into her writing. Sanora's family is depicted in her work in intricate human terms and not idolized or demonized. This acceptance of human frailty was a cornerstone of her character, along with her rejection of rigid belief systems that would require her to give up freedom in her personal life or her literary endeavors. Her writing reflects detailed inquiry and an empathy for those who also resided on the margins, whether they were Okies in migrant work camps in California, subjugated groups of immigrants, or the complex members of her own family, with whom she maintained simultaneously exasperating and loving relationships.

The trajectory of Sanora Babb's life was grounded in the hard times of her youth, her early ambition for a career in writing, and a strong desire for freedom to explore the wider world. Because of her personal resilience and strength, her earliest aspirations were realized. Babb's difficult experiences served not to defeat her, but instead to propel her forward into what she later referred to as "a living life," one in which she was able to embrace new places, people, and experiences joyously (Babb, letter to Dorothy Babb 1952).

WORKS CITED

Primary Sources

Babb, Sanora. Interview with Douglas Wixson. 1990. Sanora Babb papers, Harry Ransom Center, University of Texas at Austin, Austin, TX.

———. Letter to Dorothy Babb. 23 July1952. Sanora Babb papers, Harry Ransom Center, University of Texas at Austin, Austin, TX.

———. Letter to Joanne Dearcopp. 21 August 1998. Personal collection of Joanne Dearcopp.

———. Letter to Lillie Pollard. 17 July 1935. Sanora Babb papers, University of Texas at Austin, Harry Ransom Center, Austin, TX.

Ivy, Carol. Oral interview of Sanora Babb. *Long Beach Telegram*, Sanora Babb papers, Harry Ransom Center, University of Texas at Austin, Austin, TX.

Secondary Sources

Babb, Sanora. *An Owl on Every Post*. Muse Ink Press, 2012.

———. *An Owl on Every Post*. Afterword. Muse Ink Press, 2012.

———. *The Lost Traveler*. Muse Ink Press, 2013.

Campbell-Sills, Laura, Sharon L. Cohen, and Murray B. Stein. "Relationships of Resilience to Personality, Coping, and Psychiatric Symptoms in Young Adults." *Behavior, Research and Therapy*, vol. 44 (2006): 585–89. https://doi.org/10.1016/j.brat.2005.05.001.

Gumpbrecht, Blake. "A Saloon on Every Corner: Whiskey Towns of Oklahoma Territory, 1889–1900." *Chronicles of Oklahoma*, vol. 74, no. 2 (1996): 146–73.

Kempler, Jennie Babb. Letter to Sanora Babb. 18 October 1943. HRC.

Kirby, Laura D., and Mark W. Fraser. "Risk and Resilience in Childhood." *Risk and Resilience in Childhood*, edited by Mark W. Fraser, pp. 10–33. National Association of Social Workers, 1997.

Liu, Ya, Zhen-Hong Wang, and Zheng-Gen Li. "Affective Mediators of the Influence of Neuroticism and Resilience on Life Satisfaction." *Personality and Individual Differences*, vol. 52, no. 7 (2012): 833–38. https://doi.org/10.1016/j.paid.2012.01.017.

Shiner, Rebecca L., and Ann S. Masten. "Childhood Personality as a Harbinger of Competence and Resilience in Adulthood." *Development and Psychopathology*, vol. 24, no. 2 (2012): 507–28, https://doi.org/10.1017/S0954579412000120.

Werner, Emmy E. "Resilience in Development." *American Psychological Society*, vol. 4., no. 3 (1995): 81–85. https://doi.org/10.1111/1467-8721.ep10772327.

Wixson, Douglas. *On the Dirty Plate Trail: Remembering the Dust Bowl Refugee Camps*. University of Texas Press, 2007.

———. "Radical by Nature: Sanora Babb and Ecological Disaster on the High Plains, 1900–1940." *Regionalists on the Left: Radical Voices from the American West*, edited by Michael C. Steiner, pp. 111–35. University of Oklahoma Press, 2013.

DARYL W. PALMER

7
SANORA BABB'S *AN OWL ON EVERY POST* IN THE CANON OF AMERICAN LITERATURE

In 1913, when Sanora Babb was six years old (decades after Conestoga wagons began crossing the American prairies), she and her family left the Oklahoma Panhandle to settle in a dugout on the plains of eastern Colorado and farm without irrigation. It was a doomed, yet unforgettable experiment. Like Willa Cather and Laura Ingalls Wilder, Babb was haunted by her pioneer memories and felt compelled to turn them into something more powerful than simple memoir. Babb began writing some of the story in the late 1930s. In the 1960s, she returned to this material as *An Owl on Every Post* began to take shape. Decades after the classic fiction of Cather and Wilder, *An Owl on Every Post* was published in 1970, but Babb's belatedness should not be viewed as a shortcoming. In fact, in the case of *An Owl on Every Post*, belatedness actually begets innovation in ways that help make the work a classic, worthy of a place on the shelf alongside Willa Cather's *My Ántonia* (1918), F. Scott Fitzgerald's *The Great Gatsby* (1925), Ernest Hemingway's *In Our Time* (1925), and Wilder's *The Little House on the*

Prairie (1935). Though the book has yet to earn such recognition, Babb's story of life on the Colorado plains deserves to be part of the American literary canon.

In 1970, *An Owl on Every Post* entered the world auspiciously enough. Babb's literary contemporaries praised the book, Ralph Ellison summing it up in glowing terms on the jacket of the Signet edition: "Thought-provoking description of the mystery, wonder and poetry of growing up in a pioneering environment. A vivid restoration of an important phase of American history." The reviewer for the Paterson, New Jersey, *News* praised the novel's "charm and pathos," noting, "Sanora Babb . . . has long been quietly recognized as one of the finest writing talents in America today." Carol Ivy, writing in the Long Beach, California, *Independent*, noted that the novel "has been highly acclaimed by critics here and in England, where portions of it were dramatized on BBC." Others around the world echoed this assessment. The *London Times* was impressed by the work's lyricism: "Masterly. Hers is a small song, and not grand opera. But hearing it is a significant and salutary experience." The *Pretoria News* rightly emphasized the author's powerful depiction of beauty in hardship: "The author has achieved a small miracle with this book for she has turned hunger, poverty, loneliness and depression into incomparable beauty by the magic of her writing." When the third edition was published in 2012, Linda Patterson Miller described Babb's achievement: "On a par stylistically and thematically with Willa Cather's *My Ántonia* the book is a classic that deserves to be rediscovered and cherished for years to come." Arnold Rampersad made a strong claim for the work's place in the American literary canon: "An unsung masterpiece—I was completely blown away. . . . Her ageless story deserves a permanent place in our nation's literature."[1]

With such accolades, why has this "classic" not found a "permanent place" in the American literary canon? One important answer is belatedness. *An Owl on Every Post* appeared in the same year as Judy Blume's *Are You There God? It's Me, Margaret* and the English translation of Gabriel García Márquez's *One Hundred Years of Solitude*. By the time Hunter S. Thompson's *Fear and Loathing in Las Vegas* (1972) and Thomas Pynchon's *Gravity's Rainbow* (1973) were published, Babb's *Owl* was a rare prairie bird in a changed landscape. Perhaps, as it did for Fitzgerald's *Gatsby*, only hindsight can reveal Babb's achievement.[2]

In the case of Babb's *An Owl on Every Post*, hindsight in 2020 may have something to do with human hardship. Acknowledging that canons have always been imperfect, even flawed versions of artistic ideals, critical authority, and popular taste, I suggest a deeper notion of canon formation. What if well-tended literary canons are ultimately rooted in human need? What if literature, with all its craft on display, is great because it offers us experiences such as compassion, perspective, wisdom, feeling, and inspiration? Neuroscientists tell us that mirror neurons fire when we read fiction, making our reading experience indistinguishable (in the brain at least) from the experiences we have in the external world.[3] Perhaps, then, our sense that certain works of literature must be cherished has something to do with what our brains need in order to live good lives in hard times. As Abigail G. H. Manzella observes, Babb always affirmed "the need to respect the people and space around you and stand up collectively for justice" (108). In *An Owl on Every Post*, Babb tells a story of people nurturing these values through failure, suffering, deprivation, and death. In so doing, she implies that respect and justice depend on resilience, wonder, learning, empathy, and imagination.

Because canons often honor niches, it also matters that Babb's story unfolds under the vast skies of the American West. Problems of perspective, climatic extremes, ridiculous expectations, bold gambles, and the smell of sage sharpen every word of Babb's narrative. Failures spin like dust devils in a dry land. A long time ago, Walter Prescott Webb pinpointed aridity as the underlying and defining facet of a region that began at the ninety-eighth meridian: "At this fault the ways of life and of living changed. Practically every institution that was carried across it was either broken and remade or else greatly altered" (8). Suffice it to say that Babb understood Webb's point as well as anyone who has ever written and lived on the Great Plains. In her hands, the pioneer memoir was remade into what we now call creative nonfiction, one of the most popular narrative genres of the twenty-first century, a genre that makes strong claims about telling the truth while emphasizing literary craft and imaginative daring.[4]

Like Cather's novel *My Ántonia*, Babb's memoir begins on a train crossing the plains: "All the way on the train from the Indian country of Oklahoma to the flat plains of Colorado east of the Rocky Mountains, my mother and I were sad; she to leave household and friends, and a town, however small; I, to leave my pinto pony and Oto [sic] Indians near Red Rock, my other family, my other home" (7). Babb's narrator, Cheyenne, like Jim Burden in Cather's novel, embodies a good deal of the author's consciousness, giving voice to the experience of displacement that many settlers felt. Like Cather in *My Ántonia*, Babb was remembering her own shock at arriving "in a place without trees" (7).

But Babb strikes distinctive notes in her opening paragraphs, beginning with Cheyenne's sense of time. Wilder's *Little House on the Prairie* begins in 1873, Cather's *My Ántonia* in the early 1880s, Sandoz's *Old Jules* in the 1890s. By contrast, Babb's novel of homesteading starts in 1913. The narrator establishes the setting of the tale: "This was an empty land. A primordial loneliness was on it; the train carried us backward in time" (7). Babb is clearly preparing her readers for a vertiginous vision of the pioneer experience they may assume they already know from reading Cather and Wilder. In other words, Babb is claiming the belatedness of her family's experience and marking it as time travel, a magical movement that ripples through the whole work. When ghosts begin to appear in the book, savvy readers will be rewarded.

Cheyenne's remembered relationship with the Otoe tribe is another way Babb sets her novel apart. Where Cather tends to erase Native American experience and Wilder describes fraught engagements, Babb writes out of a lifelong "dedication to Native American issues" (Manzella 77). Many stories of settlement out West involve a character's recollections of eastern ways, but Cheyenne upon arriving in Colorado mourns the loss of her Otoe friends in Oklahoma: "I would never again be known or called by my Indian name: Little Cheyenne Riding Like the Wind. I tried to imagine that I was back there with them, in old Edie's big lap or held tenderly against Chief Black Hawk's tobacco-smelly chest" (9). In this way, Babb tells an uncommon story of lost kinship.

In such recollections, the narrator's distinctive voice begins to emerge and claim a spot alongside some of the great narrators in American fiction. Like Jim Burden in *My Ántonia* and Nick Carraway in *The Great Gatsby*, Cheyenne simultaneously captures youthful perception and mature reflection. Recalling their grim arrival, the narrator explains, "Although the air above the ground was sharp and dry, in the dugout a dank earth dampness pressed into our breath, chilled our bones. The slant door had been let down. We were trapped" (13). The narrator's rhythms make the trauma vivid even as she concludes the chapter lyrically by looking toward the sky for the first of many times throughout the work: "Papa pushed up the door, and it seemed that the stars were falling down upon us" (14).

In fact, Babb's narrator is downright poetic, suggesting the voice of Kansas poet William Stafford in "Across Kansas": "Once you cross a land like that / you own your face more: what the light / struck told a self" (105). Babb somehow manages to voice this fine mingling of imagery and self-analysis through a young person's perspective. After their first trip to the little town of Two Buttes, the family walks home through the dark. The narrator sets the scene: "We were all silent within a great silence. The air was sharp, cool. No insects sang. We met no one" (33). A paragraph break allows the narrator to slip into a more Staffordian voice: "This moon was not the one I knew, not an ornament of summer evenings, or the reassuring lamp of winter dark. It was a world of liquid light, magnetic, overpowering, rousing in my child's mind a furtive knowledge not yet lost. I was awed; kept silent by a wondering stir of beauty, a longing of spirit asking a first and eternal question of the universe" (33). Using the skills of a novelist, the narrator (to apply Stafford's language) "owns her face more" in both the present and the past.

If Babb's brilliant craftsmanship is embodied in Cheyenne's voice, the author's thematic commitment is apparent in her focus on hardship in the American West. With this emphasis, she claims a place in revisionist western historiography that had not been invented when she wrote her book. As Patricia Nelson Limerick argued in the 1980s, "the history of the West is a study of a place undergoing conquest and never fully escaping its consequences" (26). More recently, Alex Trimble Young and Lorenzo Veracini have identified this discussion of oppression, failure, and epistemological ambivalence as "the field of settler colonial studies" (Young and Veracini 3). Unlike any of its Great Plains companion works, *Owl* seems to embody crucial elements of this conversation. Cheyenne makes the orientation clear and distinctive: "While other parts of the United States moved swiftly ahead, the hopeful or desperate people who filed claims on these high western grazing lands were plunged a hundred years backward in our history, to live and struggle again like the early settlers in other states" (8). Babb's *Owl* depicts an improbable history of hardship rooted in the aridity of the Great Plains.

The family's first Christmas is a particularly effective treatment of this theme, especially for those readers who have Cather's *My Ántonia* in mind, with Cather's beautiful portrayal of a country Christmas enforced by heavy snow. Babb's narrative seems pointed in that direction after the family's magical visit with Fred and his parents. The narrator recalls, "On Christmas morning Marcy and I woke to see our long white Christmas stockings nailed to the windowsill, and they were not empty. They were not stuffed full as in other years, but the contents were far more enjoyed" (73). The message here is a familiar one: doing without helps people appreciate simple things more. With this suggestion, the novel seems to have more in common with the Christmas story in Wilder's *Little House on the Prairie*.

But Babb's scene takes a sad turn indeed when Ginny sits down to play her piano, the only possession she managed to bring from Oklahoma: "She arranged herself at the piano, smiled at us all, rubbed her chilly hands together and placed them on the keys, just touching them with affection. She rubbed her hands again, tried her voice, then began to play and sing. No music came from the piano. The keys went down with a plop" (74). Moisture in the dugout has seriously damaged the instrument. Ginny begins to sing and cry. In shock, no one sings with her: "'Time to clean the chimney and fill the lamp,' she said to me'" (75). Walt convinces everyone to sing a round of "Jingle Bells," and they let Bounce, the dog, in the cave to share the holiday warmth. With a Victorian sensibility that Dickens would have appreciated, Babb captures holiday feeling and failure.

As times grow harder, the novel becomes powerfully modern. We know that the Cratchitt family is undernourished, but Babb allows us to experience starvation. It is early spring and the family has "had nothing to eat for seven days" (197). The narrator recalls, "All we had left was salt and red and black pepper. From these we made 'pepper tea,' which was hot water with a sprinkling of pepper" (197). Because Babb's readers may not understand how poverty really works, the narrator offers context: "We grew weak, not alone from the seven days fasting but from the long periods over the years when we had less than we needed, and almost none of the fresh vegetables and fruits we craved" (197). As the chapter unfolds, the narrator recalls the dangerous dizziness they all experience: "We were shaky and light-headed. I felt very tall and fluffy and it seemed to me I was taking great steps above ground, walking on air. In a way it was lovely. Every sight and sound was delicately intensified. At any moment I should fly or float into the crisp morning air and find myself across the creek, drifting on and on. This treacherous euphoria followed days of intense hunger, stomach cramps, and headache" (198). The psychological realism of this passage, when set against other stories of pioneer life, is remarkable. From the perspective of literary craft, the reversal in the passage is striking. Like so many of Cheyenne's experiences, it is marked by visionary appreciation in the midst of suffering, an attunement to possibilities in a landscape that seems to promise nothing of the kind. Then, just as the reader embraces this magical vision, real suffering once again cuts through the luminosity.

At this juncture, a less ambitious author might have contented herself with sketching recollected scenes of family life on the Colorado plains, as John Ise does with the memories of Howard Ruede in *Sod-House Days* (1937), but Babb writes dynamic scenes worthy of the best American fiction that carry her readers along an inevitable arc of small victories and larger failures and finally on to the family going back to life in a country town. The author demonstrates her ability in the first pages of the book, when the family's happy talk of prairie animals is interrupted by a giant rat. Papa chases the creature around the tiny dugout, but the rat "turned and this time he fought, lunging at Papa, dodging his blows, running about the room and back to the steps" (49). The battle is vivid and ends with consequences. Papa kills the rat, and the narrator recalls, "We felt unclean, as we had felt the rat to be unclean" (49).

Death drives turn after turn in the arc of the memoir, but nowhere is it as blunt as when Cheyenne's mother, Ginny, barely survives a miscarriage. Babb's prose seems emphatically modern as the narrator recalls the burial of the stillborn baby: "The night air was sharp with the smells of sage and sun-baked land released by the rain. A last-quarter moon was going down. Stars swung through the curving dark. For all that had happened, I could not ignore the beauty of the night; I was glad to be in it, free of our room. Papa carried the spade and the baby" (120). The last sentence carries its burden like the short, simple sentences of Ernest Hemingway's *In Our Time*. In the midst of the scene, the narrator turns her philosophical gaze on her father: "Did the very brevity of this child's life have a purpose, and was that purpose to shake his bare soul in this bare night and leave it wondering?" (121).

In fact, a reader could ask the same thing about every death in *Owl* as Babb shakes souls and leaves them wondering. On the first visit to the Royal Cafe, we learn that Mrs. Denny's dead husband returns from time to time. The revelation prepares us for later hauntings. Just as Ginny is beginning to recover from her ordeal, the narrator's favorite horse, Fred, dies. Cheyenne is inconsolable, and so her grandfather, Alonzo, takes her "on a little jaunt" out into the night (132). A young bay horse appears out of nowhere and begins to play in front of them. He runs this way and that—until he runs straight off a cliff, "screaming all the way down" (137). As they begin to walk home, Alonzo tries to explain why Cheyenne should not be sad: "'I wanted to see if you could see Daft. You saw him first. Now Daft ran over that cliff and killed himself two years ago'" (137). And then they look up to see Daft in front of them, "standing a little way off looking at us in a peaceful, browsing way" (138). When Cheyenne runs to touch him, the horse disappears. In a work that seems to be built on principles of realism, the scene is striking. It probably should not work, but we can gauge Babb's accomplishment by the way it does. Introducing the latest edition of the book, William Kennedy declares, "I love and believe this ghost story. I believe every word of Sanora Babb's book, for what she has written has not dated" (2). Babb maintained to the end that it all was real, and many contemporary readers will feel that they are safely in the realm of creative nonfiction.

The imagination, disability, and death of Fred Shibley in this atmosphere allow Babb to explore mortality in surprising ways. Fred invents an ingenious version of the game "Streetcar" in which the children wheel off in his chair to Sumatra and Ceylon in search of cinnamon. At Christmas, he sends them to "Samarkand to see the tomb of Tamerlane" (70). In the midst of Baca County, Colorado, having never been anywhere, Fred reminds them, "'Your mind is better than a thousand legs, but it is no good with the door closed'" (71). As they depart for home, Fred urges them to come the following Saturday or any Saturday: "'I'm always home. That is'—he turned to Marcy and me—'that is, unless I'm in Makassar'" (32). Perhaps geography is not destiny out West. When Fred dies, the girls try to make sense of it. Marcy asks, "'Is Fred dead the way our cat was dead that time?'" In an exchange that could come from a Carson McCullers novel, Cheyenne recalls: "'He has gone to Makassar, the way he said, remember?' I knew he was dead, but Makassar sounded like a foreign heaven, and Fred was always traveling to strange places" (95). Near the end of the book, Babb turns to Cheyenne's grandfather to distill the vision: "After supper, Grandfather told us a story of old times, of people long dead who lived in our minds as alive as we" (221).

If Babb's book offers a remarkable vision of life and death in the American West, it also lights out for uncharted territory when Cheyenne and her sister encounter the man everyone calls Old Loony. In an age where we speak more openly about abuse and violence, contemporary readers will find these scenes particularly unsettling and relevant. As Loony lurks about the prairie countryside, adults give him a wide berth. The gossip says that he killed his wife, but the ever-curious Cheyenne wants to know more: "'I would like to see what crazy really is,' I said" (160). Great heroines are driven by this kind of intelligent recklessness.

Not surprisingly, Cheyenne and her sister, Marcy, eventually find themselves invited into the man's dark dugout, where he convinces the girls to try on the hair of his dead wife. The girls manage to escape with civil conversation, Cheyenne assuring the old man that she will call him "Sir Loony" from now on. Viewed from one angle, the ambitious narrator has introduced a bit of Gothic on the Colorado plains. Viewed from another angle, the heroine has taken dangerous chances in her exploration of mental illness, and contemporary readers will rightly worry that we may be missing all the facts in the story. In this way, the book seems decidedly of our time.

By the end of the book, Grandfather Alonzo turns out to be one of Cheyenne's most surprising discoveries. When she first encounters him in the middle of the night in the damp dugout, he seems to need unearthing. As everyone tries to sleep, bedbugs begin to bite. Cheyenne's father explains, "'They came in the new lumber. Dad's lived alone so long he doesn't care, didn't even try to get rid of them'" (14). In the days that follow, Alonzo retreats to the barn, "aloof, humiliated, criticized by the swift changes; he mended harness, cared for the horses, and read a book. Papa had warned us not to go near him (and yet he and I shared a cot!) because of the vivid red spots on his face" (17). The reader's expectations have to be low at this point, but Cheyenne remains attentive. She is drawn to him because he is lean and brown and reminds her of her beloved Otoe chief.

But Alonzo ultimately wins her over with his learning and penchant for philosophical inquiry. He teaches her and her sister to read from a biography of Kit Carson and the Denver newspapers pasted to the dugout walls. Observing that their primer ought to be the Bible, he explains, "'Once, when I was a Socialist, I threw my Bible away. I was afire with Socialism; you won't understand that now. I thought they had the answers to all the injustice of the world'" (78). In telling the story of her education, Cheyenne begins to reveal her grandfather's complexity. Far from being a dirty, ignorant hermit, Alonzo is a Great Plains intellectual of sorts. Having discovered that Socialism did not have all the answers to injustice, he has revised his notion of God and tells the child, "'You can't throw God away, he's in your hand still, and your hand is in God'" (79). In suggesting that stories of pioneer life might pivot on philosophical musing, Babb is reimagining the American West.

By this point in the novel, careful readers have noticed how Cheyenne's father, Walt, has shaped our negative perceptions of his father. Great writers, it goes without saying, always manage these filters deftly. Over the years, the two men have lived together, fought, separated, and found each other again. Their exchanges give the novel's dialog the kind of visceral quality we associate with classic American drama in the mode of Arthur Miller's *All My Sons*:

> "You think I have no more pride than that?"
> "More than your share likely."
> "Well, it keeps me going in a place like this."
> "You came out here of your own accord, son." (67)

What responsibility do parents have for the hopes and dreams of their children?

> "I thought you'd have your own place, remember. It didn't turn out that way and we'll make the best of it."

"I don't want to make the best of it," Papa said. "I don't mind to work hard but I want to make a living at it."

"We'll plant in the spring. We'll have crops."

"It's too dry here." (67)

What responsibility do parents have for their children in a world of too little rain and inevitable hardship? What does it mean for migrants "to make the best of it" in the company of their parents? Babb's dialog captures such questioning with the open-ended clarity of the best American fiction and creative nonfiction.

Inevitably, Babb's work must find closure, as so much American fiction does, in the choice between what Susan Stanford Friedman calls "roots and routes" (154). Over and over again, the question for pioneers was a simple one: Should we stay or should we go? Settlers dream of putting down roots—only to be driven back to routes. In Cather's *O Pioneers!* Carl abandons homesteading to travel and make his fortune but eventually returns to celebrate the power of roots and settle down with Alexandra. In Wilder's *A Little House on the Prairie*, Pa promises to stay put but ultimately leads the family away from their failed homestead at the end of the book. It is important to read *Owl* against this backdrop to appreciate its innovative take on the familiar choices. In Babb's vision, imagination transcends simple binary oppositions like routes and roots.

The author makes this point emphatically by how she ends her work. Most readers will assume they are approaching the ending of this familiar story when, after four and a half years of unsuccessful farming, the parents finally agree to leave for a new town in Kansas called Elkhart. But the story goes on in what we could call the Elkhart Coda, six chapters that describe the family's return to "civilization."

Having ventured in a strange, luminous, and painful country, Cheyenne and her family reinvent themselves in Elkhart. Walt finds a job as a baker. Cheyenne's education in the dugout has done enough to prepare her for progress in school with a teacher named Miss Temple, who truly cares about her. But Cheyenne has already guessed that her father's commitment to roots in the new town may be temporary: "Was Papa already thinking of other places after Elkhart?" (233).

In the end, Cheyenne's education, thanks to her philosophical grandfather and her new teacher, will allow her to transcend her own story's belatedness. Miss Temple tells Cheyenne that she will soon be reading great writers like Emerson. The narrator recalls, "I put her words away to get them out at another time. There was something familiar here. An image of Daft came to me. Who was Emerson?" (240). In ways that belong distinctively to Babb's belated imagination, the ghost horse and the American philosopher are inevitably joined.

If *An Owl on Every Post* really does find its place on "the shelf" alongside *My Ántonia* and *The Great Gatsby*, those of us who cherish it will want to keep a volume of Emerson's essays nearby. More than any other writer who influenced Babb, Emerson offers language for the novelist's achievements. We can, for instance, turn to "The Over-Soul" for a powerful summation of Babb's ambitious vision in this novel: "There is a difference between one and another hour of life in their authority and subsequent effect. Our faith comes in moments; our vice is habitual. Yet there is a depth in those brief moments which constrains us to ascribe more reality to them than to all other experiences." In ways no other novelist has managed, *An Owl on Every Post* sounds the depths of Emerson's "brief moments."

NOTES

1. Ralph Ellison, review on jacket cover of *An Owl of Every Post*, by Sanora Babb, Signet, 1972; "Remembers Hard Life with Joy," *Patterson, NJ, News*, 12 July 1973, p. 23; Carol Ivy, "A Heritage of Love for Land Long Lost," *Long Beach, CA, Independent*, 12 July 1973, p. 32; *London Times*, 1 November 1971; *Pretoria News*, 29 March 1972; Linda Patterson Miller, email interview, received by Joanne Dearcopp, 19 July 2012; Arnold Rampersad, email interview, received by Joanne Dearcopp, July 2012.

2. Corrigan explains, "By the time Fitzgerald died, in 1940, his greatest novel had pretty much disappeared" (12). Corrigan devotes the rest of her book to describing the forces that helped lift *Gatsby* to such enduring fame. For more on Babb's belatedness, see Manzella, *Migrating Fictions*, pp. 70–71.

3. See, for instance, Heister.

4. Nearly a quarter of a century after *An Owl on Every Post* was published, Lunsford offered one of the first scholarly explorations of the rising popularity of the genre Babb anticipated. For a lively discussion of truth and fiction in creative nonfiction, see Anderson.

WORKS CITED

Anderson, Donald. "Necessary Lies: The Expedient Blurring of Fact/Fiction in Creative Writing." *English Now*, edited by Marianne Thormählen, pp. 137–49. Lund University Press, 2007.

Babb, Sanora. *An Owl on Every Post*. Muse Ink Press, 1994.

Corrigan, Maureen. *So We Read On: How the Great Gatsby Came to Be and Why It Endures*. Little, Brown, 2014.

Friedman, Susan Stanford. *Mappings: Feminism and the Cultural Geographies of Encounter*. Princeton University Press, 1998.

Heister, Hilmar. "Mirror Neurons and Literature: Empathy and the Sympathetic Imagination in the Fiction of J. M. Coetzee." *MediaTropes*, vol. 4, no. 2 (2014): 98–113.

Kennedy, William. Foreword. In *An Owl on Every Post*, pp. 1–3. Muse Ink Press, 1994.

Limerick, Patricia. *The Legacy of Conquest*. W. W. Norton, 1987.

Lunsford, Andrea. "'Creative Nonfiction': What's in a Name?" *Conference of College Teachers of English Proceedings*, vol. 55 (1995): 41–48.

Manzella, Abigail. *Migrating Fictions: Gender, Race, and Citizenship in Internal Displacements*. Ohio State University Press, 2018.

Webb, Walter Prescott. *The Great Plains*. University of Nebraska Press, 1931.

Young, Alex Trimble, and Lorenzo Veracini. "'If I Am Native to Anything': Settler Colonial Studies and Western American Literature." *Western American Literature*, vol. 52, no. 1 (2017): 1–23.

CHRISTOPHER BOWMAN

8

"TODAY IS A TERROR"

Whose Names Are Unknown and the "New" Dust Bowl Novel

> Migration is as old as humankind and as recent as today.
> —Douglas Wixson, *On the Dirty Plate Trail*

Since the long-delayed publication of Sanora Babb's *Whose Names Are Unknown* in 2004, there have been a number of sensationalized reports on the relationship between Babb's novel and John Steinbeck's *The Grapes of Wrath*, which was first published in 1939. Of course, both authors were involved with the Farm Security Administration (FSA) migrant labor camps, and both were also close with one of the leading figures of this organization, Tom Collins, who encouraged them to write on the subject.[1] Yet despite similarities in the content of their books, as both Steinbeck and Babb wrote about the Dust Bowl migration, the strategies each writer deployed are remarkably different: Steinbeck couched his migrant family, the Joads, in layers of American mythologies and biblical symbolism, while Babb portrayed her family, the Dunnes, in a more straightforwardly realist approach. As a result, Steinbeck's narrative strategies permitted basic mischaracterizations of the Dust Bowl region, while Babb's drew upon her deep knowledge of this area to more accurately portray the devastating effects of this environmental disaster on those who lived there.

Even though many critical responses to *Whose Names Are Unknown* position this novel as a rival to *The Grapes of Wrath*, this essay begins with the premise that the two novels are better served by being placed in conversation—rather than in competition—with one another. For while the narrative strategies utilized by each author are remarkably different, both Steinbeck and Babb were motivated by a genuine concern for the Dust Bowl migrants, and both approached their novels as projects with which they could cultivate public support for the "Okies" in California. To this extent, Steinbeck's symbolism and mythological references inspired sympathy for the Joads on the basis of their white American identities (Wald 54), whereas Babb highlighted the extreme environmental conditions of the Dust Bowl to establish a sympathetic portrayal of her hardworking family, the Dunnes. Steinbeck's Joads leave Oklahoma as a result of their being "tractored out" by their corporate landlords, while Babb's Dunnes ultimately travel west because of the accumulating effects of living in this harsh environment. As this essay will argue, Babb's portrayal of life in the Dust Bowl goes further than Steinbeck and enables her novel to contribute to the discourses in fiction on climate change now referred to as "cli-fi."

Perhaps due in part to Steinbeck's omission of details on the Joads' life in the Dust Bowl, it is often difficult for contemporary readers to imagine the environmental realities of the Southern Plains in the 1930s. In the hardest hit areas, the sky often grew dark in the middle of the day as great clouds of dust blossomed and rolled across the countryside. As the dust storms blew through, nothing was left untouched, as it entered houses through windows, doors, and cracks in the walls and accumulated in piles often big enough to warrant the use of shovels. Dust covered fabrics and linens and scraped paint off surfaces. It also blinded animals and lined their lungs until they suffocated. The Red Cross distributed dust masks, though many people still suffered from dust pneumonia. For several years, this was life in an environmental disaster on the Great Plains.

Some folks remained on the plains throughout the 1930s in spite of these hardships, but conditions pushed approximately 350,000 migrants west in what is referred to as the Dust Bowl migration. In this regard, the Dust Bowl shares much in common with contemporary climate change, as both environmental phenomena drastically alter relationship to place and force people to relocate to different regions. The 1930s exodus from the plains to the West Coast remains among the largest internal migrations within the United States, though the global scope of climate change and the uneven distribution of its impacts will likely affect communities around the world in a greater order of magnitude in the coming years. In addition to these disastrous environmental effects on communities, the Dust Bowl and climate change also have much in common with regards to their origins, as both emerged through the combination of cultural behaviors and natural processes (Worster 13). Whereas the Dust Bowl was the result of unsustainable agricultural practices and the region's recurring drought cycle, the current climate destabilization is largely driven by unchecked emissions on our global climatological and environmental systems. In this sense, neither crisis can be attributed solely to natural or cultural sources but emerge instead as the nexus of these forces.

And while we currently struggle to address the challenges of climate change, so too did folks in the 1930s struggle to respond to the Dust Bowl, until they came to identify with the migrants through John Steinbeck's *The Grapes of Wrath*. Although Steinbeck's book is firmly lodged in public consciousness, it is nevertheless not the sole or even the best Dust Bowl novel to consider in light of the growing challenges of climate change—particularly since it did not actually portray life in the Dust Bowl, instead providing a thorough critique of corporate landownership. By contrast, Babb highlights the realities of living in a Dust Bowl region in the first part of *Whose Names Are Unknown*, which establishes the motivations of the Dunnes before they subsequently flee to California in the second part of the novel. By emphasizing life before the migration, Babb humanizes her characters' plight, a technique often used today as climate change fiction grows increasingly popular among writers and readers alike. As such, although Babb's novel was precluded from contributing directly to the public discourses of that time, its portrayal of climate refugee migrants is just as relevant now in a time of accelerating global climate destabilization as it was when Babb completed the first draft in the late 1930s.

Although readers typically encounter the Dust Bowl through Steinbeck's Joads, critics have long taken issue with the verisimilitude of the novel's portrayal of geographic locations, environmental conditions, and life in Oklahoma. Steinbeck completed famously little research on Oklahoma, as he placed the Joads "more or less at random" in Sallisaw (Loftis 152) after first locating them in Shawnee (Steinbeck, *Working* 31)—both of which are outside the area most heavily devastated by the Dust Bowl. Despite this lack of accuracy, Steinbeck's portrayals of life in Oklahoma were nevertheless incidental to the overall success of his novel in shaping public perceptions of the Dust Bowl migration. By contrast, Babb knew and depicts the region intimately. She was a child of the plains, spending her earliest years in places such as Red Rock, Oklahoma; Baca County, Colorado; Elkhart, Kansas; Forgan, Oklahoma; and Garden City, Kansas, before moving to California in 1929. Although the precise boundaries of the Dust Bowl are difficult to pinpoint, as it varied from year to year (Worster 29), many of the places in which Babb grew up lie within the area that was later hit the hardest by the dust storms—which her family experienced and her mother described in a series of letters, which are discussed later in this chapter—and her firsthand knowledge of the area proved invaluable in the composition of this novel.

Indeed, Babb pulled heavily from her childhood experiences on the Southern Plains in part 1 of *Whose Names Are Unknown*. Perhaps surprisingly, the novel's exact geographic location was a point of debate up until its publication, as Babb and her editorial reviewers considered a variety of options for locating the first part of its narrative—including references to real places, which was the early preference of Douglas Wixson (2), or using fictional names instead, which Babb and her agent, Joanne Dearcopp, eventually agreed upon (Dearcopp 1). Through its first couple of drafts, the story was set in the fictional "Lafar, Colorado" (Babb, "Working Copy, Carbon"), which was then changed to the real "Lamar, Colorado" (Babb, "Working Copy, Photocopy"). To avoid repetition with Babb's memoir, *An Owl on Every Post*, the setting was then shifted from Colorado to Oklahoma in the third and fourth drafts, with consideration given to Boise City (Babb, "Revised Draft #3") and Forgan (Babb, "Revised and Edited Draft #4"), respectively. Ultimately, the story was set in the general area of the Oklahoma Panhandle, with references to the fictional towns of Riding and Flatlands (Babb, *Owl* 13). Despite this debate, and the final decision to use fictional settings, *Whose Names Are Unknown* has avoided criticism of geographic and environmental inaccuracies through its locating the story within a High Plains area most heavily affected by the dust storms.

In this regard, Babb's familiarity with this region where she had lived ultimately enables her environmental descriptions of the High Plains to be among the most evocative passages in the novel. This feature of Babb's writing is perhaps counterintuitive, considering the inherent challenges of effectively portraying what Wixson describes as "the unbounded, featureless physical space of the Great Plains" (*Dirty* 9), or what Erin Royston Battat suggests is "a landscape characterized by the *absence* of physical features" (54). Yet in its depiction of the Dunnes, *Whose Names Are Unknown* not only brings the sights, sounds, and smells of the Southern Plains alive for the reader, but it also reveals that this region, which has often been dubbed "no-man's land," is a place in which people lived and developed a deep sense of place.

In portraying this close relationship between the Dunnes and their farm, Babb skillfully navigates the passage of time in the first part of the novel, compressing it at times to emphasize the duration in which they have been there, and expanding it elsewhere to highlight the extent of the challenges that arise from living in this area. For example, the novel's second chapter spans the first year in which the Dunne family plants winter wheat and establishes their connection to this land through regular descriptions of environmental conditions. As the Dunnes plant wheat early in the chapter, the "sharp high air of western autumn came into their noses, penetrated their clothes, made them go about their chores briskly" (6). After this brief description, which introduces the extent to which the Dunnes literally internalize their surroundings, the novel swiftly transitions into the "long cold winter" (6–7).

Time is further condensed at this point in the chapter as the narrative quickly shifts to the end of winter, despite this season's initial characterization as a protracted and harsh experience. As Babb writes, "Late snow melted under the tepid spring sun, the rutted byroads held muddy brown water for days, and the yard was wrinkled deep with wagon tracks and pocked by dog paws and animal hooves. The pure white world of winter—with its noble stillness, its grand and awing beauty, its mighty storms—slipped deftly into a wild and windy spring" (7). If the winter receives little contemporaneous description in this chapter—by this point in the narrative, the season has turned to spring—its beauty is nonetheless elevated in this passage through anaphora and dramatic language, both of which enable the reader to interpret this "long cold winter" as one that is also filled with appreciation and admiration for this place.

As the spring transitions into summer, the capricious conditions of life on the plains are focalized through the anxieties of the Dunnes, though the weather in this season ultimately proves benign. In addition to occasional dust storms, the narrator notes that rainstorms arise with regularity, which enables the wheat crop to grow, and the season produces a strong yield. In this manner, the Dunnes' well-being is shown to be closely intertwined with the year-round environmental conditions of the Panhandle, which not only emphasizes their connection to this place, but also enables readers who have perhaps never encountered conditions like those on the Southern Plains to share the experience in these positive moments. In this way, the second chapter of *Whose Names Are Unknown* compresses time in order to provide a complete picture of life in a successful year of raising wheat, offering a snapshot of a "good" year against which the subsequent hard years can be judged.

In addition to portraying the Dunnes' deep connections to the Panhandle through the manipulation of time across seasons, Babb also depicts them through access to the Dunnes' thoughts about farming. For example, after switching from broomcorn to winter wheat, "they looked at the land they had planted the day before, and the land they would plant this day, and they felt a sense of possession growing in them for the piece of earth that was theirs. But these unformed thoughts never came to words" (6). Later on, Milt Dunne thinks that "nothing was quite like the satisfaction he felt after he planted or harvested a crop. *This kind of feeling is one of the things a man lives for*, he told himself on one of the long walks to a neighbor's farm, *the feeling that I made something, I made something with the soil, together we made a crop grow in order and loveliness*" (58). In these moments, the Dunnes' thoughts and feelings—even when they elude language—highlight the sense of partnership and cooperation that they feel with the land, which is subsequently threatened and strained by the prolonged drought and the persistent dust storms that soon become a constant presence in their lives.

As Wixson notes, "Ecological disasters occurring on the High Plains are associated in Babb's writing with broken dreams, human tragedies brought about by false expectations, speculation, and the restless demand for land" (*Dirty* 4). In *Whose Names Are Unknown*, as precipitation decreases, Milt grows anxious, saying, "If the dust storms get any worse next year we won't have a field. We'll be starved out. This land is going back to desert" (42). In this passage, Milt's concerns that have heretofore remained in the background are finally expressed, which introduces the possibility that the Dunnes will be forced to move if conditions do not change. These fears continue to escalate over the winter, despite last year's winter being characterized as having had a "noble stillness." Instead, this year, "there was a dust storm in January earlier than any had come before, and apprehension blew over the land with the brown wind" (67). Although this particular storm is ultimately inconsequential for the crops, it nevertheless foreshadows the severity of the dust storms that arise the following summer, while further establishing the physical presence of these storms as manifestations of the constant anxieties felt by the farmers on the High Plains.

Of course, these fears are soon realized, as the dust storms grow in regularity and severity with the warming summer air. As the Dunnes work in the field one afternoon, Julia watches from the yard as a dust storm develops on the horizon: "Along the north sky was a pale yellow, the strange dead color of a lamp flame through a window in daylight. This dull inert mass had been lingering on the horizon for the last hour, but now she saw it take the shape of a curved wall rising slowly in the air" (75). Here, the storm's physical development mirrors the Dunnes' fears, as it looms ominously in the background. This lingering anxiety intensifies as the cloud grows closer, and they watch as it hits their land:

> "Look!" he said again, and they stood together not saying anything, awed by this new attack of nature. It was an evil monster coming on in mysterious, footless silence. It was magnificent and horrible like a nightmare of destiny towering over their slight world that had every day before this impressed upon them its vast unconquerable might. Grains of dust sounded against their shoes in a low flurry. The open land beyond was blotted out as the brown mass struck the edge of his field. (77–78)

Through the manifestation of this dust storm, the persistent anxieties associated with the dust that have been present throughout the novel manifest in this singular "evil monster" that reduces the expansive High Plains to a "slight world." Thus, the scope and severity of the dust storms are literally brought from the background to the forefront of the narrative, which not only portrays the sheer extent of this "nightmare of destiny" and the sense of inevitability that accompanies it. The narration also shows the reader how to feel about these storms through sinister descriptions. In this regard, while Steinbeck's Joads are not subjected to dust storms before leaving Oklahoma—as he instead relies on other narrative techniques to craft a sympathetic portrayal of them—the experiences of Babb's Dunnes as they encounter and survive these storms actively portray the harsh realities of the 1930s Dust Bowl. Being presented with specific details of their plight, we have sympathy for them as they struggle to survive in this place they have grown to love.

Following the appearance of this first dust storm of the season, which begins in a "monotonous soundless deluge" (79) in chapter 14, the dust's effects on the Dunne family become clear in the following chapter, as the "fine dark loam was drifted like snow" and "the smell of dust was everywhere" (81). In chapter 16, "the sky was obliterated" by the dust's mid-morning arrival, which then hung around for days (86–87). In these chapters, the events of the novel emphasize the inescapable realities of life in the Dust Bowl, which disturbs the Dunnes' daily lives. Indeed, after introducing the dust storms in these chapters, Babb pays particular attention to the storms' accumulating effects on the Dunnes as they endure these conditions for an extended period of time.

Babb's portrayal of the Dunnes' experiences of the dust storms, however, is not uncomplicated in the novel. With consideration to the Dust Bowl's origins in the combination of farming practices with natural drought cycles, Babb makes clear that the Dunnes are not blameless for the part they inadvertently played in this disaster. Indeed, in the first chapter, the Dunnes transition from broomcorn to wheat—the crop primarily associated with the Dust Bowl—though this decision was not made lightly, as Milt wanted to plant wheat despite his father's reluctance (3). On the other hand, despite their switch to wheat, it is important to remember that it is difficult to assign culpability to individuals for regional phenomena with dispersed impacts. As Worster argues, it is "unjust and misdirected to blame everything on the Dust Bowl residents themselves, for they were largely unwitting agents—men and women caught in a larger economic culture, dependent on its demands and rewards, representing its values and patterns of thought" (43). And near the end of part 1, as the Dunnes prepare to travel to California, Babb includes a direct critique, through discussions of the Brownell brothers, Max and Pete, one of whom had attended college to study agriculture, of the system that encouraged this behavior (14). After Pete argues that "this may be rich farmland well enough, but first it's grassland, and if we don't keep enough grazing country the soil will blow" (97), Max points out that farming "takes more than a strong back. We're getting more and more scientific. We want improved farming, and we want improved conditions to lessen the gamble" (102). In this conversation, Babb acknowledges the unsustainable approach to agriculture in the Southern Plains at this time, while arguing for more responsible and better-informed farming practices moving forward.

From a narrative perspective, the portrayal of the dust storms as consistent disruptions to everyday life risks becoming overly repetitive, considering the regularity with which these storms hit, and the forced mundanity of life trapped inside the Dunnes' dugout. However, Babb navigates this challenge through the skillful interjection of Julia's diary in chapter 17, which provides variety in the structure and content of the narrative, as well as the ability to condense months' hardship into a few pages. These entries vary in length from abrupt phrases, such as *"April 5.* Today is a terror" (90), to entries that span two full paragraphs, such as the description of April 10 (91–92). Since the narrative format of a diary entry allows for this variety in the accounts of each day, Babb integrates even more experiences of the dust storms into the novel, which further conveys to the reader the extent of the hardships the Dunnes face while living through these conditions. Moreover, since these diary entries shift the perspective of the narration from third-person omniscient to first-person, these descriptions of the lived Dust Bowl experience are thus rendered in the characters' own words, which makes them even more personal for the reader.

It has been well-established that Julia's diary entries in chapter 17 were largely based on an actual journal kept by Babb's mother, Jennie, during the dust storms of 1935. As Battat writes, although "Babb borrowed the language, structure, and content of her mother's own diary" (55), she also "significantly alter[ed] the final entries in order to use Julia's domestic struggles as the family's motivation for leaving the dust bowl. Whereas Jennie's factual diary ends on a positive note with an April morning 'warm and nice,' Julia's fictional diary concludes with the death of a neighbor and the 'dust still blowing'" (56). That is, while Jennie Babb weathered the storms, Sanora Babb's revision of the diary emphasizes the cumulative effects that the Dust Bowl had on the people who called no-man's land home, and provided the impetus for the Dunnes to search for better conditions in California, as climate refugees. The diary entries thus provide a coherent transition from Babb's portrayal of life in Oklahoma—from which she drew on her childhood on the plains, as well as the experiences of her immediate family who lived through the Dust Bowl—to her depiction of the Dust Bowl migrants in California, from which she also drew upon her own experiences volunteering alongside Tom Collins in the FSA.

As a novel that centers around a migration, *Whose Names Are Unknown* has strikingly little detail about the move from Oklahoma to California. Whereas much of the Joad narrative takes place on Highway 66, there are virtually no details of the Dunnes' experiences between the Oklahoma Panhandle and California, though Babb had initially considered placing them in Maricopa County, Arizona, for a while to earn money en route to California ("Untitled Notes"). Instead, Babb emphasized the aspects of these experiences with which she was familiar, focusing first on life on the High Plains and then on the challenges of migrant life in California. Since Babb wrote about what she knew, the Dunnes are rather efficient in finding the novel's version of the FSA camps in California, where they quickly meet a fictionalized version of Tom Collins, known in the novel as Woody. When Babb "went to the fields," as she later termed it, she and Collins traveled throughout California valleys, setting up sanitary tent camps, facilitating supplies, and providing information to newly arrived migrants (*Dirty* 29). Collins wrote to Babb estimating that she had visited in total the "tents, shacks, cabins, and homes" of "472 families or 2,175 men, women, and children" and that she had met with a total of approximately 781 families, or about 3,640 individuals, during this time ("SRA"). On several occasions, Babb later described these experiences as one of the most rewarding times of her life.[2]

While volunteering with Collins, Babb was inspired by the courage that she witnessed in the Okie migrants, despite the challenges they had faced, which was further shaped by Collins's influential "democracy functioning" approach to the FSA camps.[3] Indeed, it appears likely that Babb's approach to *Whose Names Are Unknown* was heavily influenced by her time with Collins and that she moreover intended for her novel to be an extension of her volunteering efforts. For example, as Babb describes in a letter to Wixson, Collins gave her a copy of Archibald MacLeish's *Land of the Free* as a gift, with the inscription "For Sanora, whose birthday for 1938 has a particular significance because of the *Power* she gave the thousands of homeless workers—farmers as she visited them in their hovels, and tents and counselled with them at their meetings. / They now have hope—hope that this will yet be the land of the real free, a functional democracy!" (9). In this inscription, Collins identifies Babb's ability to form connections to these people and emphasizes that she (and, by extension, Collins himself) treated them with radical empathy, which they generally did not receive elsewhere in California. This is a powerful reminder for readers of climate fiction today, since climate change refugees and migrations are expected to grow in frequency and magnitude in the coming years.

Despite this praise, Collins ultimately argues that Babb's most effective contributions to the migrants' cause is not through her volunteer work, but instead with her pen. As he explains to her in a letter:

> At this time I believe it to the point to make some suggestions to you ON YOUR REAL WORTH TO THE PROBLEM OF THE WORKERS, HERE AND ELSEWHERE. Frankly, I feel that you can do your very best work for the agricultural and industrial workers by and through the power of the written word. You have the unusual ability possessed by so few writers to do a POWERFUL bit of work. The field is rapidly being filled with organizers. Whatever you write will be of great assistance to the workers and organizers. I would like to see you WRITE and WRITE. It is your profession. You

are nobly fitted for it. May you DO IT. We all HOPE YOU WILL. WE WANT YOU TO DO SO. (Collins, letter to Babb 2)

Despite Babb's months of experience working alongside Collins, he argues here that her "real worth" to this cause is not through direct action, which he implies can be done by anyone, but instead through her unique ability to shape others' perceptions of this issue. Moreover, Collins concludes this letter with further references to his hopes for Babb's literary contributions to this issue: "To you, for your efforts, your cooperation your interest and sympathy, for helping us on the road to a united front, the many thousands of us express our thanks. We greet you, warmly, and hope to have you assist us in the bigger job to come" (8). While the conclusion of this letter shares the spirit of the passage above, it is noteworthy that Collins furthermore refers to a "bigger job to come" with regards to the Dust Bowl migration.

For while there is no reason to question the sincerity of Collins's encouragement of Babb, his enthusiasm was not reserved only for her writing abilities, as it was moreover a characteristic of his correspondence with Steinbeck during the same time period. For example, in "Bringing in the Sheaves," Collins, writing under the pen name Windsor Drake, describes a meal with Steinbeck during one of the author's trips to the migrant camps, in which Collins says, "What you want to do, John, is to keep your impressions in your mind and when the time is ripe DO something about those conditions. If you fail to do that then you are letting those thousands of people down" (225). While the total number of days that Steinbeck spent with Collins in the fields was markedly shorter than Babb's—albeit Steinbeck's was spread out over a longer period of time—the implication of this exchange is nevertheless remarkably consistent: for both writers, Collins argued that writing about the subject would have more impact on public opinion and therefore on state and national policy than direct action. Steinbeck clearly internalized this message, as Collins reports that Steinbeck proclaimed to him that he had "'a big job to do and when that is done you will realize I'm always there to do what I can for your work among the rural poor'" (226). Babb is absent from Collins's account in "Bringing in the Sheaves"— though it is likely that she was present during the very trip it describes.[4] Nonetheless, Collins's encouragement of both writers, and the unshakable empathy expressed by both Steinbeck and Babb in their respective Dust Bowl novels, clearly reflect his influence on both projects. Both writers were progressive, activist individuals and approached their novels with a "job" in mind: to cultivate positive public and political perceptions of the migrants through their literary texts. This approach to their narratives emphasizes the potential of literature's capacity to inspire social and cultural change, which is particularly relevant today as more and more climate change narratives are published.

Of course, these "jobs" necessitated accuracy in the portrayals of the 1930s migrants in California. To this extent, Collins furthermore acted as a facilitator of information for the two writers, and both Steinbeck and Babb used their time with him to collect material for their writing. While Steinbeck first visited the FSA camps in 1936 to gather material for his journalistic endeavors (Benson 173–82), Sanora Babb reports in a letter to her sister, Dorothy, that helping Collins take applications at the Porterville office was "a good chance to talk to people, because they do not know I want to write of them" (4). Moreover, both writers relied on Collins for accuracy in their portrayal of the growing seasons in California, with Steinbeck noting in a letter to Collins that he would "have to appeal to you for help again and again for details. Will you give me please a list—a family arrives in Bakersfield in August. What camps will they hit and what wage until the winter and spring," before further reiterating his aims of shaping public opinions of the migrants: "Please help me Tom. If I can do this book well enough and honestly enough it will help the people" (1). Meanwhile, Babb requested similar information from Collins while she worked on her novel, asking, "I will list the places you gave me before, and will you please fill in the crops, the months, and trace the movement into California as they would most likely go in order to live along the way?" (1). In this regard, although much of the critical discourse surrounding *Whose Names Are Unknown* focuses on Steinbeck's possession of Babb's notes and reports from her time with Collins, the often neglected central figure in this exchange is, in fact, Collins. His interest in seeing publications about the Dust Bowl migrants precluded any concerns over notions of intellectual property, or acknowledgment of the unlikelihood that two novels on the same subject would be published so close together.

Although the paths of Steinbeck and Babb crossed a couple times, it appears unlikely that Steinbeck was aware of *Whose Names Are Unknown*'s fate, as there are no known references to it (or Babb) in Steinbeck archives.[5] On the other hand, Babb was adamant throughout her life that she held no ill will toward Steinbeck for her novel's delayed publication.[6] While there is no question that Random House's acceptance and subsequent rejection of *Whose Names Are Unknown* in 1939 was unfortunate, antagonism simply did not exist between the two writers. The mischaracterization of a rivalry between Steinbeck and

Babb has unfortunately distracted critics from focusing on other ways in which Babb's novel is relevant to contemporary literary discourses, particularly, as this essay has argued, in a time of global climatological destabilization.

Although Babb's novel was unable to contribute directly to the Dust Bowl migrants' cause, its recent publication and subsequent recovery is appropriately timed. When it was published, a year before her death, Babb told her agent and friend, Joanne Dearcopp, "This is the most meaningful book I've written" (quoted in Conklin). Because Babb focused on the effects on ordinary people during an environmental disaster, contemporary readers today hear prescient warnings. With the likely increase of more environmental refugee narratives in the near future, consideration of both Babb's and Steinbeck's Dust Bowl novels offers a variety of insights to writers, scholars, and teachers engaging in ecocritical discourses surrounding climate change, environment, and migration. For while many Californians resented the influx of Dust Bowl migrants in the 1930s, Babb sought to restore their humanity through her sympathetic portrayals of their lives of hardship and loss before and after they arrived in California. Babb's approach to *Whose Names Are Unknown* is an important lesson in empathy as climate change migrations grow in the decades to come.

NOTES

1. The Farm Security Administration was a New Deal agency created in 1937 that replaced an earlier program called the Resettlement Administration, created in 1935. These programs oversaw temporary shelters and camps for Dust Bowl migrants and were managed by Tom Collins from 1935 to 1941. For more details, see Benson and Steinbeck, "'To Tom, Who Lived It'"; and Babb and Babb, *On the Dirty Plate Trail*.

2. Babb often wrote, in her correspondence and notes, about how special her time volunteering with Collins was to her. Examples include her letters to Barbara Guth, Mary Howard, and Temple Lee Reed, and in her biographical sketches from December 1957 and March 1978.

3. For more information on Collins's DF approach, see Battat, *Ain't Got No Home*, 47–48; and Babb and Babb *On the Dirty Plate Trail*.

4. The details of the story suggest that the meeting most likely took place during Steinbeck's trip to visit Collins in February 1938, during which Babb was volunteering with him (Babb and Babb, *On the Dirty Plate Trail*, 26–30).

5. In a letter to Wixson, Babb notes that Steinbeck "came down a couple of weekends and made the rounds with us" (9), and has a similar note in her biographical notes from December 1957 (3). In her notes from March 1978, she expands on this a bit more: "I knew John slightly. He had come out to the fields two weekends, and he had tramped around all day with Tom and me; we had talked a lot, eaten together" (2).

6. A particularly clear example is in a letter to John Short in which Babb grants Short permission to quote her with regards to *The Grapes of Wrath*, "so long as you do not write anything that makes me sound like sour grapes. I don't feel that way, as I wrote you" (1).

WORKS CITED

Primary Sources

Primary sources listed below are archived in the Sanora Babb papers, Harry Ransom Center, University of Texas at Austin, Austin, TX (HRC).

Babb, Sanora. "Biographical Information." December 1957. Box 58, Folder 7, HRC.
———. "Biographical Information." March 1978. Box 58, Folder 7, HRC.
———. Letter to Barbara Guth. 28 May 1995. Box 36, Folder 7, HRC.
———. Letter to Dorothy Babb. May 1938. Box 18, Folder 5, HRC.
———. Letter to Douglas Wixson. 12 November 1996. Box 55, Folder 1, HRC.
———. Letter to John Short. 23 March 1975. Box 23, Folder 6, HRC.
———. Letter to Mary Howard. 17 May 1973. Box 37, Folder 4, HRC.
———. Letter to Temple Lee Reed. 1 August 1978. Box 37, Folder 4, HRC.
———. Letter to Thomas A. Collins. Box 18, Folder 8, HRC.
———. "Revised Draft #3, March 2003." Box 22, Folders 1–2, HRC.
———. "Revised and Edited Draft #4, Photocopy, September 2003." Box 22, Folders 3–4, HRC.
———. "Untitled Notes." Box 18, Folder 6, HRC.
———. "Working Copy, Carbon with Handwritten Corrections, Also Additional Loose Chapters, 1938." Box 19, Folders 8–9, HRC.
———. "Working Copy, Photocopy, Circa 2000s." Box 20, Folder 4, HRC.
Collins, Thomas A. Letter to Sanora Babb. Circa 1938–1939. Box 18, Folder 8, HRC.
———. "SRA Form 101: California State Relief Administration Transmittal." 18 March 1938. Box 18, Folder 7, HRC.
Dearcopp, Joanne. Letter to Julie Shilling. 3 August 2003. Box 22, Folder 4, HRC.
Steinbeck, John. Letter to Thomas A. Collins. Box 18, Folder 11, HRC.
Wixson, Douglas. Letter to Sanora Babb. 24 July 1999. Box 23, Folder 2, HRC

Secondary Sources

Babb, Sanora. *Whose Names Are Unknown*. University of Oklahoma Press, 2004.
Babb, Sanora, and Dorothy Babb. *On the Dirty Plate Trail: Remembering the Dust Bowl Refugee Camps*, edited by Douglas Wixson, University of Texas Press, 2007.
Battat, Erin Royston. *Ain't Got No Home: America's Great Migrations and the Making of an Interracial Left*. University of North Carolina Press, 2014.
Benson, Jackson, and John Steinbeck. "'To Tom, Who Lived It': John Steinbeck and the Man from Weedpatch." *Journal of Modern Literature*, vol. 5, no. 2 (1976): 151–210.

Collins, Thomas A. and John Steinbeck. "'Bringing in the Sheaves,' by 'Windsor Drake.'" *Journal of Modern Literature*, vol. 5, no. 2 (1976): 211–32.
Conklin, Mike. "'Whose Names Are Unknown' Finally Becomes Known." *Chicago Tribune*, 12 October 2004, www.chicagotribune.com/news/ct-xpm-2004-10-13-0410160157-story.html.
Loftis, Anne. *Witnesses to the Struggle: Imaging the 1930s California Labor Movement*. University of Nevada Press, 1998.
Steinbeck, John. *The Grapes of Wrath*. Penguin, 2006.
———. *Working Days: The Journals of The Grapes of Wrath*, edited by Robert DeMott. Penguin, 1990.
Worster, Donald. *Dust Bowl: The Southern Plains in the 1930s*. Oxford University Press, 1979.

TRACY SANFORD TUCKER

9

FARM FICTION
Cather, Wilder, and Babb

In a 1921 interview with the *Omaha World Herald*, Willa Cather said, "Whenever I crossed the Missouri river coming into Nebraska the very smell of the soil tore me to pieces. I could not decide which was the real and which the fake 'me'; I almost decided to settle down on a quarter section of land and let my writing go" (Bohlke 37). When this passage is cited, it's almost universally used to express Cather's love for Nebraska and its importance in her writing and her life; it clearly demonstrates Cather's palpable homesickness and the lifelong connection she felt to the people of Webster County. The tension between the "real" and "the 'fake' me" that Cather identifies, however, rarely receives full attention. Its inclusion seems to suggest a prolonged struggle between versions of Cather's created selves or even an aspect of self-promotion.

The idea of embodying a version of herself, particularly as a certain type of storyteller, had become a pattern for Cather. In an 1896 letter sent from Pittsburgh, Cather tells a friend in Nebraska that she had improvised "Indian stories" to please the children of her employer and believed that Pittsburghers expected her to "fulfill [that] role" because she "come[s] from the West" (letter to Ellen Gere). Cather's belief in the necessity of her performance of the role hints at an important aspect of Cather's career. Because it addresses her feelings about herself, as a westerner living in the East, the passage also allows us to consider her motivations in writing farm fiction. More importantly, it invites a broader comparison between Cather and Laura Ingalls Wilder and Sanora Babb, two writers who share subject matter and certain life events with Cather. Examining each author's connection to agriculture and the farm novel allows readers to understand an author's intentions—and therefore her writing—more fully. In many ways, these comparisons also establish Babb as a successor to Cather and Wilder in the genre.

Our understanding of farm fiction has evolved, and along with it our understanding of why the genre attracted authors like Cather and Wilder and remained relevant to authors like Babb well into the 1970s. In 1965, critic Roy Meyer attempted to define the farm novel as a genre. The novel, he said, would be set on the farm and deal primarily with farm life, realistically depicted in physical detail and in rendering of speech. Meyer believed that farm fiction would reflect the particular "attitudes, beliefs, and habits of mind" that were typical of farm folk, like conservatism, anti-intellectualism, and hostility toward town and town life (7–13). Thirty years later, William Conlogue argued that many novels that otherwise fit that definition defied the importance of conservatism by positively depicting socially progressive ideas like rural electrification and farmers' cooperatives. Instead, Conlogue suggests that farm fiction is identified more by its nuanced exploration of relationships between farm and nature, the health of the farm and the community, and attitudes toward technology (19–21). Florian Freitag, in 2013, noted the important contributions of farm fiction to national ideas of self-conception and myth making (5–6). His work complicates a clear definition of what counts as a farm novel. While Freitag provides reasons for the genre's sudden proliferation between 1900 and 1940, Meyer dismisses them as simply inevitable and nearly spontaneous. Meyer does indeed credit Cather with "rais[ing the farm novel] to the level of high art" with 1913's *O Pioneers!* (47).

Of the work of the three authors, Cather's fiction appeared in print first. Her first novel was not a farm novel; rather, she published *Alexander's Bridge*, a drawing room novel about a bridge engineer. In a telling interview, Cather tells Latrobe Carroll of *The Bookman* about important advice she received from New England regionalist Sarah Orne Jewett:

> I never abandoned trying to make a compromise between the kind of matter that my experience had given me and the manner of writing which I admired, until I began my second novel, *O Pioneers!*. And from the first chapter, I decided not to 'write' at all—simply to give myself up to the pleasure of recapturing in memory people and places I had believed forgotten. This was what my friend Sarah Orne Jewett had advised me to do. (Bohlke 21–22)

By February 1908, when she became acquainted with Jewett, Cather had been working for two years at *McClure's* magazine, one of the most read muckraking magazines in the country. Nascent farm fiction was already being published, though much of it was poor. That same year, President Theodore Roosevelt created the Commission on Country Life to address concerns raised by the Country Life movement, an outgrowth of the nationwide Progressive movement. Under the leadership of Liberty Hyde Bailey, it was charged with "mak[ing] rural civilization as effective and satisfying as other civilization." The commission was a fierce proponent of a number of initiatives: establish a national extension service to share improved agricultural techniques; develop rural studies in universities and the federal government; and create a campaign for rural progress—based on Roosevelt's concern that "the welfare of the farmer is of vital consequence to the welfare of the whole community" (Roosevelt 6). Within the next few years, the commission would hold thirty public hearings across the nation, circulate over half a million questionnaires, and issue a final report—all before the publication of Cather's *O Pioneers!* in 1913.

Cather doesn't mention the Country Life movement in her letters or writings, but archival evidence suggests that Cather could scarcely have avoided knowledge of it. Whatever her thoughts on the Country Life Commission, she *was* very pleased with a September 4, 1913, review in the *Nation*, which positively compared her work favorably to another farm novel, Frank Norris's *The Octopus*. The reviewer writes, "It is the same big primitive fecund American which engages Miss Cather's imagination. She dwells with unforced emotion upon the suffering and the glory of those who have taught a desert to feed the world" ("Current Fiction"). Cather writes, in a letter to her sister, "Here is a notice from the "Nation" which you might read and send back to me. I like to beat those two flossy boys, Norris and [David Graham] Phillips" (letter to Elsie

Cather). Two weeks later the *Nation* published "The West and the New Agriculture," which mentions Cather's work in direct connection to the work of the commission: "Is the West thus energized because the despondent, short-sighted farmers of Willa Sibert Cather's *O Pioneers!* have given way to a sturdier, more enlightened race?" the article asks. "While the notion that the new agriculture is to be credited with every favorable turn that may be noted in the crop situation is an illusion, the impression . . . is not wide of the truth. The new agriculture is making a new earth" ("The West"). We know that Cather regularly read her press clippings and shared them with friends and supporters. She undoubtedly knew that parallels were being drawn between her work and the Country Life Commission's proposals.

Recent archival acquisitions have revealed that Cather was also interested in Nebraska for business reasons. Cather, as an independent career woman, kept her hands firmly on the financial reins of her affairs. Soon after leaving Nebraska, she began sending money to her father Charles, who ran a small farm loan and insurance business, for investment, earning 4 percent interest on her cash (Charles Cather Ledger). Later, she invested $8,000 in the purchase of three rental farms. She considered letting some of these properties revert to the county over past due property taxes, telling her farm manager, Willard Crowell, "I repeat that if I were twenty years younger I would certainly hold on to the farms, for I have not lost faith in that country. But as the facts actually are, there are two considerations of chief importance in my situation: 1) Not to send good money after bad, and 2) To give all my time and strength to my own profession and to the many demands which it makes upon me" (letter to Willard Crowell). Cather's frustrations surrounding this investment niggled for decades, but contrary to the sentiments in her 1921 interview, she gave no thought to giving up her writing and taking up farming.

Cather's other letters suggest that her knowledge of farming was, in fact, quite limited. While working on her Pulitzer Prize–winning novel *One of Ours*, she writes to her father, "Please tell me, father, is it a binder or a reaper that has a big wheel at one side with wooden slats across it? That's a poor enough description, but I think you will know what I mean. Maybe it isn't a wheel, but it looks like one, and it's never taller than the rest of the machine" (letter to Charles Cather). Though the Cather family were farmers, they had employees, and it is unclear if Cather herself, raised in a genteel southern family, ever participated in any physical labor on the land. Instead, for Cather living on the East Coast, western farms were a location of investment and source material.

This is quite distinct from the life experiences of Laura Ingalls Wilder, who was critically involved in the day-to-day work of farms. In *Prairie Girl: The Annotated Autobiography*, Wilder describes her love of the prairie in ways that are similar to Cather—but she goes on to describe her strong preference for farm chores like milking and gathering eggs to the social activities of De Smet, South Dakota (Fraser 118; Wilder 231–37). Cather was still toddling around Willow Shade, her family's Virginia sheep farm, when Charles Ingalls was suffering consecutive crop losses outside Walnut Grove, Minnesota (Fraser 70–77). While Cather was yet a schoolgirl, Laura Ingalls had married Almonzo Wilder and began to prove up their own claim, sharing the labor of sowing and harvesting and planting the required acreage of trees on Almonzo's timber claim. The young couple was first plagued by drought and storm and later struck by diphtheria and then, worst of all, by a debilitating stroke that left Almonzo Wilder with limited physical endurance. Laura's contributions, both in labor and in cash, were significant, despite the Wilders' ultimate failure on the claim (Fraser 133–55).

The Panic of 1893 illustrates the differences between Cather and Wilder. Cather used the circumstances of the prolonged economic downturn as writing material in her book *A Lost Lady* (1923). She focused on the loss of social status that accompanied monetary losses. Wilder, on the other hand, suffered directly. Financial instability, poor grain markets, and widespread weather disruptions across the northern Great Plains once again forced the young Wilder family to start over. Desperate and enticed by advertising for the "Land of Big Red Apples," the Wilders made the heartbreaking decision to leave behind their families and relocate to Missouri, where the struggle to build a successful farm continued (Fraser 169–76).

Though possessing all the earmarks of yet another disaster for the family, the Panic ultimately helped to save the Wilders. "Unable to do a full day's work," Almonzo Wilder encountered two instances of good fortune: first, a gift from his father that resulted in the Wilders' outright ownership of their house in Mansfield, Missouri, and later, finding work as a deliveryman and driver (Fraser 197–98). During this time spent living in town, Laura Ingalls Wilder, perhaps for the first time, joined social clubs. Though these clubs preceded the creation of the Country Life Commission by a decade, Eastern Star and associated Masonic groups were important for the exchange of ideas and development of skills like public speaking. Shortly after, grassroots "farmers' clubs" began to usher in any number of progressive ideas—voting rights for women, the pure food movement, fairness in farm lending—and Mrs. A. J. Wilder found herself at the heart of it all (Fraser 199, 214, 221).

While Cather was living in East Coast cities and investing her money in Nebraska farms, Wilder was personally affected by the issues brought to the fore by the Country Life Commission. Encouraged by her work in social clubs and the Missouri Woman's Home Development Association, Wilder penned "The Small Farm Home" for the Missouri Home Makers' Conference. She had written other materials for the *American Food Journal* and several small newspapers, but in this piece, Wilder asserts that the invention of labor-saving devices and the availability of rural mail delivery, public libraries, and farmers' associations and clubs all contributed to a way of life that was, in nearly every way, superior to life in the city (Fraser 223). Yet despite her claims in "The Small Farm Home," the Wilders were unable to eke out a living on their small acreage. The family's income increasingly relied on Wilder's published columns and later on the commissions on each farm loan she wrote for the newly created Mansfield National Farm Loan Association (Fraser 240–42). The work of the Country Life Commission, through the creation of the Federal Farm Loan Act in 1916, directly impacted the Wilders' lives.

When her father died in 1902, Wilder had begun "that 'story of my life' thing," as her daughter Rose Wilder Lane called it, a project that would form the backbone of the *Little House* books we know so well today (Fraser 230–42). She returned to recording her memories following the deaths of her mother in 1924 and her sister Mary in 1928. Adding to the trauma this time was Wilder's failed candidacy for Mansfield tax collector and the return of her daughter, Rose, who subsequently suffered a nervous breakdown (Fraser 286–87, 307–11). After each event, Wilder renewed work on her writing, leaning on the memories of her family, their recipes and traditions, and the hardships they had faced together, particularly during their early frontier experiences.

In the spring of 1930, Wilder shared *Pioneer Girl* with her daughter, who was quick to collaborate and share the work with own professional publishing contacts (Fraser 315–16). The published versions of the *Little House* books rely heavily on this original *Pioneer Girl* manuscript, though they omit some disturbing moments in Wilder's childhood. Some episodes were simply too gruesome for the intended age group, such as having a sow that ate her piglets, and some too sad, like the short life of Wilder's brother Freddie Ingalls (Fraser 322; Wilder 84–85). Other episodes, though, seem to have been omitted to preserve the image of Charles Ingalls that Wilder hoped to capture. For example, the worst instances of frontier hardship were removed from *Pioneer Girl*, with little mention of the desperate hunger and fear that surely had been present in her Dakota childhood. Most notably, a failed land claim on disputed Osage land south of Independence, Kansas, was reversed, with Wilder suggesting that her father and other white settlers were the wronged parties, instead of the Native Americans whose land was illegally squatted upon in 1870-71 (Fraser 322; Linsenmayer 169).

The most significant differences between Wilder's written memories and the published versions relate to mythmaking, the type of national storytelling that Florian Freitag identified in farm fiction. Despite Wilder's belief in Progressive-era policies and her role in writing farm loans for the Federal Farm Loan program, Wilder's *Little House* books deliberately reject those progressive values, emphasizing instead the rugged independence, self-determination, creativity, stubbornness, and humor that was used to characterize her father and other family members (Fraser 405-40). Like Cather, Wilder selectively utilizes episodes from her life to create fictionalized characters that embody the individualistic and nationalistic ideals of an earlier era, despite Wilder's apparent embrace of progressive ideas in the twentieth century. Unlike Cather, who creates a role for herself as a western storyteller, Wilder is creating a role for a larger-than-life father with a heart of gold.

The overlaps between Wilder and Cather have been well-documented and well-researched over the years, though recent archival discoveries have helped to document many new biographical details. Comparisons with Sanora Babb have been fewer, despite two well-regarded farm novels of her own: *An Owl on Every Post* (1970) and *Whose Names Are Unknown* (2004). Important connections exist between Babb and the two older authors. Babb's childhood too, in Oklahoma, Colorado, and Kansas, was marked by an early dislocation to a frontier land claim that was both isolating and exciting. All three women observed firsthand the terrible toll that the frontier could take on women, witnessing as their mothers grieved lost children, lost friendships, and lost health (Fraser 36-46; Wixson "Radical" 117-18; Woodress 36-43). But as Cather and Wilder had done before her, Babb waxed eloquent about the landscape itself. Babb recalls an early impression of eastern Colorado, from her seven year-old's perspective:

> The air was of such purity that we stood breathing deeply for the simple pleasure of breathing. Its fragrance was unlike the softer, leafy air we had known. Strong plants that lived in a land of little rain gave into the

winds their pungent smells, sagebrush more powerful than all others. We turned around and around to see the full circle of horizon, the perfect meeting of earth and sky. Two pointed buttes to the northwest were the only blemish on the plain. . . . We were at once in a grand and endless space, and enclosed, locked in. (*Owl* 15)

Cather had described her Nebraska landscape as "nothing but land: not a country at all, but the material out of which countries are made. . . . the complete dome of heaven, all there was of it" (*My Ántonia* 7), while Wilder describes their claim on Silver Lake as having "no trees. . . . with the great, new country clean and fresh around us" (Wilder 158–60). Babb admits that "this was an empty land" when she first sees it, but comes to appreciate its loneliness (*Owl* 7, 18). A love of the land, its plants and animals, is perhaps the easiest commonality to find among these accounts.

The three authors' publication timelines complicate comparison. Cather experienced the Nebraska frontier between 1883 and 1890 and published her farm novels between 1913 and 1923; Wilder's frontier life predated Cather's by more than a decade, but her farm fiction publication was delayed until 1932. Babb's childhood homesteading years between 1913 and 1917 seem anachronistic by comparison. As Babb and her family faced near starvation on their isolated Baca County, Colorado, claim, Cather was living a cosmopolitan life in Greenwich Village, and Wilder was proposing the ease with which a family might support itself on a mere five acres with every modern convenience. Though the Country Life Commission's work was largely completed, any resultant improvement is difficult to find in Babb's depiction of their lives in *An Owl on Every Post*. *Owl*, though at least partially drafted in the 1930s alongside her Dust Bowl novel *Whose Names Are Unknown*, was not published until 1970.

The Country Life Commission, dedicated to the improvement of living and cultural conditions in rural parts of the country, was a prominent part of both Cather's and Wilder's adult lives. Not so with Babb. Her frontier experience seemed unchanged by it. Following a difficult childhood, Babb was plunged into the lean years of World War I; after her 1929 move to Los Angeles, Babb experienced homelessness and unemployment as the country slid into the Great Depression. In the 1930s, Babb spent time documenting labor conditions and helped to run camps for dispossessed migrant farmers in California, people who reminded her of the struggling farmers of her childhood (Wixson, "Radical" 113–20). Her novel *Whose Names Are Unknown* portrays the hardships of farming in the Dust Bowl and the equally hard times as migrant farm workers in California. As Nicholas Coles points out in his examination of farm fiction, both Cather and Wilder write mostly of successful efforts on the frontier; Babb does not (Coles 217–18).

Further complicating comparisons between the three authors may be a question of literary classification. In the introduction to a special issue of the *European Journal of American Studies* focused on contemporary western literature, editors David Rio and Øyunn Hestetun hoped to contrast postfrontier writing with that of the frontier, which they deem "casually exploitative in its attitude towards nature, invidiously hierarchical in its approach toward women and minorities, and above all, un-self-critical." Though the contributors to that edition did not represent Babb's work, Rio and Hestetun suggest that "postfrontier literature not only has abandoned archetypal male-biased imagery and ethnocentric prejudices associated with the Old American West, but also often addresses the problematic legacy of western myths" (Introduction). In this context, Cather's and Wilder's farm novels embody the frontier mentality, while Babb's work can be considered postfrontier. Her *Owl* and *Whose Names*, as well as the nonfiction *On the Dirty Plate Trail*, strongly focus on the traumas and impacts felt by the women and children of the frontier. And though portions were drafted earlier, *Owl* falls well outside the heyday of farm fiction. Still, frontier, postfrontier, and farm fiction share a messy liminal space within the western literary canon.

Babb's actual farming experience was limited to helping her parents plant and harvest broomcorn sorghum as a child, but through her work with displaced Dust Bowl farmers in the California government camps, she gained a great deal of secondhand knowledge about many types of agriculture and the social and economic factors that affected it. This distinguishes Babb from authors like Frank Norris and Willa Cather, who engaged in something like voyeurism in tackling the farm as subject. In a 1914 letter to Elizabeth Sergeant, Cather writes that harvest is a sight she "has not beheld in years." Wilder, on the other hand, had ample, lifelong, firsthand experience of every aspect of farm life, but she chose to revise her memories to promote a national ethos that relied upon stubborn independence, self-reliance, and hard work. A comparison of these writers reveals Babb's vision of the world of agriculture as, in many ways, much broader than either Cather or Wilder.

The salient question, it seems, is the deliberateness with which each author approaches her farm fiction. It is significant that all three women came to literary careers partly through journalism, and later, more intuitively, took on other genres. Cather's early efforts in poetry and fiction were heavily allusive and seldom use Nebraska as their subject. Conflicting statements in Cather's correspondence mean that scholars may never fully be able to know whether she intended *O Pioneers!* to be a farm novel, one that propelled the genre forward, or if she was, again, merely enacting the role of westerner to her advantage. Wilder's motivations are clearer than Cather's. All of her writing, from her earliest journalism, took for its topic the farm, the farm home, and the superiority of rural living, and the payments for these publications sustained her struggling family (Fraser 250–53).

Babb's purpose seems as clear, but it also seems purer in purpose. Her Dust Bowl novel, *Whose Names Are Unknown*, was based on her collected accounts of farming and dispossession from the migrants of Weedpatch Camp, eastern California (Wixson, "Radical" 128). She, like any writer, held high hopes for the work and was bitterly disappointed when Steinbeck's *The Grapes of Wrath* effectively cornered the market on novels about dispossessed migrant farm laborers (Wixson, "Book Review"). Despite this, Babb never abandoned the strategy of speaking for and through the working class people she met—whether in a Farm Service Administration camp or in sharing her own thoughts and memories of her prairie childhood. Babb helpfully tells us herself of the importance of that hardscrabble childhood on her grandfather's farm claim as depicted in her memoir *An Owl on Every Post*: "Years have passed since my life on the plains, but living in a true wilderness as a child had a profound influence on me. . . . The impact of those years is still potent. . . . It gave me tolerance. Perhaps it was the bigness of the plains and the sky that stretched my thoughts" (Afterword). Though this passage talks about *Owl*, the "bigness" of Babb's thoughts is what allows her to translate her own childhood farm and frontier experiences into literary work that speaks to the experiences of other women and children. Unlike Steinbeck, whose work, like Cather's, elevates the migrant story to the level of literary epic, Babb retains the "intimate, familiar sense of who the people are" (Wixson "Book Review"). Undoubtedly, Babb was influenced by the progressive and indeed radical social movements of the 1920s and 1930s, but she had an authentic connection borne of experience that Cather lacked entirely and that Wilder chose to omit. That guilelessness, that lack of contrivance that comes between the lived experience and the reader is what truly sets Babb's work apart from not only Steinbeck, but Cather and Wilder as well.

Because of the pervasiveness of the Country Life Commission's work across the plains, we may assume that all three authors knew and shared Roosevelt's opinion that the welfare of the country depended on the welfare of the farmer. For Cather, that concern was largely financial. The politics of the Progressive era, despite her work on *McClure's* magazine, may have passed her by, even though the ideas shared by the commission—indoor plumbing diagrams, whitewash recipes—were so significant to Cather's father that he pinned those articles into his ledger. Babb's grandfather and father were homegrown prairie socialists; she herself became a communist in the 1930s (Wixson "Radical" 124). Wilder and Babb thoroughly absorbed the populist, progressive thinking that hovered in the air of the plains states, though Wilder portrayed little of it in her writing. In the end, only Babb fully embraced progressive politics and portrayed them in a form that fused the postfrontier to the farm novel, reflecting Conlogue's and Freitag's definitions of the farm novel with a self-aware and progressive agricultural population.

Though Cather and Wilder have long been considered canonical authors of farm fiction, I believe that Babb deserves equal consideration. An inclusive view of farm fiction's range, including work that falls outside the early twentieth century and work which complicates the genre's standard classifications, demands Babb's inclusion. Given Babb's prolonged work in the genre, her farm fiction feels both more deliberate and more intimate than Cather's. It reads like the work of a writer who not only experienced the hardships of a frontier farm childhood, but recognizes her own trauma in the faces of struggling farmers and their families. While the work of Wilder and Cather remain important cultural touchstones, Babb's work embraces that tradition and expands it, in her own unique and genuine style.

In giving a voice to those who suffered most—the displaced, the disenfranchised, the impoverished women and children of the West—Babb's work modernizes and humanizes farm fiction in new and important ways. She is able to do this without artifice or play-acting; she writes of social ills and political movements without propagandizing. Her stories are, at their heart, the stories of Babb's chosen community. "Her writings . . . dignify the ordinary," says Douglas Wixson, Babb's biographer ("Harry Ransom Center"). But the genre of farm fiction *needed* a writer like Babb, someone with a bigness of thought and heart, to give dynamism and materiality to those ordinary and overlooked lives. The recovery of these voices through Babb's work is critical if farm fiction is to remain a viable study of American life and culture.

WORKS CITED

Primary Sources

Cather, Charles. Ledger. WCPM Collection. Willa Cather Foundation Collections & Archives at the National Willa Cather Center in Red Cloud, NE.

Cather, Willa. Letter to Charles Cather, 28 December 1918. Philip L. and Helen Cather Southwick Collection, University of Nebraska-Lincoln.

———. Letter to Elizabeth Sergeant, 10 August 1914. Morgan Library and Museum, New York, NY.

———. Letter to Ellen Gere, 29 June 1896. Willa Cather Collection, Nebraska State Historical Society, Lincoln, NE.

———. Letter to Elsie Cather, 31 October 1913. Susan J. and James Rosowski Cather Collection, University of Nebraska-Lincoln.

———. Letter to Willard Crowell, 11 December 1938. Willard Crowell Collection. Willa Cather Foundation Collections & Archives at the National Willa Cather Center in Red Cloud, NE.

Secondary Sources

Babb, Sanora. *An Owl on Every Post*. Muse Ink Press, 2012.

———. *Sanora Babb: Stories from the High Plains*. Harry Ransom Center exhibition. www.hrc.utexas.edu/exhibitions/web/babb/. Accessed 7 July 2020.

———. "Welcome." Sanora Babb website, www.sanorababb.com.

———. *Whose Names Are Unknown*. University Oklahoma Press, 2006.

Bohlke, Brent. *Willa Cather in Person*. University of Nebraska Press, 1987.

Coles, Nicholas. "Working the Fields: Love and Labor in Farm Fiction from 1890 to the Dust Bowl." In *A History of Working Class Literature*, edited by Nicholas Coles and Paul Lauter, 215–31. Cambridge University Press, 2017.

Conlogue, William. *Working the Garden: American Writers and the Industrialization of Agriculture*. University North Carolina Press, 2002.

"Current Fiction." *The Nation*, vol. 97, no. 2514, 4 Sept. 1913, p. 210. Hathi Trust, https://hdl.handle.net/2027/chi.32142195. Accessed 3 June 2019.

Fraser, Caroline. *Prairie Fires: The American Dreams of Laura Ingalls Wilder*. Metropolitan Books, 2017.

Freitag, Florian. *The Farm Novel in North America: Genre and Nation in the United States, English Canada, and French Canada, 1845–1945*. Camden House, 2013.

Linsenmayer, Penny T. "Kansas Settlers on the Osage Diminished Reserve: A Study of Laura Ingalls Wilder's *Little House on the Prairie*." *Kansas History* (Autumn 2001): 168–85.

Meyer, Roy Willard. *The Middle Western Farm Novel in the Twentieth Century*. University of Nebraska Press, 1965.

Rio, David, and Øyunn Hestetun. "Introduction: Storying the West in Postfrontier Literature." *European Journal of American Studies*, vol. 6, no. 3 (2011).

www.researchgate.net/publication/273183776_Introduction_Storying_the_West_in_Postfrontier_Literature.

Roosevelt, Theodore. "Special Message." United States, Congress, Senate. *Report of the Country Life Commission, February 9, 1909*. Government Printing Office, 1909, https://www.fca.gov/template-fca/about/Report_of_the_Country_Life_Commission.pdf.

"The West and the New Agriculture." *The Nation*, vol. 97, no. 2516 (18 September 1913): 255. Hathi Trust, https://hdl.handle.net/2027/chi.32142195.

Wilder, Laura Ingalls. *Pioneer Girl: The Annotated Autobiography*, edited by Pamela Smith Hill, South Dakota Historical Society Press, 2014.

Wixson, Douglas. "Book Review: *Whose Names Are Unknown* by Sanora Babb." *Western American Literature*, vol. 40, no. 2 (Summer 2005): 215–17.

———. "Harry Ransom Center's Web Exhibition Explores Work of Novelist Sanora Babb." Harry Ransom Center, www.hrc.utexas.edu/press/releases/2009/sanora-babb-exhibition.html. Accessed 14 September 2020.

———. "Radical by Nature: Sanora Babb and Ecological Disaster on the High Plains, 1900–1940." In *Regionalists on the Left: Radical Voices from the American West*. University of Oklahoma Press, 2013.

CHRISTINE HILL SMITH

10
THE RADICAL VOICE OF SANORA BABB

This essay was inspired by the American radicals of the 1930s, when progressive, anti-racist, anti-fascist writers and artists banded together in loose confederations across the country to improve social justice and employment abuses. Sanora Babb, 1907–2005, was one of these people and used her journalistic and fiction-writing skills for advocacy on many fronts, for many decades. This essay explores the trajectory of Babb's activism and connections to the Communist Party, taking her from an inherited homegrown midwestern socialism to a blazing, ardent communism in her twenties in the 1930s, to a less political and more introspective and literary focus in the 1950s and afterward.

Babb wrote no political theory, but we can glean her ideas from her three novel-memoirs; over seventy short stories and hundreds of poems published in literary "little magazines"; letters; and a small but worthy output of journalism about labor, mining, and migrant farming issues for leftist journals. With the latter, she was in good company, sharing the pages with mid-twentieth century writers such as William Carlos Williams, Theodore Dreiser, John Dos Passos, Upton Sinclair, Richard Wright, Ralph Ellison, Genevieve Taggard, and Ernest Hemingway.

Many factors contributed to Babb's acquiring a progressive, leftwing mindset. As a very young child, her parents allowed her to visit and indeed spend weeks alone with the local Otoe tribe on their reservation near the tiny town of Red Rock, Oklahoma. She played with the Otoe children, slept in the tipis with the families, rode the pinto pony the chief gave her, and participated in their communal lifestyle. Although very young, this unusual experience for a white child in the early twentieth century made a lasting impact on her.

Like the family of Laura Ingalls Wilder, Babb's family struggled to get by on various frontiers of the American West. Her father's small bakery failed in Red Rock when Sanora was seven, after which he quixotically moved the family to the dry eastern plains of Colorado to farm broomcorn sorghum. Babb's memoir, *An Owl on Every Post* (1970), tells the sometimes beautiful, sometimes desperate story of their five-year fight with the land—once going for seven days without food. Many of her proletarian short stories set in the dry Midwest depict the helplessness of individuals against bad weather, starvation, isolation, and the fragile class system rife in rural areas. In her more radical journalism and stories from the '30s, she explicitly depicts workers' getting together to fight for rights and better conditions and wages. When Babb taught at a one-room schoolhouse in western Kansas after college, she describes the experience as "quite a proletarian occupation," what with having to walk to work through blizzards, carry coal, and build fires, all the time boarding in a half room with an indifferent family ("Typescript Note on Teaching School"). All this instilled in her a great empathy in later life for the poor and outcast. If she later saw Pare Lorentz's dark documentary "The Plow That Broke the Plains" in the mid-1930s, she would have agreed with his populist and environmentalist analysis of the Dust Bowl, since she knew firsthand about conditions of American deprivation in general and climate disaster in the Dust Bowl states specifically.

Babb came by her progressive politics honestly, first from her freethinking father and also from her grandfather, "Konkie," with whom the family lived in a tiny dugout on the Colorado prairie. Babb's grandfather took the *Appeal to Reason*, a weekly socialist newspaper out of Kansas. The early twentieth century saw plenty of socialist publications and elected officials in the Midwest; thus Konkie's politics were not unusual. By the early 1910s, over a thousand card-carrying socialists held office around the country, including mayors of industrial worker cities like Butte, Montana, and Flint, Michigan (Woods 6). The Industrial Workers of the World and the Communist Party of the United States attracted middle-class immigrants and other Americans due to its pro-labor and anti-imperialist work (Woods 8).

That the Babb family held socialist and incidentally agnostic ideas was not at all uncommon for that era. As Evelyn Funda has shown in relation to views depicted in Willa Cather's 1918 *My Ántonia*, nonmainstream political and indeed anti-religious sentiment were the norms in some immigrant and ethnic groups in the Midwest and were associated with ideas of American nationhood and liberty (Funda 9, Ramirez-Rosa). Babb's grandfather apparently used to take her father Walter to Socialist meetings as a boy, though later, young Walter eschewed groups, insisting that he was a "free man" (*Owl* 175). Sanora inherited that independent streak, which, coupled with a nascent feminism, prompted her to drift away from the Communist Party in the late 1940s. After that, she refused to conform to male-dominated party politics and focused instead on her memoir and creative writing as more satisfying than polemic journalism and stories.

Babb started working at the local newspaper in Forgan, Kansas at aged twelve as a printer's devil, progressed to being a reporter, and became accredited with and filed stories for the Associated Press. After high school and two years of college, she ran out of money and took a train to Los Angeles at age twenty-two to escape a bad love affair and her narrow world (Joanne Dearcopp, telephone communication). As this was just a few months before the 1929 stock-market crash, she found only unsteady employment in Los Angeles and was poor for many years afterward (interview with Danny Mann). Doing site visits and research on articles for leftwing magazines during that period, she saw firsthand how carelessly the rich capitalist owners of film studios, factories, mines, and farm conglomerates treated the working poor. She notes, "In the early 30s I was in and out of jobs, sometimes without a room or apartment (5 of us slept in a park once for a week), so I was personally aware of the Depression, and attracted to the subject of people in desperate straits. That was the real life then, on a larger scale" (letter to Wixson 18 September 1983). She notes to a female friend that she does not mind being alone or doing with less because, "I learned so early how to live with the harshest realities" ("Three Page Letter").

In LA, Babb worked at day jobs writing copy for the Warner Brothers radio station KFWB and doing other short-term office and journalistic work. She says, "Of course, I soon became aware of and interested in and active in the

Left. . . . Those were rich, good years and I have no regrets" (letter to Wixson 18 September 1983). Revolutionary poets Ralph and Lucia Trent made her aware of political issues (interview with Wald). Although Sanora went to meetings of the John Reed Club in LA, she was "never active," but she did join the Communist Party in 1938 (letter to Wixson 1996).

With other compassionate observers in the 1930s, Babb took the Great Depression as proof of the fatal failure of capitalism. Babbs was not alone, and she found herself part of an international, Depression-era community of writers and activists who wrote about and organized for progressive, socially conscious causes. Her close friends included writers Carlos Bulosan and William Saroyan, communist organizer John Howard ("Jack") Lawson, feminist and union activist Tillie Lerner (later Olsen), and, later, science fiction writer Ray Bradbury. She became friends with Jack Conroy, novelist, folklorist, and editor of *The Anvil* and defended him and others against being dismissed as "proletarian hacks" (letter to Alan M. Wald). She explains how dire conditions were in the factories and mines; these were times "when workers' pay and conditions were inhuman. Men were hanged for acting [striking] for an 8-hour day. Strikes were one-sided wars: electrified fences, hired goons, incredible brutality" (letter to Alan M. Wald). She details the genesis of worker-writers like herself: "Many young writers, especially the Depression generation . . . had our education interrupted or stopped; we became self-educated from love of books; we were wandering all over the USA looking for any little job for survival" (letter to Alan Wald). They became part of the so-called Popular Front, the burst of American leftwing creative output between 1935 and 1939, when World War II started (Denning). This "coalition of Communists and liberals against the threat of fascism" had different emphases and meanings depending on the situation and era (Balthaser 254, n. 8). Babb was involved in many capacities during these activist times.

A large part of leftists' attraction to communism in the mid-1930s grew out of a fear of the fascist movements' gathering momentum in the United States and abroad, particularly in Spain and Germany (Folsom). Anti-fascism was not mainstream in the mid-1930s, though it seems to us now that it would be. The Hollywood studios were careful not to make films too anti-fascist since many American business interests, including the studios, were still cozy with Germany (Harmetz 67). Babb worked for the Anti-Nazi League and founded the Spanish Aid Committee in Los Angeles (interview with Wald), both of which raised funds to get refugee writers out of Germany and Europe and to send money and clothes for the Republican volunteer brigade against fascist

Generalissimo Francisco Franco. The leftists condemned fascism while praising Soviet nation building and were of course dismayed and brought up short by the German-Soviet Nonaggression Pact of 1939. As Alan M. Wald explains, American communists emerged from our democratic soil but then morphed and split over the years: "Simply put, being a Communist is very complicated and the meaning changes over time" (email correspondence).

Babb was in the thick of it for some years. The rhetoric in her journalism in the mid-1930s is full of communist jargon—disdain for "the reactionaries" and a "decadent minority" running the country into the ground, sympathy for "the oppressed," and praise for organizations run on "a cooperative basis" and financed "cooperatively" ("The Los Angeles" 22). Writing about a brutal putdown of a strike by Latinx miners in Gallup, New Mexico, in 1935, she explains that she and her associates had to slink into the mining camp after dark to avoid harassment by the mine owners' security people, "the company-hired terrorists" (3). In an unpublished article titled "Extras," Babb details the poor wages and uncertain job prospects of extras in Hollywood movies but notes that now that they are unionized, the studios cannot abuse them as much: "Actors are waking up to the fact that they are *workers* and will have to organize . . . To what degree of militancy they [the actors] have made up their minds is yet to be seen. It is at any rate a hopeful sign that they have come out of their individual comas and recognize the need for mass protest and mass action" ("Extras" 7, 8). Collective communistic defiance seems to her the only way to force the studios to treat people with respect.

Babb never stopped writing short stories during her journalistic decades. Many were published in the leading leftist and literary magazines of the day, including *The Anvil*, the *Daily Worker*, *New Masses* (1926–1948), *Mainstream*, *Black and White*, *The Clipper*, and *California Quarterly*. Her subject matter ranges from impoverished piecework girls to starved-out farmers, from random old men on the street to stolid, working-class midwesterners. All have seen better days and feel frustrated by their fate but are not usually revolutionary toward the system. In fact, they are often politically unaware or unsophisticated, even if made miserable by the failures of capitalism. Babb lets readers fill in the blanks, to realize that similar goals and solidarity among workers is sometimes all they have against the bosses.

This awakening comes to the white migrant farmer Milt in Babb's Dust Bowl novel *Whose Names Are Unknown* (2004), where his knee-jerk racism against Filipinos and Mexican workers evaporates when he see the necessity of a unified front against the greedy farm owners. Erin Royston Battat calls such moments in leftist novels of the era "conversion to class consciousness," noting that authors often "used migration and interracial exchange to set up" characters' transformations (4). Benjamin Balthaser claims that often there were some local attempts by communists to connect poor whites in the California camps with the political goals of the Spanish-speaking workers. Babb presents scenarios in which this cross-cultural affiliation might inform the downtrodden and get them to unite against the considerable repressive forces against them, even though this was not usually the case historically (Manzella 71).

Worker solidarity is a common theme in Babb stories, sometimes combined with depictions of the excesses of Depression-era fat cats. In an unnamed story fragment from the 1930s, young Lynn starts at a temporary job where convivial young women work at tables in a shabby room signing a man's name on invitations to a fancy gentlemen's club ("Short Story Fragment"). We hear that "the recipients of the carefully worded message, would know they would find [at the club] all kinds of gambling, drinks and obliging 'hostesses'" ("Short Story Fragment").

Hapless Lynn feels alienated from this mindless work but continues working because she is desperate for a job. Later in the story, when the club has been shut down after a government raid, the young women wonder if their jobs will continue. One single mother comments that she hopes she will still be able to buy her six-year old an outfit. The narrator describes the moment: "Suddenly in Lynn there is a warmth and understanding, something more than pity. Something angry, without sentimentality" ("Short Story Fragment"). A worker connection has been made where Lynn's lone deprivation and misery is put in context by that of her fellows and their deeper need.

The mid-1930s were years of hope if also of violence for workers, as 1934 strikes by San Francisco longshoremen, Minneapolis's teamsters, and auto workers in Toledo were successful (Denning xiv). September 1934 saw four hundred thousand workers walk off the job in a huge national textile strike (Denning xiv). The country seemed poised to improve the plight of lower-level workers. The next year, Babb drove from LA to New York City with two writer colleagues, Tillie Lerner (later Olsen) and Olsen's boyfriend Harry Carlisle, to the first American Writers' League Congress. This Communist Party–sponsored conference was organized to encourage writers to use their energies in the causes of justice and social change. Franklin Folsom, longtime executive secretary to the league, describes the optimism and fervor of leftwing writers coming together at League congresses to learn best practices and get inspiration from their often lonely activist work. Major American and British writers attended these congresses, including Theodore Dreiser, Dashiell Hammett, Lillian Hellman, Langston Hughes, Ernest Hemingway, Upton Sinclair, Dorothy Parker, John Steinbeck, and William Carlos Williams (Folsom).

The leftists in that era were notorious for their fragmentation along doctrinal lines, and the East/West divide between California and New York was pronounced (Wald "The End"). While all American communists supported antifascist and anti-racist work, the East was more connected to Soviet communist theory and orthodoxy, while the West was more independent and practical, going out to aid strikes and refugees. Babb notes that Hollywood fundraising surpassed that in the East, so New York could not feel entirely superior in their ideological purity (interview with Wald). She expressed disdain for the "New York Intellectuals & *Partisan Review*," preferring homegrown Western cultures (interview with Wald). The seeds of Babb's rejecting communism actually emerged at the conference. She explains, "That trip that began so happily did not end so. . . . [at the Congress] I was [considered] a 'mere radical, an individualist' and was rather too often scorned for not being a Marxist" (letter to Wixson 18 September 1983).

In 1936, Babb took a trip to the USSR with left-wing *New Theatre* editor Herbert Kline and a few fellow Angelino drama and literary types. She observed Soviet collectivization and took away enthusiasm for this new idealistic experiment in communality and equality, particularly in relation to women's rights. Apparently the Soviet Union was full of idealism and hope for the future at that time, even though ten to fifteen million peasants and others had starved in Stalin's early 1930s agricultural collectivization, and his Moscow "show trials" of 1936–38 were just beginning while Babb was there (Keller). As evidenced from Babb's letters directly after her visit to the USSR, she knew that the trials were ongoing but neither their full import nor the devastation of the kulaks was clear to her. We don't know what Babb knew and when she knew it. Now we know that during 1936–38, over one and a half million people were arrested for anti-Soviet activities, and about a million were executed (Keller).

Babb was certainly blinded by her belief in and enthusiasm for communist ideals as she saw them lived out in the USSR, but we cannot deny what she saw with her own eyes. We have to respect that in her several-month trip, not all she experienced could have been orchestrated by officials eager to have Westerners on board with their agenda. In letters from London in September 1936 to her sister Dorothy and cousin Lillie directly after returning from the USSR, Babb explains that she and her small group were allowed to go all over unaccompanied. She writes excitedly about happy, marching, singing Red Army soldiers, the model kindergartens, the collective farms functioning well, so we have to acknowledge that despite Stalin's murderous excesses, some Soviet efforts and citizens were honestly building a new society of trust into a new kind of future. In her September letter she effuses, "I am so filled with enthusiasm for the whole country" and "Coming from Russia made us all wish we were going home to Soviet America, instead of the long struggle to make it come true there" (26 September 1936, 4, 5).

Others visited the Soviet Union in that decade and also found it congenial. Langston Hughes went to observe how the dominant ethnicity treated people of color, noting that Turkmenistan [in the mid-1930s] was less "a primitive land moving into the twentieth century [than] a *colored* land moving into the orbits hitherto reserved for whites" (quoted in Balthser 92, emphasis in the original). The revered longtime *New York Times* Moscow bureau chief Walter Duranty defended Stalin until the end, even denying the liquidation of the kulaks and subsequent severe famine in the early 1930s (Applebaum). Henry Sigerist, a Swiss medical historian, professor at Leipzig, emigrated to the US but visited the Soviet Union in 1935 and saw a model freezer-cutting tool plant in Moscow with good ventilation and lights, live martial music on the loudspeaker, and thousands of workers productive and happy. He praised what he saw: "You come to realize what work can be, and what it must eventually become everywhere if there is to be a real civilization" (Sigerist 1937, 156, in Bynum).

So Babb felt confident in her happy views of the USSR. A typescript manuscript from 1936 after she returned from the Soviet Union, titled "There Are No Fences in Russia: Collective Farm," celebrates what she saw there, starting with her assertion that all over the Ukraine, "there are no fences in Russia to divide one man from another." She details a successful collective farm where she stayed for several weeks recuperating from appendicitis, with its varied crops and animals and good pay, perks, and educational opportunities for the farmers-workers. She insists that "the relationship of these people is intimate, neighborly, something possibly requiring a new name, the old ones having been so much abused, for a new and healthy kind of relationship" ("There Are No" 3). In another piece, Babb extols the optimism and forward-looking spirit of Soviet Russia; she glows that once in the USSR, she is "looking at the idea of socialism functioning, not as a dream in the minds of men but as a fact in a real, not imaginary, country" ("Dr. Fera" 23).

"Dr. Fera of Moscow" is a striking profile of a Soviet female surgeon, written in 1937 but published in the *Clipper* in 1941. As of 1945, we know that besides eighty thousand doctors, 75 percent of whom were women, thousands of both sexes were trained in the USSR to be *feldshers*, "field barbers," doctors' assistants (Scott 3). Babb went to a Moscow hospital to be treated for appendicitis, where she met Dr. Fera, head surgeon. The two women traded stories. Fera had been born a poor country girl, had run away from home, and had become a prostitute. After the 1917 revolution, she and others were gathered up and sent to a rehabilitation home, a *prophylactoria* (Bynum et al. 363). There she was cured of her venereal diseases, and after it became clear that she had a talent for medicine was sent to medical school. Fera was grateful that she had a new, fulfilling life, but she also soon came to believe that it was "her right—to be happy and to serve my people" (24). She tells Sanora, "If my country is left in peace to grow, the whole world will hear us working and singing" (24).

Babb was excited about women's opportunities in the Soviet Union. In *The Clipper* article, she celebrates that women were being treated equally and "were competing equally with men in every field of work. I rode on a train completely run by women. I talked to a 22-year-old woman engineer who was directing a crew of a hundred men in the construction of a bridge" ("Dr. Fera" 23). Farm women had communal daycare for the children so they could become horticulture experts. "It was a good sight that everywhere women had the respect of men as equals" (23).

When Babb returned to the US from London in 1938, local communist leader Jack Lawson asked her why, since she worked so hard for leftwing causes, she hadn't formally joined the Communist Party (letter to Wixson 18 September 1983). So she did. Most Americans in these later years cannot conceive of the Communist Party as realistic in our country, but in the 1930s, it was "a legitimate political party that placed candidates in elections and fostered labor reforms" (Wixson 123). Reflecting back in an interview with Alan Wald when in her early 80s, Sanora notes "a wonderful camaraderie" about the Communist Party. She made sure to point out that, "No one was making bombs to overthrow the government. We were doing all the best things to be done then" (interview with Wald 1989). American communists did not feel disloyal to the United States. They adopted American "icons of popular culture—Hollywood, Mom, the Dodgers, Abe Lincoln" to make their proletarian goals fit into a North American ethos (Rabinowitz 55).

Babb was idealistic and believed a new political order might emerge from the depths of the Depression. In 1938, she "went to the fields" of eastern California, as she termed it. She volunteered for eight months with the Farm Security Administration (FSA) in California helping set up sanitary and self-governing camps for the migrants, many of whom were displaced Dust Bowl farmers. Sanora insisted in later years that she did not do this as a directive from the American Communist Party (CP-USA), but Alan M. Wald and Doug Wixson suspect she did (Babb letter to Richard L. Wentworth, Wald email to Joanne Dearcopp, Wixson *Worker-Writer* 395). Wald notes that "she obviously did it for political reasons planning to write an empathetic, exposé novel. It may have been her friendship with Bulosan, who was connected to the Filipino migrant pickers" (email correspondence). In the camps, Sanora worked directly under but also independently from the rarely sleeping, indefatigable Tom Collins, head of the FSA, a federal agency founded in 1937 that was an enlargement of President Roosevelt's New Deal program for the rural poor, the Resettlement Administration. This enhanced agency was only funded after American-born white farmers fled the Dust Bowl devastation in the Midwest for California and ended up destitute. The similar plights and decades of horrendous working conditions by the traditional farmworkers, Mexican and Filipino men, had not prompted Washington to action. But media pieces by John Steinbeck and others and images taken by FSA photographers, such as Dorothea Lange and Walker Evans, of starving Anglo farming families, the descendants of pioneers, finally lit a fire under Congress in 1937.

Babb was appalled by the primitive conditions in the grower camps, the starvation wages, and the prejudice of California locals to these fellow Americans down on their luck through no fault of their own. It turned her rabid for union organizing and collective action. Her short stories, letters, and notes are filled with anger at the cruel and indifferent powers that be. Her passionate feelings comes through in her ca. 1939 grant proposal for a Guggenheim Fellowship that reveals Babb's views of the deep flaws in capitalist society. She noted that "all people suffer alike in varying degrees from the sickness of a time when civilization is threatened with its own decay." She continues, "As in other periods of darkening history, there remains or newly grows the healthy, hopeful nucleus of society in which the future is germinating. . . . I want to write books about these people in the various phases of their own personal history, expressing them as truthfully as I am capable of doing" (*Guggenheim* p. 2). She did not get the grant but continued to write about the dire conditions around her.

Through her life and her writing, Sanora Babb exhibited an openness to the intrinsic value of others' ideas and a belief in racial equality. This is a point of distinction between *Grapes of Wrath* and her Dust Bowl novel, *Whose Names Are Unknown*, in which she is more colorblind and inclusive of immigrant farmers than Steinbeck. The white Okies in *Whose Names* come to understand their solidarity with the earlier migrants of color in the squalid picking fields in ways that Steinbeck's farmers do not.

Babb was a "fellow traveler" and then a card-carrying Communist for just over two decades, 1929–52. Stalin's crimes were not exposed until 1956, but Babb had become disillusioned earlier. In a 1946 letter, she still calls herself a Marxist, but sometime in 1952, she rejected party conformity and control (letter to Albert Maltz 3). She was friends with Albert Maltz, who was heavily censured in 1946 by his fellow communists for daring to write in *New Masses* that communists valued ideological purity over artistic merit in the arts (Maltz "What Shall"). His humiliation damaged her belief in communist workings in the United States (Wald, email correspondence). On top of that, in 1946, Soviet leaders criticized American communists for their wayward tendencies, which put a crimp in Americans' independence from the USSR. (Wald, *The New York Intellectuals*, "100 Years").

Nevertheless, Babb is still radical and fiery in 1947. In that year, she wrote a review of sociologist Ruth D. Tuck's *Not with the Fist*, an exposé of racism against Mexican-Americans, who unlike African Americans and Asian Americans were free of laws explicitly limiting their integration with mainstream American society (*New Masses* 11 February 1947). Surprisingly, Babb's typescript manuscript is much more radical and critical of the causal and structural racism in US society than the shorter review published in *New Masses*. For some reason, perhaps merely space, the editors cut much of her leftwing verbiage, such as "We have practiced caste thinking against the immigrant stereotype from the Irish, through the colored races, to the Okie" (Typescript of Review, p. 2). In the manuscript, Babb excoriates the history of segregation in housing and unions in the United States and addresses the CIO's and AFL's support (or not) of social justice progress during World War II (Typescript of Review, p. 2).

Babb's drift from party activism was accelerated by her year-long self-exile from the US in 1949 so that her husband, cinematographer James Wong Howe, would not be blacklisted in Hollywood. Relocating to Mexico City, and by all accounts thriving there, Babb became friends with leftwing writers and other artists, such as the mysterious anarchist B. Traven, the dancer Waldeen, translator Asa Zatz, and other intellectuals. She continued to write about the downtrodden, this time in Mexico, though she also began her second novel about her teenage years, *The Lost Traveler* (interview with Wald). While in Mexico, she edited the *California Quarterly* (Steiner 124), a literary magazine that had started out communist but later jettisoned rigid ideology (letter to Douglas Wixson 1996). It was good that Babb left the United States, since we now know that she was mentioned as a communist (as "Sonora Babb") in a 1952 House Un-American Activities Committee meeting, ratted out by a hapless musician named George Bassman who had attended only a few Communist Party meetings in 1938 (*Communist Infiltration*, 2366, 2369).

Babb's commitment to her writing and to intellectual freedom motivated her to move away from the CP-USA. Once back from her Red Scare exile in Mexico City in the early 1950s, she dutifully submitted an early draft of *The Lost Traveler* to the local CP in L.A. This was by no means mandatory for party members, but she must have felt obliged to do so. She was told by her friend, hardliner Jack Lawson, "you write like an angel" but "put the book in a drawer" because "it isn't in the mainstream and doesn't have any social consciousness" (interview with Wald). This purity stance by the CP-USA was part of a longtime ideological position that a good communist's writing or creative endeavor should educate the audience about class inequities rather than probe personal circumstances or psychology (Maltz).

Ignoring Lawson's paternal dismissal, nevertheless she persisted with the novel; *The Lost Traveler* was published in 1958. Babb noted wryly in a later interview, "And then I got all kinds of letters about feminism and social consciousness" (interview with Wald). Kate Weigand notes that some female American communists in this heyday prepared the groundwork for second wave feminism, to which Babb subscribed in her own, quiet, unsung way. In later years, Babb emphasized her longtime independence from political or communist coercion, asserting that "I was never amenable to authority and dogma and finally rebelled against dogma-interference with my writing" (letter to Wixson 18 September 1983). In her seventies, looking back on her writing career, Babb stated that "I never wrote then or now in any expected, that is politically expected, or to the commercially expected, formula. I write the way I can. And I love doing that" (letter to Wixson 18 September 1983). Babb admitted that it had been "very difficult" to write articles for *New Masses* on the assigned social consciousness themes but that she had dutifully done so (interview with Wald). It may be that the party-line rhetoric of her mid-1930s journalism sounds so strident because it is put on and forced. Babb's strength as a writer was her attention to detail and her sympathy with down-and-out people. She came to understand the larger political aspects of why people were poor or disadvantaged, but her focus still remained on individuals, not ideologies.

Reflecting back in her early eighties, Babb remarks in a 1989 audio interview with Alan Wald, with a little laugh, "We were all taken in" by communism. In a later letter, she states similarly, "I disliked politics, save that I was just naturally a liberal" (letter to Wixson 1996). In that same correspondence, she answers a question about whether politics or the John Reed Club was helpful for her writing:

> Heavens, no. I was and always have been and still am an independent writer. One of the disagreements I always had with the Left was their ideas about writing, and telling one how to write. Same in USSR & China.
>
> It is true I learned a lot in the Left movement about politics, economics, class struggle, history, left philosophy, etc. and wanted to become active and did so.
>
> Michael Gold was not an influence. The only influences on my writing were all the good writers I had read over the years. I don't like narrow slanting. I just want to write about human beings and other animals as truthfully as I can." (letter to Wixson 1996)

Babb was cagy with interviewers later in life about her communist years, so it is difficult to know exactly when her views changed and why. As Wald notes, "Many things that she says here about being independent, no Communist coercion on writing/activities, no dogma, etc., are standard boiler plate that everybody says and learned to say later on. Very few will admit to doing things under social pressure, especially in their art. The reason is that they WANTED to help the movement and believed in its ideas—so it didn't feel like pressure and coercion until they began to doubt the political commitment" (email correspondence). To Douglas Wixson, her potential biographer, she insisted, "We did a lot of good. I could never be ashamed of all that work, although I'm as disillusioned in communism as in all other politics. Power still corrupts, no matter where. I just try to support the most democratic, the most liberal actions" (letter to Wixson 1996).

It is not surprising for Babb to be vague about her prior affiliation with the CP-USA. Since the 1950s McCarthy hearings and Premier Nikita Khrushchev's

1956 revelations about Stalin's genocide in the USSR, the entire discourse in the United States has demonized communism. Michael Denning himself notes that after the Red Scare and "purges" of the 1940s and 1950s in the US, much of the culture and attitudes of those idealistic 1930s have been eradicated (xvi). Wald explains how we can barely comprehend what people thought back then, since records and memories have been so assaulted by anti-communist thinking over the decades ("The End of 'American Trotskyism'").

Babb's legacy is that she was part of the proletarian, worker-writer force in the 1930s and 40s that reflected the changes in American culture from Euro-centric and East Coast–centric to that of the ordinary, western American people and their regional, ethnic, often uneducated, idealistic concerns. Along the way, she became politicized. She wrote about real and imagined disenfranchised people in accurate settings, detailing the indignities and triumphs of lives lived with few resources and little autonomy. She knew firsthand the details and humiliations of poverty from her childhood and coming of age during the Great Depression. I now no longer see Babb as a pleasant regionalist but as a fighter for the underdog against the rulers of the American economic system. Her deft hand at both journalism and fiction, written so many decades ago, reveals the racism, prejudice, and injustice that has constantly been part of this country's political and social history.

WORKS CITED

Primary Sources

Babb, Sanora. "Dr. Fera of Moscow." *The Clipper*, September 1941. Typescript in Sanora Babb Papers, Harry Ransom Center, Austin, Texas (hereinafter, HRC), Box 26.6 s.

———. "Extras." ca. mid-1930s. Typescript with handwritten title. Box 27.6. HRC.

———. *Guggenheim Grant Proposal*. p. 2, no. 3, ca. 1939, typescript. Box 19.5. HRC.

———. "High School Journal," typescript. Box 30.11, HRC.

———. Interview with Alan M. Wald, July 1989. Audio file C3058. HRC.

———. Interview with Danny Mann. 1982, p. 18, Academy of Motion Picture Arts and Sciences Library. Transcript. MS. Box 28.6. HRC.

———. Letter to Alan M. Wald. [Summer 1989]. Box 54.8. HRC.

———. Letter to Albert Maltz. 23 January 1946. Box 37.1. HRC.

———. Letter to Douglas Wixson. 18 September 1983. Box 54.8. HRC.

———. Letter to Douglas Wixson. 1996, p. 7. Box 55.1. HRC.

———. "Lora." *Daily Worker*, July 20, 1935, p. 9. Box 2.7. HRC.

———. "Morning in Imperial Valley." *Kansas Magazine*, 1941 [in Babb's hand, in pencil]. Box 3.1. HRC.

———. "No Lamps Lighted." *The Daily Worker*, 28 April 1936, p. 8 [copy]. Box 4.1. HRC.
———. "Short Story Fragment." Box 30.11. HRC.
———. "The Terror: New Mexico" 1935. Published in the USSR in *Reportage: International Literature*, according to handwritten note by Sanora Babb. Box 5.2. HRC.
———. "There Are No Fences in Russia: Collective Farm" (typescript). Box 30.14. HRC.
———. "Three Page Letter." Box 30.11. HRC.
———. "To the Nazis in Kiev." *The Clipper*, October 1941, pp. 6–7. Box 26.6 s. HRC.
———. "Typescript Note on Teaching School." Box 30.11. HRC.
———. Typescript of Review of Ruth D. Tuck, *Not with the Fist: Mexican-Americans in a Southwest City*, Harcourt Brace, 1946. Box 26.6. HRC.
Dearcopp, Joanne. Telephone communication. 2 February 2020.
Wald, Alan. Email correspondence. 19 April 2019.
———. Email correspondence to Joanne Dearcopp. 18 April 2020.

Secondary Sources

Applebaum, Anne. "How Stalin Hid Ukraine's Famine from the World." *Atlantic*, 13 October 2017. www.theatlantic.com/international/archive/2017/10/red-famine-anne-applebaum-ukraine-soviet-union/542610/. Accessed 23 November 2019.
Babb, Sanora. "Dealing with Major Catastrophes." *New Masses*, vol. 31, no. 9 (23 May 1939): 17–18, www.marxists.org/history/usa/pubs/new-masses/1939/v31n09-may-23-1939-NM.pdf. Accessed 17 November 2019.
———. "Farm in Alaska." *New Masses*, vol. 26, no. 2 (9 July 1935): 19–20, www.marxists.org/history/usa/pubs/new-masses/index.htm#start. Accessed 19 October 2019.
———. Review of *Not with the Fist: Mexican-Americans in a Southwest City*, by Ruth D. Tuck, Harcourt Brace, 1946. *New Masses*, 11 February 1947.
———. "The Los Angeles WPA Theatre Project." *New Theatre*, June 1936, pp. 22–23.
———. "Young Boy, the World." *The American Century: An Anthology*, edited by Maxim Lieber, pp. 21–24. PaulList, 1955.
Balthaser, Benjamin. *Anti-imperialist Modernism: Race and Transnational Radical Culture from the Great Depression to the Cold War*. University of Michigan Press, 2016.
Battat, Erin Royston. *Ain't Got No Home: America's Great Migrations and the Making of an Interracial Left*. University of North Carolina Press, 2014.
Bynum, W. F., Anne Hardy, Stephen Jacyna, Christopher Lawrence, and E. M. Tansey. *The Western Medical Tradition: 1800–2000*. Cambridge University Press, 2006.
Communist Infiltration of the Hollywood Motion-Picture Industry—Part 7, Hearings before the Committee on Un-American Activities, House of Representatives.

82nd Congress, 2nd sess., January 24, 28, February 5, March 20, April 10, 20, 1952. United States Government Printing Office, 1952. Internet Archive, https://archive.org/details/communistinfiltro7unit/page/2368 Accessed 21 July 2019.

Denning, Michael. *The Cultural Front: The Laboring of American Culture in the Twentieth Century.* Verso, 1998.

Dijkstra, Bram. *American Expressionism: Art and Social Change 1920–1950.* Abrams, 2003.

Folsom, Franklin. *Days of Anger, Days of Hope: A Memoir of the League of American Writers, 1937–1942.* University of Colorado Press, 1994.

Funda, Evelyn. "*Rekindled Fires* and *My Ántonia:* The Bohemian Immigrant Novels of 1918." *Willa Cather Review*, vol. 61, no. 1 (Summer 2018): 5–15.

Harmetz, Aljean. *Round Up the Usual Suspects: The Making of Casablanca—Bogart, Bergman, and World War II.* Hyperion, 1992.

Keller, Bill. "Major Soviet Paper Says 20 Million Died as Victims of Stalin." *New York Times*, 4 Feb. 1989. www.nytimes.com/1989/02/04/world/major-soviet-paper-says-20-million-died-as-victims-of-stalin.html.

Maltz, Albert. "What Shall We Ask of Writers?" *New Masses*, 12 Feb. 1946, pp. 19–22.

Manzella, Abigail G.H. *Migrating Fictions: Gender, Race, and Citizenship in U.S. Internal Displacements.* Ohio State University Press, 2018.

"Martin Berkeley." *WikiVisually*, 12 November 2019. https://wikivisually.com/wiki/Martin_Berkeley.

Newmark, Julianne. *The Pluralist Imagination from East to West in American Literature.* University of Nebraska Press, 2014.

Post, Charlie. "The Popular Front Didn't Work." *Jacobin*, 17 October 2017. www.jacobinmag.com/2017/10/popular-front-communist-party-democrats.

Rabinowitz, Paula. *Labor & Desire: Women's Revolutionary Fiction in Depression America.* University of North Carolina Press, 1991.

Ramirez-Rosa, Carlos. "Democrats Ignore the Left at Their Peril: Midwesterners Aren't Scared of Socialism—They're Hungry for It." *NBC News*, 9 July 2018, www.nbcnews.com/think/opinion/democrats-ignore-left-their-peril-midwesterners-aren-t-scared-socialism-ncna889741.

Scott, J. A. "Venereal Disease in the Soviet Union." *British Journal of Venereal Diseases*, 1 March 1945, https://sti.bmj.com/content/sextrans/21/1/2.full.pdf. Accessed 14 October 2019.

Wald, Alan M. "100 Years of U.S. Communism." *Against the Current*, January–February 2020, pp. 11–14.

———. *Exiles from a Future Time: The Forging of the Mid-Twentieth-Century Literary Left.* University of North Carolina Press, 2002.

———. "The End of 'American Trotskyism'?: Problems in History and Theory." *Trotskyism in the United States: Historical Essays and Reconsiderations*, edited by George Breitman, Paul Le Blanc, and Alan Wald, 45–52. 2nd ed. Haymarket Books, 2016.

———. *The New York Intellectuals: The Rise and Decline of the Anti-Stalinist Left from the 1930s to the 1980s*. University of North Carolina Press, [1987] 2017.

———. *The Responsibility of Intellectuals: Selected Essays on Marxist Traditions in Cultural Commitment*. Humanities Press, 1992.

Weigand, Kate. *Red Feminism: American Communism and the Making of Women's Liberation*. Johns Hopkins University Press, 2001.

Wixson, Douglas. "Radical by Nature: Sanora Babb and Ecological Disaster on the High Plains, 1990–1940." *Regionalists on the Left: Radical Voices from the American West*, edited by Michael C. Steiner, 111–33. University of Oklahoma Press, 2013.

———. *Worker-Writer in America: Jack Conroy and the Tradition of Midwestern Literary Radicalism*. University of Illinois Press, 1994.

Wood, Gioia, editor. *Left in the West: Literature, Culture, and Progressive Politics in the American West*. Nevada University Press, 2018.

CAROL S. LORANGER

ERRATIC ORBIT
Sanora Babb, Poet

Sanora Babb's career as a poet spanned seventy years. She wrote her first poem, precociously titled "How to Handle a Man," at the age of eleven; at ninety, she published *Told in the Seed*, a slim selection of poems published between 1932 and 1990, along with some new and previously unpublished work.[1] As a young woman Babb did all the things aspiring poets do: entered contests, sought publication in little magazines, and imitated poets she admired. Over the years as her voice emerged and technique grew, she developed a characteristic set of images and poetic subjects and sought publication in increasingly respectable venues. Even as she turned to short fiction in the 1930s and to the longer prose forms of the novel and memoir during the middle part of the century, she continued to write and submit poems for publication regularly, with bursts of new poetic activity after the successful publications of the prose works *The Lost Traveler* (1958) and *An Owl on Every Post* (1970).

Like any poet, Babb ranged among subjects, including love and sex in the abstract, intimate personal and familial relationships, encounters with and observations of the natural world, particularly the California landscape, and, occasionally, current news and politics. Although Alan Wald's observation that Babb "did not see her art as the primary means to fulfill her political commitment" (xi) holds generally true about her poetry as well as her fiction, the Spanish Civil War, that brutal morality play of the twentieth century where socialism and fascism first fought it out on the world stage, and US nuclear testing in the 1950s drew from her two long poems drafted, but never finished.[2] The first, [It is the way the deep lush grass], a strangely prophetic poem about aerial bomb warfare, is dated January 19, 1937, mere months before the German Luftwaffe bombed Guernica on April 26 of that year. But these poems are outliers. Like many of her contemporaries in the left literary scene, Babb could not not write about the Spanish war; ultimately, however, she did not put her thoughts into a final poetic form that satisfied her.

Notes and draft manuscripts in the Sanora Babb papers at the Harry Ransom Center at the University of Texas Austin show Babb drafting individual poems over the course of days and sometimes years, writing notes to herself listing ideas for poems,[3] maintaining clippings files for potential poetry topics,[4] and turning to poetry in times of personal stress.[5] In short, poetry accounts for a substantial part of Babb's lifetime literary production. Clearly, Babb took herself seriously as a poet, and Babb scholarship should as well. To begin, we must trace the development of her craft over the decades she plied it, marking out clear stages and identifying characteristic themes, concerns, and gestures. Babb's poetic work falls into three periods: an early derivative or naïve period, the California middle period of artistic growth and experimentation, and the later, fully developed, mature and individual style. Like the seeds that so fascinated Babb, her earliest poems, however light and inconsequential, burst with potentiality that finds its final form in the mature work.

POET OF PRAIRIES

By the time Sanora Babb was twenty, her fame as a regional poet had spread throughout the prairie states as her collection of clippings from 1927–28 shows. Elmer E. Kelley's Kansas Grass Roots column in the *Topeka Capital* references the growing fame of one Sonora [sic] Babb, "a talented young woman" with "the genius of industry."[6] Similar pieces appeared in the *Garden City Herald*, where she worked as a journalist, the *Elkhart Tri-State News*, *Wichita Eagle*, and *Dodge City Globe*. Another from 1928, "Poet of Prairies," referred to her as "one of the poetic geniuses of the country" (occasioning a scrawl of "! How embarrassing!" on the clipping by Babb). These newspaper pieces occasionally included Babb's portrait or reprinted one of her published or prizewinning poems. The portrait, which accompanied Babb's own regular column in the *Garden City Herald*, "Household Hints and Timely Recipes," shows a slender young woman with short dark curly bob, big eyes looking directly at the viewer, a generous mouth. A white Peter Pan collar atop a dark tucked blouse marks her as a serious young professional woman of the day.[7]

Drafts of individual poems and clippings from this period reveal Babb as intently cultivating her reputation as a poet and alert to opportunities to publish, though not always sophisticated in understanding how those two ambitions might be in conflict. The themes of these early poems are typical for a young poet, whether male or female: navigating love and lovers, questing for an identity of independent modernity, and imagining the voice and experience of one's future self. Her handling of these topics reflects Babb's interest in and admiration for contemporary poets such as Edna St. Vincent Millay and Sara Teasdale, two American women at the height of their careers in the 1920s, whose personal freedom and literary successes surely fired her ambitions.[8] Well into the 1930s, Babb was producing short, personal, lyric poems like theirs, rhymed and metrical, with passion and lost love and love affairs as the predominant subject matter. Like Millay, and to a lesser extent Teasdale, Babb's tone in these is one of wry self-reflection and world wisdom.

Her handling of relationships in these early poems is mostly abstract and formulaic: love, passion, and loss occur in a contextual vacuum, wrapped up with an aphoristic couplet. Her speakers have no actuality outside their bright, impersonal voices and youthful zest. In these early works, Babb rhymes with ease and favors a graceful iambic tetrameter, relying when necessary on an inverted syntax already going out of date in American poetry, which she herself would abandon, along with rhyme, as her confidence grew. "For Future Reference," published in the *Stratford Magazine* in 1928 and anthologized that same year in *The Grub Street Book of Verse*, is characteristic of her early verse:

If I must lie within a grave
Dug from a measured plot of ground,
The customary six by three,

> With tombstones grinning all around,
> Let there be nothing else to crowd
> My body tense for final rest,
> For I have loved above all things
> The tang of mellow dark earth best.
> My dust will take too long to settle
> If I must lie in silk and metal.

Here Babb maintains a steady iambic beat, rhyming every other line for the first eight lines, then closes with a clever and memorable couplet. Despite a bit of padding at the start—two lines spent on the familiar size of a grave, for example, necessitated by the scheme she has set herself—in the final five lines, Babb plays with the tension between opposed states, in this case between rest and restlessness, captivity and growth. The free-spirited speaker of "For Future Reference" can accept interment in the "mellow dark earth" she loves and, as "dust," is part of, but not enclosure in funeral trappings that crowd and separate her from the world. This brief exploration of the opposition between captivity and growth and expressed connection with the natural world, nascent in this clever early verse, will fully develop in Babb's more mature poetic oeuvre.

Another funerary effort of that year, "When I Am Dead," cheerfully instructs the reader to "plant above my fresh heaped grave / Some flowering plant or tree / That I may nourish beauty from / The flesh and dreams of me" (5–8). Here Babb touches on another theme, transformation or potentiality, one that will run through her later work. Other poems published in 1928 celebrated individuality and the freedom of youth, such as "Escape" (which shared a page with sister Dorothy Babb's poem "Unanswered" in *The Prism*) or offered a self-deprecating twist on the familiar trope of the world as a stage, as in the quatrain "Life":

> The past is a story I cannot mend,
> The present, a scene that I know must end,
> The future, the rest of this uncertain play. . . .
> And I have forgotten my lines for today.

The 1920s were a boom time for aspiring poets, with dozens of new little magazines springing up every year. During her Kansas years, Babb placed poems in local and regional little magazines including *Jayhawk*, *The Harp*, and *Will o' the Wisp*, as well as in farther-flung journals including Boston's *Stratford Magazine*, the *Lantern*, *Poet's Scroll*, the *Prism*, and Harrison's *Grubstreet*, which reprinted her *Prism* poem "I Wish I Could Remember" ("Wins Prize"). The widening range of these little magazines indicates young Babb's ambition as well as her affinity for left and iconoclastic literary presses. As Cary Nelson has observed, even from the hinterlands of western Kansas, one could, "via the Postal Service, receive some of the dozens of new or newly radicalized magazines . . . of the times" (147). And Babb did find them, publishing regionally in the "socially committed" little magazine the *Northern Light*, out of Minnesota, one of a few literary journals that "helped break the isolation of a new generation of literary radicals west of the Hudson, who were widely separated geographically" (Wixson 119–20). Nationally, she placed poems in new New York City–based journals *Contemporary Poetry* and *JAPM* (*Just Another Poetry Magazine*), both published by progressive Catholic poet and publisher Benjamin Musser, who had himself been published in the *Northern Light*.

Babb's poems in these left literary magazines were not political, nor even especially socially conscious, but acceptance by these journals helped her define the sort of connections she needed in order to network to more publications and to widen her circle of young fellow progressives. Like many a young poet before and after, Babb did not always differentiate between legitimate (if short-lived and obscure) journals and vanity publishers, such as Henry Harrison, inclusion in whose anthologies required poets to sell a certain quantity provided to them at half price (Freed) and whose prizes, economically, consisted of volumes of his other publications ("Wins Prize"). Harrison, though, did also possess a left pedigree, having published the *Sacco-Vanzetti Anthology of Verse* anthology pamphlet in 1927 (Nelson 143).

Though the majority of Babb's early poems feature a first-person speaker, they shy away from the autobiographical specificity found in her later work. A notable exception is "Divorce," an unpublished poem bearing the handwritten notation "About Mama & Papa." Using a rare naturalistic image, Babb depicts the impact of divorce on the entire family, which, like a worm, may suffer when divided but grows each part singly whole again: "Sufficient as each severed piece of worms / That lies on the wet walk after rain" (4–5). In general, though, the poems of the Kansas years are not grounded in a closely observed natural world and tend to employ a bright, impersonal voice when handling intimate matters.

A HOLLYWOOD ADDRESS

The move to Los Angeles in 1929 had an explosive impact on Babb's poetry. She began to write more explicitly and personally on matters of love and sexuality, dropped the bright tone of the eager young poetess, and reduced the quantity of breathless ellipses that punctuated her earliest poems. Poem manuscripts that previously had been signed or initialed and dated now began to include her address; at first simply "Hollywood," then her street and city when she gained a fixed address. The California poems increasingly drew on specific locales, incorporating naturalistic details. Babb's deepening interest in the natural world as worthy subject for poetry can be seen in poems where nature is not simply emblematic of inner states, though nature continues to serve that purpose for a while. By the 1940s and '50s, the natural world itself becomes the subject, not just the setting, of poems, and Babb's specific history begins to be a subject of poetic exploration. The poems from the Kansas years could have been written anywhere about any place, but having left the Midwest, Babb soon found herself comparing the prairies to the golden state of California. In several valedictory poems from 1929–30, the former midwesterner looks back at prairie grasses with new eyes or considers the differences between the quality of rain in Kansas and California. Babb crows in "Conquest," shortly after her arrival in California "I, of the prairies, have conquered a mountain" (1). Her manuscript of the poem is dated "September First 1929," which was soon after her August arrival, and includes the first of her California datelines: "Mt. Lowe California."[9] In "Conquest," the speaker stands on that iconic spot, on the "breast of a sage mountain" (5), taking in the panoramic view of the city she would make her own for the rest of her life. At the poem's close she vows to "fling this wild song [and] have no fears" (8).

Written at roughly the same time, "Kansas Prairie" ruminates on the impact of landscape on the self. This short poem begins with the speaker's geographic biography: she has lived all over: "where the hills rolled the skyline / Too close to the edge of the town" and "where the tall steel man-made towers / Cut the horizon" (1–3), but longs for a third terrain, one with a horizon as open as her spirit, which hungers "for miles of clear view / Instead of mountains that I hoped to see through—/ A tan grass prairie, a Kansas plain" stretching "To the end of the sky, unmarked with trees" (5–7, 10). "The Restive Plains," from June 1930, offers a stunning word painting of a prairie sky "where violent clouds lie down / and lightning reaches fiery arms" (10–11). Another, from six months later, employs Imagist technique, a new development in Babb's style.[10] It is spare and economical and, notably, unrhymed. The focus is visual and external, scenic and distant rather than interior and relational: in the California winter rain "Outlines are sharp / Against the fog" ([Today] 2–3). The fog brings with it an air of unreality: far off houses look like toys on "a card board hill" (6). The final image hearkens visually to Pound's "In a Station of the Metro," even to the final three stressed syllables:

> tall eucalyptus trees
> along the slopes
> fringe their peaks
> like paper cut-outs
> pasted on
> a wet mauve sky (7–12)

On the typescript for this poem Babb has carefully circled the plosive consonants of *peaks-paper-pasted*, suggesting that in moving away from the security of rhymed, metrical verse, she is considering how other devices, in this case consonance, can unify a poem.

Babb swiftly found a California market for her poems, publishing regularly in local journals *Rob Wagner's Script* and the *Hollywood Talk of the Town*, as well as in little magazines nationwide from Boston to Washington, DC, and the greater Midwest, including the *Lantern*, *Visions*, and *Contemporary Vision* (formerly S*cepter*), several of which, like *Contemporary Vision*, leaned left. By 1932, she had written and published the earliest of the poems she would include in *Told in the Seed*, "Captive." Babb notes on a typescript that the poem appeared in *The Harp* in 1931 and was included in the spring 1932 anthology from Mitre Press. These Spring Anthologies, published 1930–45 and 1960–73, promised "Representative Poems of the World's Living Poets." Like Henry Harrison's anthologies, this "well-meaning but unambitious series" cast a wide net (*British* 47). Nevertheless, "Captive" is an accomplished poem, deserving of its gold medal from Mitre Press. In the familiar mode of youth imagining itself to be old, "Captive" is not the first of Babb's forays into that territory. In sixteen irregularly rhymed lines, Babb's elderly speaker laments that spring has left her and that lusty young people assume wrongly that she is unmoved by "soft nights," lovers' gay laughter, and "the courage of a fledgling taking wing" (5). But the speaker is not unmoved, merely held captive in her aged body. Affected by "the scent of spring and footsteps on the grass," she sends "my venturing soul far in the night" while she sits "at dusk alone and still" (10–16). That Babb included this youthful imagining of old age in *Told in the Seed*, published in her ninety-first year, suggests that she felt it well captured her state of mind as she entered her tenth decade.

Another notable publication of the 1930s is "Essence," the first of her poems to appear in *Prairie Schooner*. An unrhymed free verse poem of twenty-four short lines broken into four irregular verse-paragraphs, "Essence" employs its repeated metaphor "I am a wind" to advance its theme of potentiality. The wind blows "over flowers / That are yet to spring" (4–5). It is "fragrant with swollen seeds [and] the breath / Of things unborn" (9–12). While "Essence" was not included in *Told in the Seed*, it offers another early example of her interest in seeds as metaphors for potential or visual emblems of transformation.

From 1936 until well into the 1940s, Babb's travels, growing relationship with James Wong Howe, work with Tom Collins in the Farm Security Administration migrant camps, stints as a labor organizer and as chapter secretary of League of American Writers, and various other affairs appear to have pulled her attention away from poetry, with the result that there are few poems in manuscript or print for this period. Babb spent much of 1938 and 39 on her first novel, *Whose Names Are Unknown*, and was also busy writing and publishing short fiction and working "tirelessly on behalf of the Spanish Republic and the Anti-Nazi League" (Wald ix). Thus, the unfinished poem on aerial bombing from the Spanish Civil War is an important document of her political thought at the end of her first decade in California.

MEMORY'S DOOR

The 1950s saw a burst of new poetry production and another period of growth in craft and subject matter. As Babb sifted through family history for the writing of *The Lost Traveler*, she wrote more autobiographical poetry, drawing on events that would make their way into that novel and into *An Owl on Every Post*. As a result, people who appear in the poems begin to have pasts and, often, recognizable identities; they are no longer the generic "young boys" and "old women" or disembodied lovers of the early poems. In the fifties, too, Babb became more selective in seeking publication, placing poems in established national and university-supported literary journals. Several poems that would be collected in *Told in the Seed* were written and published in the 1950s, among them "Bird of Night" and "I Ride a Runaway Horse," in the *University of Kansas City Review* in 1955; "Why Does the Dog Howl on the Midnight Hill?" and "I Ride a Runaway Horse" (retitled as "Allegro Con Fuoco") in Canada's *Dalhousie Review*; and "Old Snapshots" in *Prairie Schooner*.[11] In the 1950s, she moved almost entirely to a limber, unrhymed form that allowed her to mix naturalistic detail with reflexive commentary within poems of varying line lengths, often built on stacked or run-on phrases, creating an air both measured and conversational.

Both "Allegro Con Fuoco" and the unpublished "My Lost Name" recount Babb's childhood friendship with Oklahoma Otoe leader Black Hawk and his gift of a half-wild pinto pony, offering an early glimpse of the story she would later recount in *An Owl on Every Post*. A short poem of just thirteen lines, "Allegro Con Fuoco" is divided into two uneven verses comprising three sentences.[12] In *Owl* and in "My Lost Name," the focus is on how "Little Cheyenne Riding Like the Wind" earned her Indian name. In "Allegro Con Fuoco," though, the focus is on the physical sensation of wild freedom engendered by the ride—the commingling of horse and rider into one being composed almost entirely of energy and memory. The pounding hooves, flying mane, and flattened ears of lines 2–4 are distinctively equine, but line 4's "eyes fire" removes the distinction between horse and rider—both have fiery eyes, wild hearts, and quivering thighs. From the third through the eighth lines, the focus travels backward from the horse's mane to its tail "streaking air / Like a broken star" (7–8). Point of view in the second verse-paragraph moves from singular "I" to the plural "we"—the conjoining now complete as horse and rider "flash" as pure energy. At poem's end, the focus lingers on the residue left by time: the dust of horse and rider's passing and the trace of this wild ride retained in the speaker's memory. Babb's decision to change the poem's title from the circumstantial "I Ride a Runaway Horse" to the musical directive, literally "briskly, with fire," links this wild ride with Dvořák's *New World Symphony*, with its evocation of Native American musical themes, underscoring Babb's lifelong affinity for Native Americans.

The autobiographical sequence "Old Snapshots," written during early 1965, consists of one poem for each member of the Babb family, with a fifth for "Bakeshop the town's tramp dog."[13] *Prairie Schooner* published the snapshots of Sanora, Dorothy, and Walter in its Winter 1964–65 issue; Babb restored the Jennie snapshot to the grouping for *Told in the Seed*. The poems are set in a closely described Oklahoma Panhandle town during the immediate post–Great War years. The snapshot conceit allows for a leisurely observation of each family member in an informal and thus "true" representation—these are snapshots after all, not formal portraits. In each poem, the subject is captured in a characteristic moment, revelatory of self, whether as the hero of a town ball game or involved in imaginative play. Here, too, as in "My Lost Name," photographs open "a door closed on memory" (4).

Although the entire grouping is worth close study, the first poem, featuring young Sanora, is indicative of Babb's increasing move toward naturalistic detail and increasing willingness to write directly about herself in the mature poems, as well as her continuing interest in themes of transformation and potentiality. Captured on film in "a panhandle town in Oklahoma" is the speaker's younger self, standing in front of a dilapidated house. The first six lines quickly sketch the Babb family's poverty and fecklessness—the house paint is worn and peeling, "cut to the board." The clothesline sags. Bakeshop the dog is there as well, panting on this hot day. In the second half of the poem, the adult speaker comments on the hopeful dreams of her younger self—so carefully put together in contrast to the ramshackle house and property, elegant in carefully sewn clothing, self-consciously displaying the fashionable, "thin, graceful walking stick" (9). The power of this girl's dreams temporarily transforms the weedy garden into a Parisian street. But the affectionately dismissive tone of the last line—"Such were the dreams I had!"—effectively undercuts the remembered imaginings of the girl in the snapshot. The exclamation point emphasizes the instability of the girl's transformative plans, as seen from the present day, but does not dismiss her potential to transform, as the speaker is clearly different from her younger self. Whatever she may have become, the speaker reminds us from the vantage point of forty years' distance, it was not a Parisian fashion plate. Still, the poem acknowledges, as do the other three poems in "Old Snapshots," that the desire to transform is powerful and innate, even as the results may be unpredictable. Like teenager Robin Tannehill of *The Lost Traveler*, this Oklahoma girl is a seed not yet having "burst its shell" (273).

TOLD IN THE SEED

The title Babb eventually selected for her poetry collection, from a poem appearing in the *Southern Review* in 1966, foregrounds the classic Babb themes of potentiality and transformation central to many of the poems collected within, including "Aristolochia," "Old Snapshots," "Allegro Con Fuoco," "Giant Sequoia," and the title poem itself.[14] These poems, too, offer a wealth of concretized naturalistic detail in service of their theme. Capturing specific place and time is important as well, from "Santa Cruz" and the Carmel property "Above Malpaso Creek" to a southern California January day on the "34th Parallel" and the innermost moon of Uranus. In the title poem, the speaker sits quietly at her desk on an early spring evening, in touch with the natural world around her: "Tonight I hear the first crickets on the hillside, / A big brown spider sits on my dictionary, / The moon is full, o, moon pulling at my tides" (1–3). Here the linkage between speaker and nature is both sensual and physical; the speaker hears and sees the insect life that exists both within and without the room and feels the pull of the moon on her body. Out of this seeing-hearing-feeling arises an intimacy transcending species; she feels the cold as the bees do. Thus attuned to the earth's cycles and creatures, the speaker understands that completions are coded into origins, a "covenant": "flowers are waiting: they have come up / From their secret seeds, no seed confused in its image / No matter how I mix them" (5–7).

According to Babb, the covenant nature makes is that all potential is contained within the embryonic thing. Thus, the flowers that will eventually grow will be exactly what they will be, not "confused." Things become what they are because they are "persuaded" by the natural elements that surround them to become so—although, as with "Old Snapshots," what they become may surprise us. This is the "secret" told in the seed. The second poem in the volume, "Aristolochia," hammers home the terms of the covenant, which the speaker finds both delightful and alarming: "The seed wears the design of its leaf / Drawn on its shell!" (8–9).[15] And in "Giant Sequoia," the speaker confesses herself "in awe of this small seed / Its perfect design and the design within: / The great sequoia tree sleeping" (1–3). Intimacy with the natural world is not without peril, however. In "Lean Away from the Tree," Babb reminds us that just as seeds contain within themselves the substance of the living things they will become, those living things contain within themselves spirits alien to us: "Trees are unfriendly at night" though they may "comfort you by day" (2–3).

Babb's early funerary poems featured blithe instructions to her readers given from beyond an imagined grave. By contrast, in "At Mama's Grave," drafted within a month of her mother's interment in 1961 and in "The Last Year," "A Circling Wind," "Before Sleep," and "Night Visit," all begun within four months of her husband James Wong Howe's death in 1976, Babb presents death as inevitable transformation from flesh into memory and, potentially, from memory into art and solace for the bereaved.

In "A Circling Wind," a prized artifact reminds the speaker that memory, like art, ensures eternity. Enumerating the busy bejeweled elements of the Chinese screen, she notes, "This screen, a thing of beauty, made by man, / Is not a man and yet you both endure" (17–18). Beings in the world may die or decay, but given time may resolve themselves into new things of beauty and value: "The wood and you who had a name will turn to ash, / Perhaps to jewels some other day"

(19–20). Or the dead simply become part of the natural world: "the sweet round wind, / The you that is you" (22–23). In contrast, Babb chooses an image from nature in "The Last Year," employing an acacia tree as a metaphor for Howe, who

> longed to be with the growing,
> Not the dying, so you lay in the sun
> And the wind where every tree
> Spoke in its way of moving. (19–22)

The tree's double trunk ("two strong trunks / Joined near the earth" (2–3)) does double duty as a figure for a long marriage with its tribulations and infidelities, tenderness and strife:

> our love more eloquent
> Than in the passions of our youth
> That cannot know how deep the roots
> How high old branches range the air
> How beautiful love is full of years. (25–29)

Much of the work in *Told in the Seed* strikes a similarly elegiac note, despite an occasional whirlwind like "Allegro Con Fuoco," as Babb looks back over the experiences and losses of a long life. But the volume closes with a comprehensive and joyous final image descriptive of the poet herself. Inserted late into the manuscript as its closing poem and separated from "Captive," by "Being" (a poem constructed almost entirely of present participles), "Miranda" shows just how far the Captive's "venturing soul" could fly. Babb seems to have followed Voyager 2 news closely, amassing a pile of clippings covering its flyby of the Uranean moon in 1986 and copying out the phrases "chaotic orbit, tumbling lurching erratically" and "cliffs, craters & oddly stacked terraces" on scraps of paper. Both lines appear in the poem. "A free spirit," Miranda whirls

> The opposite of nature's whirls,
> Lurching, tumbling; it's called erratic orbit.
> She even wobbles in fun sometimes,
> That is, for millions of years,
> And wanders on impulse. (5–9)

"Miranda" combines the celebration of impulse and nonconformity that characterized the speaker of Babb's earliest poems with the careful naturalistic detail of her later poems. Miranda's erratic orbit is like the poet's own: "How she escapes celestial rules / Is a mystery not even science can understand" (3–4). This seems as apt an analogy as any for the long poetic career of Sanora Babb.

NOTES

1. "How to Handle a Man," as Babb once told Joanne Dearcopp. J. Dearcopp, February 19, 2020.

2. See the untitled drafts [It is the way the deep, lush grass], and [No gods will rive the earth but man].

3. See, for example, "Notes for a poem taken while walking on our land south of Carmel" and other untitled notes (ca. 1950s).

4. See especially Babb's file of news clippings of the Voyager 2 fly-by of Uranus for her late poem "Miranda," Box 30, Folder 9, HRC.

5. See, for example, untitled note dated 28 February 1950: "I began writing poems as soon as I woke. . . . Last nite [sic] too I read the latest pronouncement of scientists on the hydrogen bomb. I sent Truman a wire and wrote a letter. I put my drop in the murky sea." And, humorously, on marital woes, see "Some Doggerel Lines."

6. Babb has jotted "1928? / 1929?" on the clipping, but internal evidence suggests 1928 as it describes her as still employed by the *Garden City Herald*. Babb was in California in 1929.

7. See, for example, "Poet of the Prairies"; "Wins Prize of Books on Poem"; "Teacher Near Garden City Writes Poetry"; "Miss Sanora Babb Visiting the Tri-State News Family"; and Sanora Babb, "Household Hints and Timely Recipes."

8. Letter to John Crawford.

9. Spelling out the date is also unusual for Babb, who typically used numerals when dating poem manuscripts, and is perhaps indicative of her elation.

10. The manuscript bears four titles: "Southern Rain" is crossed out, as is "Winter Rain"; "Rain" and "Out of Winter" remain as possible titles.

11. "Allegro Con Fuoco" retains this musical title in *Told in the Seed*. See letter of acceptance from W. Graham Allen, editor, *Dalhousie Review*.

12. The new title references the unusual tempo marking of the fourth movement of Dvořák's popular Symphony No. 9 in E minor, also known as the *New World Symphony*.

13. Who appears as Tobey in *The Lost Traveler*.

14. And included later that year in Stevensen, *Best Poems of 1966*.

15. *Aristolochia* is a genus of ornamental plant, both striking and toxic, popular with gardeners in Europe and the United States for its spectacular blooms or use in arbors.

WORKS CITED

Primary Sources

Allen, W. Graham (editor, *The Dalhousie Review*). Letter. 14 March 1956. Box 23, Folder 12. Sanora Babb papers, Harry Ransom Center, University of Texas at Austin, Austin, TX (hereafter, HRC).

Babb, Dorothy. "Bird of Night." *University of Kansas City Review*, vol. 21, no.4, June 1955, 301. Box 82. HRC. Reprinted in *Told in the Seed*, West End Press, 1998, 7.

Babb, Sanora.

———. "Captive." *The Harp: A Poetry Magazine* (n.d.). Box 23, Folder 8 and Box 24, Folder 7. HRC. Reprinted in *The Spring Anthology 1932*. Mitre Press, 1932: 170.

———. "Conquest." Box 23, Folder 10 and Box 24, Folder 6. HRC.

———. "Divorce." Box 76. HRC.

———. "Escape." *The Prism*. 1928. Box 24, Folder 6. HRC.

———. "Essence." *Prairie Schooner*, vol. 7, no. 2 (Spring 1933), 93. Box 79. HRC.

———. "For Future Reference." Box 23, Folder 8 and Box 24, Folder 7. HRC.

———. "I Ride a Runaway Horse." *University of Kansas City Review*, vol. 21, no. 4, June 1955, 269. Box 82. HRC.

———. "I Wish I Could Remember," Box 24, Folder 6. HRC.

———. [It is the way the deep, lush grass]. Box 23, Folder 13. HRC.

———. "Kansas Prairie." Box 23, Folder 13. HRC.

———. Letter to John Crawford. 1 October 1997. Box 18, Folder 4. HRC.

———. "Life." *The Harp: A Poetry Magazine*, vol. 4, no. 3, September–October 1928, 10. Box 75. HRC.

———. "My Lost Name." Box 23, Folder 11. HRC.

———. [No gods will rive the earth but man]. Box 23, Folder 12. HRC.

———. Notes for a poem taken while walking on our land south of Carmel. Box 23, Folder 12. HRC.

———. "Old Snapshots." *Prairie Schooner*, vol. 39, no. 4, Winter 1965–66, 302–3. Box 79. Sanora Babb papers, Harry Ransom Center, University of Texas at Austin.

———. [Today]. Box 24, Folder 7. Sanora Babb papers, Harry Ransom Center, University of Texas at Austin.

———. "Some Doggerel Lines on the Nuptial Maze." February 28, 1957. Box 23, Folder 10. HRC.

———. "Unanswered." *The Prism*. 1928. Box 24, Folder 7. HRC.

———. Untitled note dated 28 February 1950. Box 23, Folder 12. HRC.

———. "When I am Dead." Box 24, Folders 6 and 7. HRC.

Kelley, E. E. "Kansas Grass Roots." *Topeka Capital* (n.d.). Box 58, Folder 8. HRC.

"Poems from Sanora Babb's Pen Appear in Magazines." *Garden City Herald* (n.d.). Box 58, Folder 8. HRC.

"Poet of Prairies." Associated Press (n.d.). Box 58, Folder 8. HRC.

"Teacher Near Garden City Writes Poetry." *Dodge City* (n.d.). Box 58, Folder 8. HRC.

"Wins Prize of Books on Poem: Sanora Babb's Verse Is Best in 'The Prism' Says New York Publisher." n.d. Box 58, Folder 8. HRC.

Secondary Sources

Babb, Sanora. "A Circling Wind." *Told in the Seed*. West End Press, 1998, 28.

———. "Above Malpaso Creek." *Hawaii Review*, vol. 12, no. 2 (Fall 1988). Reprinted in. *Told in the Seed*, pp. 21–22.

———. "Allegro Con Fuoco." *Dalhousie Review* (Spring 1956). Reprinted in *Told in the Seed*, p. 8.
———. *An Owl on Every Post*. Muse Ink Press, 2012.
———. "Aristolochia." *Told in the Seed*, p. 4.
———. "At Mama's Grave." *Told in the Seed*, p. 41.
———. "Before Sleep." *Told in the Seed*, p. 29.
———. "Being." *Told in the Seed*, p. 62.
———. "Giant Sequoia." *Told in the Seed*, p. 19.
———. "Lean Away from the Tree." *Told in the Seed*, p. 5.
———. "Love Song I, II, III." *Told in the Seed*, pp. 50–53.
———. "Miranda." *Told in the Seed*, p. 65.
———. "Night Visit." *Told in the Seed*, p. 30.
———. "The Last Year." *Hawaii Review* no. 21, Spring 1987. Reprinted in *Told in the Seed*, p. 27.
———. *The Lost Traveler*. Muse Ink Press, 2013.
———. *Told in the Seed*. West End Press, 1998.
———. "Told in the Seed." *Southern Review*, vol. 2, no. 1 (January 1966). Reprinted in *Told in the Seed*.
———. *Whose Names Are Unknown*. University of Oklahoma Press, 2006.
———. "Why Does the Dog Howl on the Midnight Hill?" In *Told in the Seed*, p. 6.
British Poetry Magazines 1914–2000: A History and Bibliography of "Little Magazines." Compiled by David Miller and Richard Price. London: British Library, 2006.
Freed, Hannah, and Russell Maloney. "Vanity Publisher." *New Yorker*, 10 July 1937, 9–10.
Nelson, Cary. *Revolutionary Memory: Recovering the Poetry of the American Left*. Routledge, 2001.
Stevenson, Lionel, editor. *Best Poems of 1966: Borestone Mountain Poetry Awards*. Pacific Books, 1967.
Wald. Alan M. "Soft Focus: The Short Fiction of Sanora Babb." In *Cry of the Tinamou: Stories*, by Sanora Babb. University of Nebraska Press, 1994.
Wixson, Douglas. *The Worker-Writer in America: Jack Conroy and the Tradition of Midwestern Literary Radicalism, 1898–1990*. University of Illinois Press, 1994.

JEANETTA CALHOUN MISH AND CULLEN WHISENHUNT

12
TRANSCENDING REGIONAL LITERATURE
Teaching Sanora Babb

The diversity of Sanora Babb's oeuvre, which crosses many genres, may have contributed to her works' not being widely recognized and taught. However, that same characteristic can be a benefit to teaching her works in the classroom, where they fit into a wide variety of courses. Babb's published works are deserving of literary recovery of the kind which feminist scholars and scholars of working-class, Native American, African American, and Latinx literatures have accomplished for authors in their fields. We will provide theoretical context and curriculum units that will facilitate inclusion of Babb's work in college syllabi, thereby introducing her work to future scholars and general readers. Babb's writings can be incorporated into a wide range of courses, such as American regional literature, western American literature, western literature by women, migrant/immigrant literature, great depression literature, the proletarian novel, literature of the environment, Oklahoma literature, and courses on memoir and biographical fiction.

We will contextualize Babb's polyvalent works within four thematic approaches: regional, leftist/working-class, migrant, and environmental/place writing. In the appendix, we include a list of Babb's works assigned to the thematic categories and a link to a Google Drive folder that contains sample course units and writing prompts, extensive lists of companion texts, critical texts, and contextual resources such as historical and cultural texts and multimedia websites. The resources are available at: bit.ly/BabbCompanionTexts.

THE LITERARY WORLDS OF SANORA BABB: REGIONS

> Regionalism was the stinging word used by certain influential New York groups to keep writers outside New York in their places. It was a patronizing putdown, but I don't think any real writers were stopped by it. Just annoyed.
> —Babb in Wixson, *Worker-Writer* 377

In the 1930s, literary regionalism, as Babb notes, was, and had been widely considered less important, less literary, and tending toward nostalgic, if not retrograde, reactionary politics. By contrast, we will treat regionalism positively and celebrate its use by men, women, and American leftists as socially conscious literature.

Generally, there are two opposing viewpoints on regional writing, that it's reactionary or progressive (Steiner). Women's regional writing in particular was "minimized, ignored, and disparaged," by "either relegating [it] to the category of 'local color' or describing [it] as a subset of realism by the phrase "regional realists" (Fetterley and Pryse 4). By the early twentieth-century, male writers based in rural areas began to make inroads in the genre, but the literary elite eschewed them too, considering their writing narrow, provincial, and not conforming to modernist aesthetics. For example, before World War II, Faulkner was called a "fascist" by critics Robert Penn Warren and Maxwell Gardener—his purported fascism was based on his novels' regionalism and the characters in his writings. However, after World War II, critics recuperated Faulkner out of regionalism and happily into modernism. Steinbeck was also a regionalist, but both he and Faulkner were, and are, described as modernists rather than regionalists and defended as such by critics who insist on the universality of their writing. As Edwin M. Yoder wrote in 1997, sometimes "Faulkner's fiction seems to echo the pasteboard conventions of the magnolia-and-moonlight school of fiction, with its stereotyped figures. But Faulkner is too discerning a student of human nature to imagine that origins or labels are useful predictors of human behavior" (n.p.). More recently, critics have returned to twentieth-century regionalism with nuanced examinations that demonstrate how Faulkner, Steinbeck, and other early to mid-twentieth century regionalists, including women like Babb, were accomplished writers whose approach to human nature is both regionalist and universal.

In the 1920s appeared a new regionalism, a national literary and intellectual movement that was decidedly progressive and leftist. It included many western practitioners such as Oklahoma folklorist, poet, and literary critic Benjamin Botkin, who served as editor of the *Folk-Say* anthologies of regional writing; historian Angie Debo; and Cherokee playwright Lynn Riggs.[1] In Oklahoma, new regionalism was a home-grown intellectual movement that corresponded to the radicalism of Oklahoma farmers and workers (see below).[2] We view Babb's *Whose Names Are Unknown* and *An Owl on Every Post* as philosophically aligned with this new regionalism due to its articulation of "the economic situation of ... diverse, unpropertied, underprivileged" whites as well as sympathetic portrayals of African Americans and other people of color and a sensitivity to the ecosystems of the regions (Pryse, "Literary Regionalism" 70).

Moreover, Babb situates *Whose Names* within national cultural and political conversations about leftist politics, race and class, environmental and gender issues, the Great Depression, World War I, migrant movements, and labor unrest. Tom Lutz asserts that regionalist texts like Babb's are cosmopolitan texts in that they "represent both sides of the major debates of their time" (28). Similarly, Ken Hada writes that "Babb, like her fellow Oklahoma writers, is keenly aware of the nonwhite perspective, and her novel [*Whose Names*] reminds readers of the greater world in which her story exists" (76).

THE GREAT PLAINS

Much of Babb's writing, and all of her early works, are set on the Great Plains of Oklahoma, Kansas, and Colorado. Plains literature has been described as representing "psychopathic loneliness, soul-crushing melancholy, stultification of tender sensibilities, physical brutalization of men and spiritual destruction of women," though we could also include the physical brutalization of women (Saum 579). Babb often depicts some glimmer of hope or personal agency that helps her characters rise above the diminished life circumstances they've been dealt. Even when Babb leaves the Great Plains, she remains, literarily speaking, with refugees from the Great Plains (and elsewhere) who live in the seamy cities or migrant worker camps in California. She explores and challenges themes commonly found in Great Plains literature: The myth of the garden and the happy yeoman/agrarian, manifest destiny, and taming the wilderness.

Among the Oklahoma and Great Plains authors we suggest for companion texts are Oklahomans Ralph Ellison, John Joseph Matthews (Osage), and Edwin Lanham. For Great Plains companion texts, we suggest, among other authors, Lawrence Svoboda, Mari Sandoz, and Pulitzer Prize-winner Josephine W. Johnson (Willa Cather is listed in Immigrant Literature).

THE DUST BOWL

The Dust Bowl, while influenced by geography, topography, climate, and culture, is not exactly a region in the same sense that the Great Plains, the Southwest, or the Midwest are. The environmental and human stories of the Dust Bowl and its people brought it into the national consciousness—stories shown in newsreels, printed in national newspapers and magazines, represented in art, photography, music, and literature, announced on the airways, and investigated by teams of government employees. The effects of the Great Depression and the Dust Bowl on the Great Plains are not only directly represented in Babb's work, they also serve to represent the struggles of the people, flora, and fauna surviving in the demanding, often punishing, landscape, endless sky, and unreliable climate.

While some Great Plains literature and much contemporaneous literature of the Dust Bowl are usually categorized as realist, Dust Bowl literature, especially in its leftist incarnation, often approaches naturalism in its focus on socioeconomic and environmental causes for the struggles of working-class and the poor. Dust Bowl literature portrays the disenfranchised fighting to survive a noble but sometimes fruitless effort with a modicum of humanity and a sense of class solidarity. As evidenced by current environmental concerns and the ongoing conversations about the Dust Bowl in Ken Burns's PBS documentary, the study of Dust Bowl literature is essential to understanding how Americans represent and conceptualize region, bioregion, poverty, and government responsibility. Among the writers we suggest for Dust Bowl literature are Oklahomans Caroline Henderson and Woody Guthrie, and Great Plains writers Lois Phillips Hudson and Frederick Manfred.

CALIFORNIA

Babb's writings can also be considered California literature, a huge category too broad to explicate here. *On the Dirty Plate Trail: Remembering the Dust*

Bowl Refugee Camps and part 2 of *Whose Names Are Unknown* are certainly "California literature," as are several of the short stories in *Cry of the Tinamou*. Babb's poetry, too, as gathered in *Told in the Seed*, evokes Oklahoma, the Great Plains, and California. Our suggested companion texts include writings by recognized writers such as Carlos Bulosan, William Saroyan, Mary Austin, and, of course, John Steinbeck.

RURAL

Finally, Babb's work, including *Whose Names*, *An Owl on Every Post*, *The Lost Traveler*, and several of her short stories, fit into courses on rural literature. While "the rural" may not be a single place on the map, it is, like bounded geographical places, a space "invested with cultural meaning." The rural is also "grounded in its opposition to 'urban,'" an opposition deeply felt by country inhabitants and by some city inhabitants as well (Leyda 21). Teaching rural literature, especially to high school or college students living in rural places, can introduce students to their own worlds from different, more analytic perspectives. They may confront issues of power and marginalization, as well as their often sidelined place in urban-dominated contemporary cultural and economic structures (Mitchler 3).

Introducing texts that set rural and urban literature in conversation with one another can challenge students from any background to "call into question the ways that the rural is represented in American literature texts" and reveal stereotypes of class and culture (Mitchler 4). Cather's *The Professor's House* and Sinclair Lewis's *Main Street* would be an interesting pairing for urban versus the rural, as would a discussion of tropes based on Aesop's country mouse–city mouse folk tale such as those in *The Beverly Hillbillies*.

WORKING-CLASS AND LEFTIST/PROLETARIAN

> Few who did not live through The Great Depression realize the suffering of millions of people deprived of earning a living. Their dignity was insulted in every way, yet I observed alongside the humiliation and pain more dignity than in easier times. As for me, I was young, unemployed, and starved with the others.
> —Babb, Foreword, *The Dark Earth* 8

Sanora Babb's works reveal the world of working-class people starkly yet empathetically. Scholars and historians have noted that Babb's writing fits into the category of "working-class literature." She is included in Laura Hapke's short discussion of Babb in *Labor's Text: The Worker in American Fiction* (2000), Coles and Zandy's *American Working-Class Literature* (2007), and Wixson's biographical essay in Steiner's *Regionalists on the Left* (2013). Babb's *Whose Names Are Unknown* is also a proletarian novel since it conveys "an anticapitalist, pro-socialist message" (Libretti). Many of her short stories, set both in rural and urban areas, also fall into this category.

Much of the Midwest, as well as Oklahoma, has strong working-class, leftist traditions, now not much in evidence. We recommend that instructors educate themselves about these movements and introduce students to the history of radical farm and labor organizations and events in the Great Plains and other rural areas of the United States between 1900 and World War II. Farmers in the eastern parts of Oklahoma—known as Indian Territory before statehood—were radicalized as early as the mid-1870s by the Farmers' Alliance (O'Dell). During the three years before and after statehood (1907), major unions organized Oklahomans, among them the Industrial Workers of the World and the Socialist Party's Oklahoma Renters' (tenant farmers) Union (O'Dell). The Socialist Party in Oklahoma "consistently ranked as one of the top three state socialist organizations in America," opposing "the disfranchisement of blacks, supported women's suffrage, worked closely with organized labor, and condemned American involvement in the European war" (Bissett).

However, many farmers—mostly tenant farmers—joined the Working Class Union, which was more radical than the others in its use of direct action: night riding, lawsuits against landowners, barn burnings, dynamiting, and the 1917 armed insurrection known as the Green Corn Rebellion. To protect its members from persecution and prosecution, its membership list was secret. The union was interracial and included whites, African Americans, and Native Americans (Chang 184).

Babb's beloved grandfather—Konkie in *Whose Names* and Alonzo in *Owl*—was a socialist who subscribed to the *Appeal to Reason*, an influential socialist newspaper published in Girard, Kansas (Wixson 124). Babb's grandfather gave her "her political grounding, not in any formal way but as the spark that ignited her natural inclination to side with the outsider: minorities, the poor, the oppressed" (Wixson, "Radical" 124). This deep belief in worker solidarity led Babb to include a conversation in *Whose Names Are Unknown* between smallholder-farmer characters about organizing themselves to agitate for government assistance, price controls, and dams for water access. Old Man Dunne, the character based on Babb's grandfather, takes part in the conversation that composes the majority of the chapter. The setting for the conversation is the local schoolhouse, where mourners are gathering for the funeral of Mr. Starwood who died in a dust storm. The conversation is followed shortly thereafter by Mrs. Starwood's skunk protest at the bank and the suicide of Mr. Flanery, who, in a radical act of solidarity, has burned all the farmer's bills. These sections of *Whose Names* are important to understanding dispossessed farmers' political views of the era and the leftist leanings of Babb and her grandfather. References and topics in the men's conversation suggest 1916 and 1917 farmers' strikes and revolts in Oklahoma and across the nation.

During World War I, radicalized citizens throughout the United States were further agitated by conscription, and Oklahoma farmers' already-factious relationships with banks and landowners became more contentious. Borrowing from the Civil War's southern draft resistors, leftists throughout the country used the rallying cry "Rich Man's War, Poor Man's Fight" (Sellars, *Oil* 86). A similar sentiment appears in the post-funeral discussion in *Whose Names*, when old Gaylord states, "I'm blamed if I think duty is going off and fighting and killing other people in a war" (100). This volatile combination of grievances spurred the Green Corn Rebellion, the armed insurrection organized by Working Class Union members in the southeastern Oklahoma counties of Seminole, Hughes, and Pontotoc (Sellars, "Green Corn Rebellion"). Rube Munson, the acknowledged leader of the rebellion, was "a friend of the Socialists at the *Appeal to Reason*" (Dunbar-Ortiz et al.).

Oklahoma leftism and Babb's grandfather Konkie's influence were important to Babb's own sociopolitical ideals, and as a free-thinking adult, she continued to gravitate to the political left. Douglas Wixson (in both Steiner's *Regionalists* and *The Dirty Plate Trail*) and Erin Royston Battat offer discussions of Babb's participation in the Communist Party, the LA John Reed Club, and the League of American Writers. Babb's work with leftist organizations, her support of leftist writers and journals, and field notes from her time in migrant camps all indicate that Babb was influenced by leftist ideals and philosophy.

In addition to Babb and Woody Guthrie, other left-leaning Oklahoman writers of the period include Benjamin Botkin, Ralph Ellison, William Cunningham, and Jim Thompson (who wrote *Oklahoma Labor History* while employed by the Oklahoma Federal Writers' Project). Other Great Plains/Midwest leftist writers of the period include Meridel LeSueur, Tillie Olsen, and Jack Conroy. In all, this preliminary but impressive lineup indicates a rich tradition of leftist writing in the region, adding further context for Babb's work.

Teaching Sanora Babb's *Whose Names Are Unknown* would be beneficial not only for its frank depiction of an under-represented era in American history, but also to highlight women's radical writings like those of Meridel Le Sueur and Tillie Olsen, among others. Other companion text authors for this category include Richard Wright, William Attaway, and Edwin Lanham.

MIGRANT LITERATURE

> First "Orientals" were brought in for building railroads, mostly Chinese and Japanese. Mexicans were gradually brought in and displaced Oriental farm labor. [Then] Filipinos. Dust Bowl refugees gradually [are] replacing all other farm labor, although Mexicans and Filipinos still have high numbers.
> —Babb, "Field Notes," *The Dirty Plate Trail* 55

While immigrant/migrant literature has long been a recognized thread in American literary studies, the early twenty-first century political climate has reinvigorated recognition and discussion of migrant issues. Moreover, the many parallels between the current Mexican border crisis and the migration of Okies during the Great Depression have been pointed out in recent articles published in, among others, the *Daily Beast*, the *Bakersfield Californian*, *This Land Press*, and the *Guardian*. Babb's *On the Dirty Plate Trail*, with her daily notes from California picking fields, adds intimate experience to historical texts, and *Whose Names Are Unknown* offers an authentic representation of Okie migrants that enriches and often challenges historical accounts and perceptions of Dust Bowl migrants. Discussions of historical and prehistorical migrations in North American are a pedagogically sound method of contextualizing the study of twentieth and twenty-first century migrations like the Okie migration represented in Babb's *Whose Names Are Unknown* and *The Dirty Plate Trail*.

Historical migrations mirror and are given new urgency by the current situation of Mexican and South American migrants, and the contemporaneous situations of Chinese, Japanese, Filipino, Mexican, and African American workers are similar to the abuse and challenges of Okie migration. Okies were not only white but also mixed white and Native American—or full Cherokee, like Florence Owens Thompson, Dorothea Lange's "Migrant Mother" (Nardo 23). And, as Geta LeSeur reveals in *Not All Okies Are White*, many African Americans of the period were also economic and environmental refugees. It was, however, the flood of comparatively white poor workers into California who displaced

Mexicans and Filipinos that finally drew national and federal attention to the Dust Bowl crisis (Battat 43).

Battat argues that in *Whose Names Are Unknown*, "Babb explicitly racializes Okie" and that in the story, the slur "Okie" leads migrant children to "experience a sudden awareness of their social difference" and, for "Babb's protagonist Milt Dunne, the experience of being called 'okie' erodes his sense of racial superiority and awakens him to class consciousness" (64–65). The use of terms like "Oklahoma coolies" (*Dirty Plate*) and the slur in the following passage from *Whose Names Are Unknown* suggest that racializing Okies may have backfired on the powerful—at least sometimes—by creating solidarity across racial lines:

> Milt waited automatically to hear the 'suh' and when it did not come, he was relieved. He had been wondering how he would say it, tell him not to. *We're both picking cotton for the same hand-to-mouth wages. I'm no better'n he is; he's no worse.* The memory of being called a white nigger in Imperial Valley lay in his mind unforgotten, sore, like an exposed nerve. Milt looked at him. Garrison looked back, his eyes straight, and there was no difference. (185)

It is widely accepted that categorizations of "nonwhite" and "white" are based on class as well as race, a theory for which Okies' "oscillations" of whiteness can serve as an example (La Chapelle 25). Furthermore, in *The Wages of Whiteness*, David Roediger asserts that as pacification for their exploitation as workers, whiteness confers advantages for white laborers, such as better, higher-paying jobs and the ability to purchase a desirable home where they want. Nell Irwin Painter posits a series of "enlargements" of American whiteness starting in Revolutionary days that incorporated ethnic, racial, and religious groups formerly considered "nonwhite," as the Okies were in California.

Whose Names Are Unknown and *The Dirty Plate Trail* do not, in the end, represent a perfect praxis of class solidarity and action. Both texts suggest the possibility of solidarity across race and gender divides. Battat states that Babb's most radical stance is her "working-class feminist consciousness," and that, through her foregrounding of "Julia's domestic labor, using reproductive metaphors for class struggle, and envisioning gender equality as a prerequisite for class solidarity, Babb places the C(ommunist) P(arty)'s Woman Question at the center of the class struggle" (61). Babb also identifies multiracial working-class solidarity in *Whose Names*, where African Americans and a Filipino man are represented as leaders in the class struggle.

It can be difficult to teach immigrant literature in twenty-first century America. Mary Francis Pipino writes that "students' resistant responses" to migrant literature may reflect "compassion fatigue" and that the "failures" inherent to many migrant/immigrants narratives are felt as a "threat to the optimism with which they regard their own futures" (178–79). Pipino also suggests three strategies for overcoming student resistance to migrant and ethnic narratives: assigning readings that "foreground(s) the notion of the 'moral imagination'"; incorporating "discussion of literary conventions and students' expectations as readers" to introduce foundational critical vocabulary while at the same time encouraging the awareness to "confront unconventional stories in a more thoughtful and productive manner"; and by engaging in "explicit discussion of cultural values and expectations that students bring to their reading of immigrant narratives" (186–87). In short, with instructor guidance, students can learn the necessary literary and cultural skills to read and discuss immigrant narratives.

When taught with migrant/immigrant companion texts, both *Whose Names Are Unknown* and *The Dirty Plate Trail* could engender discussion of historical and contemporary American migrants' stories as well as the creation and shortcomings of working-class solidarity. Among the companion-texts authors for this theme are Pietro DiDonato, Willa Cather, Henry Roth, Hisaye Yamamoto, Richard Wright, and Ralph Ellison.

ENVIRONMENTAL/NATURE WRITING

> I love being alive on this earth. A generous earth on which we damage its soil and its atmosphere, its plants, birds, insects and animals, all of which we are an ignorant part. An earth on which we war and starve and sing and live.
>
> —Babb, Foreword, *The Dark Earth* 7

Perhaps the first time Sanora Babb's writing was explicitly categorized as environmental/ecological writing was in a 1973 book review published in the *Winona* (MN) *Daily News* (Quimby and Cushman). *An Owl on Every Post* was reviewed alongside Charles Lindbergh's *Boyhood on the Upper Mississippi* and Ralph L. Henry's *St. Croix Boyhood*. The reviewers noted that *Owl* "shares with the others a slowly awakening understanding of the land's special beauty and of the fragile interdependence concealed by nature's awesome power (Quimby and Cushman 16). Markers of an environmental text include stories in which human affairs and concerns are not the only focus and our stewardship of ecosystems is a given (Buell, *The Environmental Imagination* 7–8).

Both *Whose Names Are Unknown* and *An Owl on Every Post* have environmental themes. Babb does not merely use the environment as a framing device, nor is the human interest the only legitimate interest in the settings. Manzella notes that in *Whose Names Are Unknown*, Babb's dialogue and characterizations

> demonstrate the connection between the self and the environment, anticipating an ecocritical ideal not to be theorized as such until decades after Babb wrote her text—that identity and place are interrelated. . . . The farmers not only better understand themselves through their association to nature but also realize that they are able to empathize with those not directly like themselves—in this case, animals and inanimate objects in nature. (81)

Sarah Wald observes that in the novel, agriculture "[is] . . . a partnership between humans and the earth. The earth is generous; it has agency. . . . The earth provides the foundation for the Dunnes' political and philosophical analysis of the human condition. . . . A partnership with the land brings dignity and purpose that capitalist land relations deny them (68). In *Whose Names* and in *Owl*, the earth has agency rather than existing only as the object of human industry, management, and efforts at control; instead, in Wald's terms, the people of Babb's works see themselves in a partnership with the earth, and when the earth is treated poorly by humans, they have invalidated the partnership. In *An Owl on Every Post*, the grandfather expresses what is a contemporary ecocritical understanding of human's place in the world: "Man is the only one out of kilter. . . . And the chances are he has it in him to get back when he finds out he's a part of nature and not its lord and master. Right here, now, if we plow up all this grassland and kill off all the wild animals, there'll be a hard price to pay" (174).

In *Whose Names* and in *Owl*, Babb contextualizes the Dust Bowl as a function of a variable environment—a short (in earth-time) period of plentiful rain followed by the land's reversion to form as a semiarid ecoregion. In *Writing for an Endangered World*, Buell posits that "nothing conduces to a livelier sense" of the environment "than contemplation of scenes of rapid environmental change" like the Dust Bowl (170).

Babb's characters live within a complex, intertwined social, economic, and environmental frame "within which a great many things about the characters . . . an be understood" (Buell, *Endangered* 173). In fact, it may be impossible to fully grasp Babb's characters' motivations and choices without understanding, or at least being introduced to, Great Plains' climatology, Oklahoma/Kansas/Colorado geography, history, settlement patterns and farming practices of the time, and the national (worldwide) economics of the Great Depression. Companion texts authors for this theme include Mari Sandoz and Wallace Stegner as well as several fine anthologies, such as *African Americans on the Great Plains* and *The Tallgrass Prairie Reader*.

Though our pedagogical study originally regarded Babb's work within a strictly Oklahoman aesthetic, as we've shown here it soon became apparent that hers is a catalogue which embodies and then transcends not only a singular regional context but the entire category of "regional literature" itself. A writer keenly aware of her moment in history, Babb's writing crisscrosses a variety of genres, literary themes, and theories in order to respond to the most pressing questions of her times. What's more, these questions, and indeed her responses, remain as pertinent as ever, as evidenced by the border crisis and ever-growing concerns about climate change.

APPENDIX: TEACHING SANORA BABB—BABB COMPANION TEXTS

Accessing Resources

The table accompanying this appendix serves as a key for accessing and utilizing resources available in a Google Drive folder. The list of Babb's works is tagged, indicating thematic areas that correspond to spreadsheets for each theme. Resources available include sample course units with writing prompts, companion texts, critical texts, and context-resources such as historical and cultural texts and multimedia websites. The resources are available at this link: bit.ly/BabbCompanionTexts.

Principle of Selection for Companion Texts

Selections are chosen for their relevance to each thematic topic, with preference given to those texts that treat the same era written by authors whose writing-career chronologies correspond roughly to that of Babb's and which can complement, in theme or approach, Babb's work. Texts written during or shortly after events or periods represented will be privileged over those composed at much later dates. (Oklahoma author Rilla Askew is an exception.) Because we are creating the list to be used in both undergraduate and graduate courses,

WRITINGS BY SANORA BABB

Babb Texts	Thematic Areas
Told in the Seed (poetry)	Various
Whose Names Are Unknown (fiction)	Oklahoma/Regional Great Plains Dust Bowl The Great Depression Working Class California Environmental Regional
The Dark Earth (stories)	Oklahoma/Regional Great Plains California? Dust Bowl The Great Depression Migrant/Immigrant Working Class Environmental
On the Dirty Plate Trail (nonfiction)	The Great Depression Migrant/Immigrant Working Class California/Regional
An Owl on Every Post (fictionalized memoir)	Great Plains Colorado/Regional Working Class Environmental
The Lost Traveler (fiction)	The Great Depression Great Plains/Regional
Cry of the Tinamou (COTM) See individual stories below.	
COTM, "The Larger Cage"	Working Class Mexico

(continued)

WRITINGS BY SANORA BABB *(continued)*

Babb Texts	Thematic Areas
COTM, "A Scandalous Humility"	California Migrant/Immigrant
COTM, "Reconciliation"	California/Regional
COTM, "The Meeting"	California
COTM, "Aslant the Moon"	California Migrant/Immigrant
COTM, "Run, Sheepy, Run!"	Oklahoma/Regional Great Plains
COTM, "Love Be My Destiny"	California
COTM, "The Vine by Root Embraced"	California Migrant/Immigrant
COTM, "Matriarch of the Court"	California
COTM, "William Shakespeare"	Dust Bowl/Regional Great Plains
COTM, "The Tea Party"	Great Plains?
COTM, "The Santa Ana"	California/Regional
COTM, "The Wild Flower"	Great Plains/Regional
COTM, "Davy"	Great Plains/Regional
COTM, "Cry of the Tinamou"	Mexico

we have included anthology excerpts and short stories as well as monographs. We do not expect that our companion texts and unit plans will comprise entire syllabi; rather, they serve as springboards toward the design of courses that include the works of Sanora Babb.

NOTES

1. Botkin left Oklahoma in 1942 to head the Archive of American Folk Song at the Library of Congress; see Hirsch, in *Regionalists on the Left*, for more on Botkin. Published yearly from 1929–32 by the University of Oklahoma Press, the anthologies included writers such as Mary Austin, Mari Sandoz, Sterling A. Brown, and Langston Hughes

and Kiowa artist and storyteller Tsa-to-ke. Riggs wrote "Green Grow the Lilacs," a play that became the musical *Oklahoma!*

2. See Jackson, "Locating Oklahoma," for a rhetorical analysis of Oklahoma regionalism, *Folk-Say*, and the Green Corn Rebellion.

WORKS CITED

Babb, Sanora. *An Owl on Every Post*. Muse Ink Press, 2012.
———. *Cry of the Tinamou: Stories*. University of Nebraska Press, 1997.
———. *On the Dirty Plate Trail: Remembering the Dust Bowl Refugee Camps*. University of Texas Press, 2007.
———. *The Dark Earth and Other Stories from the Great Depression*. Capra Press, 1987.
———. *The Lost Traveler*. Muse Ink Press, 2013.
———. *Told in the Seed: Poems*. West End Press, 1998.
———. *Whose Names Are Unknown*. University of Oklahoma Press, 2004.
Battat, Erin Royston. *Ain't Got No Home: America's Great Migrations and the Making of an Interracial Left*. University North Carolina Press, 2014.
Bissett, Jim. "Socialist Party." *The Encyclopedia of Oklahoma History and Culture*. Oklahoma Historical Society. www.okhistory.org/publications/enc/entry.php?entry=S0001.
Braithwaite, Charles A., and Bruce A. Glasrud, eds. *African Americans on the Great Plains: An Anthology*. University of Nebraska Press, 2009.
Buell, Lawrence. *The Environmental Imagination: Thoreau, Nature Writing, and the Formation of American Culture*. Belknap Press of Harvard University Press, 1996.
———. *Writing for an Endangered World: Literature, Culture, and Environment in the U.S. and Beyond*. Belknap Press of Harvard University Press, 2003.
Chang, David A. *The Color of the Land: Race, Nation, and the Politics of Landownership in Oklahoma, 1832–1929*. University of North Carolina Press, 2010.
Coles, Nicholas, and Janet Zandy, editors. *American Working-Class Literature: An Anthology*. Oxford University Press, 2007.
Dunbar-Ortiz, Roxanne, and John Womack, Jr. "Dreams of Revolution: Oklahoma, 1917." *Monthly Review*, vol. 62, no. 6 (November 2010).
Fetterley, Judith, and Marjorie Pryse. *Writing Out of Place: Regionalism, Women, and American Literary Culture*. University of Illinois Press, 2003.
Hada, Ken. "Voices in the Earth: How Regional Writing Validates the Other." *Journal of the American Studies Association of Texas*, vol. 37 (November 2006): 69–78.
Hapke, Laura. *Labor's Text: The Worker in American Fiction*. Rutgers University Press, 2001.
Hirsch, Jerrold. "Theorizing Regionalism and Folklore from the Left: B. A. Botkin, the Oklahoma Years, 1921–1939." *Regionalists on the Left: Radical Voices from the American West*, pp. 135–56. University Oklahoma Press, 2013.
Jackson, Rachel C. "Locating Oklahoma: Critical Regionalism and Transrhetorical Analysis in the Composition Classroom." *College Composition and Communication*, vol. 66, no. 2 (December 2014): 301–26.

La Chapelle, Peter. *Proud to Be an Okie: Cultural Politics, Country Music, and Migration to Southern California*. University of California Press, 2007.

LeSeur, Geta J. *Not All Okies Are White: The Lives of Black Cotton Pickers in Arizona*. University of Missouri Press, 2000.

Leyda, Julia. *American Mobilities: Geographies of Class, Race, and Gender in US Culture*. Transcript Verlag; Columbia University Press, 2016.

Libretti, Tim. "Proletarian Literature." *The Encyclopedia of Literary and Cultural Theory*, edited by Michael Ryan. Wiley, 2010, http://doi.wiley.com/10.1002/9781444337839.wbelctv3p006. Accessed 2 October 2019.

Lutz, Tom. *Cosmopolitan Vistas: American Regionalism and Literary Value*. Cornell University Press, 2004.

Manzella, Abigail G. H. *Migrating Fictions: Gender, Race, and Citizenship in U.S. Internal Displacements*. Ohio State University Press, 2018. www.jstor.org/stable/10.2307/j.ctt2204rsp.

Mitchler, Sharon J. *Towards Using Critical Rural Pedagogy with Rural Community College Students in Undergraduate American Literature Classes*. University of Washington, 2015. https://english.washington.edu/research/graduate/towards-using-critical-rural-pedagogy-rural-community-college-students.

Nardo, Don. *Migrant Mother: How a Photograph Defined the Great Depression*. Compass Point Books, 2011.

O'Dell, Larry. "Labor, Organized." In *Encyclopedia of Oklahoma History and Culture*. Oklahoma Historical Society. www.okhistory.org/publications/enc/entry.php?entry=LA003.

Painter, Nell Irvin. *The History of White People*. W. W. Norton, 2011.

Pipino, M. F. "Resistance and the Pedagogy of Ethnic Literature." *MELUS: Multi-Ethnic Literature of the United States*, vol. 30, no. 2 (June 2005): 175–90. doi:10.1093/melus/30.2.175.

Price, John T., editor. *The Tallgrass Prairie Reader*. University of Iowa Press, 2014.

Pryse, Marjorie. "Literary Regionalism and Global Capital: Nineteenth-Century U.S. Women Writers." *Tulsa Studies in Women's Literature*, vol. 23, no. 1 (April 2004). doi:10.2307/20455171.

Quimby, Charles, and Susan Cushman. "Cover Column." *Winona Daily News*, 2 April 1973, p. 16. Newspapers.com.

Roediger, David R. *The Wages of Whiteness: Race and the Making of the American Working Class*. Verso, 1999.

Saum, Lewis O. "The Success Theme in Great Plains Realism." *American Quarterly*, vol. 18, no. 4 (1966). doi:10.2307/2711384.

Sellars, Nigel. "Green Corn Rebellion." In *The Encyclopedia of Oklahoma History and Culture*. Oklahoma Historical Society. www.okhistory.org/publications/enc/entry.php?entry=GR022. Accessed 25 Mar. 2020.

———. *Oil, Wheat & Wobblies: The Industrial Workers of the World in Oklahoma, 1905–1930*. University of Oklahoma Press, 2012.

Steiner, Michael C. Introduction. *Regionalists on the Left: Radical Voices from the American West*, University of Oklahoma Press, 2013, 1–20.

Wald, Sarah D. *The Nature of California: Race, Citizenship, and Farming Since the Dust Bowl*. University of Washington Press, 2016.

Wixson, Douglas. "Radical by Nature: Sanora Babb and Ecological Disaster on the High Plains, 1900–1940." *Regionalists on the Left: Radical Voices from the American West*, edited by Michael Steiner, University of Oklahoma Press, 2013, pp. 111–33.

———. *Worker-Writer in America: Jack Conroy and the Tradition of Midwestern Literary Radicalism, 1898–1990*. University of Illinois Press, 1994.

Yoder, Edwin M., Jr. "Faulkner and Race: Art and Punditry." *Virginia Quarterly Review*, vol. 73, no. 4 (1997), www.vqronline.org/issues/73/4/autumn-1997#toc.

CAROLINE JOHNSON AND MARIAH WAHL

13

NO LONGER UNKNOWN

Exploring the Archive of Sanora Babb

In March 2019, the Harry Ransom Center at the University of Texas at Austin offered a Women's History Month event featuring American author Sanora Babb. With the opportunity to view otherwise restricted manuscripts and collection artifacts as part of a group experience, about sixty members of Austin's community filed into a room on the second floor of the Ransom Center to view the small exhibition. The group was there for Ransom Readers, a presentation and discussion focused on Babb's *Whose Names Are Unknown* (2004), her Dust Bowl novel first written in the 1930s.

The Harry Ransom Center's Ransom Readers event is a bimonthly opportunity for public engagement with rare archival and special collections material.[1] Outreach efforts are conducted specifically to engage members outside of the University of Texas's student, faculty, and visiting fellows community. Centered around a specific text, the program offers a unique opportunity for nonacademic visitors to deeply engage with primary-source materials and research methodologies. Each Ransom Readers presentation begins with an hour-long discussion of archival material, during which members are exposed not just to rare items, but also to the connections and insight researchers might make about their historical and literary context. Participants have time to engage with the objects on their own, asking questions about them and the processes used to analyze them. This presentation is followed by an hour-long discussion of the text and the objects. Throughout the session, presenters are interested in engaging participants in history, literature, and the author's biography. This follows the guidelines and best practices established by the Society of American Archivists for public educational engagement in primary-source literacy.[2] In the last fifteen to twenty years, archives, museums, and special collections have grown increasingly invested in public outreach and education efforts.[3] This includes prestigious institutions such as the Victoria and Albert Museum, whose recent outreach initiative "invite[s] the public to play within the institution and challenge existing conceptions of knowledge and knowing."[4] Their public education effort is aimed at promoting the democratic engagement of their expansive collection outside of a formal exhibit space. The University of Idaho's special collection takes an innovative approach to outreach, using a 3D printer to help the public re-create and more directly engage with artifacts in their collection. Increasingly, this kind of informal access is becoming the standard of public engagement.[5]

We focused on *Whose Names*, which presents a portrait of a family trapped in the conditions of the Dust Bowl and aftermath of the Great Depression, because of the novel's historical relevance and unique publication history. The Harry Ransom artifacts written and saved by Babb reflect her deep understanding of history in the making. The collection material on this particular novel is a direct result of Babb's journalism and her dedication to reflect historical accuracy even in a fictional work. They illuminate the narrative surrounding the novel's unique publication history.

The March 2019 presentation featured materials from Sanora Babb's expansive collection at the Harry Ransom Center, which traces her life and her writing from her young adulthood until her death in 2005. The collection was acquired, in part, because of Babb's association with Douglas Wixson, professor emeritus of English and American Studies, a well-regarded associate of the Harry Ransom Center. Wixson first wrote of Babb in his *Worker-Writer in America*

(1994) and subsequently in academic conference papers, most recently "Sanora Babb: Stories from the American High Plains."[6]

Beginning with scrapbooks that contain pictures of her childhood, notes from her high school education, and her earliest writings, Babb's collection reveals a woman with an early gift for writing and an immense heart for people and activism. Her correspondence is especially impressive. Babb maintained deep and lasting writing relationships with many authors, acquaintances, family members, and friends. Spanning over thirty-two linear feet, the collection was opened for public use and research in 2009.

Considering the size and significance of her collection, an exhibition of materials for the Ransom Readers book club required specific consideration of public history, archival access, and artifact selection. In this chapter, we use Sanora Babb's collection and curated materials for the Ransom Readers event to elucidate the value of archival access in promoting a person and her work. Although archives and materials are frequently made available for professional and academic researchers, those readers often require specialized knowledge or status to enter and engage with them. As an effort to reach wider audiences, archivists promote "public history," a chance for nonacademics to acquire a deeper understanding of historical or literary work that often goes unnoticed or unappreciated. Babb's archive offers the perfect example of how the act of public history can transform hidden treasures into public knowledge. Through a transparent discussion of the collection's processing with our book club, as well as the curation of Babb's collection materials and the role of cultural institutions such as the Harry Ransom Center in allowing audiences to experience her story, we demonstrate that public history efforts are paramount to ensuring that canon-worthy work such as Sanora Babb's does not remain unknown.

We first provide background on public education, situating the Babb collection within the efforts of staff at the Harry Ransom Center. Next, we frame our work within a feminist methodology that seeks to dismantle the distinctions between the private and public lives of women. Third, we offer an analysis of the Babb archive itself to understand its provenance and organization, as well as the artifacts specific to *Whose Names*, detailing the historical narrative they produce and uncover. Finally, we propose how the artifacts of Sanora Babb's *Whose Names* are read in relation to additional archives within the Harry Ransom Center to highlight Babb's work within a historical context and to unearth her stories not yet told.

PUBLIC INSTITUTIONS: EDUCATION AND OUTREACH

In order to understand Sanora Babb's work in relation to both the archive and the general public, we must consider the role access plays in cultural heritage institutions such as the Harry Ransom Center. Since the Ransom Center is at once a library, a museum, and an archive, we had the option to display Babb's papers in two small cases or to hold an interactive session as part of the book club presentation. Often, people who are unfamiliar with the specific missions and procedures of a cultural institution like the Ransom Center assume galleries are available for all to see but are unaware that access to archival materials is open to more than academics or specialists. Our goal, then, was to provide an overview of Babb's archive and invite others to return and engage with the materials on their own.

With an eye to attracting nonspecialists, we felt the choice of the novel *Whose Names* reflected Sanora's goal to inform the public through detailed research and compelling narrative. We chose to hold an interactive session as part of our presentation of the Babb archive. Placing materials under glass would have created a barrier that would have reaffirmed the exclusiveness associated with major archives that we sought to challenge. The presentation, direct engagement with materials, and the added element of requesting visitors to read *Whose Names* promoted interactivity, such that our nonacademic Ransom Readers were "no longer passive but [could] take an active role in an exhibition."[7] Taking into account Babb's extensive work as an activist for working-class Americans and immigrants and the intimate descriptions of her Dust Bowl subject matter, we opted for an access that promoted the themes involving collective reckoning with the American history and institutions best represented in *Whose Names*.

An archive's ability to affect an emotional response provides part of its strength as a tool of public history. The most powerful public histories are ones in which the public feels emotionally invested, and where people have the freedom to think critically and draw their own conclusions about history and its narrative (Frisch). Best practices include creating a "shared authority" in which museum and archival professionals find opportunities for creating history *with* members of its public, rather than creating public histories *for* those publics.[8] Archival collections such as Babb's provide a unique opportunity for this kind of thinking and discourse, opening up opportunities for public history both because of the collection's content and Babb's own personal connection to the important historical events of her time. Her role as both a historical figure and a creator of fiction that represents historical moments means that a consideration of her collection is vital to both literary and historical endeavors.

WOMEN'S PUBLIC HISTORY AND ARCHIVAL ACCESS

In unearthing the stories of a twentieth-century American female author, we framed the discussion and our curation of materials with specific consideration of feminist approaches to public history. By 1983, scholars used the newly founded field of public history to understand the role of women within historic preservation efforts. Nineteenth and early twentieth-century women's organizations often led the way with cultural and historic preservation, though "such women were rarely credentialed historians and were increasingly disregarded as the movement became more professional."[9] Babb was an investigative journalist and writer rather than a historian, but she nonetheless left an archive of much historical value. Accessing Babb's collection at the Harry Ransom Center, then, allows for a deeper understanding of how her work reflects longer trends of historic documentation and preservation efforts by women.

With the adoption of "separate spheres" for men and women during the Industrial Revolution of the late eighteenth and nineteenth centuries, there was a stark differentiation between the private and public lives of middle- and upper-class women. By the twentieth century, scholars determined that the separate spheres ideology was too narrow an approach and did not accurately reflect the historical experience of all women. Adopting the 1960s slogan "the personal is political," we too assert that women's "private lives are shaped by political realities."[10] Through increased access to an archival collection, individuals can reach their own conclusions about the extent to which women's work and home lives impacted one another. With the inclusion of details based on personal experience, including Babb's relationship with her Great Plains family and her volunteer work in the migrant camps in California, *Whose Names* captures the harsh lived experience and the political and environmental realities of men and women of the 1930s.

ANALYSIS OF THE BABB ARCHIVE

Many sections of Sanora Babb's archive at the Harry Ransom Center relate directly to *Whose Names*. The Harry Ransom Center acquired Sanora Babb's archive between the years 2000 and 2008.[11] When historians and scholars examine archival collections, we sometimes erase the archival science that makes these objects available to us and to the public. In Babb's case, we owe a debt to archivist Amy Armstrong, who organized and described her collection, making it publicly available and navigable. Armstrong, who processed the collection from 2008–09, organized the materials into 32.84 linear feet, a fairly sizable collection. Babb has a substantial record of correspondence, having maintained deep friendships with notable friends all over the world, including Ralph Ellison, B. Traven, and Ray Bradbury. Babb was committed to these relationships and her letter writing, a direct result of her empathy as an author and friend. Her archive communicates her personality as someone "warm and compassionate," in Armstrong's view of the collection.[12] In addition, the correspondence in the Babb collection was iterative and layered. Many drafts of her writing pulled directly from her correspondence or notes about her family's life and the events unfolding around her.

Some of the most notable material in Babb's collection relates to the research and writing of *Whose Names Are Unknown*. Babb worked as an assistant to Tom Collins in several migrant camps, including Arvin (nicknamed "Weedpatch") during the Great Depression. Located just south of Bakersfield, California, this camp was built by the Works Progress Administration and managed by the Farm Security Administration to house migrant workers during the 1930s in the aftermath of the Great Depression and the Dust Bowl. Babb took meticulous notes and carefully preserved records about her time serving the laborers there. She captured their stories—their sorrow, their suffering, and their resilience. At the same time, she communicated with her mother and sister back home in Oklahoma about their hardships there, capturing the difficulty of the Dust Bowl as it was unfolding. Reading Babb's words, one can see how she saw herself as both an author and a conduit, sometimes placing the stories of her family and the Weedpatch camp directly onto the manuscript page for her audience to absorb. Many objects in her archive are striking in the immediate affective response they inspire: the fragile, dirtied dust mask Babb saved from her time in Oklahoma (too delicate to circulate), to the long, claustrophobic writings from her mother describing life and dust storms on the Kansas plains and in dugouts.[13] These objects speak to Babb's mission in writing *Whose Names*, which was to capture the voices of those who could not speak for themselves. Babb's personal mission as an activist-author is revealed at the Ransom Center archive, since her extensive field notes and many drafts preserve the lives and stories of real people and real-world crises. Perusing her collection shows the often-buried kind of work it took to write an important story like *Whose Names Are Unknown*. Our Ransom Readers' choice of book was a gesture to recover Babb's life and history for wider literary and cultural memory.

ARTIFACT ANALYSIS OF *WHOSE NAMES ARE UNKNOWN*

Though Babb's whole collection in its entirety is impressive and worth exploring, the section of the archive specific to *Whose Names* offered a unique opportunity for exhibition and a detailed look into the life of the work and the historical importance it carries. Each artifact we selected for the Ransom Readers presentation represented a part of history tied directly to the research, writing, and momentousness of *Whose Names*. We offered full transparency regarding our selections, yet we also encouraged readers see what tales they could derive from seeing part of her archive.

In addition to considering our audience's relationship to women's history, we presented the artifacts for *Whose Names* using a methodology of public history. We had to consider the best way to bring the experience of writing and reading the novel alive through interaction with her archive. In his work championing Neil MacGregor's *A History of the World in 100 Objects*, Trevor Jones explains how an object-centered interpretation of materials makes for some of the most complex and interesting historical work. Jones notes that "every museum possess[es] artifacts that can tell significant and emotionally charged stories that resonate with the present."[14] Following this challenge, we carefully selected and paired objects that best represent the deeply personal work of *Whose Names*, while tying their interpretation to relevant themes for today's audience. These interactions are visible in the object-level analysis that follows.

With such a rich and exhaustive archive as Babb's, it becomes difficult to decide which objects are most useful—because, of course, each object is valuable for some potential audience. Several objects resonate with affective significance, however, for the ways in which they connect Babb's writing and life to her audience. Chief among these, perhaps, is the eviction notice that inspired the title of Babb's novel. The impersonal broadsheet, pinned to an abandoned home outside of the Weedpatch Camp, reads: "To John and Jane Doe, whose True Names are Unknown," and continues on to tell them of their eviction from (an apparently long-forgotten) encampment.[15] It's not hard to imagine why Babb kept this notice. The cruelty of the migrant labor system, both outside and within the labor camps, is represented succinctly in this one stark note. When audience members glanced over it, many noted how the hopelessness of the notice is palpable—where have these people gone, and what good can possibly come of declaring their eviction now? Babb's novel attempts to provide some of the answers to this real-world mystery.

The original complete manuscript of *Whose Names*, never submitted for publication when it was written in the 1930s, is another especially affective part of Babb's story. The manuscript is labeled "Restricted," meaning it is too fragile to be brought to the reading room for general public use. Though this conservational measure is in place, different modes of access are still available for using this work for public history: public presentation, physical exhibit, and digital scanning are all reliable methods of ensuring this piece is made available without compromising the object itself. One of the most intriguing differences between this manuscript and the work eventually published in 2004 is the dedication. The contemporary publication has a dedication to "The People of the Western Plains," but the original manuscript includes a dedication to Babb's husband, James Wong Howe, and to the people she'd met at the Weedpatch Camp: "To JWH, and the people and races who do the work of the Western Plains, especially my okie friends."[16] Babb's original dedication explicitly foregrounds the people and the labor she wishes to honor in her book, making the human connection explicit and contemporary.

Babb saved a wide range of published materials that informed her personal research conducted at the migrant camps. A pamphlet from the US Department of Labor dated 1937, for example, contains a table showing "Returning Californians and Out-of-State Migrants 'in Need of Manual Employment' Entering California, by Months, June 1935-Mar. 31, 1938." As the table shows, in June 1935, 3,454 out-of-state migrants entered California looking for work. By September 1936, this number had nearly quadrupled to 12,549. Such materials provide quantitative historical context and undergird Babb's meticulous study efforts in reflecting the personal realities of the statistics. As Ransom Readers glanced at the numbers, they made small exclamations of "Wow!" or "I had no idea it was that many." Though fictional, the Dunne family in *Whose Names* represents just a few of the numbers shown in the labor pamphlet.[17]

To elucidate the personal experience of these statistics, we juxtaposed the pamphlet with Babb's field notes, full of her meticulous attention to detail in describing her findings while working at migrant camps in 1938. Showing the more human element of the labor pamphlets, Babb records the events of the day or general findings. Dated October 29, 1938, one series of notes reads:

> 144 camps in Kern Co. now. Squatter camps not allowed thru stricter health rules. Most families now live in private camps on owners places, where cabin is 'free' rent, but lights are $6.00 a month! In order to be allowed to live in a cabin, each cabin must show daily picking of cotton no lower than 900 lbs. This means at least three persons, more likely four. In most cases, this means two or more families live in a cabin. Ave. picker picks 250# a day, 10 hrs. At 75c—$1.87 per day. Many cannot pick more than #200 per day. Many women pick as much as men per day.[18]

Babb includes these facts in the second part of *Whose Names*, providing accurate data for the experience of the Dunne family and many others living in private camps on growers' land. Upon reading the sections, the audience members in the Ransom Readers were able to immediately place the facts within the second part of the novel itself. Their faces lit up as they realized how her field notes were directly evident in the details of the plot. The Readers saw how Babb's work takes on an element of moral and factual authority unmatched by other novels about the Dust Bowl. Her reporting skills transfer directly into her narrative, painting a realistic and historically accurate picture of migrant experience.

In addition to written sources, Babb's archive contains many photographs that helped audience members to visualize her written prose. Taken by Sanora's sister, Dorothy Babb, one photograph depicts Tom Collins in the Weedpatch Camp. Weedpatch is the camp detailed in John Steinbeck's *The Grapes of Wrath*, which Steinbeck dedicated to Tom Collins. While Steinbeck certainly visited the camps, Collins and Babb actually worked there, Collins for several years, Babb for almost a year.

The Ransom archive has a letter from Collins to Babb encouraging her to write about what she saw during her field work. The Ransom Center also holds Babb's typed and handwritten correspondence with Tom Collins, which reflect her commitment to detail and accuracy of experience. She enlisted his assistance when she was writing the book, sending him point by point questions to make sure her narrative for *Whose Names Are Unknown* was accurate. "It is almost done," she writes. "Almost all of it is taken up with the midwest, and the last is going to be concentrated stuff on California."[19] Babb requests Collins's help filling in the specific seasonal crops and movements of migrant workers in California. She asks, "Where and about how far would be the most inviting place to go in the summer months after they either come thru or stop in Imperial Valley?" Writing back in orange pencil—which contrasts drastically to Babb's black typescript—Collins provides his responses. In addition to crossing out "or stop," he also creates a brief migrant itinerary chart, detailing the months of July through January, the best locations, including Hollister in July, Gridley in August and September, and "Kern Co" [County] in October and November. He lists the crop, such as apricots, peaches, cotton, or grapes, that apply to each region.[20] Book club members gathered around to peer at the personal correspondence, elated by each detail they recalled from *Whose Names*. They noted how the storyline carries the family to Kern County for cotton picking, which is reflective of Tom's notes. The evidence of Babb's journalistic method in her archive provides credibility to the stories she tells.

As Babb's collection documents, her fictional account of the Dust Bowl was pieced together thoughtfully through a combination of her own careful observations made as she served families living in the FSA camps, Collins's letters, first-person accounts, and letters from her mother and sister back home in Oklahoma. She created a copious amount of research material from her time working in California, preserved in her archive, including her correspondence with Collins. We read Collins encouraging Babb to communicate the conditions of Weedpatch Camp to the outside world. Ostensibly, this is why Collins invited John Steinbeck to visit the camp in late 1938. Collins handed over several sets of notes from camp workers, Babb's among them. According to the National Archive, where these reports that passed from Collins to Steinbeck are held: "The reports feature numerous 'items,' from major to minute, that appear in the novel. . . . Sometimes these were inserted whole-cloth into *The Grapes of Wrath*, but more often they were reconfigured or 'built-out' to serve the creative purposes of the novel."[21] Babb was aware that Collins was passing her reports on to writers, but it is unclear if she knew that the reports were going to Steinbeck for his own fictional account of the camps and other Dust Bowl representations. Steinbeck had previously published a nonfiction series called "Harvest Gypsies," which highlighted and credited the field reports of various Alvin/Weedpatch workers. It's possible Babb thought her report would be part of this effort, as well as another project Steinbeck was promoting to publish these accounts as their own work of nonfiction. We have no evidence that Babb knew her work was being used to publish a Dust Bowl novel. Babb herself had just entered into a contract to write her own novel with Random House, the manuscript that would become *Whose Names Are Unknown*.

BABB'S ARCHIVE IN CONTEXT

When readers can interact with Babb's materials in an archive, her life's narrative gains a larger context. For the book club, we chose to include photographs from the Farm Security Administration, a US government photography project, headed at the time by Roy Stryker, that captured stunning portraits of American life from 1935 to 1944. Some of the most prominent photographers in this project include Dorothea Lange and Arthur Rothstein. Together, two collections at the HRC hold ten gelatin silver prints documenting the 1930s.

These jarring photographs contextualize Babb's archive of *Whose Names* by visually depicting the aftermath of the Great Depression, the dust storms, and the setting of the novel itself. There are also diary entries from Sanora's mother, Jennie Babb, in a box labeled "Family letters and journal regarding Kansas dust storms, 1935–1937." Jennie Babb writes, "It looks like the desert you read about in books . . . no food cattle dying and people imprisoned with windows and doors covered to keep out the fine, choking dirt."[22] As Ransom Readers noted, these passages echo the descriptions of dust storms found in chapter 17 of *Whose Names*. In the book, the matriarch of the Dunne family, Julia Dunne, keeps a journal of her experiences. Her diary entries reflect near identical ones written by Sanora Babb's mother. Jennie Babb's diary reads, "You have read of april showers. . . . We are having april showers all right but of the finest of dust you ever saw."[23] Chapter 17 in *Whose Names* reads, "*April 4* . . . Everything covered with dust."[24] Babb's use of her mother's original diary entries reflect her personal relationship to the Dust Bowl and the lived experiences of her family used in the characters of *Whose Names are Unknown*. By including these diary entries in *Whose Names*, readers see that Sanora's writing is based not only in researching historical accuracy, but also in personal and family sources.

In addition to pairing these artifacts with FSA photography, Babb's collection includes an assortment of scrapbooks and photo albums that bring her world into focus. Contrasting the bleak depictions of the Dust Bowl in *Whose Names*, Babb's photographs present a multidimensional life from her childhood in Oklahoma, Colorado, and Kansas, relocation to Los Angeles, trip to the USSR in the mid-1930s, up through her partnership and marriage to cinematographer James Wong Howe. Ransom Readers noted how her life seemed happy and engaged. By presenting this evidence of a long life lived on many fronts, we sought to show that an author is not defined by one work or even the entirety of his or her works. Rather, a more complete and complex vision of a person is available through perusal of such a rich archive. They see that such depth of archival knowledge is useful for understanding *Whose Names* within the larger context of Babb's life story.

Employing practices of public history and initiating discussions of Babb's work in relation to museum studies, historic preservation, and archival science, we are helping recover Babb as a part of larger cultural memory. Archives provide the chance for readers to evaluate independently Babb's historical narrative as well as her work. Though during our presentation to the Ransom Readers, we suggested interpretations for each piece, our book group members' direct engagement with Babb's archive challenged the process and authority of individual analysis normally performed by scholars. A large part of our charge was and is to encourage personal engagement by nonprofessionals. By championing affective engagement and personal connections over prescriptive paradigms, we encouraged the Ransom Readers of Babb's *Whose Names Are Unknown* to reconsider how the past is recorded and the work's relationship to modern day writing and circumstances.

One goal of public history projects is to effect contemporary understanding of literary as well as political and economic history. *Whose Names Are Unknown* engendered ideas within our Ransom Readers about how the United States' past has affected contemporary issues such as the migrant crisis and attitudes toward climate change. By enacting the accessibility of Babb's collection at both the archival and artifact level, we produced a framework for opening cultural conceptions of women's history, writing, and activism. Sanora Babb's collection offers an example of the nuances involved in uncovering the work of many women, people of color, and other marginalized figures within our historical narrative. In the case of Babb, a public presentation and explication of part of her archive gestures to its many uses for the public—not just for academe. Ultimately, we asked our audience to consider what figures are elided from our contemporary understanding of history, as Babb herself often has been. Though many narrative and personal stories of non-elite people have been erased from our cultural legacy, public engagement with Babb's work ensures that at least Sanora Babb's name will no longer be unknown.

NOTES

1. The authors wish to extend their gratitude to Lisa Pulsifer, head of public programs and education at the Harry Ransom Center, for initiating and maintaining the Ransom Readers Book Club.
2. "Guidelines for Primary Source Literacy." 2019. *Society of American Archivists*, www2.archivists.org/sites/all/files/GuidelinesForPrimarySourceLiteracy-June2018.pdf.
3. Traister, "Public Services and Outreach."
4. Segall and Trofanenko, "The Victoria and Albert Museum."
5. Passehl-Stoddart et al., "History in the Making."
6. Wixson, "Sanora Babb."
7. Glines and Grabitske, "Telling the Story."
8. Frisch, *A Shared Authority*.
9. Mayo, "Women's History and Public History." Edith Mayo connected the intricacies of public history to women's history, explaining that there was first a divergence between historians and antiquarians. The former were considered trained scholars who worked in the academe, while the latter were historical enthusiasts who lacked specialization in historical methods or interpretation.
10. Keohane, "Preface." In her preface to the collection of essays from the Seventh Berkshire Conference on the History of Women in the early 1990s, Keohane explains the use of the slogan "subverts the public/private separation by denying that it operates as it is usually supposed to."
11. Sanora Babb's literary executor, Joanne Dearcopp, inventoried and sent Babb's collection during this period of time. She has been responsible for getting Babb's books back in print and others newly published. For decades she has promoted Sanora's work in academic and public spaces and continues exploring film opportunities. A screenplay of *Whose Names Are Unknown* was a finalist at Sundance a few years ago and the 2020 Nantucket Film Festival's screenplay competition.
12. Armstrong, Amy, Ransom Center manager for archives cataloging, description, and access. Interview with Mariah Wahl. Austin, TX, 7 October 2019.
13. Cvetkovich, *An Archive of Feelings*. Our definition of affective archive draws primarily on Cvetkovich's relation of affect to public cultures.
14. Jones, "Telling Stories with Objects in the Starring Role."
15. Original Eviction Notice (1938). Box 18.6, Sanora Babb papers, Harry Ransom Center, University of Texas at Austin, Austin, TX (hereafter, HRC).
16. Manuscript of Whose Names Are Unknown (1938), Box 92, HRC. Emphasis is the author's.
17. Bureau of Labor Statistics: United States Department of Labor, "Refugee Labor Migration to California" published August 1938, Box 19.2, HRC.
18. Field Notes on California camp sanitation and costs. 29 October 1938. Box 18.6, HRC.
19. Sanora Babb's exchange with Tom Collins, Box 18.8, HRC.
20. Ibid.

21. Nealand, "Archival Vintages for Grapes of Wrath."
22. Jennie Babb's Writing on Dust Storm, Box 18.5, HRC.
23. Ibid.
24. Babb, *Whose Names Are Unknown*, 90.

WORKS CITED

Babb, Sanora. *Whose Names Are Unknown*. University of Oklahoma Press, 2004, 90.

Cvetkovich, Ann. *An Archive of Feelings: Trauma, Sexuality, and Lesbian Public Cultures*. Duke University Press, 2003.

Frisch, Michael H. *A Shared Authority: Essays on the Craft and Meaning of Oral and Public History*. State University of New York Press, 1993.

Glines, Timothy, and David Grabitske. "Telling the Story: Better Interpretation at Small Historical Organizations." *History News*, vol. 58, no. 2 (2003): 5.

"Guidelines for Primary Source Literacy." Society of American Archivists, 2019. www2.archivists.org/sites/all/files/GuidelinesForPrimarySourceLiteracy-June2018.pdf.

Jones, Trevor "Telling Stories with Objects in the Starring Role." *History News*, vol. 69, no. 2 (2014): 23–26.

Keohane, Nannerl O. Preface. In *Gendered Domains: Rethinking Public and Private in Women's History*, edited by Dorothy O. Helly and Susan M. Reverby. Cornell University Press, 1992.

Mayo, Edith P. "Women's History and Public History: The Museum Connection." *Public Historian*, vol. 5, no. 2 (1983): 63–73. doi:10.2307/3377251.

Nealand, Daniel. "Archival Vintages for Grapes of Wrath." *Prologue*, vol. 40, no. 4 (2008). www.archives.gov/publications/prologue/2008/winter/grapes.html.

Passehl-Stoddart, Erin, Ashlyn Velte, Kristin J. Henrich, and Annie M. Gaines. "History in the Making: Outreach and Collaboration between Special Collections and Makerspaces." *Collaborative Librarianship*, vol. 10, no. 2, article 8 (2018). https://digitalcommons.du.edu/collaborativelibrarianship/vol10/iss2/8.

Segall, Avner, and Brenda Trofanenko. "The Victoria and Albert Museum: A Subversive, Playful Pedagogy in Action." In *Adult Education, Museums, and Art Galleries: International Issues in Adult Education*, edited by Darlene E. Clover, Kathy Sanford, Lorraine Bell, and Kay Johnson, pp. 53–66. SensePublishers, 2016.

Traister, Daniel. "Public Services and Outreach in Rare Book, Manuscript, and Special Collections Libraries." *Library Trends*, vol. 52 (2003): 87–108.

Wixson, Douglas. "Sanora Babb: Stories from the American High Plans." Exhibition Brochure. University of Texas at Austin, Henry Ransom Center, September 10, 2017. https://web.archive.org/web/20170906045541/; www.hrc.utexas.edu/exhibitions/web/babb/career/.

ACKNOWLEDGMENTS

Unknown No More is a fitting culmination of an interesting and sometimes lonesome mission to gain greater recognition for the work of Sanora Babb, and there are many people to thank. We are indebted to David Wrobel and the twelve contributors to this book who generously offered their time and expertise even before we had a publisher—such was their belief in Babb's work. Enormous gratitude goes to Douglas Wixson for his passion and early contributions to Babb scholarship and for being a stalwart colleague on our shared endeavor. Several others from academia lent their support in the early days and deserve much appreciation. Michael Steiner readily agreed to chair the first academic panel on Babb at the American Studies Association conference and then tried to convince Joanne that an audience of six wasn't bad; Erin Battat bravely joined that panel, traveling cross-country to Los Angeles while seven months pregnant. We offer our thanks to the other panelists at this and Western Literature Association conferences for bringing a variety of perspectives and spreading the word about Babb's significance.

As with any successful endeavor, personal friends deserve credit for their candid advice, support, and encouragement. Judy Gediman and Beverly Hall provided keen critiques of our prose; John Michaan engaged us with stimulating conversations and shared Sanora memories; William Kennedy's enthusiasm—"Her books are a gift of voracious eloquence"—has meant a lot. Creating this collection was a first for us, and we are lucky and most grateful having had Chuck Rankin as a mentor along the way.

Thanks also go to the many good people at the Harry Ransom Center, University of Texas, Austin: Michael Gilmore, Ransom Center visual materials circulation coordinator, and the charming Kathryn Millan, reader and viewer services administrative associate. We also owe gratitude to Mary Lynn Woodard, who provided Christie with housing and family warmth during her several stays in Austin while researching the Babb archive at the Harry Ransom Center.

We want to thank the University of Oklahoma Press, which had the foresight to publish *Whose Names Are Unknown* in 2004 at a time when Sanora herself was quite unknown. Publication of this now quite well-known book gave impetus to her rediscovery, as did the Ken Burn PBS documentary *The Dust Bowl*. Special gratitude goes to him for featuring Babb and her novel *Whose Names Are Unknown*, which soared to number one on Amazon the day after it aired, reaching thousands of new readers. With publication of this first collection of essays on Babb and her literary contributions, we hope to broaden recognition of her work both in academic circles and among a growing audience of general readers. We also hope to stimulate continuing explorations of her work and life.

If *Unknown No More* achieves our goal, it will have been ably assisted by the talented and professional publishing team at University of Oklahoma Press, who made this book a reality. When we initially reached out to Alessandra Jacobi Tamulevich, she enthusiastically responded to our query and championed the project throughout the acquisitions process. After that, others helped bring it all together: Dale Bennie, a longtime supporter of Sanora's work; freelance copyeditor Richard Feit, who can spot an errant comma from thirty thousand feet; Sherry Smith, a thorough indexer; Amy Hernandez, who kept things moving smoothly; Katie Baker, the publicist who works creatively and energetically to get out the word; and the wonderfully talented Tony Roberts with his arresting design. We consider ourselves very lucky to have had managing editor extraordinaire Steven Baker to guide and advise us throughout this journey. His patience and responsiveness made the creation of this book both fun and painless. Our grateful thanks and deepest appreciation to one and all.

CONTRIBUTORS

ERIN ROYSTON BATTAT received her PhD in American studies from Harvard University. She currently teaches in the Writing Program at Wellesley College, and she has taught in Harvard's History and Literature Program and at Penn State Harrisburg. Her book *"Ain't Got No Home": America's Great Migrations and the Making of an Interracial Left* (University of North Carolina Press, 2014) examines how writers, artists, and activists used stories of migration and itinerancy to fight for economic and racial justice amid the capitalist collapse of the 1930s. She lives in Natick, Massachusetts, with her husband and three children.

CHRISTOPHER BOWMAN is a PhD candidate in the English Department at the University of Minnesota. He specializes in twentieth- and twenty-first-century American literature and film, with research interests in ecocriticism, environmental humanities, and climate-change fiction. He is currently working on his dissertation, titled "Climate Change of Mind: Revisiting Dust Bowl Narratives in a Time of Anthropogenic Climate Change." He would like to thank the University of Minnesota's Graduate School for supporting his research on Sanora Babb at the Harry Ransom Center.

JOANNE DEARCOPP is a writer's coach and Sanora Babb's literary executor, agent, and longtime personal friend. She has worked at Simon & Schuster, McCall Books, and Grolier Publishing. Now, as the publisher of Muse Ink Press, she has brought Babb's previously published books back into print. Joanne has presented papers on Babb at American Studies and Western Literature Association conferences and continues to work on Babb's recovery. A coauthor, with Alexander Platt, of *The Nature of Joy* (Xlibris, 2004), she has written for *British Airways* and *Greenwich* magazines and published motor racing photographs in a variety of media. Joanne has a BA from Gettysburg College.

IRIS JAMAHL DUNKLE teaches at Napa Valley College and is the poetry director at the Napa Valley Writers' Conference. She received her PhD in American literature from Case Western Reserve University and her MFA in poetry from New York University. The biography *Charmian Kittredge London: Trailblazer, Author, Adventurer* is her most recent book (University of Oklahoma Press, 2020), and her newest collection of poems, *West : Fire : Archive*, is forthcoming from the Center for Literary Publishing in 2021. Her previous books include *Interrupted Geographies* (Trio House Press, 2017), *There's a Ghost in this Machine of Air* (WordTech, 2015), and *Gold Passage* (Trio House Press, 2013). She is currently working on a biography about Sanora Babb.

JESSICA HELLMANN grew up in western Colorado and is an independent researcher and scholar. Her essays have previously been published in *Consequence*, *The Willa Cather Review*, and the *War, Literature & the Arts Journal*. Her work focuses on the environment of the American West and how it shapes those who live there. She is a former Air Force officer and taught English at the United States Air Force Academy for three years from 2015 to 2018. She has a BS in English from the United States Air Force Academy and an MA in English from Colorado State University. She currently lives in Montana with her husband and son.

CAROLINE JOHNSON is a doctoral candidate in American studies at the University of Texas at Austin where she focuses on the histories of women, labor, and technology. She has worked as a graduate research associate at the Harry Ransom Center in Austin, Texas, and served as a Smithsonian National Air and Space Museum fellow. She is currently completing her dissertation on women commercial airline pilots, titled "Clouds Like Glass: The Gendering of U.S. Airline Pilots, 1973–2010." Ms. Johnson received her MA in history and BA in history and anthropology from Miami University.

CAROL S. LORANGER is associate dean of the College of Liberal Arts and associate professor of English at Wright State University in Dayton, Ohio, where she has taught nineteenth- and twentieth-century American literature, with a focus on literary naturalism, proletarian writing, and neglected texts since 1993. Her most recent scholarship addresses underlying elements of literary naturalism in the works of various early twentieth century American poets.

JEANETTA CALHOUN MISH, a native Oklahoman, completed her PhD at the University of Oklahoma with a dissertation on late-twentieth-century working-class women poets. She has published critical essays, three poetry collections, and a collection of personal and cultural essays. Mish directs the Red Earth MFA in creative writing at Oklahoma City University and is the current Oklahoma State poet laureate.

DARYL W. PALMER is a professor of English at Regis University in Denver, Colorado. His most recent book is *Becoming Willa Cather: Creation and Career* (University of Nevada Press, 2019). His articles on Willa Cather and the American West have appeared in such journals as *American Literary Realism*, *Great Plains Quarterly*, *Kansas History*, *Theory & Event*, and the *Willa Cather Review*.

AMY STRICKLAND SMITH is a native Oklahoman and holds a degree in history from Oklahoma Baptist University and an interdisciplinary master's degree in women's and gender studies from the University of Oklahoma. She owns a pharmaceutical research company that conducts clinical trials in psychiatry and neurology.

CHRISTINE HILL SMITH is professor of communication/humanities at Colorado Mountain College, Glenwood Springs. She has a BA from Tufts University and an MS and PhD from the University of Denver in English with an emphasis on American studies. She is the author of *Social Class in the Writings of Mary Hallock Foote* (Nevada University Press, 2009). In 2003, she coedited with James Lough and contributed to *Sites of Insight: A Guide to Colorado Sacred Places* (University Press of Colorado). She presents on western women writers and American singer-songwriters at Western Literature Association conferences.

TRACY SANFORD TUCKER is the education director and certified archivist at the National Willa Cather Center in Red Cloud, Nebraska. She holds degrees in literature and creative writing from Kansas State University and the University of Nebraska-Lincoln and a specialization in Great Plains studies. She is an associate fellow with the Center for Great Plains Studies. Tucker has published work in the *Willa Cather Review* and *Old Northwest Quarterly* and presents regularly on topics related to Great Plains literature and life.

MARIAH WAHL is a former graduate research associate at the Harry Ransom Center and holds a master of science degree in information studies and a master of arts in English literature from the University of Texas at Austin. She studies digital and analog collections, considering how institutions can make their information ethical, accessible, and inclusive for different audiences. Her thesis project, "Mapping AILLA'S XML MODS, MADS & Custom Metadata to Dublin Core," considers how open data can make an archive of indigenous languages more interoperable and accessible for other institutions.

ALAN M. WALD is the H. Chandler David collegiate professor emeritus of English literature and American culture at the University of Michigan. He is the author of a trilogy from the University of North Carolina Press about writers and communism in the United States, as well as an editor of *Against the Current* and *Science & Society*.

CULLEN WHISENHUNT, a native Oklahoman, completed his MFA in creative writing with a creative thesis of poetry and a secondary concentration in Oklahoma literary history. Whisenhunt is the honors program advisor at Southeastern Oklahoma State University in Durant.

KATHERINE WITT is an Air Force officer who taught English at the United States Air Force Academy from 2016 to 2019. Her literary interests include contemporary literature, feminist studies, and personal narrative/memoir. She holds a BS in English from the United States Air Force Academy and an MA in literature from Texas State University. Her work has previously been published in *Santa Clara Review*, the *Laurel Review*, *Hot Metal Bridge*, and *War, Literature & the Arts*. She currently lives in Alaska with her husband and two children.

DAVID M. WROBEL is dean of the College of Arts and Sciences and the David L. Boren professor of history at the University of Oklahoma, where he holds the Merrick chair of Western history. A historian of the American West and American thought and culture, David is the author of *America's West: A History 1890–1950* (Cambridge University Press, 2017); *Global West, American Frontier: Travel, Empire, and Exceptionalism from Manifest Destiny to the Great Depression* (University of New Mexico Press, 2013), winner of the Western Heritage Award for Western Nonfiction; *Promised Lands: Promotion, Memory and the Creation of the American West* (University Press of Kansas, 2002); *The End of American Exceptionalism: Frontier Anxiety from the Old West to the New Deal* (University Press of Kansas, 1993); and numerous articles and essays. David is currently working on a new book, "John Steinbeck's America, 1930–1968." He is past president of the Western History Association, Phi Alpha Theta: The National History Honor Society, and the American Historical Association–Pacific Coast Branch. David received his BA from the University of Kent at Canterbury, England, and his MA and PhD from Ohio University.

INDEX

"Above Malpaso Creek" (Babb), 149
"Across Kansas" (Stafford), 86
Adams, Andy, 55–56
The Adventures of Kit Carson, 67, 69, 78
age, in Babb's poetry, 146
agreeableness trait, as resilience factor, 73
alcoholism, A. Babb's, 67, 74
Alexander's Bridge (Cather), 111–12
Alexandra, in *O Pioneers!* 92
Algren, Nelson, 2
"Allegro Con Fuoco" (Babb), 147–48, 151
The American Century (Lieber, ed.), 20
American Exodus (Lange and Taylor), 6
American Food Journal, 115
American Working-Class Literature (Coles and Zandy), 160

American Writers' League Congress, 128–29
Amster, Lew, 20, 25n25
Anderson, Sherwood, 17
anger, W. Babb's, 74, 77
ant activity scene, in *Owl on Every Post*, 34
anti-fascism, 21, 126–27
Anti-Nazi League, 21, 126
The Anvil, 2, 126
Anzaldúa, Gloría, 51n3
"The Apostate" (London), 60
Appeal to Reason (newspaper), 124, 160
Are You There God? (Blume), 84
"Aristolochia" (Babb), 150
Aristolochia (plant), 152n15

INDEX

Armstrong, Amy, 177
Askew, Rilla, 166
Atlantic Monthly, 7
"At Mama's Grave" (Babb), 16, 150
Attaway, William, 162
aural imagery, in *Owl on Every Post*, 44. *See also* natural world imagery, Babb's uses
Austin, Mary, 43, 56, 159
The Awakening (Chopin), 48–49

Babb, Alonzo: environmental perspectives, 37, 43, 165; and frontier myth, 42; ghost scene, 89; and Ginny's miscarriage, 44; homesteading decision, 31, 67, 75–76; mothering role, 63, 64, 66, 67–68; parenting failures, 67, 74; socialist perspective of, 91, 124, 160; son relationship, 90–92; as teacher, 9, 37, 67–68, 69–70, 78, 91
Babb, Dorothy: adaptability failures, 73–74; adult struggles, 18, 79–80; childhood damage, 77; Howe's restaurant, 25n27; photography of, 6, 180; poetry of, 143; sister's correspondence, 106, 130
Babb, Ginny: dugout chores, 63, 64; gender statement, 45; loneliness of, 35, 65; mothering challenges, 65, 66, 71; piano scene, 87–88; pregnancy and miscarriage, 35–36, 44, 45, 69, 89. *See also An Owl on Every Post* (Babb)
Babb, Jennie, 77, 103, 182. *See also* Babb, Ginny
Babb, Sanora (biographical highlights): birth, 74–75; formal schooling, 76, 78–79; literary importance, 10–11; scholarly attention, 2, 6–8; writing career overview, 1–6, 54–55. *See also specific topics, such as* gender expectations, Babb's treatment; land ethic principles; *An Owl on Every Post* (Babb); poetry career, Babb's; *Whose Names Are Unknown* (Babb)
Babb, Walter: adaptability failures, 74; beliefs about animals, 37, 43; Christmas scene, 88; Elkhart move, 92; family move to Colorado, 76; farming failures, 74; father relationship, 91–92; gambling impact, 70, 76; marriage, 74; mistreatment of family, 77; patriarchal beliefs, 64–65, 68, 69; political beliefs, 125; rat scene, 89; Red Rock life, 74–75; and wife's pregnancy/miscarriage, 35–36, 44, 45
Babb family, in poetry, 148–49
Bailey, Liberty Hyde, 112
Bakeshop (dog), 148, 149
Balthaser, Benjamin, 128
Bassman, George, 134
Battat, Erin Royston: biographical highlights, 189; chapter by, 40–53; comments on, 8, 17, 98–99, 103, 128, 161, 163
bedbugs, in *An Owl on Every Post*, 91
"Before Sleep" (Babb), 150
"Being" (Babb), 151
Belle, in *The Lost Traveler*, 46, 51n6, 78
Best American Short Stories (Foley, ed.), xi
Bible, in *An Owl on Every Post*, 68, 78, 91
"Bird of the Night" (Babb), 147
Black and White, 21
Black Hawk, Chief, 86, 148
Blackie, in *Lost Traveler*, 48, 49
blues, in *An Owl on Every Post*, 65
Blume, Judy, 84
Booklist, 5
The Bookman (magazine), 112
Botkin, Benjamin, 157, 168n1
Bounce, in *Owl on Every Post*, 88

Bowman, Christopher: biographical highlights, 189–90; chapter by, 95–109; comments on, 9
Boyhood on the Upper Mississippi (Lindbergh), 164
Bradbury, Ray, 2, 5, 55, 126
Braiding Sweetgrass (Kimmerer), 29–30
Brennermann family, in *Whose Names Are Unknown*, 33
"Bringing in the Sheaves" (Collins), 105
broomcorn farming, 31, 75–76, 100
Brownell brothers, in *Whose Names Are Unknown*, 102
Buell, Lawrence, 165
buffalo story, in *Owl on Every Post*, 43
Bulosan, Carlos, 2, 18, 48, 126, 132, 159
burial scene, in *Owl on Every Post*, 89
Burns, Ken, 6

Cadillac Desert (Reisner), 32
California literature, value of Babb's writings, 158–59
California Quarterly, 2, 21, 134
California Women (Jensen and Lothrop), 56
Callahan, John F., 17
Capra Back-to-Back, 56
"Captive" (Babb), 146, 151
caregiving portrayals. *See* gender expectations, Babb's treatment
Carl, in *O Pioneers!* 92
Carlisle, Harry, 128
Carroll, Latrobe, 112
Cather, Charles, 113
Cather, Willa: business interests, 113; farming interests/experience, 112–13, 118; female autonomy vision, 43–44; literary categorization, 56, 159, 164; literary worthiness argument, 83, 84; as migrant literature, 159, 164; nonfarm novels, 111–12, 114; publication timing, 111–12, 117; storyteller identity, 110–11, 118–19; womanhood portrayal, 36
Ceplair, Larry, 17
Cerf, Bennett, 3
Cheney, Ralph, 17
Cheyenne, in *An Owl on Every Post*: ant activity scene, 34; blues feelings, 65; death experiences, 89–90; grandfather relationship, 63, 64, 90–91; Old Loony visit, 90; recollections of Otoe friends, 86, 148; schooling, 67–68, 69–70, 78–79; Shibley friendship, 80; time statement, 87; train trip, 85; wedding ring scene, 66. *See also* Babb, Alonzo
Chicago Tribune, 5
Chinese American protagonist, in "A Scandalous Humility," 56–57, 61
Chopin, Kate, 48–49
Chris, in *Lost Traveler*, 49, 52n11
Christmas scene, in *Owl on Every Post*, 87–88, 90
"The Chrysanthemums" (Steinbeck), 60–61
"A Circling Wind" (Babb), 150–51
Clark, Effie DuBeau, 29
Clark, Walter Van Tilburg, 55–56
class consciousness themes. *See* migrant literature, value of Babb's writings; radical perspectives, Babb's
climate change, Dust Bowl similarities, 96–97, 104, 107
The Clipper, 2, 21, 131
Cockburn, Claude, 21
coffee, in *An Owl on Every Post*, 65
Coles, Nicholas, 6, 7, 118, 160
collective respect concept, Manzella's, 34
collectivization, Soviet Union, 129–31
Collins, Tom, 21, 103–6, 107nn1–2, 132, 180–81
Combahee River Collective, 51n3
Comer, Krista, 50n1
Commission on Country Life, 112, 117

Communist Party: and anti-fascism, 126–27; Babb's membership, 16–17, 19–20, 126, 131, 133, 134–35; demonization of, 135–36; fragmentation of, 127, 129; Midwest region, 125; political legitimacy of, 131–32; Red Scare period, 134, 135–36; restrictions for writers, 24n7, n21, 133, 134–35; writer's conference, 128–29

Community on the American Frontier (Hine), 7

community support, as resilience factor, 73, 78–79

Conklin, Mike, 5

Conlogue, William, 111

Conner, Marc C., 17

"Conquest" (Babb), 145

Conroy, Jack, 126, 161

conscientiousness trait, as resilience factor, 73

Contemporary Poetry, 144

Contemporary Vision, 146

coping abilities, as resilience factor, 73

Corrigan, Maureen, 93n2

Country Life Commission, 112, 117

Crane, Hugh, 4

Crawford, John, 20

Crenshaw, Kimberlé, 51n3

Cross Section of New American Writing, 59

Crowell, Willard, 113

Cry of the Tinamou (Babb), 3, 4, 56, 159

Cunningham, William, 161

curiosity trait, Babb's, 78

Daft (horse), in *An Owl on Every Post*, 89, 93

Dalhousie Review, 147

Damon, in "The Journey Begun" (Babb), 59–60, 61

The Dark Earth . . . the Great Depression (Babb), 14, 56, 59, 159, 164

"The Dark Earth" (Babb), 4

"Davy" (Babb), 57–59, 61

Dearcopp, Joanne: Babb communications, 98, 107; Babb friendship, 3–4; chapter by, 1–13; executor activity, 184n11; promotion of Babb's writings, 10

death scenes, in *An Owl on Every Post*, 44, 89–90

death themes, in Babb's poetry, 142–43, 150–51

d'Eaubonne, Francoise, 51n4

Debo, Angie, 6–7, 157

dedications, in *Whose Names Are Unknown*, 179

Delores, in "The Journey Begun," 60

Denning, Michael, 136

Denver Post, 67–68

Des, in *The Lost Traveler*, 46–48, 49, 78, 80

diary entries, in *Whose Names Are Unknown*, 36, 102–3

DiDonato, Pietro, 164

Dirty Plate Trail. See *On the Dirty Plate Trail* (Babb)

"Divorce" (Babb), 144

Dodge City Globe, 142

domestic violence, 46–47, 51nn6–8

dominant individualism theme: in Babb's short stories, 56–62; male tradition, 55–56. *See also* female protagonists; rugged individualism myth

Drake, Windsor, 105

"Dr. Fera of Moscow" (Babb), 131

dugout scenes, in *An Owl on Every Post*, 67–68, 76, 86–91

Dunkle, Iris Jamahl: biographical highlights, 190; chapter by, 54–62; comments on, 8

Dunne family, in *Whose Names Are Unknown*, 95–96, 98–103, 160–61. *See also* Milt Dunne

Duranty, Walter, 130

Dust Bowl, climate change similarities, 96–97, 104, 107. *See also* migrant entries
Dust Bowl literature, value of Babb's writings, 9, 107, 158, 177–78. *See also The Grapes of Wrath* (Steinbeck); *Whose Names Are Unknown* (Babb)
dust storms, 36, 96, 100–101, 102–3

ecofeminist vision, Babb's: overview, 8, 40–42, 50, 51n4; in *The Lost Traveler*, 46–48, 49–80; in *An Owl on Every Post*, 42–46
Edna, in *The Awakening*, 48–49
Elisa Allen, in "The Chrysanthemums," 60–61
Elkhart, Kans., 69, 92–93
Elkhart Tri-State News, 142
Ellison, Ralph: accolades for *An Owl on Every Post*, 5, 84; Babb relationship, 17, 18, 48; as companion text for teaching Babb's works, 158, 161, 164; *Invisible Man* novel, 7; as leftist writer, 2, 124
Emerson, Ralph Waldo, 92–93
"The Environmental Displacement of the Dust Bowl" (Manzella), 34
environmental literature, value of Babb's works, 159, 164–66. *See also* land ethic principles
"Escape" (Babb), 143
"Essence" (Babb), 147
European Journal of American Studies, 118
eviction notice, in Babb collection, 178–79
"Extras" (Babb), 127
extraversion factor, resilience, 73

family characteristics, as resilience factor, 73
Farmers' Alliance, 160
"Farmers without Farms" (Babb), 45

farm fiction genre: Babb's contribution, 116–18, 119–20; Cather's contribution, 112–13, 118–19; definitions debate, 111; Wilder's contribution, 114, 115–16, 118, 119
Farm Security Administration (FSA), 95, 107n1, 132, 177, 182
fascism, 126–27
father characters, in Babb short stories, 57–59, 60, 61
Faulkner, William, 156–57
Fear and Loathing in Las Vegas (Thompson), 84
Felksi, Rita, 51n9
female friendship themes, Babb's, 35–36
female protagonists: absence in Western literature, 55–56; in Babb's short stories, 8, 56–60, 61–62; in Steinbeck's short story, 60–61
Feminism and Community (Held), 67
field notes. *See On the Dirty Plate Trail* (Babb)
Fitzgerald, F. Scott, 83, 93n2
Flanery's suicide, in *Whose Names are Unknown*, 161
Folk-Say anthologies, 157, 168n1
Folsom, Franklin, 128–29
"For Future Reference" (Babb), 142–43
Forgan, Okla., years, 76, 79, 125
Fox, Carly, 6
Franco, Francisco, 127
Fred (horse), in *An Owl on Every Post*, 89
Freitag, Florian, 111, 116
Frentress, Myrtle Blake, 29
Friedman, Susan Stanford, 92
frontier mythology: Babb's revision of, 46–50; elements of, 42–43; and farm fiction, 118; as pioneer patriarchy, 45–47. *See also* rugged individualism myth
FSA. *See* Farm Security Administration
Funda, Evelyn, 125

Gaard, Greta, 43
gambling, W. Babb's: family impact, 76; learning experience, 74
gambling portrayals, Babb's: in *The Lost Traveler*, 46, 77; in *An Owl on Every Post*, 70; in short stories, 57, 59, 60, 61
Garden City Herald, 141–42
Gardener, Maxwell, 156
garden in wilderness concept, Kolodny's, 41, 43
Garrison, in *Whose Names Are Unknown*, 49
Gathering Moss (Kimmerer), 29–30
Gaylord, in *Whose Names are Unknown*, 161
gender expectations, Babb's treatment: archival access presentation, 176; in *The Lost Traveler*, 46–50, 51n6, 77; in Moscow article, 131; in *An Owl on Every Post*, 8–9, 44–45, 63–71; in *Whose Names Are Unknown*, 163. *See also* ecofeminist vision, Babb's; female protagonists
Germany, 126, 127
ghost visions, in *An Owl on Every Post*, 89, 93
"Giant Sequoia" (Babb), 150
Giants in the Earth (Rolvaag), 7
The Girl (LeSueur), 51nn6–7
Gold, Michael, 135
The Grapes of Wrath (Steinbeck): and Babb's Dust Bowl novel, 2, 5, 9; Babb's responses to, 108n6, 119; Joad family treatment, 36, 95–96, 101; Oklahoma life treatment, 97–98, 101. *See also* Steinbeck, John
Grass Roots column, *Topeka Capital*, 4, 141
Graulich, Melody, 41, 51nn6–9
The Great Gatsby (Fitzgerald), 83, 93n2
Great Plains literature, value of Babb's writings in, 157–58
Green Corn Rebellion, 160, 161

Grey, Zane, 55–56
growth fostering, as mothering responsibility, 64, 67–68
The Grub Street Book of Verse (Harrison, ed.), 4, 142, 143–44
Guggenheim Fellowship, 132–33
Guthrie, Woody, 7, 158, 161

Hada, Ken, 6, 157
Hapke, Laura, 159–60
The Harp, 143, 146
Harrison, Harry, 143–44
Harrison, Jennifer Marie, 7
Harry Ransom Center. *See* Ransom Center, Babb collection
"Harvest Gypsies" (Steinbeck), 181
hauntings, in *An Owl on Every Post*, 89, 93
health problems, Babb family, 76, 77
Held, Virginia, 66–67
Hellman, Jessica: biographical highlights, 190; chapter by, 27–39; comments on, 8
Hemingway, Ernest, 2, 83, 89, 126–27
Henderson, Caroline, 158
Henry, Ralph L., 164
Hestetun, Øyunn, 118
high school years, Babb's, 76, 79
Hine, Robert V., 7
A History of the World in 100 Objects (MacGregor), 178
Hollywood actors, working conditions, 127
Hollywood Talk of the Town, 146
Hollywood Writers Clinic, 17, 24n7, 24n21
Homestead Acts, 30, 31–32, 38n3
House Un-American Activities Committee, 134
Howard Reude, in *Sod-House Days*, 88
Howe, James Wong: in Babb's poetry, 150–51; marriage, 17, 18, 48; Mexico period, 133–34; Red Scare period, 21, 133–34; restaurant of, 25n27; in *Whose Names Are Unknown*, 179

"How to Handle a Man" (Babb), 140
HRC. *See* Ransom Center, Babb collection
Hudson, Lois Phillips, 158
Hughes, Genée, 7
Hughes, Langston, 130
Humboldt, Charles, 20, 24n21
Hurston, Zora Neale, 7
hydrogen bomb, 152n5

Imagist technique, in Babb's poetry, 145–46
immigrant protagonist, in "A Scandalous Humility," 56–57, 61
Independent (Long Beach, Calif., newspaper), 84
Indian Territory, 74
Industrial Workers of the World, 125, 160
Ingalls, Charles, 114, 115–16
Ingalls, Freddie, 115
Ingalls, Laura. *See* Wilder, Laura Ingalls
In Our Time (Hemingway), 83, 89
interconnected self concept, Gaard's, 43
interracial organizations, leftist, 160
intersectional feminism, 41, 51n3
Invisible Man (Ellison), 7
"I Ride a Runaway Horse" (Babb), 147
Ise, John, 7, 88
isolation/loneliness problem, 35, 65, 70, 76
"The Isolation of Life on Prairie Farms" (Smalley), 7
Ivy, Carol, 74, 84
"I Wish I Could Remember" (Babb), 144

jail scenes in "Davy," 55–59
JAPM (magazine), 144
Jarrico, Paul, 18
Jayhawk, 143
Jeffersonian yeoman farmer myth, 30–37, 38
Jensen, Joan M., 56

Jewett, Sarah Orne, 112
Jim Burden, in *My Antonia*, 85, 86
Joads, in *The Grapes of Wrath*, 36, 95, 96, 101
Johnny, in "The Apostate," 60
John Reed Club, 16, 126
Johnson, Caroline: biographical highlights, 191; chapter by, 172–85; comments on, 10
Johnson, Josephine W., 158
Jones, Trevor, 178
journalistic work, Babb's, 125–26, 127
"The Journey Begun" (Babb), 59–60, 61
Julia Dunne, in *Whose Names Are Unknown*, 36, 101, 102–3, 163, 182

"Kansas Prairie" (Babb), 145–46
Kansas years, 69, 92–93, 125
Kelley, Elmer E., 4, 141
Kennedy, William, 89
Kentucky, 74–75
Keohane, Nannerl O., 184n10
Khrushchev, Nikita, 19, 135–36
Kimmerer, Robin Wall, 29–30
Kit Carson book, 67, 68, 69, 78, 91
Kline, Herbert, 129
Kolodny, Annette, 40–41, 43
Konkie. *See* Babb, Alonzo

labor pamphlet, in Babb collection, 179–80
Labor's Text (Hapke), 160
The Land before Her (Kolodny), 40–41, 43
land ethic principles: community as foundation, 29–30, 34–35, 37–38; Kimmerer's contribution, 29–30; Leopold's contribution, 27–28, 29, 37; in *An Owl on Every Post*, 8, 28–29, 31–32, 37–38; and rugged individualism myth, 34–36; in *Whose Names Are Unknown*, 28–29, 33; and yeoman farmer myth, 30–37
Land of the Free (MacLeish), 104

landscape portrayals, Babb's: in "Davy" story, 57–58; in *An Owl on Every Post*, 31, 44, 45–46, 116–17; in poetry, 145–46; in *Whose Names Are Unknown*, 98–99
landscape portrayals, Cather's, 43–44, 117
landscape portrayals, Wilder's, 117
Landscapes of a New West (Comer), 50n1
Lane, Rose Wilder, 115
Lange, Dorothea, 6, 38, 162, 182
Lanham, Edwin, 158, 162
Lantern, 143, 146
"The Last Year" (Babb), 150, 151
LA writing group, 55
Lawson, John Howard "Jack," 17, 22, 24n21, 126, 131, 134
League of American Writers (LAW), 21
"Lean Away from the Tree" (Babb), 150
leftist literature, value of Babb's writings, 159–62. *See also* radical perspectives, Babb's
leftist traditions, in Midwest, 160–61
Leopold, Aldo, 27–28, 29
Lerner, Tillie (later Olsen), 2, 17–18, 51nn6–7, 126, 128, 161–62
LeSeur, Geta, 162
LeSueur, Meridel, 2, 51nn6–7, 161–62
Lewis, Sinclair, 159
Lieber, Maxim, 20
"Life" (Babb), 143
Limerick, Patricia Nelson, 87
Lindbergh, Charles, 164
literary creativity, Babb's cultural context: childhood/adolescent experiences, 15–16; Communist Party relationship, 16–17, 19–22; gender expectations, 18–19, 22–23; male friendships, 17–19; personal mirror statement, 14; scholarship opportunities, 6–8, 14–15, 22–24

literary West, dominant individualism theme, 55–56. *See also* female protagonists
Little Cheyenne Riding Like the Wind, 86, 148
Little House books, Wilder's, 83–84, 85, 87, 92, 115–16
London, John, 55–56, 60
London Times, 5, 84
loneliness/isolation problem, 35, 65, 70, 76
Loranger, Carol S.: biographical highlights, 191; chapter by, 140–54; comments on, 9–10
Lorentz, Pare, 124
Los Angeles, move to, 125
Los Angeles Times, 4
A Lost Lady (Cather), 114
The Lost Traveler (Babb): and Communist Party review, 134; drafting of, 134; as ecofeminist vision, 42, 46–48; gambling portrayals, 46, 77; reception of, 2, 4; as regionalist literature, 159; as revised frontier myth, 48–50
Lothrop, Gloria Ricci, 56
"Love Song" (Babb), 16
Lutz, Tom, 157
Lynn, in unnamed story, 128

MacGregor, Neil, 178
MacLeish, Archibald, 104
Madam Bovary (Flaubert), 18
The Magazine, 1
Main Street (Lewis), 159
Makassar, in *An Owl on Every Post*, 90
male friendships, 17–19, 48–49
Maltz, Albert, 22, 24n21, 133
Manfred, Frederick, 158
Mansfield National Farm Loan Association, 115
Manzella, Abigail G. H., 7, 34, 85, 165

Marcy, in *An Owl on Every Post*, 67–68, 87, 90. *See also* Babb, Dorothy
marital rape, 47, 51n7
Márquez, Gabriel García, 84
Maternal Thinking toward a Politics of Peace (Ruddick), 63
Matthews, John Joseph, 158
Mayo, Edith, 184n9
McCall Books, 3
McClure's, 112
McGrath, Thomas, 2
Mendoza, Lydia, 7
Merchant, Carolyn, 44
Mexico period, Babb's, 20, 21, 25n27, 133–34
Meyer, Roy, 111
Midland (journal), 1
migrant camps: and Babb archive, 177, 179–80; Babb's work in, 21, 103–4, 106, 107nn1–2, 132; Collins's administration of, 103–5, 107nn1–2. *See also The Grapes of Wrath* (Steinbeck); *On the Dirty Plate Trail* (Babb); *Whose Names Are Unknown* (Babb)
migrant literature, value of Babb's writings in, 117–18, 119, 162–64
"Migrant Mother" (Lange), 162
Millay, Edna St. Vincent, 16, 142
Miller, Linda Patterson, 84
Milt Dunne, in *Whose Names Are Unknown*, 100–101, 102, 127–28, 163. *See also* Dunne family
miners' strike, New Mexico, 127
"Miranda" (Babb), 151–52
mirror neurons and fiction, 85
miscarriage, in *An Owl on Every Post*, 35–36, 44, 45, 69, 89
Mish, Jeanetta Calhoun: biographical highlights, 191; chapter by, 155–72; comments on, 10
Missouri Home Maker's Conference, 115

Miss Temple, in *An Owl on Every Post*, 69, 79, 92–93
Mitre Press, 4, 146
modernist perspective, literary regionalism, 156–57
Moraga, Cherríe, 51n3
moral well-being, as mothering responsibility, 64, 69–70
mother characters, in Babb short stories, 57–58, 59
mothering behavior: Held's argument, 66–67; in *An Owl on Every Post*, 63–65, 66–71; Rich's arguments, 65–66; Ruddick's theorizing, 64, 66, 68, 69
Mrs. Denny, in *An Owl on Every Post*, 89
Mrs. Tsiang, in "A Scandalous Humility," 56–57, 61
Munson, Rube, 161
Musser, Benjamin, 144
My Antonia (Cather), 36, 83, 84, 85, 87
"My Lost Name" (Babb), 148

The Nation, 112–13
Native American community: as Babb resilience factor, 73, 74; in Babb's poetry, 148; and Babb's radicalism, 124; Cather's treatment, 111; Debo's writings, 6–7; in *An Owl on Every Post*, 85, 86; pioneer literature comparisons, 86; pony gift, 85, 148; theft of lands from, 38n3; Wilder's portrayal, 116
natural world, grandfather's teaching, 68, 78
natural world imagery, Babb's uses: in *An Owl on Every Post*, 43, 44, 89; in poetry, 16, 144, 145–46, 147, 148, 149–50, 151; in short stories, 57–58, 59–60
nature literature, value of Babb's writing, 164–66
Nelson, Cary, 144

neuroticism factor, resilience, 73
New Masses, 2, 22, 45, 127, 133–34
newspaper jobs, 79
newspapers, childhood exposure, 67–68, 91
New Story, 56
new West, defined, 38n1
New York Times, 4
Nick Carraway, in *The Great Gatsby*, 86
night scenes, in *An Owl on Every Post*, 43, 86–87, 89
"Night Visit" (Babb), 150
Norris, Frank, 112, 118
Northern Light, 144
Northwest Review, 56
Not All Okies Are White (LeSeur), 162
Not with the Fist (Tuck), 133
nurturance, as mothering responsibility, 64, 67–68

The Octopus (Norris), 112
Odetta, 7
Of Rocks and Rivers (Wohl), 29
Okies, racialization of, 162–63
Oklahoma, leftist traditions, 160–61
Oklahoma Labor History (Thompson), 161
Oklahoma Renters' Union, 160
Oklahoma Territory, 74–75
Old Jules (Sandoz), 6, 51nn6–7, 85
Old Looney, in *An Owl on Every Post*, 90
Old Man Dunne, in *Whose Names are Unknown*, 160–61
"Old Snapshots" (Babb), 147
Olsen, Tillie (earlier Lerner), 2, 17–18, 51nn6–7, 126, 128, 161–62
Omaha World Herald, 110
One Hundred Years of Solitude (Márquez), 84
O'Neill, Natalie, 7
One of Ours (Cather), 113
On the Dirty Plate Trail (Babb): as California literature, 158–59; contents summarized, 6; as migrant literature, 162–64; as postfrontier literature, 85. See also *Whose Names Are Unknown* (Babb)
openness trait, as resilience factor, 73
O Pioneers! (Cather), 92, 111–12, 118
Otoe-Missouria Tribe, 74. See also Native American community
"The Over-Soul" (Emerson), 93
An Owl on Every Post (Babb), 124; community connection theme, 34–36; as creative nonfiction, 85; death scenes, 44, 89–90; dugout scenes, 67–68, 76, 86–91; as dynamic narrative, 88–89; as ecofeminist vision, 42–46; female friendship theme, 35–36; formal schooling, 69, 79, 92–93; gender roles in, 8–9, 44–45, 63–71; hardship themes, 45, 66, 75, 84–85, 87–88; land ethic portrayals, 8, 28–29, 31–32, 37–38; landscape portrayals, 31, 44, 45–46, 116–17; literary worthiness argument, 83–84, 93, 119; mother's pregnancy and miscarriage, 35–36, 44, 45, 69, 89; natural world imagery, 43, 44, 89; night scenes, 43, 86–87, 89; Old Looney portrayal, 90; parenting portrayals, 63–71, 91–92; poetic style, 86–87; as postfrontier literature, 118; publication timing, 84, 117; reviews at publication, 2, 4–5, 84; teaching recommendations, 157, 159, 164–65; time element, 31, 85–86, 87

Painter, Nell Irvin, 163
Palmer, Daryl W.: biographical highlights, 191; chapter by, 83–94; comments on, 9
pamphlet, Labor Department, 179–80
Panic of 1893, 114
Parker, Dorothy, 2
Parks, Anna, 74–75

Parks, Jennie. *See* Babb, Ginny; Babb, Jennie
partnership ethic concept, Merchant's, 44
peddler character, in "The Chrysanthemums," 61
pepper tea, in *An Owl on Every Post*, 88
personal mirror statement, Babb's, 14
Phillips, David Graham, 112
photographs, in Babb archive, 180, 182–83
piano scene, in *An Owl on Every Post*, 87–88
Pioneer Girl (Wilder), 115–16
Pipino, Mary Francis, 164
play productions, 79
"The Plow That Broke the Plains" (Lorentz), 124
"Poet of the Prairies" label, 141–43
poetry career, Babb's: overview, 4, 9–10, 140–41; early years, 141–44; later years, 20, 147–49; middle years, 144–47; as personal mirror, 16; themes summarized, 149–52
Poet's Scroll, 143
pony gift, 85, 148
Ponzo, Edward, II, 7
Popular Front, 19, 126
Porter, Katherine Ann, 2
poverty portrayals, Babb's: magazine reportage, 45; in poetry, 149; in short stories, 58, 61. See also *The Lost Traveler* (Babb); *An Owl on Every Post* (Babb); *Whose Names Are Unknown* (Babb)
Powell, John Wesley, 29, 30–31, 34–35
Prairie Girl (Wilder), 114
Prairie Schooner (periodical), 1, 147, 148
preservation, as mothering responsibility, 64, 66–67
Pretorian News, 5, 84
printer's apprentice job, 79
The Prism, 4, 143
The Professor's House (Cather), 159

progressive perspective, literary regionalism, 156–57
proletarian literature: London's short story, 60; teaching Babb's writings, 159–62
public domain lands, 38n3
public history opportunity: Babb archive, 172–73, 174–76; and women's history, 184n9
public opinion purpose, Dust Bowl literature, 96, 104–6
Publishers Weekly, 4

racial perspectives, intersectional feminism, 41, 51n3
racial themes: in book review, 133; in *Lost Traveler*, 49, 52n11; migrant literature, 162–64; in New Deal programs, 132; in *Whose Names Are Unknown*, 49, 127–28, 133
racial themes, Babb's treatment. *See also* Chinese American protagonist, in "A Scandalous Humility"
Radical Ecology (Merchant), 44
radical perspectives, Babb's: overview, 9, 19–21, 123–25; in book review, 133; childhood influences, 124–25; fascism's role, 126–27; impact of migrant camp work, 132–33; impact of Soviet Union visit, 129–31; in journalism work, 123, 127; legacy of, 136; like-minded colleagues/friends, 16–17, 124, 126, 128–29, 133–34; during Mexico period, 133–34; scholarship opportunities, 7; shift from political activism, 134–35; in short stories, 20, 127, 128; in *Whose Names Are Unknown*, 127–28. *See also* leftist literature, value of Babb's writings
Rampersad, Arnold, 17, 84
Random House, 3, 106
Ransom Center, Babb collection: acquisition of, 173–74, 176;

correspondence abundance, 177; Dust Bowl materials, 177–78; organization and size of, 177; poetry drafts, 141; public history opportunity, 10, 174–76, 178, 182–83; Ransom Readers presentation, 172–73, 175; *Whose Names* section, 178–82

rat scene, in *An Owl on Every Post*, 88–89

reactionary perspective, literary regionalism, 156

"Reconciliation" (Babb), 18

Red Feminism (Weigland), 7

Red Rock, 74–75, 124

Red Scare years, 20, 21, 133–34

regionalism, literary, Babb's place in, 6–7, 157–59

Regionalists on the Left (Steiner, ed.), 7, 160

Reid, Panthea, 17

Reisner, Marc, 32

religion, 78, 91

resilience trait: Babb's, 9, 72–73, 74, 80–81; research overview, 73; Shibley character, 80

"The Restive Plains" (Babb), 145–46

Rhoads-Coley, Jamie, 6

rhyme, in Babb's early poetry, 142–43

Rich, Adrienne, 65–66

Riggs, Lynn, 157

Rio, David, 118

Rivera, Tomás, 7

Robin, in *The Lost Traveler*, 42, 46, 47, 48–50, 77–78, 79, 80

Robles, Francisco Eduardo, 7

Rob Wagner's Script, 146

Roediger, David, 163

Rolvaag, Ole, 7

Roosevelt, Franklin D., 19

Roosevelt, Theodore, 112

roots and routes choice, 92

Roth, Henry, 164

Rothstein, Arthur, 182

Ruddick, Sara, 63, 64, 66, 69, 70

rugged individualism myth, 30–33, 34–36, 42, 48, 50, 51n9, 116

Rukeyser, Muriel, 7

rural literature, value of Babb's writings, 159

Sacco-Vanzetti Anthology of Verse (Harrison, ed.), 144

A Sand County Almanac (Leopold), 27–28

Sandoz, Mari, 6, 51nn6–7, 85, 158, 166

Sanford, John, 2, 20, 25n25

San Juan, E., Jr., 7–8

"Santa Cruz" (Babb), 149

Sargeant, Elizabeth, 118

Saroyan, William, 2, 5, 16, 18, 48, 126, 159

Sbardellati, John, 24n21

"A Scandalous Humility" (Babb), 56–57, 61

Schaefer, Jack, 55–56

Schneider, Isidor, 22

schooling, 67–68, 69–70, 76, 78–79, 91, 92–93

Seegar, Pete, 126–27

Seven Seas Books, 20

sexual assault, 47, 51n7

sexual freedom, 48–49

Shibley, Fred, 80, 87, 90

Short, John, 108n6

short stories, Babb's: overview, 54–55; father characters, 57–59, 60, 61; female protagonists, 8, 56–60, 61–62; gambling portrayals, 57, 59, 60, 61; mother characters, 57–58, 59; natural imagery in, 57–58, 59–60; radical perspectives in, 20, 127, 128; reception of, 4. See also *The Dark Earth . . . the Great Depression* (Babb)

Sigerist, Henry, 130

Singh, Lal, 18

Slotkin, Richard, 42, 51
Smalley, E. V., 7
"The Small Farm Home" (Wilder), 115
Small Press Magazine, 4
Smedley, Agnes, 47
Smith, Amy Strickland: biographical highlights, 191; chapter by, 72–82; comments on, 9
Smith, Christine Hill: biographical highlights, 191–92; chapters by, 1–13, 123–39; comments on, 9, 10
social acceptability, as mothering responsibility, 64, 69–70
socialism: grandfather Babb's perspective, 91, 124, 160; Midwest tradition, 124–25, 160–61. *See also* Communist Party; radical perspectives, Babb's
social isolation, 35, 65, 70, 76
Socialist Party, 160
Society of American Archivists, 173
Sod-House Days (Ise), 88
Southern Review, 1, 4, 149
Southwest Review, 1
Soviet Union, 127, 129–30, 133, 135–36
Spanish Aid Committee, 126
Spanish Civil War, 21, 126–27, 141, 147
spirituality, 78, 91
Spring Anthologies, Mitre Press's, 146
St. Croix Boyhood (Henry), 164
Stafford, William, 86–87
Stalin, Josef, 21, 129–30
starvation threat, in *An Owl on Every Post*, 66, 88
Starwood family, in *Whose Names are Unknown*, 161
Stegner, Wallace, 11, 166
Steinbeck, John: Babb relationship, 106–7, 108n6, 181–82; Collins's relationship, 105–6, 180, 181; female protagonist portrayal, 60–61; male character prominence, 55–56; matriarch portrayal, 36; narrative strategies, 95–96, 97–98, 101; regionalist labeling, 156, 159. *See also The Grapes of Wrath* (Steinbeck)
Steiner, Michael C., 7, 160
Stevie, in *The Lost Traveler*, 49–50, 79–80
storytelling, as nurturance, 68, 90
Stout, Janis, 43, 44
Stratford Magazine, 142
"Streetcar" game, 90
strikes, worker, 126, 127, 128
Stryker, Roy, 182
Sunday Telegraph (London), 5
Sunday Times (London), 4
Svobida, Lawrence, 158

Taggard, Genevieve, 2
Tang-Quan, Sharon Kristen, 8
Taylor, Paul, 6
teaching Babb's works, 9, 10, 155–56; environmental literature category, 164–66; leftist literature category, 159–62; listing of texts and thematic areas, 166–68; migrant literature category, 162–64; regionalist literature category, 156–59
teaching positions, Babb's, 55, 124
Teasdale, Sara, 142
"There Are No Fences in Russia" (Babb), 130
"34th Parallel" (Babb), 149
This Bridge Called My Back (Moraga and Anzaldúa), 51n3
Thompson, Florence Owens, 162
Thompson, Hunter S., 84
Thompson, Jim, 161
time element: in *An Owl on Every Post*, 31, 85–86, 87; in *Whose Names Are Unknown*, 99
Told in the Seed (Babb), 3, 140, 146, 150–51, 159
"Told in the Seed" (Babb), 149–50
tolerance trait, Babb's, 37, 78, 119
Topeka Capital, 4, 141

train imagery, in Babb's works, 49, 60, 61, 85
Trent, Lucia, 17, 126
Trent, Ralph, 126
Tri-State News (Elkhart, Kans.), 4
Truman, Harry, 152n5
trust bond, child-mother, 70
Tsiang character, in "A Scandalous Humility," 56–57, 61
Tuck, Ruth D., 133
Tucker, Tracy Sanford: biographical highlights, 192; chapter by, 110–22; comments on, 9
Tulsa World, 5
Turkmenistan, 130
Turner, Frederick Jackson, 42, 55
Two Buttes scenes, in *An Owl on Every Post*, 35, 89

UCLA extension program, 55
Ukraine, 130
"Unanswered" (D. Babb), 143
University of Idaho, 173
University of Kansas City Review, 147

valedictorian speech, Babb's, 70, 76
Veracini, Lorenzo, 87
"The Verge" (Babb), 16
Victoria and Albert Museum, 173
"The Vine by Root Embraced" (Babb), 18–19
violence element, frontier myth, 42, 46, 51
Visions, 146
Voyager 2, 151

The Wages of Whiteness (Roediger), 163
Wahl, Mariah: biographical highlights, 192; chapter by, 172–85; comments on, 10
Wald, Alan M.: biographical highlights, 192; chapter by, 14–26; comments on, 8, 57, 127, 131, 132, 135, 140

Wald, Sarah D., 7, 165
Walker, Alice, 7
Warner Brothers radio, 125
Warren, Robert Penn, 156
Watkins, Claire, 49
wave metaphor, feminism movements, 41, 51n3
Webb, Walter Prescott, 85
wedding ring, in *An Owl on Every Post*, 66
Weedpatch camp, 119, 177, 178, 179, 180, 181
Week, 21
Weigand, Kate, 7, 134
West, Nathanael, 2
"The West and the New Agriculture," 113
West End Press, 20
western women's narratives, 41–42. *See also* ecofeminist vision, Babb's
wheat farming, in *Whose Names Are Unknown*, 33, 99–100, 102
"When I Am Dead" (Babb), 143
Whisenhunt, Cullen: biographical highlights, 192; chapter by, 155–72; comments on, 10
whiskey towns, 74
Whitehead, Carrie Mayo (in *An Owl on Every Post*), 35–36
Whose Names Are Unknown (Babb): archival materials for, 177–83; dedications, 179; diary entry structure, 102–3; dust storm scenes, 100–103; as ecofeminist vision, 42; farming portrayals, 33, 99–100, 102; female protagonist, 36; geographic setting decision, 98; land ethics portrayal, 28–29, 33; landscape portrayals, 98–99; legacy of, 107; migrant camp depictions, 103, 104; motivations for writing, 96, 104–6; narrative accuracies, 95–96, 98; as postfrontier literature, 85; as

proletarian literature, 22; publication timing, 2, 3–4, 106–7, 117, 119; racial themes, 49, 127–28, 133; Ransom Readers presentation, 172–73, 177–82; reception of, 5; scholarly attention, 6; screenplay of, 184n11; teaching opportunities, 157, 159, 160–65; and yeoman farmer myth, 33–34. See also *On the Dirty Plate Trail* (Babb)
"Why Does the Dog Howl on the Midnight Hill?" (Babb), 147
Wichita Eagle, 4, 142
Wilder, Alonzo, 114
Wilder, Laura Ingalls: farming interests/experience, 114–15, 119; literary worthiness argument, 83–84; publication timing, 117; writing motivations, 115, 119
Williams, W. C., 2
Will o' the Wisp, 143
wind imagery, 59–60, 147, 151. See also dust storms
Winona (Minn.) *Daily News*, 164
Wister, Owen, 55–56
Witt, Katherine: biographical highlights, 192–93; chapter by, 63–71; comments on, 8–9
Wixson, Douglas: Babb correspondence, 104; on Babb's communism perspective, 19, 135; on Babb's migrant camp work, 132; and *Dirty Plate Trail*, 6, 95; discovery/promotion of Babb's writings, 6, 10, 160, 173–74; and *Whose Names Are Unknown*, 98
Wohl, Ellen, 29
women's history, 184nn9–10
Women's History Month, Babb event, 172–73
Women's Home Companion, 60
Women's Review of Books, 5
Woods, Gioia, 7
Worker-Writer (Wixson), 6, 19, 156, 173–74
working-class literature, value of Babb's writings, 159–62
Working Class Union, 160, 161
working conditions, Depression era, 124, 126, 127. See also radical perspectives, Babb's
World War I, 161
Worster, Donald, 102
Wright, Richard, 162, 164
Writers Clinic, Hollywood, 17, 24n7, n21
Wrobel, David M.: biographical highlights, 193

Yamamoto, Hisaye, 164
yeoman farmer myth, Babb's challenge, 30–37, 38
Yoder, Edwin M., 156–57
Yonnondio (Olsen), 51nn6–7
Young, Alex Trimble, 87
"Young Boy, the World" (Babb), 20, 22

Zandy, Janet, 7, 160
Zhdanov, Andrei, 20

www.ingramcontent.com/pod-product-compliance
Lightning Source LLC
Chambersburg PA
CBHW020837160426
43192CB00007B/686